PRAISE FOR HELE

THE OTHER GU

"Difficult-to-put-down thriller . . . Brilliantly characterized, boldly plotted, and boasting an ending that readers will think they have figured out only to have everything turned around. The perfect vacation thriller."

—*Booklist* (starred review)

"[A] strong psychological thriller . . . Credible characters enhance the suspenseful plot. Cooper remains a writer to watch."

—*Publishers Weekly*

"In this captivating slow-burner, dark secrets lurk beneath a luxurious lakeside resort in Italy with mysterious connections to a handsome bartender in England. Helen Cooper deftly navigates between what seems like two completely separate narratives bundled in *The Other Guest*: One involves a murder hushed up by the victim's own family, and the other involves a blossoming romance. You'll be hooked on trying to solve this puzzle!"

—*Reader's Digest*

"A luxury Italian resort with a dark side. A cast of suspicious, secretive characters. *The Other Guest* is an eerie and atmospheric mystery that kept me guessing from start to finish."

—Allie Reynolds, author of *Shiver*

"An exquisite setting masks layers of secrets. Beautifully written, powerfully conveyed, and swirling with mysteries you'll race to the last page to solve."

—Megan Collins, author of *The Family Plot*

"Teased out against the slick and stylish backdrop of Lake Garda, *The Other Guest* is the perfect combination of glamour, intrigue, and sibling rivalry."

—Polly Phillips, author of *The Reunion*

"A masterpiece of storytelling with twist after unguessable twist. I relished every delicious page."

—Lucy Martin, author of *Stop at Nothing*

"Sinister and beautifully atmospheric, *The Other Guest* lures you with the promise of a luxury island before revealing its darker, claustrophobic side. I loved it."

—L. V. Matthews, author of *The Twins*

THE DOWNSTAIRS NEIGHBOR

"Fans of British mysteries will love this debut . . . It is difficult to put down. This is one that readers may not figure out fully, if at all, in advance of the denouement, but the author ties all the secrets together in a most satisfying reveal."

—*Library Journal* (starred review)

"Perfect for fans of twisty plots that'll keep you guessing."

—*Country Living*

"A heart-pounding debut . . . Even avid suspense readers won't be able to predict all the twists." —*Publishers Weekly*

"Cooper skillfully builds a house of cards, demolishes it, reshuffles the deck, and deals an even stronger hand, while keeping a few cards up her sleeve. An emotionally charged domestic-suspense debut, perfect for fans of Lucy Foley and Ruth Ware."

—*Booklist*

"A gradual unearthing of long-held secrets wrapped in a smoothly plotted page-turner."

—Kimberly Belle, author of *Stranger in the Lake* and *The Marriage Lie*

"Powerfully displays how we often think secrets are the best way to protect those we love, but they often cause more damage than good."

—*San Francisco Book Review*

"Lock your doors, close your curtains, and sink into this claustrophobic tale of families, neighbors, and buried secrets. Tense and perfectly paced, this emotionally charged novel will keep you guessing right to the very end."

—Emma Rous, author of *The Au Pair*

"The unrelenting tension of this well-crafted debut kept me whizzing through the book. Loved the tension, the secrets, and the satisfying, unexpected conclusion. Recommended!"

—K. L. Slater, author of *The Apartment*

"An intriguing and compulsive story about family, secret pasts, and private lives. Simmering with suspense and packed with twists and tension, this expertly crafted novel kept me gripped from start to finish."

—Holly Miller, author of *The Sight of You*

"Intricate . . . Readers will be kept on their toes as they are constantly handed puzzle pieces with no idea how they will all ultimately fit together. . . . I am very excited to see what Helen Cooper does next!" —*The Nerd Daily*

"A twisty tale of secrets, murder, and revenge that keeps the reader on the edge of their seats throughout, with twist after twist revealed . . . Helen Cooper will be one to watch in the future." —*Red Carpet Crash*

THE COUPLE IN THE PHOTO

ALSO BY HELEN COOPER

The Other Guest

The Downstairs Neighbor

THE COUPLE IN THE PHOTO

HELEN COOPER

G. P. PUTNAM'S SONS
NEW YORK

PUTNAM
— EST. 1838 —
G. P. PUTNAM'S SONS
Publishers Since 1838
An imprint of Penguin Random House LLC
penguinrandomhouse.com

Published by arrangement with Hodder & Stoughton Ltd.
First published in the United Kingdom in 2023.

Trade paperback ISBN: 9780593544907
Ebook ISBN: 9780593544914
LCCN: 2023040178

Printed in the United States of America
1st Printing

Interior art by icemanphotos/Shutterstock
Book design by Ashley Tucker

For Phil, for everything

THE COUPLE IN THE PHOTO

CHAPTER ONE

PHOTOS WERE LUCY'S THING. NOT SO MUCH BEING in them but taking them, collecting them, looking back on them. Her phone constantly complained about maxed-out storage and she had albums crammed with printed pictures of Adam and the girls. Every social event, every holiday, she'd be reaching for her phone. Not to post the snaps on social media or perfect them with filters, but just to lock in the moments. Adam teased her about it, as did their best friends, Cora and Scott, but Lucy didn't care. It made her happy. And if she was honest, so did their teasing.

So that was why, when a colleague started showing off her honeymoon pictures at an otherwise mundane work party, Lucy gravitated toward her. She didn't know it would change her life, would be the difference between seeing and not seeing, knowing and not knowing. She was just drawn in by the blue skies flashing across her colleague's phone.

The small group that had gathered around Ruth shuffled to make room, and Lucy drew up a seat. She loved wedding and holiday snaps in particular, even those of people she didn't know well. She associated them with joy and sunshine, food and wine—all her favorite things. "Easily pleased," Cora would say with a laugh when Lucy got excited about cherry ice cream on the beach or her favorite Malbec on offer in Sainsbury's. Lucy would stick out her tongue—"We can't all find inner peace through yoga and meditation, Cor, some of us get it from snacks and booze and box sets"—and try to persuade her friend to treat herself, too.

Now she stared at her colleague's pictures of creamy-white sands and shimmering lagoons, and felt a familiar longing for good times, new memories, new photos in her own phone. Sometimes it was as if she couldn't get enough, was trying to max out her life as well as her iCloud.

"It looks absolutely amazing, Ruth," she said with feeling. Ruth taught history and Lucy had always thought of her as ultra-serious—unlike herself, the drama teacher with the infamously loud laugh—but seeing her in the Maldives with her new husband, glowing and relaxed, cast her in a different light. Lucy nudged her plastic chair a little closer. She wasn't sure why these work gatherings always took place in a classroom, the buffet laid out on the scuffed desks and everybody milling awkwardly. But then, if she was honest, the only socializing she truly enjoyed these days was the evenings and weekends that she and Adam spent with Cora, Scott, and the kids. She felt a yearning whenever she was in anybody else's company, like she wasn't exactly where she belonged.

Her mind had started drifting, planning their next joint movie night (what film, what theme, what food?), when she saw an image in her colleague's hand that tugged her sharply back.

"Hang on, Ruth," Lucy said. "Could you . . . flick back to the previous picture?"

Ruth looked surprised but pleased, especially as others had started to lose interest and were chatting among themselves. "Oh, we met this other *lovely* couple one night while we were there . . ."

She swiped back and thrust the phone toward Lucy. The picture seemed to come slowly into focus, everything else receding. For a weird moment, Lucy felt as if she could've taken it herself. She'd captured Scott and Cora in that exact pose many times—arms round each other, heads angled together. At parties, at their vow renewal ceremony, outside the shared Norfolk holiday cottage on the day they'd all picked up the keys . . .

Except this picture, dated only five days ago, wasn't of them. It *was* Scott on the right, with his rumpled auburn hair and photogenic features. He wore a green linen shirt with the top three buttons undone, and was smiling beneath seventies-style sunglasses even though the photo had clearly been taken at night, on what looked like a restaurant terrace jutting out over a black sea.

But the woman by his side was not Cora. It was someone Lucy had never seen before, her dark eyes shining in an aura of candlelight. Her hair was dark, too, curly and wild, whereas Cora's was ash-blonde and poker-straight, usually tied in a high bun. This woman looked slightly older than both Cora and Scott, her face beautiful but very much lived-in, her shoulders hinting at a much sturdier frame than Cora's petite, yoga-honed body.

Lucy could feel Ruth frowning at her in confusion. Her heart was pounding and it took her a while to speak.

"A couple?" she said. "Are you sure?"

"Ohhh yes! They even gave Martin and me a run for our money in the smoochiness stakes!" Ruth said. "We joked about that when we got chatting to them. We only saw them the once, though, which was odd, given that it was a tiny island. And a shame, too, 'cause they were great fun."

"How . . ." Lucy's head felt thick. "What . . . were their names?"

"Jason and Anna," Ruth reeled off with pride. "An interesting pair! Pretty drunk that night, but then so were we!" She laughed to herself, as if at some remembered in-joke, then swiped onward, reeling through more palm trees and lapping waves while Lucy sat back in her chair with bile rising in her throat.

HER THOUGHTS WERE a tangle by the time she got home. She walked up the overgrown path and into the usual chaos of the hall: Tilly's purple bike on its side, blocking the way; shoes of various sizes overflowing from the rack. In her distraction, she put her foot on a tennis ball that had been abandoned in the middle of the floor and almost went flying. She snatched it up, cursing to herself, squeezing it like a stress reliever as she made her way through to the kitchen.

Adam was preparing homemade pizzas. Always their Friday-night treat, with more and more ambitious toppings each week—Lucy would joke that the only area of his life in which he took crazy risks was cooking. There was no sign of Tilly or Fran. Their green schoolbags hung from the backs of two chairs, probably harboring important letters or forgotten homework instructions that Lucy would have to sniff out later. For once, she was glad the girls weren't in the room, rushing toward her with kisses and complaints and anecdotes from their day. She wanted to talk to Adam about the photo. All the way home, she'd been trying to think of plausible explanations. Maybe the woman was a work friend of Scott's. He *was* away on business at the moment—though supposedly in Japan, not the Maldives. He organized air shows and other aerospace events all around the world and often traveled. Perhaps the Maldives was also part of this trip, and Ruth had got the wrong end of the stick about his relationship with a colleague? Maybe she'd got it wrong about the names, too?

Jason and Anna. A run for our money in the smoochiness stakes. The floor seemed to tilt beneath Lucy's feet each time she remembered those words.

"Where are the girls?" she asked as Adam kissed her in an entirely non-smoochy way, holding flour-covered palms out to his sides. His glasses were smeared and he was wearing the floral apron Lucy had been given in a work Secret Santa two years ago and had never actually worn herself. Distractedly, and out of habit, she slipped his glasses off his face and wiped them for him on a clean corner of the apron.

"In the garden," he said as she slid them back on, "playing some incomprehensible variation of tag with Ivy and Joe."

Lucy stilled. "Ivy and Joe are here?"

It wouldn't normally have come as a surprise. Most weeks, they were here more often than they weren't. But today it sent Lucy into a mini panic. And she realized Cora and the kids hadn't been around as much while Scott had been away, as if all their routines had been thrown out by his trip, things changing already, coming apart at the seams.

"I picked them up from school, too," Adam said. "Cora's got a meeting and Scott's not back 'til later tonight. Cor should be here soon, though. I said her and the kids could join us for pizzas. I just hope I've not made this dough too"—he squinted at his handiwork, prodding it with his thumb—"well, doughy . . ."

Lucy stepped closer to Adam, laying a hand on his arm. "Ad, I saw something *really* strange today."

"Did you?" He glanced at her, still preoccupied by the consistency of his pizza bases.

Lucy gazed through the big kitchen window at the kids playing in the garden, moving around each other in a dance of utmost familiarity and absorption. So comfortable together, so accepting of Tilly's bossiness and Fran's left-field imagination; Ivy's primness and the way Joe's voice got too loud when he was excited by a game. Lucy's heart strained. She often worried about the day they might grow out of one another, grow out of wanting to spend so much time within their two-family unit, especially as Tilly approached secondary school and they all got taller by the week. But now a new fear overwhelmed her, one she'd never imagined having to face. What would happen if an upset as big as an affair tore their lives down the middle?

"I saw a photo," she said breathlessly. "Of Scott in the Maldives . . . with another woman."

Adam spluttered out a laugh that sent flour particles whirling. "*What?*"

His amusement was almost comforting. It spoke of how ridiculous the idea was. Lucy grasped at the hope that they would all chuckle about this misunderstanding in a few days, when everything had been cleared up and explained away.

"My colleague—you remember Ruth?" She barely paused for his response because he was terrible at remembering people and names, always marveling at how she recalled (and obsessed over) endless details of others' lives. "Anyway, she was showing me her honeymoon photos from just last week, and there was one of a couple she met out there, and it was *Scott*. It was Scott even though Ruth said his name was Jason, and he was with a dark-haired woman . . ."

Lucy ran out of breath, her body prickling with heat. She was fully panicking now. Panicking that saying it out loud might make it true. Cora would be devastated. Poor Ivy and Joe. The Waughs were like family to her; that wasn't just a cliché, just something you said. Lucy's parents had immigrated to New Zealand sixteen years ago, and she'd moved from Nottingham to take up her first teaching job in Leicester shortly afterward. Heartsick for her mum and dad, and knowing nobody in the city, she'd got chatting to Adam at work. The friendly, slightly awkward IT guy who'd helped her sort out a recurring problem with her emails, not resting until he'd both solved it and figured out what weird combination of glitches had caused it in the first place. He'd also embarked on an unassuming mission to convince her of Leicester's charms, telling her it was "just like Nottingham, really, but without the castle!" As if, perhaps, he'd understood Lucy's craving for familiarity.

In the process of attempting to fall in love with her new home, Lucy had also, unexpectedly, fallen in love with him. His dry humor; his lack of game-playing, lack of ego. Even his lack of much of a romantic history had endeared her to him. He'd been inexperienced and shy, joking that there'd been few girls on his IT course at university, and the women on the other courses hadn't exactly gone looking for IT guys addicted to video games on their nights out. Plus, he'd been undeniably cute. Attractive in a non-showy, grows-on-you kind of way. She still remembered the moment he'd flashed her a hopeful smile and she'd realized she properly fancied him.

After a couple of months of dating, he'd introduced her to his old university housemates. Cora Waugh with her almost-mystical air of serenity; Scott Waugh with his wide grin and all the banter. They were a revelation. A lifeline. Most of Lucy's own friends were scattered across the country, so she'd been thrilled to hit it off with Adam's, to find herself in a new intimate group of four. Since then, she'd poured boundless amounts of energy into the friendship. It was she who organized the trips, packed the picnics, implemented Monthly Movie Night and Brunchy Saturdays. The thought of being without that role infused her with terror. The thought of the sadness that might lie ahead for the people she cared about most.

And the responsibility, too. It pressed down on her like a physical force. The responsibility of being the one who had seen the photo.

"It can't have been him," Adam said. "When was it taken, did you say?"

"A few days ago."

"But he's in Japan."

Lucy nodded, biting down hard on her lip. How sure was she that it had been Scott in the photo? The sunglasses, the darkness . . . and Scott's expression. Each time she recalled it, something niggled. It was both distinctly Scott and yet not quite *him*, like someone doing an impression of his grin.

"What if he's having an affair?" Lucy whispered, glancing toward the kids again, who were now sitting cross-legged on the lawn, playing something involving a lot of piled-up twigs.

"No!" Adam said instantly. "Not a chance. I mean, I know Scott thinks he's God's gift sometimes"—there was the hint of an eye roll—"but, hell, no, he wouldn't do *that*."

"That's what I thought." And it was true, she couldn't imagine Scott being unfaithful. He adored Cora and Ivy and Joe. Lucy had a sudden flashback to something Cora had said in the early days of their friendship, when she and Lucy had started sharing confidences over coffee or wine. *Scott never looks at other women*, she'd said. Not smugly, more matter-of-factly, and Lucy had been inclined to agree. Scott was a charming, sociable guy—his job demanded it—but she'd always been confident that the Waughs only had eyes for each other. Wasn't Lucy the one who often teased them, fondly, about their frequent public displays of affection?

The trill of the doorbell sliced into her thoughts.

"Shit," Lucy said, grabbing Adam's arm. "That'll be Cora."

For the first time in fifteen years of friendship, she was dreading opening the door to her.

CHAPTER TWO

LUCY'S IMMEDIATE THOUGHT, AS SOON AS SHE SAW Cora, was that something was wrong. There were black shadows beneath her eyes, staining her enviably clear skin, and her usual yogic, smoothie-enhanced glow seemed dimmed.

"You okay, Cor?" Lucy asked, kicking some hall clutter aside so she could properly hug her friend.

Cora slipped off her ballet pumps and perched them on top of the jumble of Taylor family shoes.

"Just a long day." She let out a sigh. "Long *fortnight*. It's always hard when Scott's away."

"Oh, hon, I know." Lucy felt an extra surge of guilt that she hadn't seen more of Cora during Scott's trip, hadn't offered more support. She'd been in a whirlwind of start-of-term hecticness, but Cora had a crazy-busy job, too, as an admin team leader in the National Health Service, and always seemed to have a crisis to solve, emails to answer after Ivy and Joe were in bed. She usually maintained a Zen-like calm, though. Superhumanly so. Lucy was one of the few people who ever saw it slip, who actively encouraged Cora to rant about her incompetent boss.

She hugged her again, catching a familiar whiff of citrus and sandalwood, and ushered her through to the kitchen, where Adam had made himself scarce and gone outside to check on the kids.

"Ivy's still in that weird sleeping pattern," Cora said, sinking into a kitchen chair. "It's like deliberately designed sleep torture! And I've been away on a training course the last couple of days—the kids have been at Mum's—so they're out of their routine. And, of course, complaining that I don't let them have as many chocolate cookies as she does."

"I didn't know you had a course?" Lucy berated herself again, feeling like the world's worst friend. Had she really been so distracted?

"Late-notice thing," Cora said, waving her hand. "But unexpectedly full-on. And I haven't managed to get to yoga to unwind a bit." She gestured at her head, as if to indicate it needed clearing. Lucy felt the same, but yoga wasn't generally her method of choice.

"Drink?" she offered, cocking her wrist in the universal sign for a glass of wine. To her surprise, Cora responded with an equally universal—and emphatic—thumbs-up.

Lucy grabbed an ice-cold bottle of Chablis from the fridge door. Cora didn't drink a lot. Lucy probably drank a bit too much at weekends. Sometimes she mused that, on paper, their friendship shouldn't work; they were so different. Yet it did—Lucy helped Cora to loosen up a little, while Cora kept Lucy within her limits, reminded her to look after her health as well as just seeking fun and human connection (and karaoke, which Cora reckoned she was obsessed with) at every opportunity. It was similar with Cora and Scott, Lucy had come to realize over the years. Cora's self-control complemented Scott's big appetite for life, and vice versa. Or so she had always thought.

Lucy had to admit that, when she'd first met Cora, she'd been intimidated by her apparently unshakable serenity. But then she and Adam had gone over for dinner at the Waughs' house one evening, and Cora had been stretching up to get plates out of a cupboard when Lucy had caught sight of a tattoo on her lower back. She'd instantly recognized it as a lyric from a Faithless song, and had started humming the tune before she'd even realized what she was doing. Cora had whipped around in surprise, and Lucy had panicked that she'd offended her, but then Cora had laughed and made a joke about misspent youth, lifting her blouse to give Lucy a better look. And Lucy had realized then that there was more to Cora Waugh than met the eye. Or that there had been once—and she'd felt determined to learn more about that side of her.

Now she poured two wines and clinked her glass against Cora's. "TFI Friday."

"TFI Friday," Cora echoed, taking a glug.

"What time is Scott due back?" Lucy ventured.

Was there a flicker in Cora's expression? Her friend was holding her glass in front of her face, condensation clouding it in the warm kitchen. She was sitting in the compact, curled-up way she sometimes did—knees drawn up, feet on the edge of the chair—and Lucy felt a pang of affection; tonight it made her look vulnerable.

"He lands at half seven."

"Which airport?"

"Heathrow."

"Is it direct from Tokyo?"

"Um, I'm not sure . . ." Cora lowered the glass and looked at Lucy for a beat. Admittedly, she didn't normally fire out this many questions about Scott's business trips, or demand his full itinerary. "He didn't say. Or maybe I just wasn't listening!"

Lucy tried to rein in her directness, adopt a more chatty tone. It felt uncomfortably like a performance. "You heard from him much? Has he . . . had a good time?"

Cora shrugged. "You know he gets a kick out of the air shows, especially the big-deal ones. He'll be knackered when he gets back. We'll probably bicker tomorrow about who gets up with Ivy and Joe."

Lucy sipped her wine. She didn't generally think of the Waughs as bickerers. Occasionally she picked up on a slight atmosphere—Cora's hand on Scott's arm if he was sliding from tipsy to drunk at a party. But Adam always said she was oversensitive to other people's problems and moods, especially their closest friends'. Scott would usually win Cora over in those situations, anyway, with a surreptitious nuzzle of her neck, a joke murmured into her ear. Little moments that only Lucy seemed to notice, before turning away to give them some privacy.

She reached across the table and squeezed Cora's hand, feeling the press of her rings, the coldness left by the wine. Cora seemed to shake herself alert. "I haven't even said hello to the kids!" she said. "My Mother of the Year title will be in jeopardy."

"Neither have I," Lucy said, laughing guiltily. "Not that they seem to have noticed!"

They exchanged a smile, acknowledging that they'd both needed a minute.

"I'll be there in a sec," Lucy said as Cora got up and walked toward the back door. "I'll just put these pizzas in. Oh, and be sure to reassure Adam that the dough's not too 'doughy' when we eat, okay? Because he *will* obsess about it."

She was pleased to hear Cora chuckle, followed by the brightening of her voice as she stepped outside to greet the kids. Lucy felt a stab of longing, wanting to feel her girls barreling into her, their arms around her waist, garden-grubby hands pawing at her work clothes. Opening the oven to a blast of heat and smoke—it *really* needed cleaning—she shoved in Adam's pizzas, noting with gladness that he'd gone for Mexican-inspired toppings. Was that because Mexican was Cora's favorite comfort food, on the rare occasions she indulged herself, and he'd predicted she might need cheering up after a fortnight on her own? *That man is more perceptive than I give him credit for,* Lucy thought with a smile as she turned to follow Cora into the garden.

A phone vibrated on the kitchen table as she passed. Cora's phone. Lucy sidled toward it, her heart jumping as she saw Scott's name flashing over the top of the screen saver of Ivy and Joe.

On impulse, she answered it. "Hello!"

There was a pause. "Cor?"

"It's Luce."

"Oh . . ." He seemed thrown. Lucy could hear a bustle in the background, and what sounded like the tinny echo of announcements through a PA system.

"Have you landed already?" she asked, checking the time—quarter to seven. "Cora said half seven."

"Uh, yeah, we landed a bit early. A first! Is Cor there?"

"She's outside." Lucy started walking toward the door with the phone, taking tiny slow footsteps. "How was Japan?"

"Oh, fine, yeah, good."

"Were you in Tokyo the whole time?"

"Yeah, an air show and then the usual schmoozing . . . ate my body weight in sushi, which is actually quite a challenge . . . Luce, could I have a quick word with Cor?"

"Yes, sorry, I'm getting her. She seems a bit stressed tonight."

"Stressed?" His voice sharpened. "Why?"

"Just a busy fortnight by herself, I guess. And this training course at the end of it seems to have wiped her out." Lucy couldn't tell whether she was trying to make him feel guilty. She didn't really know what she was hoping to achieve. Hearing his voice just reminded her that she adored him, too, that he was as big a part of her life as Cora. Reaching the back door, she looked out at Cora and Adam, deep in conversation on the rickety garden bench, while the children were still sitting on the lawn surrounded by jewel-bright autumn leaves.

"Is she . . . pissed off with me?" Scott asked.

"Not that I know of," Lucy said. She kept her tone light: "Should she be?"

"Not that I know of!" he echoed, also seeming to strain for a jokey note.

There was a pause that felt vaguely awkward.

"Well, we're getting through customs pretty quickly, so I shouldn't be home as late as I thought."

"Come over here if you want," Lucy said on another impulse. She feared she wouldn't be able to sleep until she'd seen Cora and Scott together and tried to ascertain whether anything was amiss. "Cora's having a glass of wine, so she might appreciate you driving home!"

"Will it get me out of the doghouse?"

"Thought we'd established you weren't in the doghouse."

"Yeah." He laughed weakly. "Okay. Well, cheers, I'll see you in a couple of hours, then."

"D'you still want a word with Cora?"

"No. Don't worry. I'll surprise her by turning up."

"Good idea," Lucy said.

She was normally a big fan of surprises, especially with any kind of romantic slant, but her stomach knotted again as she ended the call.

THE KIDS CHATTED nonstop as they demolished the pizzas. Fran kept asking what all the toppings were, even the ones she was entirely familiar with, like peppers and sweetcorn, which the others found hilarious, so of course she spun it out for far too long. Cora seemed quiet, Adam had become obsessed with fixing a faulty striplight in the kitchen, and Lucy busied herself with topping up drinks and getting out unnecessary condiments. She didn't take any pictures of the children with tomato sauce and guacamole all round their mouths, as she normally would've done. The camera icon on her phone now filled her with dread.

The doorbell rang after they'd finished dessert, and Lucy let her spoon clatter into her bowl. She had set up an "ice cream factory" with stations for rainbow sprinkles, jelly tots, chopped fruit, and sauces—the kind of activity she enjoyed constructing as much as the kids enjoyed consuming (perhaps more so, the other adults often teased). The children's excitement had peaked as they'd piled their bowls high, but Lucy still hadn't taken any photos, was distracted listening for the door.

"Who could that be?" she said in mock bafflement when the bell did, finally, ring, and she leaped up to let Scott in.

She wasn't sure why, but she wanted to clap eyes on him before anybody else did. She opened the door in a fluster and scrutinized his tired face, his travel-crumpled suit that he was still somehow styling out. He had a light tan, but he always developed one over the summer; he was a rare combination of auburn-haired and olive-skinned ("lucky bastard," Adam would mutter). Plus, Lucy had little idea how sunny Tokyo was in comparison with the Maldives at this time of year. He didn't smell of unfamiliar perfume—she knew it was a cliché even as she sniffed for it—or look particularly altered by his trip. He was, she thought hopefully, just Scott.

"Daddyyyyy!"

Ivy and Joe hurtled into the hall and launched themselves at his legs. Lucy had to look away as he hoisted them both up high, pretending to buckle under their weight while they belly-laughed with delight. Scott was all about the rough-and-tumble with his kids, the messing around—a different kind of dad from Adam, who loved long, intense board games, or techy projects that involved taking things to pieces, then immediately putting them back together.

Cora appeared, looking surprised. "You're early!"

"Yeah, we landed a bit ahead of schedule." He put down the kids with a mock groan and came toward Cora—tentatively, perhaps?—kissing her on the lips. "You okay?"

His eyes searched her face until she nodded and smiled, fiddling with the little gold hoops in her ears. Lucy knew she shouldn't be watching them so keenly, but she couldn't help it. As she urged everybody back into the kitchen, offering leftover pizza to Scott, she had no idea whether the strange atmosphere was all in her head. She could detect frissons of energy between Cora and Scott. Could feel Adam watching her, shooting her looks that meant *stay out of it/stop jumping to conclusions.* The children were oblivious, enlivened further by Scott's unscheduled appearance and far too hyped-up for bed.

Lucy went upstairs to the toilet and splashed cool water on her face. She inhaled some of the "calming" lavender oil that Cora had bought her for her birthday ("What makes you think I need calming?" Lucy had said with a laugh when she'd opened it) and took a few deep breaths. As she headed back downstairs, her eyes fell on Scott's suit jacket in the hall. Hanging there on the coat hooks like an opportunity. Lucy listened to check that the others were all occupied in the kitchen and crept toward it. *What on earth are you doing?* said a voice in her head. Adam's voice, if she was honest. She dismissed it with a twinge of misgiving and rummaged in the jacket's pockets. The outer ones were empty. She glanced around, then slid her hand inside the jacket, patting its silk lining. There was a bulge of folded paper. She tugged it partway out, glimpsing the words *Boarding Pass . . .*

"On the rob, Taylor?"

Lucy froze, then whirled around. Scott was standing at the end of the hall, looking at her with a bemused, questioning smile. He always used her surname when he was teasing her. Normally, she saw it as a signature of their friendship, a shorthand for banter. Right now, it added a sternness.

"I—"

"Nothing but yen in there, I'm afraid!"

Lucy let her hand drop from the jacket. She wanted to throw out a question about yen exchange rates as some kind of test, but her face was burning and she thought better of pushing her luck. "I was . . ." The words scratched in her throat. "I thought I heard a phone going off."

Scott arched an eyebrow. "Can't hear anything."

"No, it's stopped now." She played dumb. "I probably imagined it. Ever since we caved and got Tilly a mobile, I'm hearing them everywhere."

Scott shook his head, smiling in a *what are you like, Taylor* kind of way, then stood there waiting, his eyes on her face, as she backed away from the pegs and strode as nonchalantly as she could to the kitchen. She thought she saw his smile drop as she passed him, his eyes darting toward his jacket, but she didn't trust herself to properly look.

I wasn't prepared for how I'd feel seeing her again. I'd thought about it, of course, in unguarded moments, on darker days. I'd imagined what might happen if she ever reappeared from wherever she's been all these years. Getting on with her life, I suppose, like me. I've tried so hard to forget about her, about everything connected to her. I've built a career, a family, a safety net for us all . . .

Until the day I heard her name again, and the cracks seemed to suddenly show.

It stayed as just a name for a while. A name with a mess of feelings attached, but only a name, at least, something I could keep at arm's length, decide what to do with. But then, seeing her. The easy way she moved, like she didn't know or remember a thing. I watched her from a distance, mesmerized, paralyzed, and then I moved toward her, small step after small step.

"Juliet?" I said, and her dark hair flew out as she spun around.

That was the no-going-back moment. A moment that seemed to have ripples gliding off it, forward and backward in time.

CHAPTER THREE

Sundays were usually spent working on the Norfolk cottage. Lately, though, Cora and Scott had been a little flakier, pulling out because Ivy or Joe had colds, or birthday parties to attend. Lucy had worried that they were losing enthusiasm for the renovation project. Adam kept reassuring her that there was no rush to get it finished, but in Lucy's head there *was*: She'd been picturing weekends in the completed cottage, beach days, cozy fires in the winter, and she couldn't wait.

This weekend, she was fully expecting an apologetic call from the Waughs, given that Scott had only just got back from his trip and Cora had seemed so tired. But the call didn't come, only a text from Cora saying, See you at HQ mid-morning??! with three kisses and a few seaside-related emojis. Normally, this would've sent Lucy buzzing around the kitchen, making sandwiches, singing to herself at the thought of the day ahead. But she was still plagued by Friday's unease. She kept dropping and spilling things as she cobbled together an unimaginative packed lunch.

Adam paused halfway through filling up the girls' water bottles for the car, and looked at her. "You okay?" he asked, rubbing her back. "You're not still worried about the photo thing?"

They'd discussed it in bed on Friday night. In the darkness, warm under the covers, Adam had reminded her of everything they knew and trusted about Scott. How they'd seen him cradling each of his newborns in the hospital, dazed and elated and suddenly without any witty asides; how they'd watched him and Cora renewing their wedding vows less than two years ago in a ceremony that had made Lucy sob into her maid of honor bouquet. *We have to rely on* those *things*, Adam had said—rather than Lucy's brief glimpse of a picture on a phone. Lucy had drifted off in the crook of his arm, telling herself he was right. Fifteen years of friendship counted for much more than an out-of-context photo that she might've got totally wrong. She had vowed to put it out of her mind, but after a night of strange, slippery dreams, she'd woken in the grip of anxiety again.

Now she leaned into Adam as they stood at the sink. "A bit, yeah," she admitted.

"Want me to talk to Scott?"

She glanced at him in surprise. Though he and Scott were good friends, as comfortable with each other as brothers—and sometimes as competitive—Lucy rarely heard their chats these days go much deeper than work and kids, cooking and gadgets. And it wasn't like Adam to volunteer to broach a sensitive subject.

"What would you say?"

"I don't know. I'd think of something. No need to look so skeptical!" He nudged her hip with his.

She laughed. “Sorry. For technical issues you’re always my first port of call . . .”

“But not so much for relationship problems.” He smiled good-naturedly. “That’s definitely more your area. Seriously, though, if it helps . . .”

“You’ve changed your tune since Friday. You thought it was all a load of nonsense.”

“I didn’t *say* that, Luce. And I still think it’s going to turn out to be nothing. But if it’ll put your mind at rest, ’course I’ll have a chat with him. See what I can suss out.”

She kissed his weekend stubble, then wiped away the sticky imprint of her lip balm. “Thank you. I love you.” She paused and then added: “Be subtle, though, Ad.”

“Subtle’s my middle name.”

“And don’t say *anything* to Cora.” Her friend’s face came into her mind, those new dark circles under her eyes, and she prayed they’d be gone when she saw her later, that all of the strangeness would somehow, magically, have disappeared.

THE COTTAGE WAS built from the honey-colored brick that characterized a lot of Norfolk’s coastal villages. It backed onto a field of scarlet and blue wildflowers, on the other side of which a footpath tumbled down to a permanently windswept beach. It was beautiful. It was also a wreck. Every time they took up a carpet or stripped a wall, they uncovered more problems to be fixed. Yet Lucy loved donning overalls and scraping back her thick hair into a headscarf, sanding floors alongside Cora while their husbands hammered at walls and the kids flitted about. Adam would murmur about costs and budgets, but she preferred not to face the reality of just how much money they were pouring into the place. She'd been so desperate to buy it with their friends, so caught up in the promise and fantasy of the project, that she'd persuaded him they could afford it. And it would be more than worth it, she kept telling herself—even today, when rain clouds hovered and she suspected everybody was a bit too tired for physical labor.

Cora and Scott pulled into the yet-to-be-refurbished driveway just after Lucy and Adam. The children spilled out of their respective cars, fell on each other with excitement, then raced off into the house.

"Careful on the floorboards in the front room, remember!" Cora called after them. "And don't go upstairs without an adult!"

"Apart from that, it's perfectly safe," Scott joked.

Lucy laughed with the others, but still found it hard to look at Scott, even as he greeted her with his signature double-cheek kiss followed by a hug. The memory of getting caught snooping in his jacket flashed back, making her pull away and hurry inside. As she put the kettle on, Scott and Cora wandered through the creaky downstairs rooms with their arms around each other, talking about what still needed to be done. Lucy felt a swell of fondness as she heard Cora speaking fervently about the potential of the layout. She could picture her framing her ideas with her hands, drawing architectural pictures in the air. When Cora came into the kitchen a few minutes later, Lucy smiled at her. "Still can't believe you never became an architect, Cor. You're made for it."

Cora blinked, then turned away, rummaging in a cupboard. When she replied, her tone was unexpectedly clipped. "Just didn't go that way, did it?"

Lucy felt taken aback. They'd talked about it a few times before, about Cora deciding not to complete her full architectural qualification, and she'd always said that getting together with Scott in her third and final year of university had changed her priorities. That she'd realized she wanted to settle down with him and have a family, not plow through "a million more years" of studying and apprenticing. She'd always sounded happy with her decision, but now there was an edge to her voice that suggested Lucy had touched a nerve.

"Sorry, hon, I know." She brushed the sleeve of Cora's coveralls, trying to keep her own voice light. "I just meant, you blow me away with your ideas for this place. We're lucky to have you."

Cora smiled, but still seemed troubled as she helped Lucy finish making the drinks. Lucy watched her, wondering for the first time whether Scott had changed her life for the better or worse. She knew Cora had seen a therapist for a little while after university. Cora didn't really like to talk about it and had never fully explained why, other than to say it had been at Scott's encouragement and had helped her with some of her insecurities. Now Lucy opened her mouth to say more, but thought better of it. She switched to teasing her friend instead, about the fact that she never trusted anyone else to make her green tea.

"There's a ten-second window in which it's exactly the right strength," Cora said, sounding more like herself again. "You know I can't trust that to you philistines!"

Lucy laughed, feeling a rush of warmth. Cora dropped her tea bag neatly into the bin and turned back around. She was still tired, Lucy saw, her eyes red and glazed. Impulsively, Lucy stepped forward and hugged her. Cora let out a surprised laugh and hugged her back, patting her shoulder as if humoring her and her random acts of affection. Lucy felt another desperate surge of hope that she'd been wrong about the photo, that nothing would have to change, no awful secrets would need to be kept or confessed.

Cora pulled back, her cheeks a little flushed. "Fuck it," she said unexpectedly, pointing at her green tea. "I'm going to have a coffee instead. I need it this morning. Don't tell the Your-Body-Is-A-Temple Police."

Lucy laughed and put both her thumbs up. "I support this plan."

"And then shall we go for a walk on the beach before we start grafting?" Cora suggested, seeming to draw herself together. "I think I could do with some air."

THE TIDE WAS so far out that the sea was a gray smudge on the horizon, leaving an expanse of wet, naked-looking sand in its wake. The kids ran into the wind, hair billowing, coats flapping, while Lucy strolled with Cora, and their husbands walked together just ahead. Lucy inhaled the briny air, inviting it to blast the tension from her sinuses. She bent down and pocketed a tiny shell, just as she did every time they came here, to add to her collection in the deep yellow bowl in their bathroom at home.

Next to her, Cora raised her arms above her head and rose onto tiptoes, her lean body stretching toward the sky. She stretched even higher, closing her eyes, straining her fingertips up and then out to the sides. Lucy watched her with fascination. Sometimes she got the feeling Cora was trying to climb out of her own body, or purge something from it. She'd seen her contort herself into impossible-looking poses, seeming to relish the pain, the twisting of her spine and limbs.

Lucy looked ahead to where Adam and Scott were walking and talking: Scott struggling to tame his floppy auburn hair as it blew about, while Adam's dark crop was too short to be ruffled. Scott took long strides, moving his hands performatively as he spoke, whereas Adam's were in the pockets of his hoodie, and he turned his head slowly between Scott and the distant sea. Lucy wondered whether they were having *the* chat. Wished she could zoom in on their body language, the movement of their lips. Pulling her eyes away, she watched the children instead. God, how they were growing. How long Tilly's legs looked in those jeans. And Fran's crazy curls bouncing around as she leapfrogged fearlessly over Ivy. Lucy gave her a cheer as she flew straight off the leapfrog and into a speedy cartwheel.

"NICE ONE, FRAN!" Lucy shouted, laughing as they all began showing off their cartwheeling skills, including Cora, who turned three elegant ones in a row. Soon the beach was covered in their hand- and footprints, zigzagging and criss-crossing, and Lucy pulled out her phone and took a photo for the first time in three days.

AS THEY RETRACED their path along the shore—following a battle to convince the kids they needed to leave or they'd never get any work done—Adam took Lucy's hand and held her back, letting the others move ahead.

"I talked to Scott," he whispered.

Lucy nodded eagerly. "And?"

"I honestly don't think it could've been him in that photo."

She took this in, realizing her heart was thudding. "What did you say to him? What did he say? Tell me word for word!"

Adam raised his eyebrows at her—his half-affectionate, half-exasperated signal for when she was being overly dramatic. "I can't remember word for word! But I asked him loads of questions about Japan, and he answered them all. He didn't seem uneasy talking about it."

"What *kinds* of questions?"

"About the air show. About which area of Tokyo he'd stayed in and what he made of it. The food, the nightlife . . ."

"And he gave you specifics?"

"Well, once I'd started pulling out his fingernails he became much more talkative."

"Very funny."

"Sorry." He brought their entwined hands up to his mouth and planted a kiss on her knuckles. "I'm not laughing at you, Lu. I just really think you can relax and forget about the whole thing. Think you *should*, in fact."

"I'm trying to, Ad. You think I want this going round and round up here?" She pointed at her own head as if holding a gun to it.

He stopped walking and took both her hands, turning so they were facing each other. A strong gust of wind made them sway slightly, as if they were on the deck of a boat. "Look, the photo is obviously weird. There must be someone out there who looks like Scott, and had a holiday in the Maldives. But that's all it is. A big, crazy coincidence. And you're letting it stress you out. Worse, you're *this* close to letting it mess with your friendships. And I know how much they mean to you, Luce."

Lucy fell silent, considering. Wanting to grasp at the lifeline Adam was offering. Maybe she was so used to seeing photos of her friends that she'd projected Scott's face onto the image of another auburn-haired man? She hugged the possibility close, leaning against Adam and smelling the absorbed sea air in his clothes. She tried to unclench her stomach, to let her worries be taken by the breeze. Up and away, past the ownerless pink kite that was dancing in the sky above.

This is your happy place, she reminded herself, *and nothing is going to take it from you.*

BACK AT THE house, as they fell into a rhythm of companionable DIY, Lucy relaxed a little more, then a little more, until it felt almost like a normal Sunday. They turned the radio up loud, despite the patchy reception, and took it in turns to choose a station, music and crackly interference echoing around the carpet-less cottage. Scott backchatted the DJs, Cora made them all do intermittent stretching, Adam raved about the tech they could install in the house, and Lucy accused him of an obsession with voice-controlled gadgets. The kids tumbled in and out as a giggly pack and were given lots of little unnecessary jobs to make them feel involved.

Just after lunch, as Lucy was sanding the skirting board in the living room, a shout made her jump out of her skin.

"Fuck!"

She whipped around and Cora did the same. Scott was at the top of a stepladder, clutching his hand. He'd been tackling the rotten molding, humming along to the Kinks just moments before, but now blood was dripping from his palm, spattering the bare floorboards below.

"Oh, God, what have you done?" Cora asked, springing up.

Scott's eruption had brought the kids running, with Adam in their wake. "Daddy's bleeding!" Ivy said. "That's my daddy's blood!"

"It's okay, darling," Cora said.

"It's *not* okay!" Scott snapped. "It bloody hurts!"

"Stop swearing," Cora said, the reprimand as automatic as her reassurance of the kids.

"You'd be fucking swearing if you'd cut yourself this deep!"

Lucy hurried to the bottom of his stepladder. "Let me help you down, Scott. Adam, get the first aid kit out of our car?"

Adam hurried off and Scott climbed down, uncurling his fingers to show Lucy the gash across his palm. "Chisel slipped and I high-fived a fucking nail," he said, wincing. "For fuck's sake! This *FUCKING* HOUSE!"

Lucy felt a weird pang of hurt hearing him lash out at their cottage. She glanced at Cora, who was tight-lipped, clearly torn between concern for Scott and annoyance at the further swearing in front of the kids. Lucy focused on Scott's injury, pushing down her slight alarm at how he was reacting. He'd always been one to yell and curse if someone cut him off while he was driving, or if he burned the garlic bread at dinner, but he'd normally laugh about it immediately afterward, make a joke at his own expense.

Now his fury was like heat steaming off him, refusing to dissipate.

"Let me see," Cora said, reaching for Scott's hand.

He pulled it away. "Watch it, Cora!"

Lucy saw the way Cora recoiled and felt her own protective instincts stir in response. She watched Cora's lips tighten again—more wounded than annoyed this time—then saw her dismiss whatever she was feeling and make another attempt to inspect Scott's palm.

"Just fucking leave it!" Scott said and stormed past his wife toward the kitchen.

Lucy and Cora exchanged a loaded glance.

"Must be bad," Cora said, her mouth twisting halfway between a grimace and a forced smile.

There was an odd pause, in which both women seemed to know their focus should be on the person with blood gushing from his hand. Yet there were other things Lucy wanted to say to Cora, and suddenly they all seemed urgent, as if Scott's injury and his temper had squeezed them to the tip of her tongue.

As though sensing—and avoiding—the conversation, Cora turned to follow Scott. Catching sight of the kids still hovering, she rushed to them. "It's okay, darlings, nothing to worry about, nothing at all!" She kissed Ivy and Joe on their foreheads, closing her eyes as she pressed her lips to their skin. Lucy gave her own girls a quick hug and a no-big-deal wink, then trailed Cora into the kitchen.

They found Scott holding his palm under the tap, growling as the water flushed out the cut.

"Do you need to go to the hospital?" Cora asked, approaching him tentatively.

Scott didn't answer. He was breathing hard.

Lucy peered over his shoulder. "Looks like the bleeding's slowing. Think you should be okay."

"I must've missed you getting your medical degree, Taylor," Scott said.

It was the kind of joke he would normally make, but it came out as a snarl, and Lucy felt another stab of hurt. *Well, I might've done, for all you know,* a voice in her head retorted, its bitterness taking her by surprise. It was somehow linked to the fact that Scott, Cora, and Adam had all been at university together, whereas none of them knew who Lucy had been back then—a theater studies student coming out of her shell—and none of them ever asked her much about it.

Adam returned and handed the first aid kit to Lucy. At the sink, Cora was trying again to look at Scott's palm while he elbowed her away. When Cora knocked the tap and accidentally turned the hot water to full blast, Scott leaped back. "Great, a fucking third-degree burn as well!" he yelled into the clouds of steam.

Adam strode forward. "Mate!" he said sharply, inserting himself between Scott and Cora. Then in a softer tone, clapping a hand to Scott's shoulder: "Take it easy, okay? This was nobody's fault."

Scott blinked at him. Adam kept his hand in place and slowly inclined his head, their eyes locking. Lucy couldn't help feeling a glow of pride. She'd always found Adam's flashes of protectiveness toward Cora endearing, even if they'd sometimes been followed by an unwelcome twinge of jealousy in the past. And there was something generally solid and steadying about him, which was what had attracted her in the first place. It seemed to be the thing that snapped Scott out of it, too. The thing that made him look up and around, recovering his self-awareness.

That was when Lucy saw it. An expression formed on Scott's face that made her freeze with recognition. It was a forced grin painted over his remaining anger. And it was the exact expression he'd been wearing in Ruth's photo, the smile that had puzzled Lucy, had seemed so distinctively Scott and yet not quite right.

Instantly, the photo was vivid again in her mind's eye. And all her self-reassurances that it probably hadn't been Scott burst like a flurry of bubbles.

He was angry, she thought. *He was smiling in the photo but he was angry.*

She stood there breathing hard, trying not to stare at Scott as awkwardness lingered in the room. Scott flicked his eyes to Cora and his face seemed to settle and become fully him again—the face that was usually primed to crease up with laughter at any moment.

"Sorry," he mumbled, pushing back his hair. "Lost it a bit there."

He let Cora blot the cut dry while Lucy snapped alert and got out some antiseptic and bandages. The kids crept forward, intrigued and unnerved by the drama.

"Hey, don't worry!" Scott said to them, reaching his non-bleeding hand toward Ivy and refinding his grin. "I've still got . . . Hang on, how many fingers am I supposed to have again?"

"Ten!" Ivy giggled, tucking herself into her dad's side.

"No, eight," said Tilly, always eager to correct people. "Two are thumbs."

"Well, I think I've got all of those, but maybe you guys could double-check?"

There was a collective exhalation as the moment passed. Lucy scrubbed spots of blood off the worktop, trying to dissolve the image of the photograph that now loomed again at the forefront of her mind. As everybody began to disperse, murmuring that maybe it was time to call it a day, she looked back from the kitchen doorway and saw Scott pulling Cora into his arms. He leaned his forehead against hers, talking to her in a soft, placatory voice, while she stood rigid, eyes closed, hands clasped against her chest in the small gap between their bodies.

LUCY WAS RELIEVED to get back that evening. Normally, she felt bereft when she had to say good-bye to the cottage and the sea for another week or two, but tonight her Leicester home was like a comfort blanket huddling itself around her. She and Adam carried their sleeping girls from the car straight up to bed, then collapsed in their usual places on the sofa, legs overlapping on the footstool they always shared even though they had two. Lucy's thoughts buzzed with the events of the day. Sawdusty rooms full of music; the kids' happy shrieks and chasing footsteps; the cartwheels on the beach. But also the blood running from Scott's hand; Cora's face when he had snapped at her . . . and his off-kilter smile, which she still couldn't stop thinking about, picturing it with sunglasses above it and an unknown woman by its side.

She turned on the news and tried to distract herself. As the headlines began, a shout came sailing down the stairs: "I CAN'T SLEEEEP!"

Lucy paused the TV and she and Adam both cocked their ears. Fran, of course. She never settled properly until past ten o'clock. Her mind was too full of stories and questions and imaginings. Whereas Tilly fell instantly into a deep slumber, as if even sleeping was a competitive matter.

"I'll go," Adam said, patting Lucy's thigh and heaving himself up.

Lucy shot him a smile as she restarted the news, then picked up her phone to text her mum. It would be morning in New Zealand and she'd be opening her curtains to her mountainous view. Lucy always asked for a glimpse of it when they video-chatted. Seeing what her parents saw made them feel less far away. But there was still a pang of longing now as she composed a cheery text. An awareness that she wasn't even in the same day of the week as her mum and dad. Perhaps it was all the more acute because things were uneasy with Cora and Scott, her found family. Lucy felt suddenly alone, not even able to hear Adam's and Fran's voices from directly above.

She was diverted by a mention of the Maldives on the TV. Her head shot up, her focus flying back to the news. Was that place determined to haunt her this week?

A chill washed over her as she saw the headline running across the bottom.

British woman missing from island resort

Then a face filled the screen that made her whole body jerk upright.

It was the woman. The dark-haired woman who'd been with Scott—or Scott's double—in the photo. Lucy's pulse thundered in her head, chopping up what the newsreader was saying.

"Juliet Noor failed to return home from a trip to the Maldives . . . Was staying by herself in a private resort, working on a novel . . . Airline has confirmed she was not on her scheduled return flight the day before yesterday . . . Police are appealing for witnesses to establish when she was last seen . . ."

Lucy pressed her fingers against her eyes with a lurch of nausea. She opened her mouth to call out to Adam but closed it again because she couldn't find the words.

When she lowered her hands, the image of the woman had disappeared, replaced by an overhead view of a horseshoe-shaped island surrounded by turquoise sea. A boat moved slowly at the edge of the shot, its sail a perfect white triangle, gliding like a ghost.

CHAPTER FOUR

LUCY SNAPPED OFF THE TV AND SAT BACK, HOLDing a cushion against her stomach. Silence rang in the living room and she became aware of sitting almost in the dark. She hadn't turned on the mismatch of lamps that would normally throw different shades of warmth from the corners.

Her hand twitched back toward the remote. Part of her wanted to see Juliet Noor's face again, to check, to make sure, but she shied away as fear blew through her. She glanced down at her phone, which had tumbled to the worn edge of the footstool. She could look up the story. Look up the woman herself. Tightness gripped her chest and she ended up recoiling from that idea, too, wobbling to her feet and running upstairs instead.

All was quiet. She peered into the girls' bedroom and saw that Adam had fallen asleep next to Fran. His mouth was open and his glasses had slid endearingly to one side. Lucy took a moment to drink in the three of them, to assure herself that they were okay, though there was no logical reason they shouldn't be. Adam flinched in the way he often did when he was in a shallow sleep, then woke.

"Ah, I've done it again, haven't I?" he mumbled, peering groggily around him. It was another running joke that he got some of his best sleeps in Fran's bed after lulling himself with his own story-reading. He was generally a restless sleeper, and sometimes went through periods of insomnia, which had surprised Lucy when she'd first learned it about him. It always made her feel protective, seeing him battle with himself over something as fundamental as sleep. He would joke grimly that he wished he could power himself down like a computer.

Now he performed a well-practiced wriggling maneuver to dismount from Fran's bed without waking her, and took Lucy's hand as they went to their room.

Lucy's thoughts were a seesaw. One second convinced the news story was no big deal—awful for Juliet Noor's family, but not relevant to hers—and the next buckling under a sense that something in her life had torn, something had been ruptured by what she had seen. The connection she had made that she couldn't seem to unmake, no matter how much she wanted to.

"You're quiet, Lu," Adam said as they settled under the covers and he picked up his book.

It was true, she hadn't spoken a word as they'd got ready for bed. Normally, she'd be chatting away even with her electric toothbrush buzzing in her mouth, ignoring Adam's protestations that he couldn't tell what she was saying. She'd be talking to herself, really. Talking through whatever had happened that day, or what the following day had in store. Tonight, she was at a loss.

"You okay?" He frowned. "Tired?"

"Tired," Lucy murmured, nodding.

He dropped the book and twisted toward her. "That's a 'something's up' tone of voice, not just an 'I'm knackered' one." He moved a little closer, adjusting his pillows. "What is it, Lu?"

The words felt stuck in the back of her throat. "The woman I thought I saw . . . with Scott . . ."

"Luce, I thought we'd decided—"

"But there's been a . . . Something's happened . . ." The more tongue-tied she became, the more Adam leaned forward in concern.

"What? What's happened?"

"She's gone missing," Lucy finally blurted.

There was a slow beat of silence. Adam shook his head as if dislodging a blockage. "*What?*"

"It was on the news. She never returned from the Maldives. Her name's Juliet Noor, not Anna. They said she was there alone . . ."

"But . . ." He took off his glasses and rubbed his eyes, a familiar sign that he was processing. Then she saw him enter the next stage of that, the bit where he assembled things in his mind like pieces of data and came to a decision about how to react. "O . . . kay," he said. "Well, two things. Like I said earlier, I really don't think Scott's been anywhere near the Maldives in the last—"

"But you're only basing that on a conversation with him."

"In which the things he said and the way he said them made me *sure* he had nothing to hide."

Lucy stopped herself from saying that Adam's reading of others was not exactly infallible. She knew it was unfair, her automatic assumption that she was the one who understood people while Adam got along better with things that could be switched off and on. Look at how he'd calmed Scott down today. And his gesture with the pizzas and Cora's favorite toppings on Friday.

"Secondly," Adam continued, "you don't *know* the woman in the news is the same one as in that photo. The Maldives thing might've just made a link in your brain. If they look alike, and there's the coincidental thing with the location..."

Lucy nodded, fiddling with the edge of the duvet. *It might not be her. Might not be him.* She kept chanting it in her head, hoping it would stick while knowing, deep down, that only something concrete, definitive, could make her truly believe it.

"I need to see Ruth's photo again," she said.

Adam wrapped his arms around her, pulling her in. She could feel concern radiating off him, could sense it in the stiffness of his jaw as it rested on top of her head. She held on to his waist and tried to relax against his bare chest, but every muscle in her body felt taut.

"Lu," he said. "Be careful. She's your colleague, and this is big stuff to go diving in with."

"But you just said yourself I might not have remembered properly. And the only way to be sure is to—"

"Sure of what?" Suddenly, his tone was sharper. "Whether our best friend of fifteen-odd years—even longer for me—has made a woman *disappear*?"

Lucy inhaled at his bluntness. Maybe that had been his intention, to shock her out of her anxiety spiral, but it had the opposite effect. A wave of worst-case scenarios crashed through her mind. What if Scott had not only cheated on Cora, but had gone to extremes to make sure she never found out? What if the hint of Jekyll and Hyde they'd witnessed in Norfolk was only the tip of an unimaginable iceberg? What if . . . *no.* Lucy shook the thoughts away. They hurt; they actually hurt. Cora's face came into her mind and made her want to sob.

"Come on, Lu-Lu," Adam said more softly, his lips now moving against her hair. "There's no way. No *way.*"

She tuned in to his voice, in to the familiar scent and solidity of him, trying to make his physical presence stronger than her fears.

LUCY ARRIVED AT work the next morning unrested and unprepared. Juliet Noor's image had stalked her thoughts and dreams all night long. She'd kept seeing her on a boat—that boat from the news, with the spooky white sail—disappearing over a dark blue horizon. And she'd dreamed of Scott's wounded palm, of blood gushing across a ripple of white sand. Next to her, Adam had seemed restless, too. Their bedtime conversation had clearly left its mark, despite his insistence that her suspicions had to be a mistake.

Now, in the swarming school corridors, the face Lucy sought was Ruth's. But her colleague hadn't been in the staffroom first thing, and Lucy couldn't find her in any of the classrooms she stuck her head into. She smiled apologetically at the teachers whose lessons she interrupted, her frustration building and building. Her only goal for the day was seeing that photo again, and it seemed an increasingly impossible task.

In the break between second and third lessons, she rushed back to the staffroom.

"Have you seen Ruth today?" she asked a math teacher, Tony, who was speed-marking tests at one of the scuffed plastic tables.

"Ruth from history?" he asked, dashing off ticks with a pencil. "I think I heard someone say she's off sick."

"Off *sick*?" Lucy felt another lurch. "Is . . . Do you know what's wrong with her?"

"No." He shrugged. "Sorry. That's all I heard."

Lucy tried to smile politely but her face was frozen. She checked her watch, realizing she was now late for her next lesson, and fled the room trying to remember who she was supposed to be teaching next, and where, and what.

IT WAS HER turn to pick up the girls from school. In her state of panic and distraction, she left her students' essays behind and had to double back, making her late as she drove through heavy traffic across town. It was only when she was nearly there that she remembered she could text Tilly. The mobile had been Adam's idea, so that their rapidly growing girl could keep in touch if she went to friends' houses or clubs after school. Tilly was always at pains to point out that she was in year *six*, top of the *WHOLE SCHOOL*, but Lucy still couldn't get used to her ten-year-old having a phone. She was glad of it now, though, as she dashed off a sorry sorry sorry text with a string of kisses.

The girls skipped toward her when she arrived, dumping their book bags into her arms, entirely unfazed that she was half an hour late. It was impossible not to smile at the random snippets they chose to report about their days at school, and their vagueness about the things Lucy actually wanted to know, like whether they'd eaten their lunch or received any Super Effort stars. She pulled them close, one on each side, as they walked to the car in a stream of uninformative chatter.

At home, Adam had just got back and was unpacking a delivery—their new smart doorbell, which he'd been excited about for weeks.

"It arrived!" he said, showing her the gadget as if he'd won a prize.

Lucy normally found his excitement about new technical purchases endearing, despite her complaints that she couldn't *move* in their house without tripping over one. His enthusiasm always reminded her of the first time she'd ever gone to his flat, when he'd cooked her chili and then spent forty-five minutes talking her through his new TV. She'd forgiven the technical monologue because the chili was so damn good. And she'd secretly awarded him extra brownie points for not assuming he needed to go easy on the spices.

Tonight, though, she couldn't muster any interest in his new toy. There was something strained between them, a woodenness to their interactions, like the aftermath of an argument that hadn't actually happened. The girls were genuinely fascinated by the doorbell, so Lucy let them pick up the job of asking him about it, as they clambered onto his knee and wound their skinny arms around his neck. Fran was desperate for him to open the box and show her how it worked, whereas Tilly just demanded to know what it was for, why you would want one in your life.

Lucy took the opportunity to check the BBC News app again on her phone. Search parties were combing the Maldives island, divers trawling the turquoise sea. All the reports still suggested Juliet Noor had been holidaying alone. There were pictures of the bamboo bungalow she'd been staying in: It had a pointy, feathered roof and levitated on stilts over the sparkling ocean. Now, of course, it was surrounded by police tape. There was a new nugget of information, too: Juliet's laptop was missing and had become an important part of the search.

Lucy glanced up to see Adam watching her over Fran's head, anxiety pinching the corners of his eyes.

He wants me to have moved on from this. Forgotten all about it.

And she couldn't blame him. She wished she *could* let it go.

"What shall we have for dinner?" she asked with false chirpiness, forcing herself to lower her phone. "Shall I do cheesy mash? Feels like a cheesy mash kind of a day."

The girls cheered and Lucy put her phone into her pocket, trying to show she was back in the room.

She knew it was far from the last time she would check the story that evening, though. But she vowed not to bring it up with Adam again. Vowed to keep her worries balled up inside until Ruth came back to work.

RUTH DIDN'T COME back. Not the following day, nor the next. Lucy constantly scanned the corridors, beginning to feel as if her colleague was the missing one, and she the single-person search party. On Wednesday, she tracked down Ruth's boss and asked after her. Anya told her that Ruth wouldn't be in work for the rest of the week.

"What's the matter with her?" Lucy asked. "Is she okay?"

"I can't say without Ruth's permission, I'm afraid." Anya was stacking books rapidly on a shelf. "I'm sure she'd be pleased to hear from you if you dropped her a message."

Lucy didn't admit that she didn't have Ruth's number, hardly knew her outside of work at all. She left the room with a cold, roiling unease in her core.

HOW COULD SHE find out more? That was the question on her mind all the way home as she fought the traffic yet again. After maneuvering into a parking space on her ever-busy terraced street, she grabbed her phone and searched for Ruth on Instagram and Facebook. She found her on Facebook, but her account was set to private, as most teachers' were. Lucy couldn't see whether she'd uploaded any honeymoon photos. She *could* send her a direct message, though. She hesitated, wondering whether to launch straight in with her fears, but instead opted for a polite opener:

> Hi Ruth, it's Lucy from school. Sorry to hear you're not well. Was hoping to chat with you a bit more about the place you went to on your honeymoon—it looked amazing! Anyway, get well soon and please let me know if there's anything I can do.

She sent the message, then followed it with a friend request, staring at Ruth's smiley profile picture of her and her new husband on their wedding day.

She was about to return to Facebook and search for Juliet, when she glanced ahead on the street and registered the car parked two spaces in front. Scott and Cora's big silver Nissan. Lucy would usually be cheered to find the Waughs here when she got back from work; this new dread of facing them was like a hole in her stomach. She hadn't texted Cora at all this week, when normally they were in contact every day, even if it was just to send a picture of a pretty morning sky (Cora, usually) or an enormous frothy coffee about to be devoured (Lucy, more often). Lately, Lucy found herself anxious and sad each time she saw her friend's name on her screen. Now she glanced at her house, worried they might all be looking out of the window, watching her just sitting in her car staring at her phone. She flung open the driver's door and tried to compose herself as she climbed out.

"Here she is!" Scott said as she discovered them sitting around the kitchen table, drinking tea. Or rather, the kids were *under* the table, playing some kind of secretive whispering game, glasses of Ribena abandoned above. Adam, Scott, and Cora all turned broad smiles toward Lucy as she perched in an empty chair and reached habitually for a cookie.

"Haven't heard from you all week, so thought we'd pop in," Cora said.

"It's only Wednesday," Lucy said, aiming for a joke but hearing it come out all wrong. She adjusted her tone: "But it's nice to be missed!"

"Well, you know the kids miss each other," Cora said. She dropped to a stage whisper, cupping her hands theatrically around her mouth. "Which is the world's weakest cover for us missing each other just as much."

"It's true," Scott said. "We get withdrawal symptoms. You guys have the best cookies."

Lucy put hers down with a sudden fear she might cry.

"How's your hand, Scott?" she blurted, nodding at his palm. It was bandaged and she noticed he kept fiddling with the edges of the dressing.

"Fine, cheers." He pulled his other hand away. "I'll live, as they say."

"Any more trips coming up?"

"No, I'll be at home for a bit now. Promised Cor." He flung a smile at his wife and Lucy felt it again, the pull of tension between them. She looked at Adam but he was wiping his glasses, not looking her way.

Lucy jumped to her feet. "Going to change out of my work stuff." As she padded upstairs, she checked her phone, but there was nothing from Ruth. She refreshed her screen twice, then caught a glimpse of herself in the bedroom mirror: her eyes wide and bloodshot, the remnants of two-day-old eyeliner smudged like bruising at the corners.

Her fingers danced back to her phone, typing *Juliet Noor* into the search engine yet again. This time, rather than poring over the articles about her disappearance, she scrolled much further down in the results. Juliet's Twitter page and LinkedIn profile sat buried beneath, her personal and professional life demoted now that she'd become Missing British Woman. Lucy clicked on the LinkedIn page, kicking off her shoes and unbuttoning her crumpled dress as it loaded.

Then Juliet's face was there again, a glossy corporate headshot, and Lucy froze as she scanned her bio.

Juliet Noor is a trade journalist in the aerospace industry.

News reports so far had only referred to her as a journalist. Aerospace hadn't been mentioned; if it had, Lucy would've leaped on the fact that it was the same industry as Scott's. The new connection was like icy water flung into her face.

"Luce!" Adam shouted up the stairs, startling her. "Scott and Cor are asking if we want to head over to theirs for dinner tonight?"

"We owe you soooo many dinners!" Cora's voice sailed up, too. "Not that anyone's counting!"

Lucy put a hand to her cheek, expecting her skin to be cold but finding it fever-hot. She plowed her mind for excuses. Adam had probably already revealed that they had nothing on tonight. The kids would already be ecstatic at the prospect of teatime together. She felt suddenly trapped by the dynamics of their socializing, which she normally treasured; trapped by the assumption that last-minute plans together were always okay.

"Uh . . . sure, yeah!" she called back, her voice so high it broke.

She glanced again at her reflection, seeing blotches of color rising on her neck. Fanning herself with her hand, she began to re-button her dress. Choosing something else to change into now seemed like too overwhelming a task. Her hands slipped on the tiny buttons as she stepped out of the bedroom and almost ran straight into Cora on the landing.

"Shit!" Lucy clapped a hand to her half-exposed chest. "You scared me!"

"Sorry." Cora laughed. "I just came to check you're okay. You looked a bit frazzled when you got back from work." She deftly fastened up the two buttons that Lucy still had left to close. "I've got a really nice new jasmine oil if you want to try it? Good for stress relief."

"Oh, no, I'm fine!" Lucy's voice remained a note too high. "Frazzled is my usual look, to be fair. But, thanks, I'm good. Aside from the heart attack you just gave me." She took Cora's arm, trying to smile, to stop talking so hectically. "Hey, is that why you *really* carry calming oils around with you? To counteract your habit of making people jump?"

"Rumbled," Cora said as they walked down the stairs arm in arm.

THE WAUGHS LIVED ten minutes away, in an area of Leicester that seemed to have an independent café or sweet-smelling bakery for every three homes. Theirs was a Victorian terraced house, like Lucy and Adam's, but it had been extended upward and backward and contained *a lot* less clutter. Cora liked clean lines, bare surfaces, rooms bathed in natural light. The only untidy corner was Ivy and Joe's playroom, which Tilly and Fran thought was the best thing in the world and were desperate to replicate at home. *Every room is your playroom at ours*, Lucy would say to them when they begged, pointing out their toys and half-finished craft projects scattered everywhere.

Scott poured them all glasses of wine and they sat in

the conservatory, September sun glinting on the glass. Lucy couldn't take her eyes off him, no matter how hard she tried to relax. She watched as he bantered semi-competitively with Adam, squeezed Cora's shoulder and got a tiny smile in response, checked his phone (twice, that she saw), performed a silly walk for the kids each time he got up to check on the Bolognese. He was in good form. Yet something simmered beneath the surface—was she imagining it again, because of what she thought she knew, or would it have struck her even if she'd never seen that photo?

The words were out of her mouth before she could stop them. "Did you guys see the news about that British woman gone missing in the Maldives?"

There was a surprised pause.

"Topic change, Luce!" Cora said.

Lucy forced a laugh. "Sorry. I just thought of it because... I read she's a journalist in aerospace. Juliet Noor. I wondered whether you knew her, Scott?"

She didn't need to look at Adam to know he was blasting warnings at her with his eyes. She kept her gaze on Scott. He had stood up to tend to the dinner again, but he paused and looked at her. "Was she? Thought the name rang a bell. I've probably seen it in the trade mags." His hand made a twitchy gesture to one side, and Lucy followed its direction to see a pile of magazines stacked neatly in the corner of the conservatory.

"Missing?" Cora said, edging forward in her seat. "I'm a bit behind with the news this week."

"She flew out to the Maldives to work on a novel," Lucy said. "And... didn't come back."

"Oh." Cora blinked. "Blimey."

"Apparently she covers air shows," Lucy pressed, "so I thought your paths *must've* crossed, Scott."

There was a pause. Cora was looking at Scott expectantly now, frowning just a little, and Lucy's heart quickened at the prospect of what she was drawing attention to.

"Not to my knowledge," Scott said eventually, with a shrug. "Our PR team tends to deal with the press. I'm always too busy trying to make sure the whole event doesn't go tits up." Ivy wandered into the conservatory just as he said *tits*, and gasped and giggled.

Cora rolled her eyes, her frown melting. "I wish I could bleep you out sometimes, Scott. Our kids are going to have the vocab of a Tarantino film."

"Sorry!" He grinned, blowing her a kiss and then shimmying away. "Should be nearly ready now," he called over his shoulder as the smell of garlic bloomed out of the kitchen.

Lucy drifted over to the pile of magazines and picked one up. She felt Adam and Cora watching her as she flicked through with feigned casualness, scouring the pages for Juliet's name.

"Wish he'd get rid of some of those," Cora tutted. "It's like being back in our student house with Scott and Ad's piles of gaming magazines everywhere!"

"Highly educational literature, they were," Adam said. "Great for reading in the toilet."

"Lovely," Cora said, pulling a face and laughing. "What a lucky girl I was with you two."

Lucy stopped on an article about the Berlin Air Show from a couple of months before. She knew Scott had been to it—she remembered him bringing back a book on the Berlin Wall for Adam's shelf of unread history books. And there was Juliet's name, against a two-page write-up of the event. Lucy looked for any mention of Scott, but there was none, even though Lucy was sure he'd been heavily involved. She stared at a photo of a huge, gleaming aeroengine with five smartly dressed people standing in its shadow. Stared even harder at an overhead shot of the fair, as if she'd be able to spot Scott and Juliet among the crowds.

"Dinnerrrr!" Scott called from inside the house, then made a noise like a gong being struck.

Lucy dropped the magazine back onto the pile, returning Cora's half-questioning smile with what she hoped was a neutral one of her own.

"YOU'RE STILL HUNG up on this Maldives thing, aren't you?" Adam said when they'd got home and settled the girls in bed.

Lucy filled a glass with water and stood with her back against the kitchen cabinets. Her stomach was a flutter of nausea. Everything seemed unsteady at the moment, constantly swaying, reminding her of when she'd gone skiing near her parents' place in New Zealand and had been unable to lose the feeling of motion even when the skis were off her feet.

"Listen." Adam turned her to face him, his hands on her upper arms. "You remember after dinner, Scott asked me to check out a problem he was having with his computer?"

Lucy nodded. Adam was forever fixing IT issues for family and friends. He'd sometimes complain—half-jokingly—about all the extra he could be earning if he charged people for the favors he was too much of a softy to refuse. Tonight, Scott had wanted him to take a quick look at something, and they'd disappeared for half an hour.

"His paperwork from his trip was on the desk," Adam told her now. "I saw his hotel *and* flight bookings. He was definitely in Japan for the whole two weeks."

Lucy's mouth fell open. A chink of light seemed to inch through the haze. "Really?"

Adam nodded vigorously, like a child who'd found the answer to a puzzle. "Really."

"Did you take a photo?"

"No!" He sounded vaguely hurt. "We're not all photo addicts, Luce! Don't you believe me or something?"

She shook herself. "Of course I do. Sorry. I just want to see it with my own eyes."

"Well, you'll have to trust *my* eyes." He took off his glasses and widened them comically, the hazel in his irises popping under the kitchen lights. "I know I'm getting blinder by the year, according to Specsavers, but I *can* still tell a boarding pass from a shopping list."

She managed a smile. Unexpected tears were filling her eyes and throat. Exhaustion, perhaps. Relief.

"It wasn't him," she whispered, trying out the words.

"Of course it wasn't, sweetheart."

"But . . ." She kept circling back to the coincidences, the connections. That strange grin from the photo, glimpsed again in Norfolk, like a visual memory dropped directly into her brain.

Adam took her hands and kissed each of her knuckles.

"Let's go to bed, Lu-Lu," he said, drawing her into a hug.

She let her cheek melt against the softness of his T-shirt,

inhaling the end-of-day smell of him. The laundry powder in the fabric, something a little more bodily beneath, a hint of cooking from when he'd been helping Scott and arguing about the best way to do Bolognese. Adam pulled her close, his arms tight around her, then led her up the stairs as she leaned against him.

Under the covers, he stroked his fingers over her hip.

"Cold hands," she said but smiled and rolled toward him, their legs tangling.

"You know what they say," he said. "Cold hands, hot sex?"

"Nobody says that," she said with a laugh.

He rubbed his palms together to warm them up, then moved them onto her back, gliding them over her spine. It was the next step in a familiar routine, but it still made her tingle, as if her nerve endings were rising to the surface. The first time they'd spent a night together, she'd been happily startled by the chemistry between them. She'd known she liked him, even though he wasn't her usual, more outgoing type, but their early dates had had a matey feel to them—curries and beers and work chat—so she hadn't been prepared for the electricity that had sparked when they eventually slept together. It had seemed to come as a surprise to Adam, too. He'd confided that he'd never thought of himself as having much sex appeal. Scott had always been his charming, better-looking friend, and Adam had hovered in the background. That was what he liked about Lucy, he'd admitted. That the things he thought made him invisible were the things she was drawn to.

Their connection had changed and fluctuated over the years, of course. But it was still there. Sometimes, when the lights were off, Adam would seem to click into a different mode: rawer, more passionate; less mild and measured than his usual self. Tonight, though, as Lucy closed her eyes and tried to lose herself in the moment, the photo was trapped in her mind's eye. Jason and Anna. Scott and Juliet. It couldn't be erased, not even by Adam's promises, or the shiver of his lips on her neck.

Juliet Noor gets inside your head. That's the thing. The undoing. And it seems to hold true whether you're in a paradise of palm trees and white sand, or in a soulless hotel room on company expenses, or a grotty student flat. She casts her irresistible spell.

Maybe it's the wildness of her hair, the way she constantly pushes it back from her face. Maybe it's the sexiness of her shape, which she seems to wear with even more confidence now. Or the fact that she comes across as uninhibited, uncrushable . . . almost untouchable, except for the few chosen people she draws into her orbit. Whether those people belong to somebody else or not doesn't seem to matter to her. And perhaps that's part of her charm, too.

I haven't been able to stop thinking about her. Despite all my attempts to stop. And second time around, it feels like something really dangerous. She *feels like something dangerous. What she knows about me, about us. What she could destroy. I've been careless, taken my eye off what's important, and things have gone too far; there's too much to lose. My family, my kids. They can never, never know what I've done.*

CHAPTER FIVE

OVER THE NEXT FEW DAYS, LUCY'S OBSESSION with Juliet Noor only escalated. Every spare moment—when she wasn't teaching or looking after the girls or trying to act normal with Adam—was devoted to finding out *everything* about her.

She'd been a journalist for twelve years, with various specialisms, but had only moved into the field of aerospace just over a year ago. She was well respected, intelligent, ambitious, according to statements from organizations she'd worked for or people who knew her. She wasn't married, had no children. There was something enigmatic about her, which drew attention from the press: this good-looking woman who'd taken herself off to the Maldives to work on a novel and vanished without a trace.

Lucy dreamed about her. Began to feel as if she knew her. Compared her to Cora, imagined her with Scott, continued to pore over photos of her online, staring into her dark eyes as if her secrets might be written there. The images began to merge in her mind with the photo she'd seen on Ruth's phone, and all the scenes she'd constructed in her imagination since.

Ruth still hadn't accepted her Facebook friend request. There was no indication she'd even read Lucy's message. This gnawed at Lucy, too, until she cracked and sent another message, sitting in her garden early on Saturday morning while the rest of her family slept.

This time, she dispensed with any attempt to be subtle.

> That photo you showed me, Ruth. The couple you met on your honeymoon—Jason and Anna. Anna looked like Juliet Noor, the journalist who's gone missing in the Maldives. Could it have been her?

She looked out over the garden after she'd sent it, watching the autumn wind teasing the red and gold trees. The swings Adam had rigged up for the girls were swaying back and forth as if propelled by invisible children. A flame-red leaf blew in Lucy's direction and she caught it, scrunching it hard between her fingers. Cora had tried to teach her about mindfulness. How to focus on the waxy texture of a leaf, the bold veins running through it. But switching off racing thoughts had never been Lucy's forte. And now she wondered why Cora needed all those soothing rituals to get through her day-to-day life.

Life with a man who was unfaithful, perhaps. Or worse. Lucy flinched even as she let herself think it.

She went back inside and made another strong coffee. Then she started again, unable to resist: googling Juliet to see if there was anything new, trying different search terms in combination with her name. It made her feel crazy, yet it was also a way of taking control, taking action, without having to do anything as drastic as reporting to the police.

And today, unexpectedly, she stumbled across a photo of Juliet on Google Images that she hadn't spotted before.

Lucy moved over to the kitchen window so she could see it better. The photo showed Juliet at her graduation, smiling in her black gown, her hat barely balancing on the fountain of her hair. Lucy read the caption and stalled on the words *Leeds University.* Where Scott, Cora, and Adam had gone, too. She clicked on the picture and went through to its host website, the alumni page for the English department. It was a feature about their graduates and what kinds of careers they'd ended up in, and it had a short description of Juliet's job and her journey to getting it.

But what Lucy fixated on was the dates. Juliet had studied at Leeds between 2003 and 2006. The exact period when Lucy's friends and husband had also been there. When *Scott* had been there, studying business rather than English, of course—but it was another connection, setting off another avalanche of questions through her head.

Before she could dwell on any of them, Adam walked into the room.

"You're up early," he said, scratching at his hairline, then at his stomach beneath his pajama top. His eyes darted to her phone and she blanked the screen. There was a moment when he seemed on the verge of asking what she was doing but it skittered away, and he kissed her instead, a very faint frown on his brow. "You know it's not 'til this afternoon?"

"What isn't?" Lucy said.

"Ivy's swimming thing. We promised Cora and Scott we'd go along to cheer her on?"

"Oh." Something colder than the morning air sank down Lucy's spine. "Shit, yes, I forgot."

"I'm just going to take a moment to celebrate the fact that *I* remembered a social engagement and you didn't," he said with a grin.

She smiled weakly as he performed a little dance, trying not to notice that even his goofy celebration felt forced. He tailed off, looking embarrassed. When they heard one of the girls stirring above, Lucy ran from the room to check.

THE LOCAL SWIMMING pool was a nightmarish place on only a couple of hours' sleep. The echoing noises, the stench of chlorine, the reflections of lights wobbling on the surface of the water. Lucy felt like passing out as they sat in their damp seats waiting for Ivy's race to begin. She was sandwiched between Cora and Scott, while Adam had ended up in the row in front with the other three children, passing them snacks as they started to get bored. Without having to ask, he knew which kid would want Quavers, who'd prefer a cereal bar, a slice of malt loaf. Lucy felt a sudden, crushing sadness as she watched him ruffle Joe's hair as fondly as he interacted with Tilly and Fran, calling him the Quaver King while Joe grinned into his packet of crisps.

"I could just jump in there," Cora said, to her left.

"Really?" Lucy blinked at the water sloshing over the edges of the pool. "I don't fancy it myself. Quite happy with dry land and a flask of coffee on a Saturday afternoon." She shivered, even though she'd been too hot a second ago, and again felt the scratch of chlorine at the back of her throat.

"I used to love swimming," Cora said, sounding almost wistful. "It made me feel so free. Especially wild swimming... *night* swimming, even..." She paused with a dreamy smile, and an image flashed through Lucy's head of Cora plunging into a starlit river, her Faithless tattoo on show, her hair long and loose like she apparently used to wear it all the time. "I don't know why I never do it anymore." Cora glanced over at Scott but he was frowning at his phone, pinching the bridge of his nose. She raised her eyebrows at Lucy and mouthed *work*.

Lucy turned to address Scott, though it made her heart thump. "Everything okay, Scott?"

"What?" he growled distractedly, his frown deepening as his eyes flickered to her. Then his face cleared, as if he'd remembered where he was: "Oh, yeah, just the usual madness."

"He's got a big presentation coming up," Cora said, switching from mild annoyance to defense of his distractedness in an instant.

Scott shot them both an apologetic smile, winked at the kids as they turned to look at him, then went straight back to his phone.

"Oh, here she goes!" Cora said, pointing down toward the pool. Ivy was lining up for her event, wearing a green skirted swimsuit, her big Cora-like eyes searching the crowd for her supporters.

When the whistle blew, something seemed to ignite in Cora. Lucy watched with amazement as her usually serene friend leaped up and began shouting wild encouragement at her daughter, flailing her arms, bouncing on her toes, attracting glances from around them. Adam caught Lucy's eye and they grinned, bonded for a moment in their mutual surprise. When her attention slid to her right, Lucy's amusement was punctured. Scott had disappeared. His jacket was left slung over his empty seat. Cora turned and noticed, too, her animation dying just as Ivy glided to the finish in first place.

SCOTT REAPPEARED AS the races were coming to an end, saying he'd had to take an important call, and Cora cold-shouldered him. Lucy had been watching her in the interim, sensing her unvoiced anger that Scott had missed Ivy's victory, and wishing she could pull her aside for a chat away from the kids. Afterward, as they shuffled out amid a slow-moving crowd, she saw Scott trying to take Cora's hand and Cora spurning him, helping Joe put his coat on instead.

Lucy glanced at Scott to gauge his reaction, but somebody else caught her eye, a little way ahead in the crowd. A shock of recognition bolted through her, immediately diverting her from the Waughs' argument.

Is that . . . ?

The woman had a familiar chestnut-colored bob, a familiar way of hoisting her handbag onto her shoulder, yet the sight of her was so unexpected that Lucy wondered if her mind was playing tricks. She stood on tiptoes and peered through the crush of parents. The woman turned her head and Lucy saw that she'd been right. It was *Ruth*. She hadn't returned to work, hadn't accepted Lucy's friend request or replied to her messages. But she was here. She was meters away.

Lucy tried to surge forward, but there were too many people between them. She had to wait a painfully long time to get to the exit, then she broke away from her friends and made a beeline for her colleague.

She clocked the exact moment when Ruth pretended not to see her. Her eyes swept over Lucy, then she averted her gaze and walked briskly toward the car park, pulling a little girl by the hand. Lucy followed, calling her name. Ruth's pace quickened but Lucy refused to give up. With a burst of energy, she got close enough to touch her colleague's elbow. Ruth stalled, turned. She looked thinner and paler, her honeymoon glow long faded.

"Oh . . ." Ruth smiled stiffly as she feigned surprise. "Lucy! Hello."

"Ruth." Lucy was too agitated for niceties. "Are you okay?"

"I'm fine," Ruth said, without stopping completely, so that they continued to move in awkward side steps toward the cars. "How are you?" she added, her smile snagging at its edges.

Lucy matched her every movement. "I'm sorry you've been ill."

"Oh, I'm fine," Ruth repeated, but there was an unmistakable catch in her voice.

"And I'm sorry if I made you feel uncomfortable . . ." Lucy tried to keep her hunger for answers under some kind of control. "Asking about the photo."

Ruth finally stopped moving. Her eyes darted past Lucy, then down to the little girl, who was clutching at her jeans. "The honeymoon photo," Lucy added, trying to leave no room for Ruth to claim ignorance. "The messages I sent you—"

"I haven't got anything more to say about the photo,"

Ruth cut in. "It wasn't . . . that woman. That wasn't who I met."

"Could I see it again? Please—just for my own peace of mind. Then I promise I'll drop the whole thing."

Ruth shook her head. "I deleted it."

Lucy's mouth dropped open. "Why?"

"It was a photo of two people I'll never see again. What's the point in keeping it?"

"Might it still be in your Deleted folder?"

Ruth stared at her. "Why are you so interested in it?"

"Because—because she's *missing*. God knows what's happened to her. And it might be evidence."

Ruth flinched and covered the child's ears. "Please. Not in front of my niece. She's sensitive. We just came here for the swimming. I don't know why you're asking me these questions . . ." She started to edge away again, pulling her car keys from her pocket and pressing the button to make a nearby Volvo's lights flash.

"Ruth—"

"I'll see you at work." Ruth bundled her niece into the backseat and folded herself into the front, slamming the door so hard the car shuddered.

Lucy took a step backward, lifting her hand to her throat. She could feel the tight vibration of her own breathing beneath her palm. When she turned, she saw the others waiting in a confused huddle where she had left them, the kids playing a game that seemed to involve a lot of barging and giggling off to the right. She composed herself and walked back over, frustration still pulsing under her skin.

"Who was that?" Cora asked, peering past her.

"Just a colleague," Lucy said.

Adam gave her a look as if he'd guessed which colleague, guessed why she'd chased her down. Lucy kept up the casual act, though it strained in her voice and her smile. "I just wanted to say hello. She hasn't been at work lately."

Scott performed a wounded expression. "Wait, you have *other* friends?"

They all tittered, but something about the joke sat uneasily. The truth was, Lucy didn't really have other friends these days. That was what was she was realizing, what was making this all feel much worse.

"Traitor, I know." She attempted to laugh along. "Don't worry, I still love you guys the mostest."

She was distracted as she noticed Scott staring across the car park. His gaze seemed to follow Ruth's Volvo all the way out of the leisure center, with much more attentiveness than he'd given to any part of the swimming meet.

CHAPTER SIX

CORA INVITED THEM ALL BACK FOR A TAKEAWAY to celebrate, looking pointedly at Scott each time she referred to Ivy's win. Lucy found herself swept along with the plans, no way to explain a sudden, drastic reluctance to hang out. But all she wanted to do, really, was analyze her conversation with Ruth.

Her friends stared at her when she said she'd have a korma. For some reason it was the first thing that came into her head, even though she was famous for her love of fiendishly hot curries.

"You coming down with something, Taylor?" Scott broke off from making a note of the orders and pretended to feel her forehead. Lucy laughed thinly, trying not to flinch at his touch.

"My heart said madras and my mouth said korma," she said. "Maybe it's begging me to stop setting it on fire."

Wine was poured, the kids disappeared to chase each other thunderously around the upstairs rooms, and Cora lit a raft of vanilla-scented candles. Lucy tucked herself into her usual spot in the crook of the corner sofa, hoping the press of cushions on either side might offer some protection. Cora sat next to her, slim legs curled toward her so their feet almost touched. She rarely wore socks, yet the soles of her feet were always soft and clean. She'd changed into a long yellow sweater, pulled her hair into an even higher topknot. Another of her rituals was frequently taking down and re-tying her bun. Lucy had seen her do it so often she could've mimicked the exact motion of her hands and the slight arch of her eyebrows.

Scott had changed his clothes, too. His cotton sweatshirt and loose trousers suggested relaxation but he seemed restless, kept getting up and peering through the blinds for the takeaway driver.

"We only just ordered, Scott!" Cora said, gesturing for him to sit down.

He retreated to an armchair, picked up his wineglass, and stretched his legs out in front of him. Cora studied him for a moment, still seeming displeased, then turned away. "Well, here's to the star swimmer of the day," she said, raising her drink to the rest of the room.

Lucy clinked glasses with her, and their husbands leaned forward from their seats to do a four-way cheers. Something about it chimed discordantly, though, and Lucy couldn't make eye contact with Scott as their glasses clashed.

"And here's to the parental cheerleader of the day," Adam said, winking at Cora.

Cora looked embarrassed. "I did get a bit caught up in the moment, didn't I?"

"It was *very* entertaining," Adam teased. "A glimpse of the old Cora."

"Ah, yes, the famous old Cora," Lucy said, trying her hardest to sound playful as she nudged her friend's feet with hers.

Cora was blushing. "It's true, I used to be much more of a badass. Back when Ad and Scott were first lucky enough to make my acquaintance!"

Lucy felt her heart rev, thinking of what she'd discovered about Juliet being at Leeds at the same time as the three of them.

"She was not to be messed with back then," Adam said, smiling meaningfully at Cora, then turning his smile to Lucy as if remembering she was in the conversation, too.

Scott was saying nothing. Just twirling his wineglass in slow circles.

"Get the old photos out!" Lucy said with all the fake breeziness she could muster. "I love seeing your dodgy noughties fashions. And how sweet you all looked in your little ménage à trois."

"Ménage à trois?" Cora's eyes widened.

"I'm joking, hon," Lucy said with another nudge of her feet. "I just meant how you all hung out together as a threesome."

"Oh, yeah." Cora laughed shrilly. "We were a bit of a triangle."

"I was always the gooseberry," Adam said. "But I rolled the best cigarettes."

"Even if you never actually smoked them yourself," Cora said, and suddenly the room seemed charged with memories that Lucy had no access to.

She began slapping her thigh, chanting, "Photos! Photos! Photos!" Her performance of lightheartedness was stretching almost to its limit. They'd had evenings before when

Cora had got out her shoeboxes full of printed snaps and the three of them had reminisced. Lucy had always tried to be a good sport, tried to hide her faint feeling of exclusion, but she'd usually found herself steering the conversation back to anecdotes that involved them all. Back to that converted barn they'd stayed in for a rainy week, which Fran had become convinced was haunted by the ghost of a cow. Or that country pub where Scott had got dragged up onstage to sing "Danny Boy" with the local band, and Lucy, Cora, and Adam had screamed like his groupies.

Tonight, though, she had a different mission. She wanted them to talk and talk about their university days, show her every careless picture they'd ever taken, just in case Juliet's name or face slipped out from among it all.

CORA BROUGHT THE shoeboxes out under some duress, shooting Lucy a bemused look as she realized she wasn't going to take no for an answer. Scott's attention seemed to snap back into the room as he saw what was happening, the photos of him with gelled hair and a handsome baby face being tipped across the carpet. The kids reappeared, apparently decided that old photos of the grown-ups were of no interest, and ran off again to play a rowdy game of hallway skittles.

"Want some more wine, Luce?" Cora asked.

Lucy hesitated, then made a decision. "No, thanks, Cor. Ad, I'll drive home if you like. Think it's my turn."

"It's been your turn for the last six," he said, smiling to show he was kidding.

Lucy took her empty glass to the kitchen and rinsed it,

upturning it on Cora and Scott's sparkling-clean draining board. She would stay sober and alert tonight. Would push down the waves of emotion that kept heaving through her, and use the one skill she had at her disposal: reading people. The people she knew best, or thought she did at least. She would keep her head and she would watch Scott, watch Cora, try to understand. Taking a deep breath, she went back into the living room and sat on the carpet to shuffle through the photos.

It was a long-running joke that Scott and Cora both looked very different now, while Adam hadn't changed since their university days, bar a few more lines around his eyes. He'd had the same uncontroversial haircut for most of his adult life (which Lucy had always found cute), the same style of glasses, the same fondness for hoodies. The three of them had been housemates for much of their time in Leeds, with Cora and Scott becoming a couple at the start of the final year. Cora burst from many of the photos, sticking out her tongue for the camera, making peace signs—or the reverse—and grinning, always grinning, her hair a rainbow of dyed shades.

When had she folded her exuberance away and decided she'd outgrown it?

As Lucy realized the photos were in roughly chronological order, she began to get a hint of the answer. The later ones, marked out by Cora's more conventional haircut and a return to her natural ash blonde, were mainly of Cora and Scott, posing as a couple with beatific smiles. They were reminiscent of pictures Lucy had taken of them in more recent years. The same angle of their heads and bodies, leaning into one another; the same sense that each picture could pass for an engagement portrait in *Hello!* magazine.

There's never been anybody else, Cora often said. Lucy was never sure how literally she meant that. Or whether she was referring to Scott as well as herself. They certainly both acted as if anything that had come before had paled into insignificance once they'd admitted their feelings for one another. Lucy recalled Scott's head touching Juliet's, mirroring his and Cora's signature pose. Even that would count as a huge betrayal in Cora's eyes. Even cuddling up to another woman a little too intimately in a picture.

The Waughs exchanged a few glances while they were looking through the old photos, Lucy noticed. But there was no hand squeezing, no nostalgic private smiles. An atmosphere swirled in the room again: uneasy body language, unspoken words. Lucy tried to keep up a pretense of casual interest in the pictures. Then she paused over one she didn't remember having seen before, one that seemed to break the mold of the later Cora-and-Scott-centric snaps.

It looked like it had been taken in a bar. Scott was in the middle, leaning forward with a half-empty pint in his hand. Adam and Cora were on either side—but *they* were looking at each other, their gazes meeting somewhere behind Scott's back. There was something in their faces that made the hairs stir on Lucy's arms. Something intense passing between them, captured by whoever had taken the photo.

She held it closer, blinking.

It's just a look. Cameras freeze-frame split seconds. People appearing sad when they're just resting their face. People seeming angry when they're just forming a word that contorts their mouth.

She put the photo aside and snapped out of her reverie to realize that she and Adam were now alone in the living room.

"Food's here," he said. "You okay, Lu? Seemed miles away for a minute."

She tuned back in to the sounds of Scott paying the driver at the door, Cora getting out plates in the kitchen. "I'm fine." Her eyes flicked back to the photo that had stalled her, but it had lost its potency now. She had to stay focused on the things she really needed to worry about. She lowered her voice and spoke quickly: "Ad, did you know her at uni?"

He frowned. "Know who?"

She paused, then breathed out: "Juliet."

He closed his eyes. "Luce, not again."

"She was at Leeds at the same time as you all."

"*Thousands* of people were."

"So you didn't know her?"

"I'd never even heard of her before your bloody obsession with her."

"Obsession with who?" asked Scott, passing through the room with a large paper bag and a waft of spicy scent. He paused and frowned at the two of them, his expression momentarily serious.

"Uh . . . Kylie Minogue," Lucy said in vague panic. "When I was younger."

Scott raised his eyebrows and shot her one of his *you're a bit mad, Taylor* looks. "Was it Cora's mum's perm in the graduation pics that reminded you of that?" he said, then chuckled and continued into the kitchen with the food.

Lucy turned back to Adam. He was frowning now, too.

"I'm worried about you, Luce," he said. "I thought you'd stopped with all this."

"Well, I *haven't*." Her defiance was undermined by the tremor in her voice, as she felt suddenly on the verge of tears. It hurt, she realized, that she didn't have his support, even if she was acting crazy, getting obsessed with something potentially damaging. It hurt that they were on opposite sides.

"Is this because you saw Ruth today?" he asked. "It *was* her, wasn't it? I could tell by the way you ran after her. You looked like you were chasing down an escaped prisoner!"

"She . . . she said she'd deleted the photo. And that it wasn't Juliet anyway."

"Well, then!" He looked exasperated. "Why can't you accept that?"

Why can't I? Lucy's thoughts echoed. They were interrupted by Cora shouting from the kitchen for them to come and help themselves. After a beat, Lucy clambered up from the floor. Her legs had gone to sleep and she staggered, planting a foot in the middle of the photos. Adam grabbed her arm to steady her, and held on to it for a moment, whispering in her ear. "Luce, please. For your own sake, for your mental health, you need to let it go. We're in Scott and Cora's house, for God's sake! You can't be thinking this stuff. They're my friends, too, and it bothers me, it really does. That you could believe—"

The kids were charging past them now, declaring themselves *totally* starving, asking how many poppadoms they were allowed each. Adam released her arm and followed them toward the strengthening aroma of the food being unpacked. Lucy stood stroking the dented skin where his hand had been, her stomach closing against the meaty, spicy smells. On impulse, she leaned down and picked up the photo of Adam and Cora exchanging a glance behind Scott's back. Without quite knowing why, she folded it into the back pocket of her jeans.

The camera never lies, that's what they say.

Except when it does. Except when it tells the wrong story or falls into the wrong hands. When a smile is ambiguous, an angle misleading.

Or maybe it's not the camera that lies, but the people who curate the photos, who interpret them, change them, even destroy them. Maybe it's the distance between a photo and the person looking at it. If you weren't there, how can you really know what happened?

But if you were there, and you were caught on camera, how can you deny it?

Because that's what I keep coming back to. It's the photo that's the problem. If that didn't exist, maybe everything could've been different, maybe the danger would've washed away on its own.

But it does exist. A permanent record, somewhere out there.

And now in my inbox, too.

A reminder? A warning? What is she playing at; what does Juliet want? The emails have been vague so far—menacing, infuriating, but vague—yet the photo is concrete, tangible, shareable. A moment turned into an object that can be passed from hand to hand.

The world can never see it. Never learn what it represents.

CHAPTER SEVEN

SHALL WE PUT THE KIDS TO BED HERE, LUCE?" Adam said after they'd finished the curry and were all sitting around the dining table amid a sea of oily, colorful leftovers.

"Good idea," Cora said. "Then we can all go to Norfolk tomorrow together."

Lucy recoiled from the suggestion. She didn't want her girls to sleep in this house. Couldn't face another day at the cottage, hammering and sanding, breathing in the dust, pretending everything was fine.

"We haven't got any of their stuff with us," she said.

"Oh, we can rustle up some PJs and spare toothbrushes," Cora said. "We've done it enough times before!"

"I know," Lucy murmured. "I'm just not feeling great."

Everybody looked toward her, their faces transforming with concern. "What's wrong, hon?" Cora asked, leaning across to touch her arm. "I noticed you didn't eat much."

Not like you, Luce was the obvious quip, but nobody made it, not even Scott.

"Just feel a bit queasy," Lucy said.

Fran, always sensitive to other people's ailments, rushed over and slid onto her lap, laying her head on her shoulder. "Poor Mummy," she said, snuggling in, clearly tired. Lucy rested her nose in her curly hair and smelled swimming baths and coconut.

"We should get going, Ad," she said. "The girls have had it."

He pushed back his chair as if having an abrupt change of heart. "You're right." Suddenly he was all briskness, collecting the plates and whisking them away to the kitchen. Cora called to him that he didn't need to tidy up. Adam shouted back, "I'm not!" over the sound of a tap gushing on.

"I'll just pop to the toilet," Lucy said, untangling herself from Fran's embrace. She could feel Cora's eyes on her as she went, and tried to aim a reassuring smile over her shoulder.

The upstairs landing was striped with shadows cast by half-open doors. Lucy padded along it, glancing into each familiar room and feeling as if nothing was quite right—the curtains hung strangely; the clocks ticked too loudly; the Waughs' bathroom didn't smell as fresh and floral as usual. Her unease was polluting her surroundings as well as poisoning her thoughts. And she was so tired of feeling this way. So desperate to have her normal life back, her normal *self*, without all the paranoia and doubt. Sitting on the toilet, she dropped her head into her hands and cried.

Only for a few moments. *This isn't going to solve anything, Lucy.* She pulled herself together, left the bathroom, and marched back along the landing. This time, at the entrance to the study, she paused. The flight bookings that Adam had seen. The Tokyo hotel reservation. If she saw *those* for herself, would she feel reassured at last? Lucy hovered, peering at the slice of the room that she could see. From below, she heard the clatter of mass tidying up, and Adam's voice calling, "Cor, are these the normal-cupboard plates or the fancy-cupboard plates?" Lucy glanced behind her, then inched into the study.

A framed photo of Scott, Cora, Ivy, and Joe was the centerpiece of the large oak desk. Lucy gazed at it with a welling of sadness: The session in a photography studio had been a gift from her and Adam when the Waughs had renewed their vows. Lucy had joked that they should have some family photos taken by a professional rather than just always by her, and Cora had said something sweet about preferring Lucy's "naturalistic style" but enjoying the novelty of posing in a studio all the same. "It's just a shame Ivy's doing her Wednesday Addams smile in almost every one," she'd joked when the prints had come back, and she and Lucy had cracked up as they'd picked out the best ones over a glass of wine. Cora, of course, looked flawless in them all. She'd framed the one in which she and Scott were beaming at each other with adoration, and Ivy's grin was huge and real because Scott had tickled her as the camera had clicked.

Now Lucy leafed through the pile of papers to the left of the picture, but found nothing relating to Scott's trip. Nothing in the pile just behind them, either. Things had gone quieter downstairs, so she sped up, turning her attention to the drawers. Her hip nudged the computer chair and it skittered to one side. Shiny, caramel-colored leather caught her eye from underneath the desk. A suitcase. *Scott's* suitcase. Lucy blinked at it for a moment, then crouched down and quietly unzipped it, the smell of leather flooding her senses. As she lifted the lid, her heart began to thunder. There was just one item inside. A sage-green linen shirt with brown buttons.

Exactly what the man had been wearing in Ruth's photo.

"Lucy?"

She stood up so fast she banged her head on the desk. Clutching it, she turned to see Scott leaning in the doorway. Arms folded, eyebrows high. Lucy waited for a joke from him, like when he'd caught her looking in his jacket, but this time he let her dangle, and this time she couldn't think of an excuse.

"I was . . ." She trailed off and realized, as they faced one another, that maybe she didn't want an excuse. Maybe this was it. Enough was enough; she couldn't go on pretending everything was okay. "Scott, can I talk to you?"

As he stepped properly into the room, closing the door behind him, her resolve wavered and her nerves took hold. The limited light that had come from the landing disappeared. Only a small desk lamp now illuminated the room, casting an amber glow that was almost like candlelight, failing to stretch to the very corners of the study.

"What is it?" he asked gruffly. "What are you doing in here, Luce? Crouching under my desk . . . ?" He looked at her as if she'd entirely lost the plot.

"Are you . . ." She paused, swallowed. Wondered where to begin. "Have you . . . Scott, have you been having an affair?"

"Have I *what*?" Shock washed over his face just as the low light seemed to shift, catching his dilated pupils.

"Were you really in Japan last week?"

"What the . . . ? Of course I was!" He straightened up tall, unfolding his arms, his whole posture indignant. "What are you looking for in here, proof that I'm not a scumbag?"

"Well, yes, actually. I mean, no, not . . ." Words even worse than *scumbag* flashed through her head and she still couldn't tell if she believed them, if she could hang them on him, make them fit. "I . . . I think you went somewhere else. The Maldives. With . . ." She faltered at the expression on his face. He looked as if the words coming out of her mouth were the most offensive ones he'd ever heard.

But she couldn't leave it. She was in neck-deep. "Do you know Juliet Noor?" she whispered.

"Who?"

She stared at him, absorbing the quickness of that *who?* Even if her name hadn't been all over the news, surely he remembered Lucy bringing her up only a few days before.

"The woman who's missing. Who's a trade journalist in *your* industry. Who went to the same university as you, at the same time. And who . . ." She paused, sensing that this was the no-going-back moment. "Who I saw you with . . ."

"*Saw* me?"

"In a photo." She was breathless. "On my colleague's phone."

For a few seconds he did nothing but blink, his mouth jerking down at the corners, transforming his whole face.

"What the fuck, Lucy?" He took a couple of steps back and raised his hands as if in self-defense. "That is *not* possible. You've got something very, very wrong here."

They ended up on opposite sides of the room and it seemed to subvert what she'd been braced for: him closing in, looming over her, scaring her. Now he was just Scott again, backed up against his own study wall by her accusations.

"What the fuck, Lucy," he repeated, the question mark falling off the end.

Lucy felt the wind knocked out of her. She held on to the desk chair but it moved again on its wheels, giving her the sensation of the floor sliding away.

"I don't know what it is you think you've seen, or what you're accusing me of," Scott continued, inching forward again. "I can't believe you would think *any* of it, given how long we've . . . how *much* we've . . . But I'm not having an affair. I don't even know that woman, so I can't have been in a picture with her. I was in Japan. Working. How dare you come in here, going through my stuff, making accusations . . . ?"

"I'm not accusing you of anything," she said, though it felt blatantly untrue. "I'm just saying, if you have any information about Juliet, you have to go to the police."

"I have *no* information about her." This seemed to whistle out through clenched teeth. "I keep telling you, I don't *know* her! Fuck, you haven't said anything crazy to Cora, have you?"

She shook her head, feeling queasy. He was still coming toward her, re-closing the distance.

"We have a trust that runs much deeper than you seem to think."

"*She* has a lot of trust," Lucy agreed as a picture of Cora's bare feet came into her mind, her curled shape on the sofa, her blush when she'd remembered cheering raucously for Ivy. And her total belief that, in her own words, *Scott would never look at another woman.* "I just hope you haven't abused that."

His eyes flashed. "Cora knows I never would. You would know that, too, if you bothered to stop and think for once!"

The sting of his words caught her off guard. As if she was now the one finding out what he really thought of her, not the other way around. Anger surged, propelled by desperation, the snowball effect of everything she'd been wrestling with over the last week.

She drew herself up taller. "Then promise me," she said. "Look me in the eye. Swear on Ivy's and Joe's lives. Swear you've never met Juliet Noor."

"Jesus, Lucy! This isn't on!"

"Swear on their *lives.*"

He looked into her face, breathing heavily, for what felt like a long, excruciating moment. "I can do better than that."

Brushing past her, he went to the desk and yanked open a drawer. Seconds later a wad of paper was shoved into her hands. She looked down through a veil of tears, seeing the words *Boarding Pass.* There they were—Heathrow to Tokyo, Tokyo to Heathrow. And underneath, a booking at a hotel in Tokyo for the full fortnight.

"Do you want to call my colleagues? Check with them? Be my fucking guest . . ." His eyes were blazing and glimmering, and she started shaking her head, filled with the sinking feeling that this was a grave mistake, after all, that she must really be losing her mind.

"Don't ever use my children in that way again," Scott said in a low, furious voice.

He put his hands on her shoulders to shift her out of his way, then stormed from the room, leaving her choked with tears, his boarding passes scrunched in her fist. And with the lingering realization that he hadn't actually sworn on their lives, in the end, and she supposed she couldn't blame him.

CHAPTER EIGHT

I CAN'T GO, ADAM. I'M SORRY, I JUST . . . CAN'T."

He stood by their bed, holding the cup of tea he'd made her. Lucy was swathed in the duvet and could smell her night sweats still clinging to it. There was a clogged feeling behind her eyes, a dryness to her mouth, like a hangover even though she'd stayed deliberately sober the night before. Maybe she *was* ill. She ran a finger over her cracked lips and let her eyes droop shut. Scott's face appeared behind her lids and made them spring back open.

Don't ever use my children in that way again.

And yet, to Lucy's disbelief, Norfolk Sunday was still going ahead. Scott mustn't have said anything to Cora about their confrontation. Both he and Lucy had acted as if nothing had happened as the two families had said their slightly subdued good-byes last night. But Lucy had been half expecting a call from Cora this morning, demanding to know what was going on. Nothing, though. Just a sense of waiting for the fallout.

"You don't look too good," Adam said, putting the tea down on the nightstand and perching on the edge of the bed. He reached out to feel her forehead and Lucy remembered how he used to rub her temples when she had a hangover, his hands gentle but firm. How he'd bring her tea and ibuprofen, then climb back into bed and the tea would end up going cold. It had always been on those mornings, snuggled in post-boozy bliss, when Adam would start talking about a hypothetical future, suggesting they could move away one day, leave everything behind. They'd never done it, of course. Their jobs and their friendship with the Waughs had kept them loyal to Leicester. But it was strange to think that if they'd ever got serious about relocating, Lucy might not be facing this dilemma, might never have seen that photo.

"You could still take the girls," she said. "I don't feel up to any DIY. Or a long car trip."

"Would it help you get some rest if I took them?"

"I think you know the answer to that," she said, mustering a smile. If the girls were in the house, they'd be bouncing on the bed, wriggling under the covers with her. The thought filled her with both longing and exhaustion. "I'm sorry, Ad," she reiterated, unsure why she felt quite so guilty.

"I'll take them," he said. "As long as you'll be okay?"

"I just need to sleep." She pulled the duvet over her head and felt Adam lay a hand on her through the fabric. He made a noise as if he was kissing the air near to her, for lack of being able to reach her, then she heard the door softly close, with what might have been a sigh from him.

SHE WOKE WITH such a jolt it was like having the covers ripped away. In fact, she *had* kicked the duvet off in restless sleep, but that wasn't what had woken her. Her phone was ringing from the bedside table.

She groped for it, her immediate thought being, *Adam and the girls.* When she saw it was Cora she hesitated, wondering if this was the angry call she'd been anticipating. But what if *she* was ringing because of an emergency in Norfolk? Lucy steeled herself and answered the phone.

"I didn't wake you, did I?" Cora said.

"It's okay. Is everything all right?"

"That means I did wake you! Sorry, hon! I'm at the door."

"Which door?"

"Yours! I didn't want to use my key and burst in! I've just come to check on you. Ad said you're not well."

"But . . ." Lucy sat up, blinking. "Aren't you in Norfolk?"

"No, I decided to stay at home, too. Let them have some man time, whatever that constitutes. And I was worried about you."

"I'll come down." Lucy swung her legs around, her feet rocking unsteadily against the carpet.

When she opened the front door, Cora's eyes widened.

"Oh, Luce, you do look ill! Which I realize is one of those things people say that makes the person feeling like crap feel even more like crap . . ." Cora held up the offerings she'd brought: a flask of homemade smoothie, a Tupperware container full of thick green soup, some herbal cough sweets. Lucy fought tears again as she sat at the kitchen table watching her friend heat up the soup. She remembered how incredible Cora had been after Lucy's C-section with Fran. Adam had been sweet, supporting her in his own way by printing off endless web pages about C-section recovery, but Cora had known the most comforting things to say, how to make her laugh even when it strained her stitches. Now, as Lucy sat in the same fluffy dressing gown she'd lived in during that time, slurping Cora's broccoli soup, she almost choked on the secrets she'd been keeping from her best friend.

Cora sat down opposite Lucy and reached for her hands. "It is just a cold, isn't it, Luce?" she asked. "There's nothing else bothering you? You've not seemed yourself recently."

Lucy couldn't meet her eye. "It's just a cold. And work's been mad."

"You *would* tell me if something else was wrong?"

A lump blocked Lucy's throat and she pretended to have a coughing fit, extricating her hands from Cora's. She had another jolting flashback to the previous night. Forcing Scott to swear on Ivy's and Joe's lives. Lucy's *godchildren*. How had it come to that?

"There's nothing, honest," she answered Cora, though she was sure her face told a different story. "I . . ." She hesitated. "I was actually going to ask you the same thing."

"I guess we've both just got a lot going on at the moment." There was something veiled about Cora's smile. She ran her slim fingers over the tabletop, and Lucy knew her well enough to be able to tell there was more she wanted to say.

"Are you worried about the cottage, Luce?" she asked eventually. "The . . . financial aspect, I mean."

Lucy was taken aback.

"What makes you say that?"

"I've seen the look on your face sometimes when we have to order materials or find something else massive to be done. The way you brush over it, especially when Adam's there . . . but *I* can tell you're worried."

"Nobody likes shelling out money!" Lucy protested, her cheeks heating. "But it's not a problem, honestly, Cor. It's an investment. Our lovely . . ." She felt choked again. "Our lovely cottage."

She looked over at the pinboard, at the collage of photos that Adam had made for her as a surprise a few months ago. He'd photoshopped them to show what the cottage might look like when the renovations were finished: brightly painted walls, new furniture, restored floorboards, and beautiful beams. Lucy had cried with delight when he'd shown it to her, imagining him spending ages getting the images just right, taking much more interest in carpet colors or curtain fabrics than he would in real life.

"We could help," Cora said, a little too brightly. "Scott and I could take on a bit more of the financial burden."

"No, you don't have to do that!" Lucy shook her head. This was not the conversation she'd expected to be having with Cora. Not the one she'd been having in her mind for the last few days. "Cora, this is all unnecessary! Thank you, but . . . unnecessary. Let's drop it, please?"

"Okay." Cora sat back in her chair, moving her hands into her lap. "Sorry, Luce." There was a pause which became awkward, neither of them looking at each other. Cora got her phone out and began fiddling with it, while Lucy put her soup bowl into the dishwasher as something to do.

When she came back to the table, ready to change the subject, she caught a glimpse of Cora's phone over her shoulder. Adam's name was at the top of the screen, visible for just a second before Cora closed her messages.

Lucy cleared her throat. "Are they . . . all okay in Norfolk?"

Cora looked up, blinking. "Oh, yes!" There was another slightly awkward pause. "That was Ad, checking how you are."

Lucy glanced at her own phone. "He hasn't messaged me." She was aware of sounding like a jealous teenager.

"He knew I was planning to call in. I said I'd let him know how you seemed. He's fretting about you." Cora smiled and put her phone away. "That man's a keeper."

"I know," Lucy said. "That's why I kept him!" It was supposed to be a joke but she felt weirdly petulant. She remembered the old photo she'd slipped into her pocket last night: Adam and Cora gazing at each other while Scott grinned obliviously at the camera. She hadn't given it a thought since her confrontation with Scott, but now she felt an urge to fetch it and look at it again.

"Hon, you look pale," Cora said, frowning, and jumping to her feet. "I'll make you another cuppa."

All Lucy wanted, suddenly, was for Cora to leave her alone. The realization made her feel wretched. She'd never had a longing to show her the door before.

Instead, she smiled thinly, doing her best impression of someone whose head was not a total mess.

"Make it a proper one, though, Cor," she said. "Just because I'm sick doesn't mean I *have* to drink herbal."

Cora laughed and began filling the kettle. After she'd made the drink ("One builder's tea, extra buildery"), she announced that she was going to leave Lucy to rest. Her departure seemed so abrupt that Lucy worried she'd upset her, being weird about Adam's message. Under normal circumstances she wouldn't give a second thought to Adam texting Cora rather than her. Why was the Juliet thing warping her entire perspective?

She hugged Cora tightly when they said good-bye, as if trying to re-seal something that might be coming unstuck. And she noticed how thin her friend felt, thinner than ever, or was Lucy imagining that, too?

LUCY WENT BACK upstairs after Cora had gone, and took a long, extra-hot bath, trying to soak away her worries. A message from Adam came through as she was dressing:

> Missing you. Hope you're feeling better xxx

He sent a photo of Tilly and Fran helping Scott to paint the living room wall.

> Only allowing them to get involved in the base coat, obviously!!

They both looked insanely cute, absorbed in the task. Lucy's eyes went to Scott and a shudder rippled through her.

Great brushwork, she typed back. In the past she might've added a joke along the lines of Scott's has room for improvement, though. But she could no longer talk about him in a lighthearted way.

She assured Adam she was feeling a bit better, then picked up her jeans from the chair she'd draped them over last night. Taking out the folded-up photo, she allowed herself one more look. She was reading too much into it. Reading too much into *everything*. It was just a freeze-frame of a moment between three close friends, years ago.

Something new drew her attention, though. Another man in the dark background of the photo, looking toward Scott, Cora, and Adam. He had a beer bottle in his hand, and a woman beside him with her back to the camera, only partly in the shot. Clearly the picture had been taken in a pub or somewhere social, but this man seemed to be ignoring any companions in favor of watching the photo being taken. Watching with an expression that, yet again, plucked at Lucy's instincts. He was extremely good-looking, about the same age as the other three, with a strong jawline, high cheekbones, and long fair hair that brushed the upturned collar of his denim jacket. But he didn't look happy. Seemed to be observing the triangle of Scott, Cora, and Adam with trouble in his face.

"Mummyyyy?"

Voices and footsteps from below. Lucy shoved the photo into her underwear drawer and turned toward the familiar but unexpected sound of her family tumbling into the house. She wrestled on her jeans, tied up her damp hair, and ran downstairs. Tilly and Fran launched themselves at her before seeming to remember she was feeling poorly and pulling away, making a big show of handling her more carefully.

"I didn't expect you back yet," Lucy said, kissing Adam. "I only just got a message from you."

"I sent that a while ago," Adam said. "Mind you, the signal seemed even dodgier than usual there today."

"You managed to get through to Cora, though," Lucy said.

"Cora?" He shot her a confused look, and Lucy hated herself again. "Yeah, I guess," he said with a shrug.

"Hey, Luce," came Scott's voice from behind Adam, making Lucy's heart vault. He was stepping through the still-open front door, a tired-looking Ivy and Joe trailing behind him. "How you feeling?"

"Um . . . okay." Lucy was thrown by his presence. His demeanor was normal, maybe a little stilted, his overalls splashed with terra-cotta-colored paint, which looked unnervingly like dried blood.

"Your coat ended up in our car," Scott said to Adam, hanging it on a peg. "Just spotted it before we turned off home; thought you might need it."

"Oh, cheers," Adam said. He glanced at Lucy, indecision crossing his face, then added, slightly cautiously, "Stay for a quick beer before you head on?"

Scott seemed hesitant, too. But the kids all perked up at the idea of a bit more time together, and soon Scott and Adam were on the sofa with beers in hand and the TV on, while Lucy sat in an armchair feeling tenser than she'd ever felt in her own living room. They filled her in on the day and attempted to include her in the conversation, but her thoughts were a silent, paralyzing loop. Ruth at the swimming pool. Scott last night in the study. Boarding passes, hotel bookings. A sage-green shirt in a suitcase. *I don't know Juliet Noor. Don't ever use my children in that way again.*

Only the familiar intro to the evening news eventually snapped her out of it. An automatic attention-grabber for her at the moment. She glanced at Scott, anxious but curious at the idea of potentially seeing a news update about Juliet while he was in the room. Discreetly, she turned up the volume until Scott and Adam's conversation petered out. An atmosphere seemed to develop as the headlines were rattled through. Then the name they were all clearly waiting for, without having acknowledged it.

The body of a woman found washed up on a beach in the Maldives has not yet been confirmed as that of Juliet Noor.

Stillness fell over the room. Lucy was barely breathing.

A body. A woman.

She felt sick to her stomach. Surely it was her. She'd wanted to test Scott's response to any updates on the search, but she hadn't expected this.

She could feel Adam looking her way. As far as Lucy knew, he was still none the wiser about her confronting Scott the night before. He seemed to be willing her with his eyes not to overreact to the latest news. Heart pounding, she looked over at Scott, whose gaze was fixed on the screen. His hands were clenched, as if he wanted to hit something, yet he looked as if he'd just been punched in the gut himself.

Seconds later, he stood up and strode out of the room. Lucy heard Ivy's voice saying, "Daddy, are you all right?" followed by the firm closing of the downstairs toilet door.

"The entire south side of the island has now been designated as a crime scene," the news report continued, "but no official police statement about the identity of the body has yet been—"

The screen switched to Sky Sports and Lucy blinked in surprise. She turned her head to see that Adam had stood up and grabbed the remote from the arm of her chair. He started flicking through the other sports channels, murmuring about catching the snooker, acting as if he could change reality simply by changing the picture on their TV.

It's all I think about some days. The moment of stillness after it happened. The slow seep of blood. And afterward, the tainted smell of the air. A new understanding of what the phrase "dead weight" really means.

Even when I manage to put it out of my mind, there's always something to remind me.

Always someone *to remind me.*

History repeats itself, so they say. Another phrase I've never really given much thought to until now.

Juliet tried to ruin my life once before. I couldn't let her try a second time. I knew it wasn't a coincidence, any of it. That she was back on the scene, with her beauty, her charm, acting like nothing significant had happened in our past. That she'd turned up in the world of aerospace, as if by pure chance. And the emails. The emails that wouldn't stop coming.

And when I saw what she'd been writing about in her so-called novel, that was when I knew, really *knew, that there was no going back.*

Except it isn't over.

It will never be over while the photo is still out there. Will never be over while people are looking for things they don't understand.

CHAPTER NINE

LUCY NEVER NORMALLY HAD HER PHONE ON HER in class. She'd switch it to Do Not Disturb and leave it in her bag, misguidedly hoping her students would follow suit. But today she kept it in her desk drawer, doing frequent, surreptitious checks of various news sites. Had the body been identified? Was it her? Was it her?

Nothing yet.

Scott had left almost straight after the news last night. He'd come back from the toilet and attempted to maintain a pretense for a few more minutes, but Lucy had noticed his beer disappearing quickly. The moment he'd finished it, he'd stood up and barked to Ivy and Joe that it was time to go home and have their baths. The color never returned to his face; he never looked Lucy in the eye.

Adam hadn't wanted to discuss it, either. He and Lucy had gone to bed almost in silence, both clearly disturbed but afraid to voice their thoughts or hear the other's. When Lucy had closed her eyes, all she'd been able to see was a body on a white beach, with soaking-wet hair splayed across the sand like black tentacles. And next to her, once again, she'd been able to feel Adam's restlessness, seeming to push him further away from her rather than bond them in their shared anxiety.

At lunchtime, she searched for Ruth again. She was nowhere to be found, and nobody who Lucy asked knew whether she was at work.

Lucy couldn't help herself. She sent Ruth another message.

Please can we talk?

There was no reply. And nothing new from the BBC News app, no matter how many times she refreshed it. Lucy could barely string a sentence together as she attempted to teach her afternoon lessons, her students eyeing her as if she was going insane.

At the end of the day, she retreated to the staffroom, attempting to finish marking some papers. Normally, she liked to sit in the middle of the room with the buzz of conversation around her, but today she hunkered in the corner, trying to tune it all out.

Until she heard the words.

"That body," somebody said, almost matter-of-factly. "It's her, apparently."

Lucy's eyes snapped to the speaker. It was Paulo, a PE teacher, looking at his phone with his feet propped up on the table in front of him. A casual pose, a casual tone, as he talked about someone's death. Lucy's heart climbed into her mouth.

"The Maldives woman?" asked Kara from Learning Support, glancing up from a cup of tea. "Juliet thingy?"

"Noor." It was only as heads swiveled that Lucy realized she'd been the one to say it, and that she'd spoken too loudly, almost territorially.

"Someone's back in the room," Paulo joked, and Lucy laughed uneasily. Her mouth had dried up. She reached for her water bottle, then changed her mind and scrambled for her phone instead. It was only a breaking story, hardly any details yet, and no indication of the cause of death.

Police continue to ask anyone with relevant information to come forward.

Juliet's face accompanied it, now with an extra quality, both haunting and haunted. When Lucy dragged her gaze away, the room swam. She swayed to her feet and rushed out.

She's dead. The finality of it kept thumping into her. The leap from "missing" was bigger than she'd imagined. She closed her eyes and felt tears prickle behind her lids.

When she opened them, she realized, with a jolt, that she was looking straight at Ruth. There she was—at last—in the nearest classroom, supervising a detention alongside another teacher. Lucy's heart revved up again. Ruth still didn't look very well, or very happy, her bob scraped back from her face with a soft white band. Lucy never had found out what kind of illness had kept her off sick. Hadn't managed to speak to her since Saturday at the pool.

Suddenly, Ruth looked in her direction. Her face transformed, passing through surprise and something like alarm, finishing unmistakably on a *you again* kind of anger. She stared at Lucy, unblinking, until Lucy dropped her gaze and reluctantly retreated.

A few steps down the corridor, she stopped. She couldn't leave it. Not after she'd spent all day on the lookout for Ruth. She spun on her heel and walked back to the classroom, knocking briskly at the same time as opening the door. Ruth looked horrified when Lucy burst in. The other teacher seemed surprised, too, turning with a stiff, questioning smile, while the two students took the opportunity to roll their eyes at each other in a why-are-we-even-here exchange. Lucy cringed at her own unprofessionalism. She could be impulsive sometimes, it was true, but she was usually on her best behavior at work.

"Sorry," she said, holding up a palm and speaking too fast. "Really sorry, but, Ruth, could I have a quick word?"

Ruth looked flustered. "I'm"—she gestured at the students—"in the middle of something."

"Two minutes, I promise."

"Not right now, Mrs. Taylor." The use of her teacher name was pointed, the politeness creaking in Ruth's voice.

"But something's come up," Lucy said, aware that she sounded desperate, "related to what we've been discussing."

"It can *wait*." Ruth's tone was steely now, and any trace of a smile, even for show, was gone.

Lucy stared at her for a couple more seconds, wondering what she was avoiding. Why she looked so spooked every time Lucy came anywhere near her. The other teacher began tapping a pen impatiently against her chin. The conversation had reached a dead end, and Lucy had no choice but to back away, feeling all their eyes on her as she did.

"IT WAS HER," she said to Adam that night as they loaded spaghetti-hoop-stained plates into their groaning dishwasher.

Adam froze, bent over with a fistful of knives and forks, then slowly straightened up, like someone with a bad back. Lucy was reminded of when he'd had sciatica a few years ago and had spent days lying on the floor. Tilly and Fran had put on a show to cheer him up, dangling homemade puppets in his face. Then the Waughs had come round for Saturday-night drinks and they'd all sat in a circle around him, Scott pretending to use him as a footstool while Cora prescribed yoga stretches and muscle rubs. Lucy remembered Adam commenting that, once upon a time, Cora would've fed him beer and slipped a joint into his mouth to help his plight. Had Scott looked slightly annoyed at that? Or was Lucy adding shades to every memory?

"The body," she said, blinking back into the present. "It . . . it was Juliet Noor."

There was a beat of silence. She had broken their unsaid agreement not to talk about the subject anymore. There was a relief in it; she hated having to censor herself around him. *Honesty, always.* It was him who'd insisted on that when they'd first got serious about each other. Who'd said lies and silence could cause more damage than anything else—and then, admittedly, had laughed when she asked if he was talking from experience, and said he was quoting a magazine he'd read in a doctors' waiting room. But, still. They'd kept coming back to the sentiment over the years. And yet here they were, in the thick of a crisis, dancing around something huge.

"I know." He glanced at her, his face solemn. "I heard." His eyes scrunched behind his glasses and he bowed his head back to their task, methodically poking cutlery into the holder.

Lucy realized her hand was shaking. A plate rattling and almost slipping through her fingers as she lowered it into the tray. Then she felt Adam's hand on hers, gripping as if to steady it. She turned her head and met his gaze.

"You're not still . . . ?" he said. "You don't still think . . . ?"

His expression was anxious. Pleading. The smell of spaghetti hoops and tomato sauce rose incongruously from below.

Lucy dropped her eyes. "Of course not," she said in a small voice. "It's just sad, that's all. For her family."

"It really is." He squeezed her hand and she felt her wedding ring press into the fingers on either side. "She probably drowned. Perhaps it was suicide. It's a tragedy. But, Lucc . . ." He squeezed again, slightly harder, and looked her in the eye. "It isn't *our* tragedy."

ADAM WENT TO bed early that night, and Lucy stayed up awhile. She sat in the garden, even though the evening had a cool bite to it, and looked up at the stars as she tried to take stock. The thought that kept returning, like a whisper in the air, was: *You have to go to the police*. Even if her fears about Scott were wrong—and God, she hoped they were—her conscience said she had a moral duty to report them. *Anyone with relevant information*, all the news reports kept saying, as if they were talking directly to her.

But she couldn't separate the simplicity of the right

choice from the mess of its potential consequences. Cora's devastation if she were to find out Scott had been having an affair, even if the truth was no worse than that. The kids' terror if their dad were to be taken into custody—whatever the outcome, it would be traumatic. And even if Lucy tipped off the police anonymously, *she* would know what she had done. Whatever it led to, she would always know she'd been the one to tear her friends' family apart.

"Fuck," she whispered into the chill, pulling her cardigan tight around herself. Whichever way she thought about it, the situation felt impossible. And yet she had to do something. She couldn't go on like this.

Tomorrow, she promised herself, staring up at the almost-full moon. Tomorrow, she would do what needed to be done.

CHAPTER TEN

LUCY HAD NEVER BEEN INSIDE A POLICE STATION before. She'd been dreading it all day at work, picturing daunting scenarios and escalating conversations. Her students had been rehearsing scenes but so had she, her lips moving as she'd sat in a corner of the drama studio preparing what she needed to say. Now she was lathered in sweat as she walked across a bright foyer toward a desk behind a high plastic screen. A slightly formidable desk sergeant swept aside some paperwork and asked how she could help in a way that made Lucy think, *If only you could.* Lucy kept her voice low, as if they were in a library or a church, though there was a charge in the air that was different from the calmness of either.

"I . . . might have information about a crime," she said, leaning into the word *might* like a crutch.

She was asked a few questions. As soon as she mentioned the name Juliet Noor, she felt a shift in the way the woman spoke to her, as if she was being moved to the front of a queue she wasn't even sure she wanted to be in.

"Please take a seat." The sergeant gestured with her pen. "Someone will be with you very soon."

The waiting area smelled of carpet cleaner and faintly of BO. There were two other people: a young man hovering on the edge of his chair, as though he might bolt at any moment, and a woman shivering in a miniskirt with no tights, who looked at Lucy with bold curiosity. As Lucy took a seat, her phone began to vibrate. She pulled it out of her bag to see that Adam was calling. Lucy let it ring, watching his name on her screen with mounting guilt. After it had rung out, she sent him a text:

Staying at work to finish a few bits. All okay with school pickup? See you at home xxxx

His response came in:

What time will you be back? X

She found herself overanalyzing it. Did he suspect she was here, or not being honest with him? How would he react if he knew? Shake his head in disappointment; close his eyes as if he couldn't believe her thoughtlessness? Lucy's stomach lurched at the idea. Yet again, she felt a surge of resentment that Scott's secrets were spawning her own, like toxic pieces breaking off and taking root where they landed.

And now she was sweating again. The sides of her phone were slick with it. As she wiped them with the hem of her dress, glad of a small task to focus on, the screen lit up once more. This time it was a Facebook message. And this time, when Lucy opened the app, she was shocked to see it was from Ruth.

> You wanted to see the photo again. Here it is. I retrieved it. I hope this confirms what we talked about and we can put the whole matter to rest.

Lucy's heart began a slow boom. She read the message for a second time. So formal. So . . . strange. Now that she was about to see the photo again—the thing she'd been trying to do from the start; the thing she needed to show the police—she tensed up with apprehension.

It took a few seconds to load. When it appeared, it was blurry for a moment, then it sharpened and clarified, took over the screen.

Her mind felt as if it was still loading, too. A couple beamed out at her: a woman with wild dark hair and bare shoulders; an auburn-haired man in a sage-green shirt and retro sunglasses.

Not Juliet. Not Scott. The same pose, clothes, backdrop, but *different faces*.

Lucy closed her eyes, then reopened them. The picture didn't change, didn't revert to her memory of it from before.

"Lucy Taylor?" A voice cut into her whirling thoughts.

It took Lucy a moment to raise her head. She stared at the police officer who had come to call her through. He was tall and silver-haired, towering over her with a whiff of coffee on his breath.

"Lucy Taylor?" he repeated, looking at her questioningly.

"I . . ." She was muddled now. Full of doubt. "I think . . . I might've made a mistake."

"Come through and talk to us," he said in a coaxing voice with the tiniest note of impatience. "It's natural to be nervous. But any information can be helpful. Even mistakes sometimes lead to useful things."

"But no, I . . ." Lucy glanced down at her phone again. When she looked back up, the man was gesturing encouragingly. She got to her feet in a daze and followed him into a small, plain room. A second police officer was already sitting at the table, a woman with fashionable, thick-framed glasses and a ponytail so glossy and neat it made Lucy feel unkempt.

"This is DC Aggarwal and I'm DC Marr," the silver-haired man said, pointing in turn. "Would you like some water, Mrs. Taylor?"

Lucy nodded mutely. He went off to fetch it and the other detective made small talk with Lucy. She was obviously trying to put her at ease, but it didn't seem to be her forte and they soon lapsed into silence. Lucy snuck her phone out of her pocket to look at the photo again. The key piece of evidence, and it wasn't what she'd thought. It should've brought a crashing tide of relief, but something wasn't right, *really* wasn't right. Keeping her phone under the desk, she zoomed in on the couple. Their expressions, their features, the outline of their shoulders as they met the velvety darkness of the background. Certainty was building inside her now. Gathering strength.

This isn't the same photo.

The picture was framed and posed in just the way she recalled. But she would never have mistaken this man for Scott. And the woman had a distinctive mole in her cheek that Lucy was sure she would've noticed and remembered; it was the kind of detail she always did.

Why would Ruth send a different, but similar, photo? Had she altered it to get Lucy off her back once and for all?

A glass of water appeared in front of her, snapping her back into the room. DC Aggarwal cleared her throat and opened her notebook with the air of somebody about to give a reading at a formal event.

"Mrs. Taylor, thank you for coming in. We understand you may have information about Juliet Noor's disappearance. This is an important investigation, being overseen by Interpol. We have instructions to ask you a few initial questions, but they may need to contact you to follow up."

Interpol? Lucy's stomach churned again. "I . . . I don't know anything for certain," she said. "I should make that really clear."

They nodded, poker-faced. Lucy felt as if she was hovering on a precipice, deciding whether to step over the edge. Knowing, really, that she'd already made the decision, had begun the slow slide downward.

"Take your time," Marr said. "Tell us exactly why you came here today."

"Well . . . just over a week ago . . . I saw a photo on a colleague's phone," she began haltingly. "Among her holiday photos from the Maldives. I thought . . . think . . ." She hesitated, doubt grabbing her by the throat again. "I think it was of Juliet Noor. With my . . . friend . . ." She couldn't bring herself to voluntarily say his name. A tiny part of her still hoped she wouldn't have to.

"Who is your colleague?" DC Aggarwal asked, pen poised.

Lucy blinked. She had forgotten she'd be bringing Ruth into this, too. So much for her attempt to throw Lucy off the scent and end her own involvement. If that was, in fact, what the fake photo had been.

"It's important we have all the information," the female detective pressed.

"Ruth Beaumont." Lucy's voice got quieter. She knew what question would be coming next.

"And your friend's name? The one pictured with Juliet?"

Lucy swallowed. "Scott." A bubble formed in her throat and she coughed. "Scott Waugh."

DC Aggarwal wrote it down, asking her to spell *Waugh*, seeming to drag out the whole thing. Even the squeak of her pen on the notepad was painful. She laid it down and looked back at Lucy. "Can you tell us a little more about the photo?"

"I can tell you my memory of it," Lucy said.

The officers looked at her as if she was being deliberately cryptic. Lucy blinked and tried to explain. "I only saw it once, quite briefly. I was pretty sure it was Scott, with a woman I didn't recognize. Ruth described them as a couple she'd met on her honeymoon. Jason and Anna. But Scott's married to my friend Cora, so obviously I was . . . confused. Then when I saw Juliet in the news . . ."

"Where is the photo now?" DC Marr interrupted her flow, and DC Aggarwal shot him a look that suggested she wasn't happy he'd done so.

Lucy paused, sipping some water. "I don't know. That's where it gets . . ." She brought her phone slowly onto the tabletop. "Ruth told me she'd deleted it. But then, just now, she sent me this." Opening the photo, she pushed it toward the officers.

They exchanged another quick glance. "This . . . *isn't* Juliet Noor," the male officer said in a slightly patronizing tone, while the woman studied the photo with a forensic gaze.

"*Yes*, I realize that," Lucy said. "But . . . I also don't think it's the photo I originally saw. It's the same in every way, except for the faces."

"This isn't your friend Scott Waugh, either?"

"No."

DC Aggarwal dropped the phone as if she'd seen enough. "You think it's been doctored?" she said, cutting to the chase.

Lucy's gut tightened. She wasn't sure if it was with certainty or fear. "I think it must've been."

The officers swapped another glance, then the woman began rapidly taking notes. Lucy felt her panic re-building. "I'm not saying he had anything to do with what's happened to Juliet . . ." she said in a rush of anxiety. "And I have no proof he was even there with her. But I just thought I should tell you . . ."

DC Aggarwal's head jerked up. "You did the right thing."

"I don't want his family to be hurt by this," Lucy said. "I couldn't bear it if—"

"We understand. But the investigating officers will need to look into this thoroughly. Talk to whoever they need to. Finding out what happened to Juliet is paramount."

Lucy held a hand over her own mouth as she nodded. She'd just put a bulldozer through the middle of her best friend's life. She wanted to flee the room, leave it all behind, but the detectives had questions. Of course they did. Was Scott supposed to have been in the Maldives at that time? Did Lucy have any reason to suspect he'd been having an affair? What was his marriage like? Did he have any history of violence?

"No," Lucy said. "No, no, no, I've never known him to be violent. And his marriage . . . it's happy. I've always thought it was happy."

"We're sorry," DC Marr said, inclining his head in what

seemed like a practiced gesture, a pace-changer in the conversation. "We know this must be hard. But we have to get the full picture. A murder investigation like this—"

Lucy turned cold. "Murder?"

DC Marr twitched, then pressed his mouth closed and slid his eyes to his colleague. DC Aggarwal looked angry, though she tried to mask it by taking a moment to smooth back her hair. Then she laid her palms on the desk, on either side of her notebook. "Yes." She nodded slowly. "My colleague has been a little hasty, but I'm sure you'll treat this with the strictest of confidence, Mrs. Taylor . . . Juliet Noor's death *is* being treated as murder."

"She didn't drown?" As she said it, Lucy realized her subconscious had been clinging to this possibility. To a version in which Scott was having an affair with Juliet, and that was bad, destructive, but it wasn't criminal. He'd had a secret trip away with her, then she had drowned. It was a terrible scenario to wish for, but wasn't that what Lucy had been doing, if she was honest, since the body was found?

"No, the cause of death was not drowning. So . . . you see why we need to question anyone who spent time with her in the days before she died."

Lucy laced her fingers in her lap. "What *was* the cause of death?"

The two police officers looked at each other again. The air felt thick with the word *murder*, and there was a new wariness in their manners. Lucy got the feeling there'd be an argument as soon as she left the room.

"That is also confidential at the moment," Aggarwal said with a firmness that seemed to be for her colleague's benefit as much as Lucy's.

Ripe images exploded in Lucy's mind's eye. Juliet being hit, pushed, stabbed, strangled . . . She inhaled and shook her head to dissolve them.

"Are there any suspects?" she asked. "It can't have been Scott. You understand that, don't you? I'm not saying I think he's capable of murder." But she had said his name in the same breath as the word, and that seemed to move the idea from impossible to minutely possible: a tiny, terrible shift.

"Interpol are following up leads."

"Speaking of which . . ." Aggarwal picked up a file that had been next to her elbow on the desk and drew out a piece of paper. She placed a printed, grainy photograph in front of Lucy. "Do you know this man?"

Lucy frowned at it, her mind still half on Scott. The man was familiar, but she couldn't place him. Longish fair hair; a handsome, sculpted face. She knew him and yet she didn't. The poor quality of the picture didn't help.

"I sort of recognize him," she said uncertainly. "I don't know who he is."

Then there was a jolt in her brain. The university photo of Adam and Cora apparently making eyes at each other behind Scott. Wasn't this the man from the background of the bar, who had caught Lucy's attention because he'd been looking at the three of them so intently? She was being shown a close-up of his face now, wearing a more neutral expression, and yet he looked the same age as he had in the uni photo; his hair was the same length and style.

"His name is Guy Everley," DC Aggarwal said, scrutinizing Lucy's reaction.

Lucy shook her head. Her heart was pounding but her brain was fogged.

"Is he a suspect?" she asked.

The officers exchanged yet another glance, layered with opaque meaning.

"No," DC Marr eventually said. "No, he's not a suspect."

"Then who is he?"

"We can't say how he fits into the investigation at the moment." They were clamming up, reuniting in their evasiveness. "As I said, he's one of a few potential leads."

"You're sure you don't know him?" DC Aggarwal seemed increasingly suspicious. It had the effect of making Lucy clam up, too. She felt overloaded; she needed time to think.

"I don't know him," she said.

That much, at least, was not a lie.

Nobody was supposed to know we were together at uni. Just like nobody can know, even more so, now. But back then, the secrecy wasn't my choice. It hurt, in fact. It angered me, bruised my pride. Pushed me to my limits.

Or what I thought were my limits. I'm learning more than I've ever wanted to about those. And more than I've ever wanted to about keeping secrets.

It's a strange feeling, not being able to shout from the rooftops about the person who consumes all your thoughts. When you want to tell everyone, but it's never "the right time"; "people wouldn't understand"; "we don't need to be conventional, we don't need to go public. We're not like that."

But maybe I was. More so than I ever wanted to admit.

Of course, the secrecy was my savior in the end. And it should continue to protect me now, with everything stirred up again, everything such a mess. So why does it no longer feel as if it's going to? Why do I wake up in the night pumped with fear, and sometimes fury; why do I dream about eyes peering in through the windows?

One significant person knew about us back then. One person was, it seems, always watching. And does it all come back to that? Who knew things then, who knows things now.

The story that the photos will never tell, or not if I can help it. But that somebody, somewhere, is clearly trying to.

CHAPTER ELEVEN

LUCY WAS SO MIRED IN HER OWN THOUGHTS AS she left the police station that she almost didn't notice him. But one part of her brain was still alert. And that part recognized the man being brought in by two uniformed officers as she was walking out.

She stopped in her tracks and turned around. She could only see the back of him now, flanked by the PCs who were talking to the woman behind the desk. But she could tell he was crying hard. The officers were having to raise their voices as his sobs became louder. When the three of them turned from the desk, Lucy saw two things. She'd been right: It *was* Ruth's husband. She recognized him from their honeymoon photos, had met him at a couple of Christmas parties. But she also saw that his smart white shirt was covered in blood.

Lucy's heart thundered. For a moment it seemed as if he'd caught her eye, until she realized he wasn't focusing on anything; he was looking around in blind panic. Lucy stepped forward just as the two police officers ushered him away, uncuffed but with their hands firm on his shoulders.

"That man," she said to the desk sergeant, feeling panicked herself.

"Do you know him?"

"I . . . know his wife."

The desk sergeant paused, looking over Lucy's shoulder. Lucy glanced in the same direction, just in time to see DC Aggarwal in the doorway of one of the back rooms, shaking her head before disappearing inside.

The desk sergeant turned back to Lucy. "I'm afraid I can't give out any information."

"Why is he covered in blood?"

"As I said—" But Lucy was already turning away, realizing it was pointless, trying to pull herself together and figure out what to do next. She could wait here for him to come out. But what if she was waiting all night?

She pulled out her phone and tried to call Ruth via Facebook Messenger. There was no answer. Ruth hadn't been online since she'd sent Lucy the message with the photo. Lucy hurried to her car, wishing she knew Ruth's phone number or where she lived. She had a vague idea it was in the same area as Scott and Cora—hadn't she and Ruth talked about that one time? And she'd been at their local swimming pool with her niece—did that mean it was *her* local, too? Lucy drove in that direction, her mind still whirring, and turned into the leisure center car park doused in sweat.

The warm, stuffy smell of chlorine greeted her as soon as she stepped in. She tried to walk calmly across the foyer, rehearsing phrases in her head just as she had for her visit to the police station. The image of Ruth's husband's bloodied shirt kept intruding, scattering her script. When she opened her mouth to talk to the receptionist, her words came out a jumble.

"My friend . . . a member here, I think . . . I need to . . . I wondered if . . ." Lucy stopped talking and mentally slapped her own cheeks, as the not-much-older-than-teenage girl behind the desk blinked attentively. "Sorry!" She forced a smile. "What I'm trying—very badly—to say is that I accidentally took home someone else's bag after a swimming lesson. I need to return it but I don't know the address. Could you see if it's in your system, please? The name's . . . Ruth Beaumont." It felt strange to recite her name for the second time that evening, unbeknownst to Ruth herself.

"I'm sorry, we can't give out members' addresses," the receptionist said.

Lucy clenched her teeth in frustration.

"If you could just give me the street, even. Or a home phone number. It looks like there's medication in the bag . . ." She was improvising now. "I'm worried it's important."

The girl frowned at this. "You could leave the bag with us. We can contact the member and let her know it's here . . . Ruth Beaumont, did you say?" She tapped at her keyboard, leaning toward the screen in front of her. "Ah, yes, we do have her details here. Do you have the bag with you?"

"Um, no. I have it at home. I'd *really* like to return it in person." Lucy could hear the desperation in her own voice, could see the slight suspicion creeping onto the receptionist's face. She shuffled to the left, darting her eyes toward the angled computer screen. Half of Ruth's name was visible. A few digits of her telephone number. The receptionist seemed to realize what Lucy was doing and adjusted the screen so she could no longer see. But Lucy had glimpsed part of the address. Enough to make a good guess at which nearby street Ruth lived on.

"I'll let her know about the bag," the receptionist said, eyes narrowed. "Can I take your name?"

"Don't worry!" Lucy said, forcing another smile. "I've just remembered we're friends on Facebook. I can message her on there and arrange to drop the bag off."

"Right . . . well, if you're sure . . ."

"Thank you so much for your help!" Lucy's voice crackled with false brightness as she backed toward the door. She found herself caught inside a big group of people, arriving with swimming kits and rolled-up towels, and she battled toward the exit with the smell of chlorine trapped in her sinuses.

In her car, Lucy checked her phone but Ruth still hadn't been online. She put the address she'd half glimpsed into her sat nav and tried to just concentrate on driving. Partway through the journey, a black car shot past her, unmarked but with blue sirens wailing. Lucy caught her breath and watched it turn off down a side street, a blur of dark metal and blinding lights. Seconds later, her sat nav directed her down the same street. She gripped her steering wheel as she followed the fading siren.

Arriving in a cul-de-sac of modern houses and neat front gardens, she didn't need her sat nav to tell her she'd reached her destination. The dread that seized her stomach was signal enough. Three marked police cars were parked straight in front of her, dominating the street. A chorus of radios buzzed in the air and a small crowd of people had gathered, a cloud of anxious energy seeming to swirl over their heads. As Lucy brought her car to a halt, she stared at the house at the very end of the road. It was crawling with officers and cordoned off with fluttering yellow police tape.

She scrambled out of her car, leaving the driver's door swinging as she ran toward the scene.

"What's happened?" she asked a police officer.

"Please stay back," he told her firmly, blocking her with his arm.

Lucy's gaze kept darting, taking it all in. Police were striding in and out of the end house, wearing gloves, their shoes covered with plastic. Her stomach pitched again when she spotted the blue Volvo parked in the driveway. It was the same car she'd seen Ruth drive off in after the swimming gala. The one Scott had watched all the way, and that Lucy now couldn't take her eyes off, either.

She shook herself and turned to a group of neighbors who were shuffling and murmuring to her right. "Does anybody know what's going on?"

"Something's happened to Ruth at number seventeen," an elderly woman said with tears in her eyes. "An accident, maybe. We don't know."

"Oh, my God," Lucy said, pressing her hands against her cheeks. "Is she okay? Has she been taken to the hospital?"

"An ambulance came," a second woman said. "But we never saw her being brought out. The police took Martin off . . . but, I mean, *he* can't have . . ." She turned to the others, as if for reassurance, and they all shook their heads.

"She's *such* a lovely girl," the older lady cut back in, growing even more upset. "Always a kind word for everyone."

Lucy stared at Ruth's front door, open just wide enough

for police officers to slip through without revealing any of the interior. She willed Ruth to come strolling out, for the nightmarish scene to melt away. The energy in her stomach had become a ball of concentrated pain.

A man in a suit and lanyard approached them. "Please, everyone, go back into your homes."

"Is Ruth okay?" one of the neighbors asked. "Just tell us that."

"Please leave the scene so my officers can work effectively." The man's expression was unwavering. His eyes swept sternly over the group. "All of you."

The crowd reluctantly dispersed, glancing over their shoulders as they retreated. Some clasped hands, offered each other cups of tea. Lucy continued to stand there, the bustle of surreal activity washing over her. The sky above was turning a violent shade of pink. A drop of rain on her forehead brought her out of a trance, and she became aware of her mobile vibrating in her pocket. Adam. Probably wondering where she was. She didn't answer and it seemed to ring on and on.

To her left, a white van pulled up, and a man in a gray fleece climbed out of the back. It took her a moment to realize what he was carrying. A camera, a tripod. The media were starting to arrive, and there was no way Lucy wanted to be caught on film here. She stirred herself and walked quickly to her car, hiding inside the dark, muffling hood of her coat.

CHAPTER TWELVE

FRAN JUMPED UP AT LUCY LIKE A PUPPY WHEN SHE walked through the door. "Mummy! You're back!"

"You're back *late*," Tilly said disapprovingly.

"I'm sorry." Lucy hugged them both, wondering if she smelled like a police station, like a crime scene. "My darlings," she murmured, hiding her face in Fran's curls so they wouldn't see she was close to tears. They hung on to her hands and led her through to the kitchen, chattering all the way. If Lucy had been paying more attention to what they were saying—something about a jigsaw puzzle, about a late teatime—she might've had more warning. As it was, she stopped dead in the kitchen doorway.

"Hey, Luce!" came a chorus of greetings from the three people sitting at the table. Adam, Cora, and Scott, with glasses of red wine in front of them. Ivy and Joe were sprawled on the floor doing a giant jigsaw. Tilly and Fran rejoined them, the four kids forming a star shape as they lay flat on their stomachs, faces hovering over the puzzle.

"We've ordered some Thai food," Adam said. "I was dithering about what to cook and then these guys called in to say hi and a takeaway plan magically formed."

"Tuesday-night takeaway," Scott said, raising his glass and swirling the dark liquid inside. "The height of decadence."

Lucy still hadn't spoken. Her heart beat wildly as she perched in the empty seat, making their adult group symmetrical again, too. She couldn't look at anyone. Were they all staring at her, or was she imagining it? Was Scott's gaze particularly intense? The table seemed smaller than usual, everyone pressed closer together.

"Get your work done?" Adam asked, giving her thigh a gentle squeeze.

"Pour her a glass of wine!" Cora said. "She's clearly shattered."

Shattered wasn't even the word. Lucy felt steamrollered. Conversation began to ebb and flow around her but she could only chime in a minimal amount. When the food arrived, she could hardly smell or taste it. Everything was numbed except for a growing sense of terror, becoming almost unbearable every time her eyes drifted toward Scott. She had called the police station on her way back from Ruth's to try to find out more information—*any* information, she had begged—but had been told that DCs Aggarwal and Marr were unavailable and the desk sergeant still couldn't tell her anything.

"You okay, Luce?" Cora asked her quietly while Scott and Adam were chatting about broadband speeds. "Are you still feeling off it?"

"Yeah," Lucy said. "Wiped out."

Cora pulled a sympathetic face and something about it

ripped through Lucy like a physical pain. She should've told Cora about Ruth's photo. About Scott, back when the photo was all it had been. She should've done everything differently.

Scott's phone began to ring. Lucy froze, the food turning to clay in her mouth. She realized she'd been waiting all night for a knock on her door or the ring of a phone, dreading having to act shocked and ignorant if the police traced Scott here. Scott pulled his mobile out of his pocket, stared at the screen, and frowned.

He looked, for a moment, as if he was going to dismiss the call. Instead, he left the room to answer it. Lucy strained to hear but all she could make out was the serious tone of his voice. At one point his volume rose, with an edge of annoyance, but she still couldn't tell what was being said. Neither Cora nor Adam seemed to have noticed. Cora glanced once toward the door, then went back to chatting and laughing with Adam as he topped up her wine.

When Scott reappeared, his face was flushed and his jaw looked clenched.

"Everything okay?" Lucy choked out.

His mouth curved into a smile that reminded her again of the grin from the photo, the one that had seemed like a mask for anger. The one she'd seen in Norfolk but that hadn't been present in the photo Ruth had sent. That version had been blandly smiley, like a stock photo. Lucy felt another welling of nausea. *Ruth, did somebody hurt you?*

"Everything's fine," Scott said. "Just a work thing. I'm afraid I need to be rude and rush off, though. Need to sort this out."

Cora looked surprised. Though Scott worked long hours

and often had extra stuff to deal with outside of that, he was usually sensitive about walking out on social events or evenings with his family—maybe because he knew it would make Cora angry. And he had people he could delegate urgent things to. Adam often joked—with a hint of sour grapes—that "at his level, you don't actually have to do anything yourself."

Tonight, though, Scott was already pulling on his jacket, kissing Cora distractedly, patting his pockets for his keys. Maybe it *was* a work problem, Lucy thought. Or maybe it was something else.

SLEEP WAS, YET again, impossible. Lucy tossed and turned, trying to escape her own thoughts, sometimes curling into a ball as if to protect herself from them. She kept seeing Ruth's husband spattered with blood. The bright yellow of the police tape. Scott's frown and hasty exit when his phone had rung. And she kept hearing the word *murder*, like an echo, kept replaying the moment it had slipped out of DC Marr's mouth. Lucy had embroiled herself in a murder investigation. And Scott. Ruth. Everyone connected to them. Eventually she could stand it no longer and she got out of bed, glancing at Adam, who was lying on his back with his eyelids flickering. In the gray light of the early hours, she tiptoed across the room and retrieved the photo she'd shoved into her underwear drawer on Sunday afternoon. Taking it out onto the landing, she sat on the top stair and stared at Guy Everley in its background.

Who are you? Why are you important?

He seemed to stare back at her for a moment, before his attention reverted to Cora, Adam, and Scott in their odd little triangle. Lucy shivered in the early morning chill as she tried to fathom his expression. Disdain? Dislike? Jealousy?

"What are you doing, Luce?"

Her heart kicked and she turned to see Adam coming out of the bedroom, bleary-eyed.

"I—"

"What's that?" He yawned and came closer, crouching behind her and resting his hands on her shoulders.

There was no way or time to hide the photo, so she brazened it out. "I took this from Cora's."

She felt Adam's fingers tighten. He used to massage her shoulders on Sunday evenings when she was stressed about the week ahead, but this was something different; he seemed to transfer tension into her muscles rather than magicking it away.

"Took it?" he asked. "Why?"

"I just thought it was . . . interesting."

"You mean Scott's bling?" He pointed at the gold chain visible around Scott's neck. It would normally make Lucy laugh—so unlike something Scott would wear these days—but she didn't react, and Adam's fingers twitched against her collarbone again.

"The way you and Cora are looking at each other," she said, feeling awkward to be saying it out loud.

His hands dropped entirely. "Hey?"

"Did you have a thing at uni?"

"No, of course not!" His tone was surprised, almost amused, but there was a note of something else, the same tension she'd felt in his fingertips.

"It's fine if you did." Lucy made just as bad a job of trying to sound nonchalant. "It was well before you met me!"

A memory flashed through her head of the first time he'd introduced her to the Waughs. How in awe of Cora's muted elegance she'd been, how scruffy and yet simultaneously overdressed she'd felt in comparison. She'd searched for signs that Adam might be comparing them, too, but had seen none. Quite the opposite, in fact—he'd kept his arm firmly around Lucy, while Scott and Cora had seemed just as affectionate with one another across the other side of the table, making Lucy warm to them.

There had been moments, though, since then. Moments when Lucy had seen Adam smiling at Cora or catching her eye. Moments that were taking on a new significance, however much she strove to keep them in perspective.

"Well, we didn't." Adam sounded more abrupt now. "Her and Scott . . . I mean, it was always them. They fancied each other from the start. It was only a matter of time before they got together."

She glanced at him. "You're blushing." It was something she might've said teasingly under ordinary circumstances, but it came out as a mild accusation.

"No, I'm not." Again, he tried to laugh it off. "Honestly, Luce, what's this obsession you have with photos? Why do you always seem to think they have hidden meaning?"

She shrugged and looked back at the image, running her free hand along the edge of the top stair, the carpet worn by four sets of feet over six and a half years in this house.

Steeling herself, she asked: "Who's that in the background?"

She sensed Adam turning stiller. When she twisted to look at him, he was staring at the photo. His troubled expression seemed to mirror Guy Everley's, making the hairs rise on the back of Lucy's neck.

"Ad?" she said, shivering again. "Who is it?"

"It could be anyone," he said. "How can you even tell it's her?"

"What?"

"I know you're obsessed with her, but how can you tell from that?" He leaned forward and jabbed a finger at the edge of the shot.

Lucy narrowed her eyes in confusion. He wasn't pointing at Guy, she realized, but at the dark hair of the barely-in-shot woman next to him.

"Wait . . ." Lucy stiffened again. "Are you saying that's *Juliet*?"

"Isn't that what *you're* saying?"

"I was talking about the man. He seems very interested in the three of you."

Adam's neck flushed. There was a strained pause, then he let out a snort of breathy laughter, entirely unlike his normal dry chuckle. "Oh! Sorry! Crossed wires!"

"Is that Juliet?"

"I have no idea!" There was something like panic in his eyes, as if he'd been cornered. "She's not even facing the camera!"

"Then why did you say that?"

"I thought that was what you were implying." He got to his feet. Lucy found herself peering up at him, seeing him from an unfamiliar angle, his proportions all distorted.

"Adam," she said, "*did* you know her at uni?"

"No, Luce. I told you. I just saw the dark hair and thought that was what you were asking about."

Bewildered, Lucy touched the smudge of black hair and the curve of shoulder in the corner of the picture. The offstage figure was becoming Juliet to her now. Another unexplained snapshot. But Lucy would never have made such a leap if Adam hadn't inadvertently made it for her. She wanted to mention Guy's name, ask more about him, but she didn't feel ready to talk about her visit to the police station. She looked back at her husband, paralyzed by the things she couldn't tell him and the things she sensed he was withholding from her.

"I'm going back to bed, Luce." He hesitated, looking at the photo as if he wanted to snatch it from her. Then he yawned in a performative way and turned to wander back into their room.

Lucy was left sitting on the top stair feeling deserted. He would usually have offered her a hand to get up, put his arm round her as they returned to bed together. She heard the familiar creak of their bed and the faint sound of Adam sighing, the bedclothes moving as if he was struggling to settle. Looking back at the photo, she felt the knot retie itself in her stomach. It seemed to contain so much, but explain nothing.

She'd left her phone in the bedroom, so she crept downstairs to get her laptop instead. It was cold in the living room; she pulled the throw off the sofa and wrapped it around her shoulders, hunching over the laptop on her knees. She'd spent so much time googling Juliet's name, it felt odd to be putting a different one into the search box. As soon as she did, a stream of news articles appeared. Lucy's breathing became shallow as she caught sight of the top headline, dated almost two years ago.

ARTIST UNVEILS TRIBUTE TO LOST SON

She clicked on it, scanning to see whether it was about the same Guy Everley. A picture confirmed that it was. The blond hair, the chiseled jaw. Lucy felt her pulse vibrating through her body as she read on.

The renowned British artist Lawrence Everley launched his latest exhibition of multimedia installations yesterday at Leeds Art Gallery. Fans were moved to see a poignant tribute to his late son, Guy Everley, who was killed in a car crash in February 2006 while studying at the University of Leeds.

Everley said, "It's taken me a long time to find the right way to pay tribute to my son. For years I've kept my grief and my work deliberately apart. But I feel some peace now that they've been able to come together."

Fans and art critics have speculated about the exact meaning behind the tribute piece, and Lawrence Everley has declined to explain, wanting people to "take what they need from it, and perhaps never understand the full complexity of my feelings about Guy and what happened to him. Those feelings are for me but the piece can still be other things to other people."

The sculpture appears to play with the idea of opposites. Hot and cold colors; light and dark hues. Parts of it are soft and cloudlike while others have an almost rocky texture, which some have speculated is a nod to the place in which Guy's fatal car crash took place, the notorious High Pass in Yorkshire. Others have said the theme of opposites shows the conflicting feelings that a huge trauma can bring, or the contradictions in Guy's character and Lawrence's relationship with him.

However you interpret it, it can't be denied that the piece is so striking as to bring tears to the eyes. Whether it would elicit the same response without the tragic context is difficult to say.

Lucy looked at photos of the sculpture and felt unexpectedly choked. There really was something about it: spikey and almost angry in places; sad and ethereal in others. She googled *High Pass* and saw images of a long, desolate road snaking through craggy hillside. It made her draw the throw closer around her shoulders, feeling exposed to imaginary elements. *Guy Everley is dead. He died on this road.* She remembered how the detectives had looked at one another when Lucy asked if he was a suspect in Juliet's murder. Of course he wasn't. He'd died long before Lucy had ever heard his name, another life cut short. *So what has any of this got to do with Juliet and Scott?*

As her head roared with confusion, something caught her eye in the corner of her laptop screen. An icon was flashing from the task bar. It took her a moment to realize it was the smart doorbell app. She hadn't really engaged with it since Adam installed it, but she clicked on it now and her screen filled with a dark image of her driveway, giving her the strange feeling of seeing her home from the outside, as if she could turn and peer in on herself.

She froze when she saw the person who had triggered the motion sensor. The broad shoulders and tousled hair, silhouetted by a streetlamp.

Scott was standing outside their house with his phone at his ear.

CHAPTER THIRTEEN

LUCY STOOD UP AND CREPT TO THE FRONT DOOR. She hovered behind it, trying to make out what Scott was saying into his phone, but couldn't hear anything. Part of her wanted to run upstairs, turn off all the lights, and pray he'd go away. But another part was desperate to know why he was here, whether he'd been with the police, what had happened.

After a few moments, she braced herself and opened the door. Scott sprang back, lowering his phone.

"Lucy," he said, in a tone she couldn't interpret.

In the pale light of the streetlamp, he looked washed-out. His eyes were raw, as if he'd been rubbing grit into them. He was wearing the same clothes as when he'd left their house earlier that evening, but much more crumpled, with sweat patches under his arms. And no jokes, no hug, not even a smile.

"I was trying to call Ad," he said. "I know it's late. I didn't want to bang on the door. I just . . . need to talk to him."

"It *is* late," Lucy said without moving.

"Was it you?" Scott said, suddenly gruff.

Her eyes snapped to his face. "What?"

"Was it *you*?" Anger leaked into his words. "Was it your fault I just went through hours of hell?"

Lucy backed into her hallway, half closing the door on him. Scott blocked it with his arm and took a big stride forward, his eyes hard, then he was inside the house, seeming to fill the narrow space.

"What's happened?" Lucy pressed herself against the soft mass of coats hanging on the pegs, wishing she could disappear into them.

"I've been at the police station all night. Being questioned about Juliet."

She noticed he only used her first name. Noticed the ring of familiarity, the crack in his voice.

"I . . ." She cast her eyes down, then raised them back to his face. "I had no choice."

"*Fuck.*" Scott smacked his fist into his opposite palm. "Lucy, why?"

"She was *murdered*."

His eyes popped. "They told you that?"

"They . . . let it slip."

Scott brought his fist up to his mouth and bit his own knuckles. Fear sparked at the base of Lucy's spine and traveled upward, tingling in her scalp. He seemed at once tightly coiled and in the process of unraveling. The same energy was steaming off him as when he'd cut his hand in Norfolk and reacted with such fury. She was suddenly aware of her vulnerability, of being alone with him in an enclosed space.

Then his shoulders started shaking, and it took her a moment to realize what was happening. He was breaking down. Sobs were heaving out of him, and he was wheezing for breath, his face contorting as if he was fighting with himself. Lucy stared at him, reminded of Ruth's husband in the police station, inconsolable, panicked.

"It's a mess," Scott choked out. "It's a fucking mess."

Lucy pressed herself further into the coats. "What do you mean?" she whispered, then felt instantly afraid of hearing the answer.

There was a pause in which his sobs turned ragged and breathless. Lucy glanced up the stairs, worried about the girls waking and seeing their uncle Scott in this state. They'd be so confused. What would she tell them? She was torn between throwing him out of the house—if she even could—and taking him into another room to hear him out. As Scott seemed to make an effort to control himself, she gestured him through to the kitchen. He sat at the kitchen table and put his head in his hands, pulling at chunks of his hair.

Lucy poured him a glass of water, spilling a few drops as she put it down. Had she just invited a murderer into her kitchen and given him a drink? Looking at the broken sight of him, she still couldn't reconcile her old friend Scott with the new version she'd been forced to assemble. Still didn't know which version was crying into his palms at her table, his legs jiggling with pent-up tension below.

"I'm going to get Adam," she said, hurrying from the room.

Upstairs, she shook her husband awake and he looked at her in bleary confusion.

"Scott's here," she whispered urgently. "He's been at the police station. I don't know what's going on, but I think . . ." She stopped and swallowed as her breath ran out. "I don't know. He says he needs to talk to you."

Adam blinked as if struggling to take this in. She got the feeling he'd only just managed to fall back to sleep since their conversation on the landing. Had he wondered why she'd not returned to bed herself?

"Ad, please, I need you down there with me. I'm . . ." She stopped short of saying, *I'm scared of him.* She still didn't want it to be true.

Adam sat up, fumbling for his glasses. "What's he said?" He reached for his phone on the bedside table and frowned at it. Then he threw back the duvet and rushed ahead of Lucy, out of the room and down the stairs.

Scott wasn't crying anymore. He was prowling around the kitchen as if he was in a cell. His hair stuck out in different directions and there was a wildness in his eyes that made Lucy regret her decision to invite him further into the house.

"Scott, mate, what the hell's going on?" Adam said.

"They asked me if I killed her," Scott said, still pacing. "They asked me how I killed her. *Why* I killed her. It went on and on and on."

"Juliet Noor?" Adam said.

Scott swung to face him. "Who else?"

Lucy looked between them, a sense of foreboding creeping over her. "What's going on? Ad, do you know something about Juliet, too?"

"No," Adam said, but his voice clashed with Scott's as he spoke at the same time: "Just *tell* her, Ad."

Adam blanched and shook his head at Scott. But Scott ignored him, stepped forward, and took Lucy by the shoulders. "I *was* having an affair with her."

She pushed his hands off. "You . . ." Even though she'd expected this part, she was speechless. There were too many competing thoughts and feelings and questions. She was aware of Adam avoiding her eye, fidgeting at the edge of her vision.

"We met through work." Scott's face twisted in anguish. "She interviewed me at the Istanbul Air Show—"

"But you'd met before that," Lucy said, trying to recover. "*Hadn't* you? At uni?"

Scott glanced at Adam. "We didn't really know her then."

"Is that true?" She looked between them again, aware of being in the middle, feeling as if they were circling her even though all three of them were still.

Scott's eyebrows sank. "*Yes*, it's true. It was something we talked about when we met again, of course. Uni days, mutual friends. But once we'd got talking"—he sighed, his hands back in his hair—"one thing led to another . . ."

Lucy almost laughed at the cliché, but felt it turn to hysteria.

"You were with her in the Maldives?" she asked.

Scott nodded, looking away. "She invited me to join her while she was working on her book."

"So, Tokyo—"

"I *did* go to Tokyo, before and after. So that I'd have the boarding passes—"

"Why?" Lucy demanded. "For the police?"

"Of course not for the police!" His voice soared and he raised his arms. "I didn't know anything was going to happen to her! How much clearer can I make that?" He brought his hands down and covered his face, as if someone had shone a bright light at him. As if *Lucy* had shone a bright light at him. "I just meant . . . in case Cora ever suspected. There had to be a trail."

Lucy swallowed hard. *Cora.* "She doesn't know?"

Scott flung another glance at Adam. Lucy turned to him. "But *you* knew, Ad?"

He stared at the floor.

"Ad! You did, didn't you? You knew this all along?"

"I . . . I couldn't tell you."

She gaped at him, anger rising. "You made me feel like I was going crazy! Both of you did! Scott, you told me you didn't even know her! And, Adam, you . . . you . . ." She couldn't even articulate yet what Adam had done. All the little lies to protect Scott, to steer Lucy away from finding out about the affair. She knew she'd go back over everything, obsessively, when she was next alone with her thoughts. But now there was just the stomach-kick of having been betrayed by the person who was supposed to be unquestionably on her side.

"What else could we do?" Adam lifted his head finally, a haunted look in his eyes.

He tried to touch her arm and Lucy pulled away from him. Her torso was rigid with fury. She opened her mouth to reply but nothing came out. All she felt ready to do was turn her back on him, dragging her focus back to Scott. "Did you . . . hurt her?" she asked, still hating the shape of the words in her mouth. "Did you kill Juliet Noor?"

Next thing she knew, Scott's hands were on her collarbones. His breath in her face as he shoved her into the kitchen wall. Lucy felt pain radiate along her spine. She struggled against him, feeling a moment of horrible helplessness as she realized how strong he was. She'd only ever witnessed his strength in a detached kind of way while they were working on the cottage. Had only ever seen his temper as a momentary, minor thing. Now she was conscious of the power in his arms, the unspoken threat that he could snap her if he wanted to. She tried to bring up her knee and jab him in the thigh. Then Adam was there, seizing him by the elbows. "Scott, for fuck's sake! Get off her, *now*!"

There was an intake of breath from Scott and he released Lucy, jolting out of it just as he had when Adam had intervened in Norfolk. He sprang back, blinking as if waking from a dream, and Lucy was left panting, rubbing her neck in shock.

"Fuck." Scott deflated into a chair. He seemed dazed, like he wasn't sure where he'd just been. "*Fuck*, I'm so sorry."

Adam shook his head at him. His face was a deep red. "Jesus, Scott! What were you thinking? Luce, are you okay?" he asked, turning to reach for her. "Luce, are you hurt?" When she swerved his touch again, he said tersely to Scott: "Maybe you should go."

"So sorry," Scott was murmuring, not even seeming to be talking to Lucy anymore. "So, so sorry. I didn't mean . . . didn't know . . ." He looked up finally, and his expression was pleading. "I didn't kill Juliet," he said, his voice frayed. "I swear, when I left the Maldives, she was . . . fine."

Lucy moved her hand to her back, sore where it had hit the wall, then to her throat again. She couldn't process what had just happened. Being on the receiving end of a burst of violence from a once-trusted friend. How might it have gone if Adam hadn't been there?

"Scott, you need to leave," Adam said. "You can't pull shit like that."

"I fucked up." Scott appealed to them both, seeming desperate, but his fingers kept flexing; he was clearly still fizzing with something he was only just managing to contain. "I just flipped. What Lucy was saying . . . It got in my head."

"You could've really hurt her." Adam's voice thickened

with emotion and it brought an ache to Lucy's chest, brief and confusing.

Scott stood up. Adam stepped toward him as if preparing to bungle him out the door. But something rose through Lucy, a kind of contrary panic. She wanted Scott out of her house, but another realization was stronger: If he went away, so would her chance to hear him finish what he'd started.

"Let him stay," she said. They both turned and blinked at her. Lucy took a breath, crossing her arms over her chest. "He's still got a lot to explain."

CHAPTER FOURTEEN

SCOTT TOOK HIS SEAT AGAIN, HIDING HIS HANDS beneath the table as if that would remove any impression of threat. Lucy kept her distance, and her eyes on him, while Adam hovered between them like a conflicted bodyguard.

"I left her on the island alive," Scott said. "Alive and well and . . . normal . . ."

Normal. The word bounced around Lucy's head. It seemed undefinable now.

"But when you saw that photo of us," Scott plowed on urgently, "and then she was in the news . . ." His eyes gleamed with more tears, and his hands reappeared to swipe them away. "I just wanted to stop you going to the police. I knew if Cora found out about the affair, she'd never forgive me. And the kids . . . I was scared you'd expose me. Destroy everything."

"But . . ." Lucy swallowed and coughed, still feeling as if her windpipe was constricted. "But the woman you were having an affair with went missing. She's now *dead*! You were the last person to see her, Scott. How could you not report that?"

Scott rocked slightly in his chair. "At first I just hoped and hoped she'd turn up. And now . . . now . . ." He broke down again, holding his stomach as if afraid it would rupture.

Lucy stared at him. Stared at Adam. Her head was full of white noise.

"Why did the police let you go?"

It took Scott a moment to compose himself enough to answer. He stared into space as if taking his mind back to the interview room, and Lucy watched him carefully, wondering if he was actually getting his story straight.

"The flight records," he said eventually. "They came through while I was there. I took a long-winded route, a plane to another island and then a boat over to where Juliet was staying . . ."

"Covering your tracks," Lucy said, her tone as cold as her body.

"It was an affair." For some reason, it was Adam who answered. "Of course he was covering his tracks."

Lucy scowled at him. Another burn of anger replaced her second skin of goosebumps. *Who are you? Whose side are you on?* One minute acting like the white knight, the next leaping in to excuse Scott's actions.

She turned at the sound of Scott thrusting back his chair. "But I was gone before it happened," he said, on his feet again, "before she was . . . before she died. The records confirmed that. *That's* why they let me go."

Lucy took a moment to let this properly sink in. *Gone before she died.* Was it true? Was that why he was here in her kitchen, not locked up in a cell? But what if this was just another lie? What if they'd released him for now but he was still at the top of their suspect list? He could even have faked his route home, just as he'd made sure he'd got boarding passes to and from Tokyo. Who knew what he was capable of?

Lucy shuddered and rubbed her neck again, answering her own question.

"Did they ask you about the photo?" she asked.

Now Scott seemed to drift, his expression opaque. "It should never have existed."

"But it does. And it—"

"I never wanted her to take it."

Lucy frowned. "Ruth?"

He nodded, closing his eyes. "It was the one night Juliet and I actually went out for dinner. The rest of the time, we stayed in, kept me out of sight. She hadn't told the resort anybody else was joining her, and we were still trying to be careful, just in case. But Juliet got fed up. She wanted to have a real date, act like a real couple . . ." His voice splintered and Lucy heard him take a rattly breath. "When we got talking to another couple in the restaurant, Juliet got carried away, inventing fake names, pretending we were on our honeymoon, too. It was"—he shook his head—"reckless. Really reckless. But we were drunk and we never dreamed the other couple would have any connection to our lives back home. Then Ruth insisted on taking our photo as a memento. It happened before I could stop it. And I was pissed off with Juliet afterward, angry about the whole stupid night . . ."

"You looked angry in the photo," Lucy said. "You were smiling but there was something . . . *wrong* about the smile. That's what I remember."

"We fought," Scott said, holding out his palms. The two simple words filled Lucy's head with images. Scott shouting. Looming. Juliet against the wall. Juliet on the floor. "But . . . I loved her." His shoulders started shaking again. "I swear, I loved her and I didn't hurt her. I didn't know I'd never see her again! That she'd wash up days later, after some psycho had beaten her brains out . . ."

Lucy couldn't listen anymore. The images were getting stronger. Juliet with her hands in front of her face. Scott lost in a haze of anger. *Flipping*, as he claimed he'd done with Lucy. She turned and ran out of the room.

"Luce?" she heard Adam call as she darted up the stairs. Then Scott and Adam started murmuring to each other, their voices indistinct. Lucy pushed into her bedroom and doubled over against the bed frame, panting hard. After a moment, she hauled herself upright. Tuning back in to her surroundings, she grabbed her phone and hurried downstairs.

They stopped talking as soon as she walked into the kitchen. Lucy swept aside another complicated wave of feeling about their collusion. She couldn't deal with it now. Instead, she opened Ruth's latest message on her phone and thrust it in front of Scott.

"I meant, did the police ask you about *this*?"

He blinked at it, saying nothing.

"Ruth sent it to me." Lucy was out of breath from sprinting up and down the stairs. "Clearly, it's been changed from the original picture. But why?"

There was another heavy silence. Scott said hoarsely, "When did you get this?"

"Earlier today. Just before I spoke to the police."

Alarm flickered dimly in his eyes. Adam stepped forward

and peered over his shoulder at Lucy's phone. He seemed only to look at the doctored photo for a split second. Lucy watched him withdraw, as if distancing himself, staring at his feet.

While she was distracted, Scott snatched her phone out of her hand. She tried to grab it back but he held on to it and scrutinized the picture, then began to scroll back through the preceding messages. Lucy swallowed, knowing he'd be reading through all her attempts to extract information from Ruth, seeing how determined she'd been. His jaw tightened and she watched him scroll back down to the end.

She was thrown by his next words. "But . . . she refused. She said she didn't want to send you this."

"What?"

"She . . ." He gestured at the phone. "She said she didn't want to get involved. That I should just face the music—"

"Ruth?"

"She must've . . . changed her mind."

Lucy took her phone back off him. Scott relinquished it and wrung his hands.

"You spoke to her about the photo?" Lucy looked at the altered version again. The memory of police officers striding in and out of Ruth's house pushed to the forefront of her brain.

"I told you, I couldn't let Cora see the original."

"You asked Ruth to send me a fake?"

"I had to do *something*." His hands lifted and Lucy instinctively flinched. "You wouldn't drop it! The real photo could've ended my marriage! Not to mention I'd have had the police crawling all over me. Imagine what that would've done to Ivy and Joe. And my job, my reputation—"

"What did you do to Ruth?"

Scott stopped in his tracks. “What?”

“How exactly did you try and persuade her?”

“How did I . . . ?” He looked Lucy up and down, as if trying to read her insinuation. “I just talked to her. I fucking *pleaded* with her. I thought I’d failed but—”

“Did you go to her house?” Lucy’s voice became high-pitched. “Did you threaten her? Did you”—she touched her own throat—“put your hands around her neck?”

“What the hell? Of course I didn’t!” His eyes blazed and for a second she thought he was going to leap on her again, and clearly so did Adam, because he moved forward. “Anything else you want to accuse me of, Lucy?” spat Scott.

They all froze in a tableau. Lucy searched Scott’s face for signs of guilt and saw the same indignation as when she’d first asked him if he knew Juliet Noor. She didn’t want to tell him what she’d seen at Ruth’s house. Wanted to feel one step ahead in something, at least. Was it *possible* he could’ve hurt Ruth? As much as any of this nightmare was possible?

“This is insane,” Scott said, turning away from her. “This is all just . . .” He whipped back around, anger reigniting. Lucy was aware of Adam lifting a palm, now with the demeanor of a teacher trying to defuse a brewing fight, but it was a beep from a phone that broke Scott’s focus. He blinked and snapped his eyes from Lucy’s face, pulling out his phone.

“Shit,” he said, seeming to scroll through several messages. “Cora. Wondering where I am. I have to go.”

“Are you going to tell her?” Lucy asked.

He didn’t answer. He was looking around as if for something he’d lost. Lucy glanced at Adam, managing to catch his eye. However betrayed she felt by him, Cora’s hurt would be a hundred times worse. Everything was hurtling forward, out of her control. And Scott's expression was so dark as he retreated into thought that she closed her eyes, longing to unsee it.

At the door, Scott paused and turned back.

"It isn't easy, you know," he said, his voice flat.

"What isn't?" Lucy asked.

"Being married to Cora. I love her. I love my family. But things . . . aren't always easy."

Lucy felt her whole body clench up. She looked him squarely in the eye. "You had an affair, Scott. Lied to your family. Held up a police investigation . . ." She stopped short of saying, *And I dread to think what else.*

"I had my reasons—"

Lucy cut him off with a jerk of her hand. "No. No. Don't you dare do that. Don't try to blame this on Cora."

All the air seemed to gush out of his lungs. In frustration or defeat, Lucy wasn't sure. His eyes slid to Adam, as they had done too many times during the conversation, then back to Lucy. "Think what you want about me and Cora, Lucy. And about my relationship with Juliet. But not about her murder. Somebody killed her, somebody *bludgeoned* . . ." He broke off and closed his eyes, then opened them and ended softly but with vehemence, the light catching his pupils, "But you have to accept now, surely, that it couldn't have been me."

The crack of the impact. The silence afterward. The slow seep of blood. It's all getting muddled. Confused with other memories, fragments, figments. Rain pattering on the ocean. The sharp click of a phone camera. A smashed mug that must've been a gift. A song I can't stop hearing.

Things are out of control now. Even I can see that. It's a domino effect, never ending, and there are still some that need to be knocked down. A cycle, a spiral, a whirlpool I can't drag myself out of.

I have to keep track of the lies. Of what I've said and to whom. That's the thing to remember. The one thing I can do now as the spiral gets bigger and spins faster and all I can do is spin with it.

CHAPTER FIFTEEN

LUCY'S LEGS ALMOST GAVE WAY AFTER SCOTT HAD left. She crumpled into a kitchen chair and tried to comprehend everything she'd heard. Adam had followed Scott to the front door to see him off, and she couldn't tell whether it was another sign of their collusion or of Adam wanting to ensure he left without any more damage. Alone in the silence, Lucy probed her own feelings as if assessing physical wounds. Which parts hurt? Which parts had gone into shock, were prickling with a nebulous kind of dread?

When Adam came back, she stood up and faced him, and the parts that hurt began to shout the loudest. It was the kind of hurt she'd hoped never to feel, especially not with Adam as the cause. He was her rock. He'd seemed to make it his mission to be that from early on. She'd never cared that it was a cliché; she'd leaned on him, wrapped herself around him.

"Why didn't you tell me, Adam?" she asked.

He moved into the space where Scott had been, leaned

on the back of a kitchen chair, and released a sigh that seemed to come from deep inside.

"All those conversations we had about Juliet," she went on. "All the times you told me to stop obsessing about—"

"I didn't know what to do!" There was a blast of defensiveness, but then his head sank, deflated. "I'm sorry. I knew you'd want to tell Cora. I thought it was best—"

"How long have you known about Scott's affair?"

He was silent. She looked at his hands, the familiar way they rested on the chair, but saw the pinched white of his knuckles, as if the bones were poking through.

"Adam!" She spoke more loudly, then caught herself, remembering the girls above. It was a miracle they'd stayed asleep, and she didn't want to be the one to wake them. "How long?"

His eyes darted. "I suppose . . . a couple of months."

Lucy let out a small moan. All the things they'd done together in that period, as two families merged into one. All the scenes she'd treasured, and often captured in photos, now painted in different darker colors.

"I was trying to protect you." Adam stepped toward her. "Luce . . . I swear . . . I knew you'd be devastated."

"I am," she murmured. "But it's so much worse that you lied to me, too. You made me feel like a shitty person, a *crazy* person, for ever suspecting Scott was cheating. You told me to forget about it, got angry with me for not being able to . . ."

He hung his head again, locking his hands behind his neck. There was something theatrical about it, not his usual style, but when he raised his head, genuine tears glazed his eyes.

"It all just got out of hand," he said. "I told him to end the affair as soon as he confessed to me about it. Okay, I agreed to keep it from Cora, and from you, and that was"—he paused as if reaching for the right description—"not fair. Not fair to *anyone*, actually, me included . . ." His expression shuttered for a moment, before he blinked and continued. "But I told him again and again that he had to end it."

"And *look* how it ended," Lucy said slowly. "Juliet was killed. And Scott was there. Right before it happened."

Adam shook his head forcefully. "You can't possibly think he did that."

"How can *you* not admit that it's—"

"The police *cleared* him, Luce. And he's still Scott! I despise what he's been doing to Cor, and what he just did to you, but—"

"Then why did you keep his secrets?" Her stomach dropped with unexpected weight as she said it. Because this was at the core of her unease, she realized: the reason Adam had protected Scott, and was still defending him, refusing to entertain the idea that he might be more seriously involved. What *was* that reason? Why did it feel like something too frightening to look at directly?

Adam's sigh was one of exasperation now. "Not for *his* sake!" he insisted. "For yours, Luce. For Cora's and the kids'. I didn't want to be the one to fuck everything up any more than you did."

His words landed on Lucy's shoulders, falling through her body. She thought of Cora heating up the soup, making her extra-strong tea, hugging her at the door. "I wanted to protect Cora, too," she said. "But—"

"Believe me, I've agonized over it as much as you have."

He'd cut her off but his voice had softened again. "It's been torture not being able to talk to you about it."

His hand left the chair to reach in her direction. The distance was too big and his fingers hovered without making contact. Lucy didn't feel like meeting him halfway. She stared past him, still fighting tears and rage. Then her gaze snagged on something on the pinboard. The collage he had made her: his vision of what their Norfolk cottage might look like when they'd finished. The series of pictures that had been expertly, lovingly photoshopped.

Cold spread in tendrils through her bones. "*You* altered the photo."

She snapped her eyes back to him, catching the flash of his guilty look.

"You didn't just keep quiet about Scott's involvement with Juliet," she continued, breathing more heavily. "You actively helped him to cover things up."

"No . . ." Desperation again; a caginess in his eyes. "No, you're twisting things, Luce."

"Ruth's my *colleague*," Lucy said. "And now she's—" A full-body shudder rippled over her. Adam was involved in dragging Ruth into Scott's mess. Now Ruth was hurt. There was a potential path from one fact to the other that was too horrible to trace.

"She's what?" Adam asked.

"You don't know?" she said, half hating herself for testing him.

"Know *what*? Luce, come on—"

"I . . . I went to her house last night. It was full of police. Her neighbors said something had happened to her."

"Seriously?" His shock seemed sincere, his hand shooting up to his face. But Lucy was no longer sure of her ability to read him.

"How did Scott persuade Ruth not to show me the real photo? Tell me, Adam."

"I have no idea!" He pushed his fingers through his hair, reminding her uncomfortably of Scott. "He asked me to change the photo as a favor. But that was as far as I went. I know nothing about . . . I don't understand . . ." He trailed off and lines scored his forehead, making him look older.

"Why was Ruth off sick after Juliet went missing?"

"How should I know?" He turned to her with a horrified stare. "You don't think that's related?"

Lucy massaged her temples. The skin felt tight over her skull. "I don't know. I don't know." She was exhausted just thinking about it. There'd been so much to take in tonight.

She looked back at Adam, tearing up again. "We always promised to be honest with each other, Ad. It was *you* who made a big thing of that when we first got together. Talking about how lies cause damage—"

"They do," he said, his chin jutting out. "I still believe that."

"Then why did you help Scott tell such a huge one?"

He brought his palm down hard onto the tabletop. "I didn't! I'm not on his side. I never have been!"

Lucy was taken aback by his outburst. It was so un-Adam. So unaligned with her image of him and Scott: buddies who had each other's backs even when one of them had done something awful. "Well, you could've fooled me," she said, unable to let go of that picture.

"You've got it all wrong, Luce. You think we've been one

big happy family all these years but—" He seemed to cut himself off, rein himself in.

"But what?" A familiar alarm rang in her ears, now that he was talking about their group as a whole. *Don't destroy my image of our lives any more than you already have. Let me keep some good memories, some happy associations.* Had she been so deluded? Were the others such skilled actors as to have feigned their easy closeness all this time?

Adam shook his head and let out another sigh. "Nothing. Shit. Ignore me. I'm so tired. I've . . . I've *had it* with all this. And I'm sorry, Luce." His eyes moved upward, rounded with sadness. "You might not believe me, but I really am."

She was reminded again of Scott—of him murmuring that he was sorry, seeming to mean it in a general rather than a specific sense. Now she couldn't tell whether Adam was talking to her or expressing some bigger regret. They were flailing in unfamiliar territory, beyond the usual apologies or compromises that followed an argument. It scared her that they didn't have a map for this.

She turned and stared at the window. The sky was copper colored as the sun rose. She chewed the inside of her cheek until she tasted the metallic tinge of blood. Then she realized she could see Adam's reflection in the glass. Could see him drawing his phone subtly out of his pocket, reading a message and tapping out what must've been a single-word reply while her back was turned. He raised his head afterward, pushed his glasses up his nose. It was a gesture she'd seen him do thousands of times, usually provoking a pang of affection, but this time she wanted to knock the glasses off his face.

"Who are you texting?" she asked, spinning round.

Adam seemed to jump. "Scott. He's . . . saying sorry again."

"So he should." Lucy pictured him getting home, waking Cora, explaining where he'd been. She could almost feel Cora's shock as a reverberation inside her own body.

"I know," Adam said. "We're on the same side here, Luce. Same team." It was something they often said: *Same team, always.* A kind of pact. Like their honesty one. But maybe he'd read that in a magazine in a doctors' waiting room, too. Maybe he'd once read a manual on marriage and had been quoting lines from it ever since.

Sorrow rushed up through Lucy's body, collecting as a lump in her throat. "It doesn't feel like it, Adam."

"Well, it still does to me." He held out his hand again. Lucy looked at it with longing, but couldn't bring herself to take it. He let it drop, cursing as if he'd just realized how bafflingly broken things were. That this wasn't a software glitch he could routinely fix.

Lucy imagined Cora and Scott in their own kitchen, in a mirroring situation, but a worse one. How much would Scott tell her? Would he use the same words he'd flung at Lucy? There were parts she could remember vividly while others had faded, like dialogue from a dream. *I loved her and I didn't hurt her. I didn't know I'd never see her again. That she'd wash up days later, after some psycho had beaten her brains out . . .*

Lucy's train of thought snagged and then froze. *Beaten her brains out.* She remembered the violence of the phrase; the mental images that had bombarded her when Scott had said it. But she had missed something at the time, which now sucked the breath out of her.

"How did he know?" she said to Adam.

He raised his eyebrows. "What?"

"How did . . ." She paused, thinking, recalling. "How did Scott know Juliet was beaten to death? The police were adamant the cause of death was confidential when I spoke to them."

"*Did* he know?" Wariness crept into his face.

"He said he had no idea some psycho was going to"—she lowered her voice—"beat her brains out. And then at the end, he said something about her being bludgeoned. Do you remember?" *Bludgeoned.* Another visceral verb. Another horror show of accompanying images.

"Not really. Luce, please, let's not—"

"How would he know those specifics?"

"I don't know." Adam held his fingertips over his eyes. "Just because the police wouldn't tell you doesn't mean they didn't tell him."

"Why would they give him that kind of information if he was being questioned as a suspect?"

"He's *not* a suspect, Luce!" Adam's exasperation was back, but Lucy's blood was pumping, her mind in overdrive.

"We don't know that, Adam," she said. "We still only have Scott's word for any of it."

"Luce!" He tried to grab her wrist. "It's in the police's hands now. Leave it. Let them do their job. It's nothing to do with us."

"It's everything to do with us."

He shook his head, sweat shimmering on his brow. "We can't get any more involved."

Finally, she stopped moving and looked straight at him. "Why not?"

"The question is, why would we? Luce, you *have* to step away." He sounded grave now, as if he was warning her, his eyes so intense they seemed to fill the frames of his glasses. "I'm begging you. I wish I'd never got involved in any of this. I wish *you* hadn't. Leave it alone, step away. I'm asking you, begging you, one last time."

CHAPTER SIXTEEN

THEY DIDN'T MAKE IT BACK TO BED. ADAM LEFT for work before the sky was even fully blue, and without kissing Lucy good-bye. She heard the sound of his car accelerating away, much faster than he normally drove, and didn't know whether to be devastated or relieved that he was gone.

For a while, she stared numbly at the wall. Parts of last night still felt like a dream. It was as if she was waking, without even having slept, in a different life from the one she'd had the day before. And perhaps Cora was feeling the same right at this moment, a thread connecting the two of them across the city. Was she okay? Was she *safe*? This was everything Lucy had wanted to protect her from since she'd seen that photo. A sense of failure settled over her, making her bones feel heavy.

She caught herself as she sank down in her chair. *You're not the one who should be feeling guilty.* And guilt was a waste of time when there were still so many gaps to fill in. She glanced at the clock: She had an hour before she needed to wake the girls and get them ready for school. Shaking off her exhaustion, she fetched her laptop from where she'd abandoned it last night on the sofa.

She took it back to the top of the stairs, the same spot where she'd looked at the university photo the night before. She'd be able to hear if the girls stirred. And sitting here reminded her of Adam's reaction to the picture, reminded her she hadn't imagined the strangeness.

Nor had she imagined the way he'd looked and sounded as he'd begged her to step away from the situation. Scared. He'd seemed scared. Lucy couldn't get it out of her head.

She thought back over the conversation with Scott, trying to get past the words *beaten* and *bludgeoned* to pick out smaller details, things she could check. After a few moments, she opened Google and typed, *Istanbul Air Show 2022.* The place he'd said he and Juliet had first met again.

There was a large number of hits. She tried refining it with Scott's and Juliet's names but it seemed to confuse the search algorithm, the results scattering from what she needed. She paused as she remembered flipping through the trade magazine in Scott and Cora's conservatory, seeing Juliet's name in the byline of an article. Closing her eyes, she pictured the front cover, then put the title into the search box. The magazine was accessible to subscribers only. Lucy checked the cost, realized she didn't actually care how much it was, and hastily signed up for a subscription. There was a faint tremor in her hands as she searched the archive for Istanbul.

There it was. Six months ago. An interview about the 2022 Istanbul Air Show, with Juliet as the interviewer, and Scott as the interviewee.

Adrenaline surged again. Even though Scott had already alluded to this part of the story, this was the first time she had actually *seen* their two names connected, side by side in black and white. If she'd been able to keep searching through the pile of print magazines in the Waughs' conservatory that night, perhaps she would've spotted it, would've known so much sooner that Scott was lying about never having met her. The interview wasn't particularly revealing—aerospace trends, new innovations, potential deals—but it was clear it had taken place in person, during the air show. Juliet asked Scott a little about himself, and his answers were confident and professional, with glimmers of the humor Lucy knew so well. A picture showed him in a light gray suit, smiling easily. Perhaps he hadn't known then how life-changing the interview would prove to be. Or even if he'd had an inkling, an idea already forming, he'd done his usual trick of smoothing it over with a smile.

There was one part of the interview that gave Lucy pause. She highlighted it with her mouse and stared at it, trying to pinpoint why it had jumped out.

Thanks for talking to me, Scott, Juliet had transcribed at the end. *I have to admit I was thrilled when I got the interview request, especially since I'm a newbie in this industry!*

It's been my pleasure, Scott had replied.

It made it sound as if Juliet had been specially selected to interview Scott at the show. Would the request have come from Scott himself, or just from someone on his team, oblivious to what they were about to set in motion? What if it hadn't been a coincidence, Juliet and Scott meeting again after all these years?

Lucy scanned a few more articles about the show and

stared at numerous photos, combing shots of milling crowds and glittery awards dinners for Juliet's dark hair or Scott's broad shoulders. Finding nothing else, she switched direction, went further back in time: *Guy Everley Leeds University.*

As before, most of the results were articles about his car crash, made bigger news by the fact that he had a semi-famous artist for a dad. Lucy read through some more of the reports, learning how he had veered off the road, hit a tree, died on impact. Lots of the articles suggested he'd been into drink and drugs, prone to reckless behavior. Some gave more prominence to the road he'd died on, quoting statistics about how many drivers had been killed by its sharp bends and hidden dips. High Pass was nicknamed the Serpent and it was easy to see why. A Google Image search for *High Pass at night* showed it winding between black hills, the moonlight giving it the oily look of a snakeskin. It had other nicknames, too. Death Pass. Death Row. One particular section was even dubbed Killer Corner.

There seemed a consensus, therefore, that the two things had come together in a lethal cocktail: Guy's drunken wildness combined with the treacherous, unlit road. Nobody seemed to know why he'd been driving through the hills at midnight. A friend was quoted as saying he liked to go out for late drives, liked to do things just because he felt like it. *Guy was Guy,* he said. *There was never any point to trying to figure him out.*

Lucy scrolled down, the articles blurring into each other, images of Guy's handsome face rolling past and almost desensitizing her. She stalled, though, when she came to his Facebook page. Sometime after he'd died, it had been turned into a public forum for tributes and RIP messages. Tears clouded her eyes as she read through some of them. It always made her cry, seeing the things people wished they could say to someone who was gone. Not so desensitized, after all. Blinking away the tears, she searched for any posts from Scott, Cora, or Adam. Any clue that they had known Guy. Their names were nowhere to be seen, but another one made her fingers stutter on the mouse pad.

I miss you, Guy, Juliet had written. The flat feels empty without you. You always predicted you'd die young and I'm so angry with you for making that come true. Sleep calmly now. Love you. J x

Lucy read it twice, her thoughts churning. Had Juliet and Guy been a couple? Was that somehow connected to her death, so many years after his?

She scrolled down further until she reached a time when Guy had been alive, his Facebook page being used by him in the usual way. He'd been tagged in some photos at a social, just before Christmas 2005. People looked merry and flushed; Christmas lights twinkled softly in the background. Guy and Juliet were in the center of a group picture in which eight people had piled onto a sofa, sitting on laps or perching with arms round each other. Juliet was wearing a low-cut red sweater, raising a glass of mulled wine; Guy had unfocused eyes and a tipsy smile. It was hard to tell from their body language whether they were a couple. Guy had both arms stretched across the back of the sofa, looking relaxed and almost smug with a woman on either side.

Lucy kept scrolling. A few weeks earlier, Guy had posted a photo of a bottle of champagne with the caption: Drinking spontaneously purchased champers at midday on a Tuesday, why not? Life's too short.

There were lots of comments underneath, mostly along

the lines of classic Guy and whose money have you bought that with??! Banter that made Lucy vaguely uncomfortable, though she couldn't put her finger on why. Then she froze as she saw a comment about halfway down.

Scott.

Is that supposed to be fucking funny?

Guy hadn't responded. Someone else had written, Who the hell are you? But the conversation had apparently stopped there. Lucy clicked through several other photos Guy had been tagged in, but Scott hadn't interacted with any of those. There was no mention of him anywhere else on Guy's Facebook page. Only that one strange remark.

She clicked into Scott's Facebook, following a slightly haphazard trail. His recent posts were all of Ivy and Joe, their cute, smiley faces, their familiar voices in funny videos. Joe looked so much like Scott. And Ivy had all of Cora's poise, but with hints of rebellion from it sometimes, like the Cora that Lucy occasionally saw. She felt another twist of sadness at the thought of what Ivy and Joe might have to deal with. The thought of not being in their lives anymore, or not in the same way she was now.

She made her way back to early 2006. When Facebook was in its infancy, the photos were low quality, and Ivy and Joe didn't even exist. There was no sign of Guy on Scott's profile. It was filled with pictures of younger Scott and Cora, and Lucy got the same feeling as when she'd looked through the printed snaps at their house: the posed nature of the images; the sense of curated coupledom.

Cora had tagged Scott in a picture in which they both wore chunky-knit sweaters over checked pajamas, captioning it cozy night in. Scott had posted another a few days later, in a shiny booth with a shared bowl of pasta: Valentine's dins with my fave person. As Lucy scrolled back a tiny bit further, the pictures seemed a stark contrast to the ones from the preceding Christmas and autumn, in which the two of them were captured among friends, looking like little more than friends themselves—drinking, dancing, hardly aware of the camera at all. Lucy checked the date of the change, something she hadn't been able to do with the physical photos. It did seem to have happened around February 2006, even though Cora and Scott always said they'd got together at the start of their final year, the previous October. Perhaps it had taken them a few months to get serious, to establish their "brand" as a couple and go public on Facebook. A brand that had never struck Lucy as at all artificial until recently.

Ideas were circling each other like boxing opponents in her brain. Dancing around the same point, drawing close, never quite connecting. Something had happened at Leeds. Something that had changed relationships, ambitions, even personalities. Something involving Guy Everley . . . whom Scott had not only known, but had clearly disliked, if that comment was anything to go by.

"We're AWAAAAKE!" came Tilly's foghorn announcement from their room.

Lucy snapped into the present, closing the laptop and jumping to her feet. "OKAAAAY!" she shouted back with matching vowel elongation.

She shook her head in a vain attempt to clear it, and hurried into the bedroom to kiss her girls and ask what they wanted for breakfast.

"Cake," Fran said, already smirking because she knew it wasn't an acceptable answer. "And cheese."

"*Cheese*cake!" Tilly said, warming to the theme.

"Why do I even ask?" Lucy said, kissing them again.

Down in the kitchen, she filled two bowls with Rice Krispies and poured two glasses of watered-down juice. Her thoughts were still buzzing as the girls whirled in and hopped onto their chairs at the table. Lucy went into autopilot, picking up dropped spoons, wiping spilled juice, fetching Ribena because "we're not wasting any more juice!" She was thinking about Scott again. Her thoughts as consumed as Juliet's might've been at the height of their affair, but presumably in a very different way.

His hands around my neck. My back against this wall. She stared at the spot where it had happened, imagining she could still see the shape of herself, pinned there.

It took her a moment to realize her phone was buzzing, too. It wasn't just the chaos in her head. She picked it up from the worktop with a slight sense of trepidation and saw that a withheld number was calling. Lucy normally dismissed them without a thought. But this one seemed to radiate importance, somehow.

"Hello?" There must've been something different about the way she answered it, too, because Tilly and Fran both looked up at her.

"Lucy Taylor?"

"That's me."

"This is DC Aggarwal, calling from Leicestershire Police."

Lucy glanced back at her girls, who had now reverted to flicking Rice Krispies at one another and shrieking with laughter. She moved away from them, feeling as if she wanted to pull down a screen between their playfulness and the conversation she was having. "Yes?"

"Could you come down to the station at your earliest convenience? We need to speak to you again."

She felt her skin growing hot. "Is this about . . ." She trailed off with a fear of saying the wrong thing, and instead asked: "What's this about?"

There was a pause. "Please come as soon as possible. We'll discuss the specifics when you arrive."

"Okay," Lucy said a little breathlessly. "I just need to take my daughters to school. And then . . . then I'll come."

Cora and Scott. Scott and Cora. The hot couple. The happy couple. The photogenic couple, people have always said . . . and I suppose there's an awful irony in that now.

But it's the way it's been for so long. An image we've projected to the world, an image powerful enough to override suspicions, make people think they must've been mistaken about any other narrative. And for long periods, actually, it's been the truth. There's been love, sex, laughter, good times, hopeful moments. A honeymoon in Italy that was an escape, a new start—or so we thought, so we hoped, so we pretended hard enough that we almost made it true.

And then there was Ivy and Joe. Our little lights in the darkness, reawakening the soft parts of my heart. There's nothing fake about how much we love them, love being parents. A family with secrets can still be a beautiful thing.

But some memories are hard to forget. Impossible to get over. They fester over time, gnaw away at the good stuff, the real stuff, even the pretending. They break out at unexpected moments and make us do things we know we'll regret.

It isn't all my fault.

Ruth should never have taken that photo in the Maldives. She shouldn't even have had the chance.

Juliet should never have sent those emails, written those things.

And she shouldn't have hurt me back then. Shouldn't have destroyed the little faith I had, made me feel so stupid, so small.

It ought to be a minor thing now, in the scheme of things; a tiny smear on the timeline of my life.

But like I say, some memories are hard to forget. Impossible to get over. Impossible to delete from the gallery in my head, especially now that she's back there, in my thoughts. Every. Torturous. Day.

CHAPTER SEVENTEEN

LUCY DIDN'T HAVE TO WAIT THIS TIME. AS SOON AS she gave her name at the police station desk, she was directed through to one of the interview rooms. It was DC Aggarwal and DC Marr again. They were noticeably more exhausted than the last time she'd been here, though it had been less than twenty-four hours ago. There was a strong smell of coffee and an extra snap of tension in the airless room.

"Mrs. Taylor," DC Aggarwal said briskly. "Thank you for coming in."

There was a pause. Lucy looked between them. Surely the ball was in their court, surely they should be explaining why they'd summoned her back, yet she felt as if the spotlight of expectation was on her. There were things she wanted from them, too, of course. To find out how much they'd told Scott about Juliet's death, why they'd released him, what Guy Everley had to do with any of it. But she was more afraid than ever of doing or saying something that would cause more harm.

"We'd like to clarify a few points," DC Aggarwal said,

flipping open her notebook and sweeping her eyes over a page of neat handwriting.

"Of course," Lucy said. "Whatever I can do to—"

"Can you tell us more about your relationship with Ruth Beaumont?"

Lucy hesitated. A few weeks ago she could've answered in the simplest of terms. Colleagues. Acquaintances. Minor characters in each other's lives. Why were the detectives asking about Ruth in such a roundabout way? The fact that she was hurt loomed unspoken over the room.

Or worse than hurt? Lucy thought, struck with fresh fear. What if that was why she'd been called back? Because Ruth was *dead*?

"I . . . I don't know her well," Lucy said. "We work in different departments. If I hadn't seen that photo on her phone, I presume it would've stayed that way. Neither of us would've had to . . ." She faltered, looking down at the table. "Neither of us would've got tangled up in all this."

"You feel tangled up?" DC Aggarwal spoke as if it was a curious turn of phrase.

"Well, of course I do," Lucy said with a swell of indignation. "It's a . . ." Her words died again, and she remembered Adam's from last night: *Leave it alone, step away.* Instead, she had plunged herself back in.

"Have you ever been to Ruth Beaumont's home?" DC Aggarwal asked.

Lucy felt the muscles tense up along her spine. Did standing in Ruth's street watching police swarm around her house count? Why did Lucy feel as if she couldn't admit to being there in the aftermath? In case it made her look too interested, too involved?

"Not socially," she said.

"*Anti*-socially?" DC Marr sounded almost amused.

Aggarwal shot him a disapproving look. Lucy remembered how she'd scowled at him last time, when he'd overdisclosed about Juliet's death being treated as murder. He'd seemed the softer, more approachable one from the start, but Lucy sometimes got the feeling he was smirking at a joke she wasn't privy to.

A rush of impatience came over her. She sat forward. "Has something happened to Ruth?"

There was another silence. DC Marr opened his mouth to answer, but an almost imperceptible hand gesture from DC Aggarwal made him close it again. He folded his arms, looking exasperated.

"What makes you ask that?" Aggarwal said in a flat, deliberately neutral tone.

Lucy didn't know why she was sweating. She'd done nothing wrong. But the room was so hot and the atmosphere so strange. She found herself wondering if Scott had sat in this exact chair, if Ruth's husband had wept in this spot.

"I . . . I saw her husband here when I was leaving last night," she said. "He had blood on him. A *lot* of blood." She winced, remembering the shocking scarlet against the white of his shirt. "He was . . . he seemed . . ." Again, no words seemed quite appropriate. "Distraught."

"Do you know him?"

"Not really. I've met him a couple of times. And I saw their honeymoon photos of course . . ." She recalled how sunny their smiles had been, the backdrop of blue skies and creamy sands, and felt a wash of regret that their honeymoon had been so tainted by what they'd become embroiled in since.

"Do you get the impression theirs is a happy marriage?"

Lucy realized she no longer felt qualified to judge. It wasn't just Cora and Scott she'd been wrong about. Hadn't she thought her own marriage was solid, too?

"They looked happy," she finally answered with a shrug. "In the pictures."

Even that sent a shiver down her spine. It reminded her of all the photos of the Waughs she'd been flicking through on Facebook only a couple of hours before. Smiles and eye contact and cute captions. Could nothing be taken at face value? Was that the reality Lucy had to accept?

She sat forward. "What happened to Ruth?"

DC Marr kept his arms folded, resolute in his silence this time. Lucy fixed her eyes on DC Aggarwal, aware of how much power this woman had over her in this moment. She could decide to tell Lucy what she desperately wanted to know, or keep her in the dark. Lucy had had the same choice with Cora. And Adam with her. Whether to share or guard their knowledge.

"Two potentially linked investigations are now underway," DC Aggarwal said, drawing a folder toward her. "One into Juliet Noor's murder and the other into injuries suffered by Ruth Beaumont. If you have any further information about either, it's essential you tell us."

"I . . . I don't." Even as she said it, Lucy questioned how true it was. Again, that decision about how much to share. The detectives were watching her as if they thought she had much more knowledge than she was letting on.

"Did you visit Ruth Beaumont last night?"

"No!" It was a knee-jerk answer. Lucy blinked as it came out of her mouth. "I was here with you for most of the evening, as you know."

"And then where did you go?"

"And then . . ." There was no way she could lie. No reason to, if she thought about it rationally, stopped panicking about how her actions might be construed. "And then, yes, okay, I'm sorry, I *did* go to her house . . ."

The detectives exchanged a glance. *They already knew I was there,* Lucy thought. It was obvious now. She'd been recognized at the crime scene and that was why they'd brought her back in.

After the crime, she tried to reassure herself as she scrambled to explain. "I saw her husband and I couldn't get in touch with Ruth, so I went to find out if she was okay. But clearly she wasn't . . ." Lucy touched her brow, feeling as if her head might explode. "You said injuries. What injuries? Was she . . . attacked?"

Aggarwal's eyes flashed down to her page. She seemed to weigh up how much to say, while DC Marr stayed tight-lipped beside her.

"She was found unconscious on her kitchen floor," DC Aggarwal said at last. "By her husband."

Lucy held her hand against her breastbone. DC Marr wrote something in his notebook and shoved it under DC Aggarwal's nose. Aggarwal frowned at him, and he upturned his palms, a silent back-and-forth zipping between them. Then Aggarwal shook her head and turned back to Lucy.

"She suffered a head injury," she said. "That's all we can disclose at this time."

There was a crush in Lucy's chest as she absorbed the

words. *Head injury. Unconscious.* Fragments of what Scott had said about Juliet mingled in: *Beat her brains out. Bludgeoned.*

"Oh, God." She felt as if she might be sick.

"Are you all right?" DC Marr's poker face morphed into one of concern, and it felt as if he was momentarily back on her side.

"We'll get you some water," Aggarwal said, seeming to soften, too—though it was Marr who got up to fetch it.

"Is she going to be okay?" Lucy wheezed. "Ruth? How bad is it?"

"We certainly hope so." DC Aggarwal left a respectful pause, but it was clear she was impatient to press on. Marr came back with the water and Lucy glugged half of it down.

"Her injuries . . ." Lucy's hand hovered near her own head, fingers rippling. "Were they . . . like Juliet's?"

DC Aggarwal sat up straighter. "How do you mean?"

Lucy snapped her mouth shut and pressed her glass against it.

"How do you know Juliet had head injuries, specifically?" DC Aggarwal asked, glancing at Marr. "We haven't broadcast her cause of death."

"I . . ." Lucy flailed for an acceptable answer. "Hasn't it been on the news?"

"No. It hasn't been disclosed outside of the investigating team."

Lucy's breath shortened again. *I heard it from Scott.* How could she say that, though, until she was certain of how *he* knew?

She tried to backpedal. "I think I just assumed . . ." And perhaps Scott had just assumed, she tried to tell herself. Or perhaps he'd inferred it from something the detectives had said? "You mentioned the investigations were linked, so I . . ."

"They're linked because of common people involved."

The subtext was almost louder than the actual words. That one of those people was Lucy. A reel of faces ran through her mind's eye: Juliet, Scott, Ruth, herself. Trapped together. Overlapping in different ways.

And then another face materialized. Floating without a clear place, upsetting any vague patterns that had managed to form.

Lucy blurted his name before she could stop herself: "Why did you ask me about Guy Everley?"

This time, both detectives cocked their heads.

"I . . . I looked him up," Lucy said, her face heating. "I know he died in a car crash."

DC Aggarwal spoke carefully. "That's correct."

"He knew Juliet? At uni?" She didn't give DC Aggarwal the chance to ask how she knew this; Lucy answered for her: "I saw her tribute to him on his Facebook page. It suggested they were close."

"They were flatmates, we believe."

"Were they a couple?"

DC Aggarwal's eyes were oddly blank. "As far as we can tell, they were just close friends. Unless you have reason to believe otherwise?"

Lucy shook her head. "No, no, I don't know anything about him. Only what I've read online. What's he got to do with the investigation?"

Aggarwal sat back in her chair. Lucy saw, unexpectedly, a slight sheen of sweat above the collar of her smart shirt.

Was it just because the room was hot, or was she as stressed by the situation as Lucy? As if following Lucy's eyeline, the detective quickly fastened an extra button. And in her moment of distraction, DC Marr seemed to wake up, to insert himself back into the room.

"In that case," he said to Lucy, "I'm assuming you've also seen the Facebook group."

Lucy's interest flared. "What group?"

Aggarwal's hand shot up like a stop signal. "We asked Mrs. Taylor here to talk about Ruth Beaumont!" She looked daggers at her colleague. "That's our priority right now. Let's stick to that, okay?"

Marr visibly deflated, and Lucy retreated into silence. Her thoughts felt too fast and too slow at the same time, like two currents pulling against each other. Somewhere in the muddle of it all, she made a mental note: *Facebook group.*

DC Aggarwal turned another page of her notebook with a crispness that suggested moving on was the only option. "Do you know of anybody else who might have visited Ruth yesterday evening?"

Lucy tried to gather herself. Was DC Aggarwal thinking of Scott? He was still the elephant in the room, not yet mentioned by name. *Why did you release him? Do you think he killed Juliet?*

A voice in the back of her head responded: *The question is, Lucy, do you?*

"I don't know," she said, as if in answer to it all. "I really don't know."

"Did you see anyone you recognized while you were there?"

Lucy shook her head, trying to remember the faces she'd seen. All she could really recall was that sinking feeling as she'd turned into Ruth's street and witnessed the kind of commotion that only ever accompanied something bad.

"What time did she have her . . . accident?" The word already seemed a euphemism. "Do you know?"

There was another silence. Another glance exchanged between the detectives.

"We're looking at a window of between five P.M. and six thirty-five P.M.," DC Aggarwal finally said.

Lucy thought back again. She must've got home just before eight, to find Scott and Cora settled at her and Adam's kitchen table. How long had they been there? She tried to picture how much wine was left in the bottle. This time, the overwhelming memory was of Scott getting the call and rushing off, claiming a work emergency. Then his demeanor when he'd returned in the middle of the night, swinging between aggression and distress.

DC Aggarwal glanced at her watch and then at the door. Lucy felt another flurry of panic at this indication that they were running out of time. She was more confused than before she'd stepped into the room. A sense of unfinished business switched off her brain-mouth filter. "You let Scott go," she threw at them, half accusation, half question.

DC Aggarwal raised her eyebrows but didn't confirm or deny. She seemed more interested in observing Lucy's body language. Lucy imagined what she'd be seeing: a bristling bundle of anxiety.

"Why?" she pressed, nonetheless. "Why did you release him? When he . . . when you . . ." She put her hands to her mouth, her confidence crumbling.

Aggarwal leaned forward. A lock of hair came loose from her ultra-neat ponytail and made her look completely different, somehow. When she spoke, her voice was surprisingly gentle. "Lucy . . ." She used her name for the first time, its consonants soft. "Do you have something more you want to say about him? Is there something you need to tell us?"

Lucy swallowed. *Did* she have more she wanted to say? The temptation to get everything off her chest, to hand over the burden. But what might that mean for Adam and for Cora?

"I . . . no," she said, hugging her elbows. "No, nothing more."

"Do you know where he was between five P.M. and six thirty-five P.M. last night?"

"He . . ." Lucy wished she hadn't said anything now. Her top was sticking to her in places she didn't even normally sweat. "He was at our house when I got home. Around eight."

"Oh?" Aggarwal's eyebrows jerked up again. Lucy wondered how it must look, that she was still socializing with Scott. That they'd seen each other right after Ruth had been found unconscious.

"I don't know what time he got there," she said. "I'm not trying to . . ." She stopped herself from finishing the sentence: *I'm not trying to give him an alibi.* And acknowledged, silently, that she hadn't told them Scott had come back later that night, that she was reluctant to, though she didn't quite know why.

DC Aggarwal had reopened her notebook and was scribbling rapidly. Lucy tried to see what she was writing but she had the book pulled close to her. Then the detective broke off, raised her head. "Thank you, Mrs. Taylor. I think that's all we need for now."

Lucy pulled the fabric of her top away from her clammy skin. She seemed to have been in this room for hours, yet now it was all wrapping up too quickly.

"Can you let me know?" she asked. "About Ruth? If she . . . if her condition changes?"

"That will depend," DC Aggarwal said, tucking the loose hair back into her ponytail. "Our hands are tied by the investigation."

DC Marr seemed to take pity on her. "You could contact the ICU at Leicester Royal. But they may not tell you anything, since you're not family."

Lucy felt sick again. *Intensive care*. She pictured Ruth in a bed, eyes closed, wired up to machines with her husband sitting beside her. In the imagined scene, his shirt was still blood-spattered. Then his face morphed into Scott's and Lucy thrust the vision away.

"I need to get to work," she said, swaying to her feet.

But she already knew, as she turned to leave, that that was not where she was heading next.

CHAPTER EIGHTEEN

THE ICU WAS QUIET, BUT WITH A SOFT HUM OF continuous activity. Phones being answered, nurses padding from bed to bed, patients shifting under thin sheets while others lay disturbingly still. Lucy half expected to be turned away, or questioned further about her relationship with Ruth, but the nurse at the desk nodded distractedly and pointed her toward the right bay. On the way there, Lucy noticed a large whiteboard of bed numbers and patient details. She sought out Ruth's name and saw the words *trauma* and *blood loss*, alongside some other medical terms she couldn't understand.

Walking on, she passed an older woman reading a newspaper at a bedside while crying silently. Lucy wanted to smile at her, show some kindness, but instead she put her head down and hurried past, feeling like an intruder. *You shouldn't be here. You've no right. You should be at work.* But she kept moving, training her eyes straight ahead, trying to walk as soundlessly as possible.

She stalled as she rounded a corner and saw Ruth's husband. Sitting next to Ruth's bed, just as she'd imagined, but wearing a black sweater rather than a bloodstained shirt. He was holding Ruth's hand as she slept, seemingly unaware of anything or anybody else. Lucy almost lost her nerve and backed away. Her eyes moved to Ruth: how tiny she looked on the bed, with a large dressing beneath her hairline, a bruise across her left cheek, a drip snaking out of her arm. It was the sight of her that made Lucy stay. She had to find out who did this to her, and why.

"Hello," she ventured, hovering at a distance.

Ruth's husband looked up, looked blank. Lucy's cheeks warmed. She really didn't belong here. Then recognition glimmered in his eyes and he looked almost relieved to see a semi-familiar face, even if they'd only met a couple of times before. Perhaps he'd been worried she was a police officer, back with more probing questions or bad news. Perhaps the break from sitting alone with an unconscious Ruth was unexpectedly welcome.

"I work with Ruth," Lucy said. "It's Martin, isn't it? I'm so sorry. I just came to see if she's okay."

"Well . . ." He sounded angry and yet defeated, as if the anger had nowhere to go. "She's not, I'm afraid."

"No. Of course she isn't. I really am sorry. Is there anything I can do? Fetch you a cup of tea? Sit with her while you take a break?"

He gazed at her, seeming confused again. His brown hair was sticking up at the back like he'd had an electric shock.

"Sorry," Lucy said. "Maybe I shouldn't have turned up like this. It's just, I heard about Ruth at work this morning, and I couldn't stop thinking about her, so when I passed by here on my way home for lunch . . ."

"It's fine." He waved a hand, shook his head. "She'd appreciate you visiting, I'm sure. If she knew." He looked back at Ruth, and Lucy wondered if she *did* have any awareness. If she could hear Lucy's voice and was yelling at her internally: *You dragged me into this mess. Put me here. Haven't you meddled enough?*

"Has she been conscious at all?" Lucy asked tentatively.

"No. It's a severe head trauma. She might wake up but . . ." He choked on the words. "Who knows what damage they've done."

"They?"

"Whoever"—she saw the muscles in his neck go taut—"whoever did this."

Lucy swallowed against the lump in her throat. Ruth slept on, motionless, maybe oblivious. What was making her look so small? Was it the lack of her usual teacherly energy and presence? She'd never been the most commanding of people but now she was a shell, and that frightened Lucy, too—how much could be taken from you in a few violent moments.

"You don't think it was an accident?" she asked, turning back to Martin.

There was a pause in which he tilted toward Ruth, as if seeking her permission to keep talking about her. He still had his honeymoon tan, Lucy noticed. His arms were studded with freckles but his nails were bitten ragged, like symbols of before and after. Martin had met Scott and Juliet, too. And yet he showed no sign, so far, of having realized the significance of that meeting. Should she ask him? Would it derail the conversation, confuse things even further?

"They say it could have been an accident," he said after a while. "The kitchen floor was wet . . . Maybe she slipped . . . But . . ."

Lucy's heart boomed. "But . . . ?" she prompted as gently as she could.

He rubbed his forehead. "If it was an accident," he said, "where's her phone?"

"Her phone's missing?"

Martin kept looking at Ruth, stroking her hand with his thumb. Lucy got the feeling he wanted to talk and yet, at the same time, was barely conscious of Lucy's presence. It was as if he was having a conversation with himself. Maybe the same one he'd been having repeatedly since he found his wife on their kitchen floor.

"She hasn't been herself lately," he said. "Distracted, a bit distant. I should've known something was going on. I just wish I knew what."

Lucy felt hideous. *You could give this poor guy some answers.* But how could she, without saying too much? That same dilemma, again and again. It was draining her.

"It must've been awful," she said. "Finding her like that."

"It was the worst moment of my life."

These words were an even bigger wrench. Lucy wanted to put a hand on his shoulder but sensed she'd be overstepping. For a moment everything felt surreal, as if that wasn't even Ruth in the bed. It was a dummy, and the real one was standing in front of a class talking about the industrial revolution.

"I got a feeling from the moment I stepped into the house," Martin said. "Something was off. The smell of our dinner burning in the oven . . . and the music playing . . ."

"Music?"

"The Alexa was on in the kitchen. I remember being surprised because Ruth doesn't normally listen to music at home. In the car she does, and when she's out jogging, but in the house she likes peace and quiet. So that felt . . . not right. And then I saw the broken mug on the floor, and the water . . . and then . . ." His face crumpled. "And then I saw her."

Lucy shook her head. "What a horrible shock. I'm so, so sorry."

Silence fell and Lucy struggled to make sense of it all—the spilled water, the music, the injuries—while her body seemed to be trying to purge it, her stomach gurgling ominously. She thought of how mortifying it would be if she vomited or fainted in this ward full of actual sick people. A smell of sanitizer hit her nostrils and made her feel even worse.

Martin turned all of a sudden. "Sorry, remind me of your name?"

"I'm Lucy."

A shadow crossed his face. "I think Ruth mentioned you. Recently, I feel like, though I can't quite . . . Did you two"—he frowned more deeply, trying to recall—"have an argument or something?"

Lucy's face flamed. "Um . . . no." She wasn't even sure if it was a lie or not. "Did she say we did?"

He lapsed into thought again. Lucy shuffled her feet, increasingly uncomfortable. It occurred to her that if Ruth's phone was found, the police would look through it, find all of Lucy's frantic messages. Did they constitute an argument? Would they look suspicious, look as if Lucy had been angry with Ruth?

Martin shrugged. "I don't know. I must've got that wrong." He turned back to Ruth, shuffling his chair closer. "I should've listened to her more. Should've asked what was bothering her. The thing is . . ." His voice gave out and he looked down. "I was too scared she was going to say it was me."

Lucy blinked back tears. "I don't think that would've been the case," she said. "I saw your honeymoon pictures." She faltered, wondering if this was the moment to bring up Juliet and Scott—or Anna and Jason, as he would've known them. Instead, she swallowed again and murmured: "I've never seen a happier couple."

He glanced over, smiling faintly. "That was the best fortnight of my life."

The contrast with his earlier phrase tore at Lucy. The best fortnight of his life, followed, a couple of weeks later, by the worst moment.

CHAPTER NINETEEN

LUCY MANAGED TO HOLD IN HER TEARS UNTIL SHE got back to her car, but they streamed down her cheeks all the way home. She knew they were a result of everything the past week or so had thrown at her, but the tangible sight of Ruth unconscious in a hospital bed was the trigger that burst the dam.

By the time she pulled up at home, her face was swollen. She fished in her bag for tissues, wiped her eyes, and went inside. The house was quiet and empty, still smelling of the orange juice Fran had spilled at breakfast. Guilt gnawed at Lucy as she thought about who she should've been teaching, remembering that her year tens had been due to do assessed performances that morning. But the ache of exhaustion behind her eyes assured her she'd been right to call in sick.

She made herself a coffee, sat in the living room, and composed a text to Cora. She'd never put so much thought into a message to her, not even in the early days when she'd been desperate to forge an intimacy that transcended *boy-*

friend's uni-mate status. Should she keep this one vague, let her tell Lucy as much or as little about what Scott had said to her as she wanted to? Or had she done enough tiptoeing around her friend?

In the end, she settled for a simple message:

Hey Cor. Are you okay? xx

The wait for a response felt like waiting for a jury verdict. Lucy's mind began to construct different versions of the conversation that might've taken place between Cora and Scott. Began to imagine Cora already miles away with the kids, never wanting to speak to any of them again. Or worse . . . what if she was hurt, too? In danger? What if the conversation had turned threatening or violent? Lucy tried to distract herself, but the only other places her thoughts would go were just as disturbing. The conversations with the police, with Ruth's husband. Trying to piece together everything she had learned.

She paused over a memory from the police station. When DC Marr had mentioned a Facebook group and DC Aggarwal had cut him off, brought the discussion back to Ruth. Lucy cradled her coffee, tracking back in her mind. They'd been talking about Guy and Juliet. Lucy had said she'd been looking up stuff online and Marr had said, *I'm assuming you've also seen the Facebook group.*

She grabbed her laptop and opened Guy's profile, his face now as familiar and triggering as Juliet's. She soon realized, though, that Facebook groups hadn't existed while he was alive. So . . . Juliet, then? Lucy tabbed over to her page, scouring the public parts of her "About" information to see what online groups she'd been part of. Perhaps a University of Leeds alumni page, or something like that? But no, the only one showing on her profile was called Workshop Your Words. Lucy tapped into it and saw that it was a creative writing forum. *Writers supporting other writers with frank feedback and advice.* It was a closed group, so she couldn't see any of the other members or posts. Lucy pondered for a moment. Juliet had been in the Maldives to write a novel. Perhaps she'd reached out to this group for help. The idea brought another wave of sadness for Juliet's wasted potential, her curtailed ambitions. Would the group contain anything of significance, though? Was it what Marr had been referring to? After a few more seconds of deliberation, Lucy shrugged to the empty room and placed a request to join.

Then she heard her phone vibrate and she dived on it, her thoughts boomeranging back to Cora.

There was no message, though. Nothing in her notifications at all. She checked her inbox, her various messaging apps, and her call record, but nothing had come through. Had she imagined the vibration?

But there it was again. It wasn't coming from her phone. She looked around her living room in confusion—one of Adam's gadgets, maybe? Edging toward the sideboard where the sound had seemed to come from, she felt as if she was playing hide-and-seek and somebody should be saying, *hotter, colder*, like Adam would do with the girls. And there, lit up in the darkness of a drawer, was a small silver phone.

Lucy's breath rasped in her throat. Clichés about husbands with secret phones flashed through her mind, followed by a cold wash of memory: *Ruth's phone is missing.* It was a huge leap but her brain was trying to make it. Trying to recall the color and model of Ruth's phone from the day she'd seen the photo. Almost fearfully, she picked up the one in the drawer.

She exhaled as the screen saver shimmered to life. Felt immediately stupid, and guilty for thinking such extreme things. The people beaming back at her were her own family. Adam pulling a silly face, the girls laughing like he was the funniest dad in the world. This was *Tilly's* phone. It was a sign of how tired Lucy was that she hadn't recognized it. And the message was just a standard one from O2 about switching to a different pay-as-you-go tariff. She didn't know why the phone was in this drawer, and not with Tilly at school in case of an emergency, but she'd ask her later. In the meantime, she *had* to calm down. Her paranoia was escalating.

Despite her best efforts, though, another buzz made her jump even more dramatically. In all the confusion, she looked toward the drawer first before realizing it *was* her own phone this time.

It was a message from Cora.

A single word:

Heartbroken

CHAPTER TWENTY

WHEN IT CAME TO IT, LUCY DIDN'T EVEN THINK about it. Cora was in crisis and Lucy needed to get to her. She left the house and headed for the NHS offices on the outskirts of town where Cora worked. Maybe she could catch her for lunch, at least for a hug. Lucy needed one as much as she suspected Cora might. On the way, though, she grew nervous again. Would Cora be angry that Lucy had known something was going on all along? Would she have questions about what else Lucy knew, or what the police had said to her?

I could ask her about Guy Everley, Lucy thought. There was no reason not to now. She didn't have to keep hiding things from Cora, trying and failing to protect her.

As she pulled into the large car park surrounded by tall trees, she was struck by unexpected longing. It was the associations she had with this place: meeting Cora on her lunch breaks, usually during Lucy's school holidays when she'd bring sandwiches and they'd eat them under the beech tree behind her office block. Or sometimes meeting her from work for an early drink if the dads were doing school pickup. The pub across the road was a little on the rough side, and Cora had always looked out of place with her goddess-like aura and smart work gear, but they'd found their own cozy corner, acquired a taste for the cheap fruity cider on tap.

It seemed a long time since they'd done any of that. Lucy realized she missed her best friend even though she saw her often. They hadn't carved out enough one-on-one time lately. They'd even missed their yearly spa weekend because they'd both been busy and distracted. Now Lucy could only hope it wasn't too late to rectify that. She had an urge to book next year's trip right there and then, like a down payment on their future friendship. But she took deep breaths and refocused; there were more important things to deal with first.

She parked where she'd always parked, and headed toward the entrance she'd always used, texting Cora as she walked:

At your work if you're able to pop out for a chat.

There was no response, so she slowed a little. She wouldn't be able to get inside without a swipe card. When there was still no reply, and no indication that Cora had read the message, she went round the side of the building to the big window that looked into Cora's shared office. She could immediately see she wasn't at her desk. It was the ultra-neat one in the corner, with framed photos of Ivy, Joe, and Scott, and certificates on the wall detailing all the training courses Cora had completed while working there. More than any of her colleagues, Lucy always noted. A reminder of how quietly driven Cora still was, even though she'd never finished her architecture qualification or gone back to do a different degree.

She walked away, checking her phone again. As she turned left toward the car park, she stalled. Cora's blonde hair and upright posture were instantly recognizable. She was sitting on a bench on the far side of the car park, visible in the gap between two trees. And next to her, with his arm around her, was Adam.

Lucy was utterly thrown. Adam looked as if he was comforting Cora, doing what she'd come here to do, and there was nothing inherently wrong with that. But why wasn't he at work? And why did Lucy feel as if she ought to scurry away rather than approach them with a casual *fancy seeing you here*?

She floundered, clenching her car keys in her fist. She could march over, see what was going on, involve herself, confront any weirdness. Or she could creep up on them, eavesdrop on their conversation. Create even more weirdness if they caught her.

She couldn't tell if Cora was actually crying. She kept shaking her head. Adam put his face close to hers to whisper something, then removed his arm from around her and took his glasses off to wipe them. When he slid them back on and glanced her way, Lucy ducked behind a tree. Adam turned back to Cora and an intense discussion restarted, with him touching her arm, then her hand. The contact was no more intimate than that. Yet intimate enough to make Lucy feel territorial about Adam's familiar mannerisms, the way he would incline his head when talking to someone who was upset. *It's usually me he saves those gestures for.* Memories of last night whirled back, of him leaving this morning without kissing her good-bye.

Lucy edged to her car and shrank into the driver's seat, hoping neither of them had noticed her.

BACK AT HOME, she paced from room to room, talking to herself out loud. It was something she used to do when she was younger, if a friend or boyfriend had upset her, or if she'd had an argument with her mum. She'd walk in circles having an imaginary conversation, trying to work out exactly why she was upset. She hadn't done it for years. Her life had felt on an even keel since she'd met Adam, had the girls. She'd found her little corner of the world, found the people she wanted to share it with.

Now she grabbed her phone and made one last attempt to reassure herself it wasn't all falling apart.

She texted Adam:

> I didn't go to work today. Are you able to come home early? We really need to talk.

To her surprise, a reply arrived quickly.

> Sorry, Luce, I'm snowed under here. Back-to-back clients all day. You not feeling well? :(

She ignored his question. Of course she wasn't feeling well. And she gave him one more chance to tell the truth:

Are you with a client at the moment?

There was a short pause, then:

Yeah, way out in Kibworth.

Lucy's heart dropped into her stomach and she threw her phone onto the sofa. It was one thing to go and comfort Cora when she was having a terrible time. It was another to lie about doing so.

She stood there for a moment, panting, staring at her phone as if it was at fault. Then, in a burst of fury, she stormed upstairs. Without any real strategy or expectation, she began searching through Adam's things: his bedroom drawers, his desk in the study. Tearing at his belongings, turning over handfuls of his clothes. She was making a mess, and messing up her own head even further, but she couldn't stop. She turned on his laptop and typed in the passcode he'd never hidden from her.

The Photoshop icon leaped out as the desktop loaded. She imagined Adam doctoring that photo, sending it back to Scott. Just a *favor* between mates. Just a piece of falsified evidence in a murder investigation. When had he done it? Late at night if Lucy had gone to bed before him? While she'd been in the shower and the girls had been in front of the TV? Lunchtimes when he'd "popped back for a sandwich"? The more she thought about it, the more devious and calculated it seemed. Not just blurting out lies in the moment, but doing something methodical, intricate, in order to pull the wool over Lucy's eyes.

Opening the app, she looked through Adam's saved projects, but of course he would've deleted the doctored photo. The only things in there were some IT-related memes, a few family pictures he'd edited, and the mocked-up images of the cottage.

Lucy closed the app. Her cursor hovered over the inbox icon on the task bar. Going through Adam's emails felt like a next-level violation. They'd always said, in the early days of their marriage, that if they ever got to a point where they were wanting to look in each other's phones or inboxes, they had to stop, had to talk about why. But wasn't their whole honesty pact proving to be a sham?

Even so, she shied away from his inbox, turning her attention to the smart doorbell app instead. She was pretty sure Adam assumed she never looked at it, or knew how to use it, and he was mainly correct. Last night had been the first time. It was easy to figure out, though, and soon she was clicking through camera footage from the last week, feeling as if she was rolling back time.

It was odd to see her own doorstep at different times of day. Neighbors wandering past, cats moseying up the drive. She paused each time she saw a person. The postman this morning; Adam leaving for work; herself with the girls, distracted and almost haunted-looking. Had Tilly and Fran picked up on her recent state of mind? Was that why Fran had been playing up at bedtimes? Lucy's worries began to spiral in that direction until an image snapped her back to the screen. Scott, last night. The agitation in his posture as he'd skulked on their doorstep trying to call Adam. Earlier in the evening, she saw the Waughs arriving as a pack, Cora holding a bottle of wine, Scott swinging his car keys from his fingers. Lucy watched them from the point of getting out of their car until someone had answered the door. Cora and Scott didn't speak once. Didn't look at each other. It was as if something had already happened, already been said. Lucy checked the time: They'd arrived at seven twenty-three P.M. She remembered what the police had said—that Ruth's "accident" must've happened between five P.M. and six thirty-five P.M.—and shifted in her seat, unable to keep still.

Flicking back further, Lucy saw Adam and the girls arriving back from Norfolk on Sunday, followed by Scott turning up with Ivy and Joe, followed by Cora, earlier in the day, knocking on the door with soup and cough sweets. There were a couple of days of nothing remarkable, until Lucy lurched forward in her chair: *Cora again*.

She had come round, alone, at four P.M. on Thursday. Wearing work clothes, glancing somewhat nervously around her. Lucy had been doing school pickup that day, which normally meant Adam worked later, but she was surprised to see his arm appear in the shot, beckoning Cora inside. Lucy drummed her fingers on the edge of the desk as she moved the time bar forward, waiting to see how long Cora had stayed. The frustration of not being able to see inside the house was intense. She could almost understand now why anxious spouses installed secret cameras or used baby monitors to spy on their partners.

Cora had stayed for less than forty minutes. Lucy wasn't sure what to read into that. She left the house briskly, without looking back, her hands buried in her pockets. And two days earlier, but slightly later in the evening, the same thing had happened. And . . . and . . . Lucy was scrolling too fast, almost missing things . . . an hour before Cora, there was Scott. The two of them had turned up one after the other that afternoon, missing each other by ten minutes. Neither of them smiled or even appeared to greet Adam before stepping into the house. Lucy didn't feel any sense of relief that it wasn't all Cora, that she hadn't caught a flirtatious smile, a surreptitious kiss. Why had she not known about any of these strange little visits?

Her mind was made up now. She straightened in her chair and clicked into Adam's emails.

Most of his inbox consisted of messages from companies he'd bought tech from. Including the purchase of an updated Photoshop package, which made Lucy seize up with anger once again. There were a few from his dad in Scotland, and some from Tilly and Fran's school, which Lucy also got. Clenching her jaw, she typed Cora's email address into the search box and pressed *enter.*

Lots of emails appeared. That was to be expected. The four of them were in constant contact, and it wasn't always constrained to the women and men communicating separately. Adam and Cora had both been obsessed with *Succession* and used to email each other after every new episode, talking in incomprehensible references to the show. Lucy felt a pang as she ran her eye over a thread of emails planning a surprise party for her birthday last year. Cora, Adam, and Scott had made it Hawaiian themed—Scott's idea—purely so they could call it Lu's Luau.

There was no recent communication between her husband and her best friend, though. Nothing in the last month. Again, this failed to relieve Lucy's anxiety. She glanced behind her with a sudden fear that someone might have snuck into the room, then typed in the email search box: *Juliet*.

No results. Lucy breathed out a little. She tried *the Maldives* and there was one result, but it was just an old marketing email from a holiday company.

She wasn't sure what she'd expected to find. Adam was surely too tech savvy to leave anything in his inbox, anyway, even if he had been keeping secrets. Tears bloomed in Lucy's eyes as she glanced to the left and caught her reflection in the mirror. A frantic-looking woman scouring her husband's computer for evidence of wrongdoing. She never thought she'd be that person, never thought they'd be that couple. This was a man who kept a folder of panda pictures on his desktop because they were Tilly's favorite animal. Who secretly played his younger daughter's *Fairy Factory* computer game to unwind in the evenings.

But who sometimes, just sometimes, seemed remote from Lucy, whether it was staring into space, drifting somewhere she couldn't reach, or in the grip of insomnia with his face pressed into his pillow. Could you ever know somebody absolutely? Did you just have to accept that you couldn't and love them anyway?

She was about to close his inbox when she caught sight of a subfolder called *J.I.C.* She paused, intrigued by the acronym, then clicked on it.

Facial recognition required.

Lucy raised her eyebrows.

Facial recognition failed. Please enter passcode.

Lucy typed in the one Adam used for the computer.

Incorrect passcode. Please try again.

She frowned and tried once more, in case she'd made a

mistake, but was denied entry to the folder again. It was the only one in his inbox that required a passcode or facial recognition. Maybe it was confidential work stuff, but why would he keep it in his personal email?

Lucy jolted as her phone buzzed on the desk. She ripped her eyes from the computer screen and opened a message from Cora.

> Sorry hon, just read your text. Out of the office today on a course. Sorry I missed you. Talk later, okay?

Lucy pressed her palm against her chest as a great bubble of hurt and anger rose up. Everybody was lying to her. Everybody who mattered. For how long had they been doing so?

A second message from Cora flashed up:

> Oh, and I'm all right. Don't worry. Sorry if I was dramatic earlier! It was a hell of a night. But I just need to focus on Ivy and Joe right now. On making sure they don't get hurt. I'm sure you understand, my fellow mum, my amazing friend xxx

Lucy absorbed this. Something about it didn't ring true. Despite Cora's efforts to maintain a constant state of yogic calm, Lucy had expected an eruption when she found out about Scott's infidelity. After all, she'd seen behind the calm before; she knew Cora got stressed and angry and upset and hurt just like anybody else. Earlier, she'd said she was heartbroken. Now she seemed to have packed away her feelings to focus entirely on her children. It was admirable, but was it real? Was it healthy?

Then a third message buzzed through.

> Please don't tell anyone else what's been happening, Lucy. Please leave it alone now. Scott and I need to deal with this our way.

Lucy dropped her phone back onto the desk with a clatter. The three messages seemed almost to have come from different people, different sides of her friend. And she had no idea how to reply.

I think back often on the time before everything went wrong.

When the three of us were the best of mates, and we'd go out dancing, raving, sometimes moshing, depending on our mood, depending on where the cheap drinks were at. And we'd hold hands and bump hips and we'd bounce off each other, stumble against each other, and it was fine because nobody belonged to anybody else; it was as if we were always meant to be a three. And, sure, there was some flirtation, there were some near misses, some potentially messy feelings floating around in the air. But it didn't really matter because nothing had to be permanent then. Nothing had to be overthought.

I think that's why we get the old photos out sometimes. Why we still keep them, even, in that tatty shoebox. It's risky, especially with Lucy always looking on; once oblivious but now—regrettably—not so much. And it's a reminder of when it all went hideously wrong, so why the fuck would we want to dwell on that? But it's also a reminder of that time before, when it was all laughter and rounds of lager; leaning on each other as we staggered home under the sunrise. And maybe that's what we're always trying to hang on to. Trying to bracket the bit that happened in between.

Things can't be undone, though, can they?

Each of us made decisions the night Guy came to our house and denied the truth. Each of us made decisions in the weeks leading up to it—small ones, so we thought, but they stacked up on top of one another, like that precarious CD pile we used to have climbing up our living room wall. And each of us has made decisions in the years since, because we have people to protect, new lives to lead.

All we can do is stand by those decisions. Shape them into the right ones even if they haven't always seemed like it.

Why does it feel, more and more, like I'm the only one still trying to do that? The only one willing to go the extra mile?

CHAPTER TWENTY-ONE

THE REST OF THE AFTERNOON DISAPPEARED IN A blur, until Lucy caught sight of the clock and swore. She was late to collect Tilly and Fran. How had so much time passed? She grabbed her phone and keys and ran to the car. As she drove, she wondered if she was even safe to be on the road. Exhaustion made her reactions slow, her judgments questionable. Inevitably, her thoughts went to Guy and his crash. She shivered as she recalled an interview she'd read with the man who'd found him the next morning. Imagine coming across a scene like that. And there was something awful about the idea of Guy sitting alone and dead in his car until someone had driven by.

As she turned the final corner toward school, she cursed again. Tilly and Fran had gymnastics club tonight; she didn't need to collect them for another hour. Where was her *brain*? She made a U-turn and was about to head home when she found herself taking a different route. Found herself heading toward Cora's house, wondering if she'd be back. Wanting to see her for reasons both familiar and strange.

Cora answered the door wearing her yoga gear, drenched

in sweat, her face so crimson it looked as if Ivy or Joe had been at it with their face paints. Lucy stared at her, realizing she'd never seen her properly sweaty before. Even on their spa weekends, Cora would emerge from the sauna with a dignified glow, while Lucy bemoaned her own tomato face and sticky thighs.

"Cora . . ." Lucy wished she'd planned what to say. Instinctive sympathy and concern were fighting it out with the anger she still felt. She listened for whether Ivy and Joe were at home, hoping they were still at their own after-school activities so she could talk to Cora alone. A sad kind of silence leaked out of the house. They'd be at soccer club, Lucy remembered. Ivy was fiercely proud of the fact that she had a higher scoring record than her brother.

Cora said nothing, but turned and walked inside. They went into the living room and Lucy hovered, standing, rather than settling into her usual spot in the nook of the corner sofa. Music was playing and a Boxercise video was paused on the TV. Cora restarted it and launched back into her workout, punching the air with increasing speed and ferocity, more sweat pouring off her, the sound of her breathing filling the room. Lucy watched in astonishment. This wasn't Cora's usual controlled exercise regime. This was like seeing her attack an invisible enemy.

"Cor . . ." she said as her friend jabbed at the air, her hand moving so fast it blurred. "Cor, easy . . ."

Cora crashed to a stop and folded forward, panting hard. When the panting became wheezing, Lucy began to panic. "Water?" she asked, but Cora shook her head. "Sit?" Lucy urged, wondering why she could only seem to speak in one-word sentences.

Cora shook her head again, and went to lean against the wall, her head thrown back, her lungs heaving.

"You okay?" Lucy asked, and Cora nodded. She didn't look it, though. Her hair, face, and cropped top were drenched, and her aura was somewhere between manic and broken.

"So . . . yes," she said eventually. "Scott told me. About . . . *her*."

The pronoun rang in the room. This should've been the point at which Lucy pulled Cora in for a hug, sweat or no sweat. She remembered holding her for almost an hour after her grandma had died, coming away with Cora's snot and tears in her hair—Cora would've been mortified if she'd known—but feeling closer to her than ever. Now Cora's yellow exercise mat lay between them like a do-not-cross line.

"Cor, I'm—"

"Like I said"—Cora straightened up, kneading at a knot in her shoulder as if trying to evict it from her body—"I need to think about Ivy and Joe right now. They're all that matters."

"Do they know?"

"No!" Her eyes flashed, then fixed on Lucy. "No, and they're *not* going to find out."

Lucy recoiled, wounded. Surely Cora didn't think Lucy would tell Ivy and Joe anything that would hurt them?

"Scott's done something stupid, and we'll deal with it." Cora's gaze flickered to the wall behind Lucy, and there was a wobble in her face. "I will not let *anything* hurt my family. My kids. They're everything."

"But—"

"There is no but, Luce. I won't let them think badly of their dad. Won't let them lose their dad. That's all there is to it."

Lucy didn't need to look to know what was on the wall that Cora kept glancing at. It was an enormous canvas of the Waughs at Scott and Cora's vow renewal, looking like the perfect family Lucy had always thought they were.

"You must feel so betrayed," she said, aware of the layers of meaning to her words. She was learning a lot about betrayal recently. And maybe she'd only scratched the surface.

Cora's fists hadn't yet unclenched from the workout. She pressed them together and stared at them.

"You have no idea," she said, her voice a crackle of emotion.

Then she blinked as if someone had clicked their fingers in her face, looked around as if remembering where she was. Lucy was reminded, jarringly, of Scott snapping out of his temper trances. "Sorry." Cora shook her head. "Let's sit down. Let's . . . let's have a drink." Her hand touched Lucy's arm for the briefest of seconds, enough to make her long for the kind of conversation they should've been having, even in dreadful circumstances.

She didn't want a drink, despite what she always told Cora: "Any time after four P.M. is acceptable if you've had a rough day." Her stomach was still unsettled. But she took the glass of red that Cora brought from the kitchen and sipped it, perching on the sofa rather than snuggling in. She still had her shoes and jacket on, as if she was in a dentists' reception, awaiting a tooth-pulling, rather than in her best friend's living room drinking Malbec.

"How was your course?" she couldn't help asking.

Cora coughed into her wine. "Course?"

Lucy looked back at her, amazed she'd already forgotten her fib. "You said you were out of the office on a course today."

"Oh, today." Cora's shoulders slackened. "Of course. It was . . . I couldn't concentrate, to be honest."

"I'm not surprised." Lucy ran her finger around the rim of her wineglass. "Where *was* the course?"

"Today's?"

"Yes."

Cora narrowed her eyes as if she sensed Lucy was prodding at something. "Local," she said. "Not far." She took a bigger gulp of wine, ending up with a red cloud around her mouth.

Lucy got the sense of butting up against a wall. She changed tack, trying to soften her voice. "What are you going to do, Cor? Did Scott tell you . . . everything?"

"It depends what you mean by 'everything.'"

She was back to staring at the family portrait. This time, Lucy did turn to look at it. Cora was majestic in a sheer white dress and a flower crown. Lucy remembered her asking if late thirties was too old to wear daisies in your hair, to which Lucy had emphatically said no. Scott had always looked good in a suit, and that day had been no exception. Joe was in a shirt with planets on it; Ivy in a rose-pink dress and a pair of fairy wings she'd insisted on sporting.

And Lucy recalled the speech Adam had given over dinner. The way he'd looked at the Waughs—at Cora especially, Lucy *did* remember observing—as if the moment had significance beyond anything Lucy could understand. *I can't remember a time when you two weren't a couple,* he had said.

Why was that the constant refrain? That Cora and Scott were some kind of sacred entity that had always been?

"It must be such a shock, Cor," Lucy said. "Especially given that you and Scott have never really been with anybody else. Never been interested in anybody else." She could feel her voice developing an edge again as she remembered Adam with his arm around Cora, whispering into her ear. She kept trying to pull her focus back to Juliet and Ruth, to Cora's broken heart and the danger she might still be in. But the sting of being directly lied to was hard to dismiss.

Cora looked at her intently. Lucy could see her chest rising and falling, slower than earlier, but still pronounced.

"I get the feeling there's something you want to say, Lucy," she said.

The silence stretched out, almost excruciating. The wine had coated Lucy's mouth with a dry film that felt like a gag.

"And there are things I need to ask you, too," Cora added. "It's all such a head-fuck. Exactly how much did you—"

They were distracted by a noise outside. Both turned their heads toward it. Footsteps were crunching in the gravel of the Waughs' driveway, and there was a murmur of unfamiliar voices unnervingly close to the house. Cora frowned and got up to look out of the window. Stripes of shadow moved across the living room as she nudged apart the slats of the blind.

"What the *hell*?" she said.

"What is it?" Lucy jumped up, too, joining Cora.

It took her a moment to register what was happening outside. Two police officers in fluorescent uniforms were peering into the windows of Cora and Scott's car. Circling it, shining flashlights into the front and back, talking and gesturing to one another over the hood. It was as if a scene from a TV drama had been dropped onto the Waughs' driveway. A pedestrian passed by and stared baldly while one of the officers crouched down and checked underneath the car.

"What are they *doing*?" Cora took hold of Lucy's arm, the friction between them briefly evaporating.

"I don't know," Lucy said, glancing at Cora and folding her hand over hers. They still hadn't established whether she knew Scott had been questioned about Juliet's murder. The shock in Cora's face suggested that, even if she had, the reality of police officers outside her house was not something she'd been prepared for. Why were they here? Why were they interested in the Waughs' car?

"They . . ." Yet again, Lucy didn't know how much to say. "Let's go and see. I'm with you, Cor, don't worry."

Cora strode to the front door and flung it open, with Lucy close behind.

"Excuse me!" Cora demanded, assertive again, her voice sailing out into the street. "What are you doing?"

The officers turned. It was two dark-haired men, strangely similar in appearance except that one was much younger than the other. Lucy was relieved it wasn't Aggarwal and Marr. There was mild surprise in their faces as they took in Cora's workout clothes still stained with sweat, the hair plastered to her head. "Ma'am. We—"

"Why are you looking at our car?"

The younger guy, who must've been no older than mid-twenties, stepped toward her. "We have a warrant to inspect this vehicle," he said, showing her a piece of paper.

Cora stared at it. There was a moment of stillness as the wind dropped and the street went quiet. "A *warrant*?"

"It means—"

"I know what it means," Cora snapped breathily. "But . . . why?" She tried to study the warrant but it just seemed to confuse her, almost to offend her. "This doesn't tell me anything . . ."

"It's part of an ongoing investigation." The man seemed unsure of himself and was clearly trying not to look too hard at Cora, with all her exposed skin and toned muscle.

The older man took over. "Is your husband Scott Waugh?"

Cora threw a glance at Lucy. There was fear in her eyes now. Perhaps connections being made. "Yes."

"Do you know where he was yesterday evening? Particularly between the hours of"—the officer double-checked his notes—"five P.M. and six thirty-five P.M.?"

Lucy's pulse raced. So that was what this was about. Why the car, though? And had they been back in touch with Scott?

"What?" Cora was blinking as if she had something in her eye. "Yesterday evening? Why?"

"We're just trying to rule him out of our inquiries into an incident."

Lucy's legs had turned to jelly. She tried to keep her face impassive, but she felt as if everyone must be able to tell that she knew what the police officers were referring to, even the woman indiscreetly spying on them from a window in the opposite house.

"What incident?" Cora looked more alarmed by the second. Her fists had re-clenched and were twitching at her sides.

"Do you know Ruth Beaumont?"

"Who?"

"You don't recognize the name?"

Cora shook her head. Lucy looked at her feet as if that would stop them from directing any questions at her. Whatever Scott had told Cora, he apparently hadn't mentioned Ruth by name. Perhaps he had told her the smallest possible amount. Perhaps all Cora had really taken in—all she'd allowed herself to take in—was the fact of his affair.

"Where was your husband—"

"I don't *know*," Cora cut the PC off. "At work, I presume. He got home about seven . . ." She paused for thought, then gestured at Lucy. "Then we went to our friends' house. Right, Lucy?" She jumped on this as if it would solve everything. "We were at yours . . . it can't have been much later than that."

Lucy nodded, still afraid to speak. The older PC noted something down while the younger one fiddled with his flashlight and glanced at the car again. "We'll need to fingerprint the vehicle. We may even need to take it away for a short while. I hope you'll cooperate . . ."

"This is insane," said Cora, shaking her head.

The vibration of a phone made them all jolt. Lucy became flustered as she realized it was hers—searching through her coat pockets; glimpsing the time; realizing, with a sinking feeling, what the call would be.

"Sorry," she said to the people on the drive as they all stared at her. "I need to . . ."

She had to repeat her apologies down the phone to Tilly's teacher. "Sorry, Mrs. Lawson, so sorry, something came up, I'm on my way."

She hung up and straightened her coat, trying to find her way back to responsible mum mode. "I have to go and pick up my kids. I'm really late." She felt dizzy again. She'd only had a couple of sips of wine but she wished she hadn't, especially now that two police officers seemed to be scrutinizing her vain attempt to get it together.

"I'll call you later," she said to Cora, trying to signal with her eyes: *Are you going to be all right?* Cora stared blankly at her. Lucy didn't want to leave her, yet at the same time she was relieved to escape to her car. As she put it into gear, she glanced back and saw one of the PCs pulling on blue plastic gloves. Cora's fists were now tucked under her chin, her eyes like saucers. A few more curious neighbors emerged from their houses as Lucy drove away.

CHAPTER TWENTY-TWO

LUCY RAN INTO THE SCHOOL FOYER, FLUSTERED and sweating.

"So sorry I'm late, my lovelies! Second time in a fortnight! Naughty Mummy!" She kissed them profusely, as if they'd been apart for weeks. "Sorry, sorry, sorry."

They looked at her as if she was slightly mad. She felt it, if she was honest. Her mind kept veering back to Cora and the police and the flashlights and the blue plastic gloves.

"I did a handstand for a whole minute," Fran said, getting into the car.

"No way!" Lucy said. "That's amazing. Didn't you wobble? Didn't all the blood rush to your head?"

"I didn't wobble," Fran said proudly.

"She wobbled," Tilly said.

"I did not!"

Predicting escalation, Lucy cut in: "And what did *you* do at gym club, Tils?"

"Loooooads on the pommel horse." She bounced high

in her seat to demonstrate, but banged her head on the car roof and shouted, "OUCH" so loudly that Fran clamped her hands over her ears in protest.

"Oops, are you okay, Tilly?" Lucy asked, glancing in her mirror to check on her daughter as she maneuvered out of the school car park. She could tell from Tilly's expression that she was unhurt but plotting to shout something else just as loudly to make Fran flinch again. It was going to be one of those evenings, and Lucy didn't think she had the strength. She tried to distract Tilly. "You forgot to take your phone to school today. Otherwise you could've rung me when I was late."

Tilly shrugged. "Mrs. Lawson rang you anyway."

"True. But just make sure you don't forget your phone, okay, sweetheart? It's important in case I need to reach you."

"I didn't forget my phone." Tilly crossed her arms and looked a little indignant. "Daddy borrowed it."

Lucy braked abruptly, spotting a red light too late, and saw both girls tip forward in her mirror. "Sorry," she said, adjusting her seat belt so it didn't feel like a knife at her throat. "But, Til . . . what do you mean?"

Tilly was gazing out of the window now, swinging her legs in their slipped-down school socks. "He borrows it sometimes."

"What on earth for?" Lucy tried not to sound freaked out, but heard her voice go up an octave.

"*I* don't know." Tilly clearly hadn't questioned Adam's motives. And a couple of weeks ago, Lucy wouldn't have, either. She sank into silence as the girls made up with a duet from *Encanto*, wondering how her life had become so alien, when so much of it was the same as it had always been.

Glancing at her phone in its dashboard holder, she saw there was nothing from Cora. The temptation to drive home via the Waughs' house was not small. But Lucy resisted, forcing a bright smile onto her face until Tilly asked her what was wrong with her mouth.

THEY GOT HOME to find that Adam was back from work and had scrubbed the kitchen until it gleamed. All it did was make Lucy feel even more nauseous. The smell of bleach. The absence of the water rings and ketchup blobs that usually marred the worktops, as if the surface mess of their lives had been scoured away. Her eyes fell on an enormous bouquet of purple and pink flowers sitting on the table.

"Who are they for?" Fran said in awe, plucking at a petal.

"For Mummy," Adam said, looking at Lucy almost shyly.

Lucy blinked at the flowers. Adam often bought her some if she was feeling down or they'd had an argument—*Another tip from the How to Be a Good Husband manual?* she now thought darkly—but this wasn't that kind of situation. It wasn't any kind of situation they'd navigated before.

"Girls, you can watch some TV before dinner if you like," Lucy said. She didn't have it in her to supervise homework or a wholesome activity. The girls looked delighted and skipped off to the living room without even removing their shoes.

Lucy turned back to Adam. "Flowers?"

"It's weak, I know. But, Luce, I'm sorry—"

"This isn't about sorry, Ad! It's so much bigger than that."

"I know." He hung his head and she saw the thinning patch on his crown, pale, vulnerable skin showing through. Part of her longed to wind her arms around him, mend things between them. She touched the flowers and felt the prick of an unexpected thorn.

"Adam," she said urgently, keeping her voice low. "The police came to Cora's just now. I was there, I saw them . . . They searched their car."

"*What?*" He'd been pulling off the Marigold gloves he was still wearing, but this seemed to send him into a spin, the rubber gloves flapping half on, half off.

"They asked where Scott was yesterday evening. During the time Ruth got taken to the hospital."

"Shit," Adam said, causing Lucy to glance toward the living room. The TV was turned up to a deafening volume, which would normally have her running in, telling them to *please* turn it down, but on this occasion she was glad of it.

"They must think he was involved in that, too," she said, her eyes filling.

Adam's eyebrows knitted low. "Involved in *what*, exactly?"

"She was hurt. She was found on her kitchen floor with head injuries."

He visibly paled. "Fuck. That's . . . How do you know?"

"The police . . ." Lucy trailed off, letting him assume she'd heard it from the police outside Cora's, rather than admitting she'd been at the station for the second time earlier today.

"They *must* just be looking to rule Scott out," Adam said.

"And what if they don't?" Lucy said with a renewed wave of horror. "Ad, what if they *don't*?"

"They will, Luce, because there's no fucking way." His voice rose back to full-force denial. "What did the police say, exactly? What did *you* say? And Cora?" He seemed worried again. Worried about what Lucy had divulged? About continuing to control how much Cora knew? An image of the two of them on the bench popped into Lucy's mind, but she pushed it away for now.

"I need to call Cora." She turned her back on Adam, rooting in her bag for her phone. As her fingers closed around it, she was reminded about Tilly's. *Daddy borrowed it. He borrows it sometimes.* She shook off that thought, too; it would all have to wait. Her phone rang and rang in her ear, until she was forced to concede defeat. When she hung up, she saw Adam was also calling someone, hanging up with a similarly frustrated sigh.

"No answer from Scott, either," he said, lifting his glasses to rub at the bridge of his nose.

They both stared into space as if they couldn't get their heads around what was happening. Lucy could hear him breathing quickly, out of rhythm with her.

"Did you see Cora today?" she asked.

That guilty look again. She was coming to know it well, the quick, dark flash of it, and she despised that.

He shrugged and began to dry the shiny-wet tabletop with a tea towel. Big, sweeping movements, like when he and the girls washed the car and they acted like it was the most fun they'd ever had.

"Yeah, actually," Adam said casually. "I popped in to see her at work. To make sure she was okay after last night."

Lucy cocked her head. "I thought you were seeing customers out of town."

"I was, for some of the day—"

"Do you two often meet up without me?"

Adam stopped drying, straightened up, and gazed at her. "I . . ." He seemed to be trying to read her subtext, solve another puzzle he wasn't used to being unable to crack. "Not in the way I think you mean . . ."

Silence swelled between them. The sound of a theme tune blared from the other room. That annoying program with the dog. Lucy thought of the way Tilly always snuck a thumb into her mouth when she was absorbed in the TV—not such a big girl when she thought nobody was watching—and her heart felt as if it was going to rupture.

"Luce," Adam said, abandoning the tea towel. "Where's all this coming from? Are you okay? Are *we* okay? Please, I *really* want us to be okay. I hate that all this crap with Scott and Cora is coming between us." He made a move toward her but she retracted into herself. "Luce, come on. Please. There's nothing between Cora and me. We're old friends. We're like siblings. And she . . . she *adores* you."

Lucy looked at him and saw tears standing out in his eyes. He tried another step toward her, reaching out to touch her arm, then unexpectedly put a hand to her waist instead. Lucy stiffened but didn't brush him off. It seemed a long time since they'd touched, and to feel his palm there, just above her hip, felt jarringly intimate.

"Adam," she said, her voice a whisper.

He looked at her almost hopefully, as if this might be the moment she forgave him, let go of everything. He'd always wanted a quiet life, she realized. That was why they didn't often fight, why he usually apologized. He just wanted everything to be simple. And maybe that was because the complicated parts had been hidden all along, only showing in the tiniest of cracks. Lucy and the girls had become his safety zone. Oblivious, perhaps, to the fact that he was grappling with much bigger, messier things elsewhere.

Lucy jerked away from him, trying not to look as his face fell.

"Do you take Tilly's mobile off her sometimes?" she asked before she could lose her nerve.

"*What?*" He pulled his hand back to his side with a mixture of rejection and surprise. "No?"

"She says you do."

He screwed up his nose in bafflement. Or an act of? Lucy really wasn't sure. "Why would I? You know Tilly gets things muddled sometimes."

"No, she doesn't," Lucy snapped as if he had no right to say anything mildly negative about his own child.

Then Fran burst in with tears on her cheeks, complaining about something Tilly had done. Lucy thought she saw a flicker of relief in Adam's face as she diverted her attention to her daughter.

"It's okay, sweetie, tell me what happened," she murmured, drawing her close but realizing she was comforting herself, not Fran, who was too cross for a hug and squirmed away.

LUCY AND ADAM barely spoke for the rest of the evening. Only via, or about, Tilly and Fran. Fleetingly, Lucy mused that maybe this was how some couples communicated all the time: through their children, or in functional phrases like, *Fran needs a tissue.* She'd always hoped that she and Adam would maintain the fun and affection of their relationship, enriched by the girls but not reliant on them. Now she was getting a glimpse of what life would be like if resentment grew but was masked for the sake of their kids.

The only thing that connected them that evening was their shared anxiety about the Waughs. Lucy called Cora six more times, with no answer, and Adam kept trying to contact Scott. By the time Adam took the girls up to bed, he and Lucy were quietly frantic. The girls seemed to pick up on the atmosphere and started playing up, whacking each other with pillows, until Adam raised his voice and reduced them both to tears. Lucy heard it all unfolding from downstairs. She had no energy to go up and help. Adam sounded immediately remorseful, rushing to make amends, but his bedtime-story voice was less melodic than usual as it drifted down the stairs. Then everything went quiet and Lucy guessed he'd done his thing of falling asleep next to them. She imagined him twitching restlessly on the edge of one of their beds, dreaming of things she hoped they'd never have to know.

As silence settled around her, an idea crept in. One that would take her over another line she never thought she'd cross, but one she couldn't get out of her mind once it was there. She tried to push it away, looking at her phone to see if Cora had texted back. Nothing. What was going on? Lucy noticed she had a Facebook notification and clicked on it just in case it was a post or a message from Cora or Scott. She was surprised by what she saw, having forgotten she'd even made the request.

Your application to join the group Workshop Your Words has been accepted by the moderator.

It had dropped out of her thoughts, slipped down in her priorities, but now her heart rate picked back up. It was something to focus on, at least, while she felt powerless in every other respect. She clicked on the group and took a moment to orient herself. It had 106 members and claimed to be an open, inclusive forum for fiction writers. Most of the posts were questions about writing, niche research queries, or requests for feedback. Lucy scrolled and scrolled, looking for Juliet's name. There were dozens of posts every day, so it took a long time even to scroll back to before she had died. But after that, she didn't have to wait much longer. Her pulse became a drumbeat as she saw that Juliet had posted in the group only days before her death.

Have you ever started writing something that you thought was about one thing, but actually turned out to be about something else?

Something much more personal than you'd realized?

Lucy looked at the responses from other members. A lot of them agreed that this had happened to them before, and shared their experiences, some going completely off topic to talk about their own work. But there was one member, Susan the Scribbler, with whom Juliet had had a bit of an exchange.

Sometimes we set out to write fiction but our subconscious has other ideas!

I think that's what's happening. It's the strangest thing. I started writing a story about a plane crash on a remote island. That's the whole reason I've come to a remote island to work on it! (Not just for the cocktails and amazing seafood, honest!) But the writing keeps pulling me away from that. Pulling me back to . . . stuff from the past. From years and years ago.

That's interesting. Why do you reckon that is?

I'm not sure. I mean, my mind has been drifting back to this stuff a bit recently because I've reconnected with someone I knew then . . . but I didn't realize I was still so hung up on it, after all this time. Not until I started writing.

Are we talking traumatic stuff from the past?

I suppose, yes.

Unresolved? Often writing's a way of resolving things in your head. Cathartic but also problem-solving, I guess?

Maybe that's it. Unresolved. Too many questions that were never answered.

Well, maybe you need to find the answers. If they don't work their way out in your writing, that is.

Maybe I do, said Juliet, and then the conversation had gone quiet. Goosepimples prickled up Lucy's spine. She felt as if she was reading Juliet's last words, even though she must've spoken others after this. But it was more than that, actually. She felt she'd just been privy to Juliet's final, short-lived ambition. To seek answers about something unnamed. Something involving a person from her past with whom she'd "reconnected"—almost undoubtedly Scott. What if that ambition, that desire for closure, had ended her life?

A loud snore from above made her jump. She looked upward, remembering what she'd been considering attempting while Adam was asleep, then dropped her gaze back to her phone screen, torn between the two. Another snore. Adam was clearly in a deep sleep, something which didn't happen all that often, especially at the moment. *It might be now or never.* Lucy put down her phone and went to the stairs.

Gingerly, she tiptoed up and poked her head into the girls' room. All three of them were fast asleep. An automatic surge of affection almost sent her running back down, mission aborted, but she steeled herself and slipped into the study instead.

Switching on Adam's laptop, she navigated back to the protected folder in his inbox. Then she untangled the laptop from the various bolt on accessories that seemed to multiply weekly, and carried it to Tilly and Fran's room. Trying not to make too much noise or knock against Fran's bed, she hovered the laptop over Adam's sleeping face. Its light shone down on him and he flinched and stirred, making Lucy spring back. He murmured something indecipherable. Twitched, seemed almost in pain. Eventually, just as she was about to reverse out of the room, he went limp. Lucy raised the laptop again, only for a second or two, not even waiting to check if it had worked. Hurrying away, she closed the door and turned the computer to face her on the landing. Her chin dropped to her chest in relief. It had worked. The folder was open.

Relief morphed into fear at the first words she glimpsed.

I know what you did.

I know what you did. I know what you did.

That's what the emails kept circling back to. Their repetitive, relentless grind. Not subtle like her "novel." Not gently probing like the questions she would ask in person, the way she seemed to steer the conversation to the edge of uncomfortable and then pull back. The emails were direct. Accusing. Uncompromising. Everything she hadn't quite come out and said elsewhere.

I know what you did, they said, in a dozen different ways, a drip-feed of head-fuckery and threat. But they never said, I know how *you did it. And they never said, I know* why.

And maybe that was the part she was trying to fill in. The part she never got the chance to, and never will.

CHAPTER TWENTY-THREE

LUCY WANTED TO SLAM THE LAPTOP SHUT, CHANGE her mind, return to ignorance. But she knew that was impossible. Instead, she shut herself in the bathroom and perched on the damp bath edge with the laptop on her knees. She took deep breaths of the humid air, still smelling of the girls' No More Tears shampoo, and read through every item in Adam's locked folder.

It was full of messages from an unidentified sender to Adam's email address. All with the subject heading Do Not Ignore. The sender's sign-offs varied from "An Acquaintance" to "An Observer" to "An Interested Party," but the email addresses were strings of letters and numbers, slightly different each time. Like spam emails, Lucy thought. Except the contents of these made her heart flail against her ribs.

What makes you think you deserve your life?

What makes you think people don't see right through it?

The ghosts of the past will always return.

Do your children know what you are?

Do your family know what you did?

I know. I could ruin you. Is that what you want?

Lucy was shaking so hard she was making the shampoo bottles quiver on the sides of the bath. Adam had been receiving these messages regularly for months. How had he managed to carry on acting normal, being a husband, dad, colleague, friend, when threats had been invading his inbox?

"Why?" Lucy whispered out loud, all the hairs bristling on the back of her neck. "What did you *do*?" She glanced at the wall between her and Adam, picturing him sleeping on the other side of it with their daughters. There had to be an explanation. Maybe Adam hadn't always been as honest as she'd thought, but there was no way he could've done anything that warranted blackmail.

It struck her that she was running through the same panicked thought processes as she'd gone through with Scott. Concocting scenarios in which she didn't have to believe the worst. She'd always been too trusting. Keen to see the best in people. Previously, she'd thought that was a good thing, a positive quality, but the last fortnight had been a nightmarish crash course in why that wasn't the case. She scrolled right to the bottom of each email, scrutinized the email addresses that lay behind the aliases, looked at the cc and bcc boxes just in case there were any clues. But there was no indication as to who might've been behind them, or why.

Then she came across one with an attachment. This

time, the subject wasn't Do Not Ignore. It was What a Charming Couple. Lucy held her breath and hovered her mouse over it, feeling as if she knew what was coming. Would this be the original photo of Scott and Juliet in the Maldives that she'd been chasing since the start? Her head throbbed and she realized she'd been reading the emails through squinted eyes so far, trying to create her own muffling filter.

She opened the email.

Am I the only one with a photo of these two people?

The only one who could prove they were ever together?

I'm certain that I am.

Lucy's finger froze on the mouse pad as the connotations dawned on her. Surely these emails couldn't be from Ruth? Why would they have come to Adam if they were? She shifted the cursor upward and opened the attachment. It was just as bewildering a moment as when she'd opened the photoshopped picture from Ruth.

This image *wasn't* of Scott and Juliet, either.

It was of Cora and Guy Everley.

CHAPTER TWENTY-FOUR

THEY WERE SITTING NEXT TO EACH OTHER ON A battered brown sofa, just the two of them. The background was dark, indistinct, but it looked like a house or a flat rather than a public space. Cora's hair was blonde but with electric-blue tips, and she was wearing a pink tie-dye sweater that Lucy recognized from some of the other university pictures she'd seen. Guy was wearing a James Dean–style white T-shirt. He had his arm across the back of the sofa and was looking at the camera, while Cora sat close to him with her hand on his thigh, gazing at him.

When had it been taken? While Cora was supposed to have been in a relationship with Scott? Was that why it was being presented as controversial? But how did that relate to Juliet? How could that possibly have led to murder, to blackmail?

Lucy ran her eye back over the other emails. The bathroom felt increasingly humid, the air too thick, too hot. Not knowing what else to do, she forwarded the emails to herself, including the photo of Cora and Guy. The thought of showing them to the police made her light-headed. She had to find out more information first, but she had no idea how, no idea if she even wanted to know.

It's not a case of wanting. It's a case of needing to. It had been the same since the day she'd taken a casual interest in a colleague's honeymoon photos. Worse and worse, like peering through her fingers at more and more disturbing things. She dropped her head into her hands, closing her eyes against the glare of the laptop screen.

"Luce?"

She shot upright. The bathroom door was rattling.

"Luce, you in there?"

"Adam . . ." She could see his silhouette through the heavily frosted door, like something out of a bad dream.

"Just . . . having a bath," she called back. She turned on the taps and water began to crash into the tub, creating clouds of suffocating steam.

"Can I come in?" He tried the door again. "How come you've locked it?"

It was true, she never normally did. He'd perch on the side of the bath and chat to her sometimes while she was in there. Trail his fingertips in the water while she flicked clusters of bubbles at him. Sometimes, when he was in the mood, he'd even slip his hand down into the water, between her legs . . . The memory made her feel faintly queasy now.

Panic climbed inside her as the air continued to cook. Even Adam's laptop looked as if it was sweating, a layer of moisture forming on its keyboard.

Just let him in. Confront him. What is there left to do?

He was still Adam, after all. Still her husband. She refused to believe she was in danger from him. Maybe he was the one who needed her help. He'd been getting threats. Was clearly tangled up in something. She remembered how scared he'd looked last night when he'd asked her to step away from the whole thing.

Standing up, she unlocked the door and opened it a crack. His face appeared in the gap, half in shadow, looking confused. "What're you up to in here? You got a man hidden away?" He was clearly going for a teasing tone, but it felt painfully incongruous.

His eyes fell to the laptop on the floor. Silently, he seemed to take in the fact it was his, that she'd got it locked in here with her, that she hadn't even put the plug in the bath.

"Luce?" he said, pushing the door and stepping all the way inside the room.

Lucy picked up the laptop and held it in front of him, the emails still visible. She saw him blanch. There was a drawn-out pause, water continuing to run straight down the plughole behind.

"I think we need to talk," Lucy said, and Adam closed his eyes.

Pictures tell a story, but they can't tell mine.

Guy's dad's artwork tells a story of aftermath, of grief. All the articles about Guy tell the facts as they appeared, with photos to make it more titillating: a car smashed against a tree, a good-looking driver with alcohol in his system, a snaking road with a deadly reputation.

A driver with a reputation, too, let's face it. That's what led to it all, I suppose. And what saved me, partly, in the end.

Perhaps Juliet could've told a story that was closer to the truth than any of the rest. Working things out, piecing them together . . . but some of the pieces live solely in my head.

A rage so overwhelming it blurred my vision. The arrogance in his face, the disrespect I could no longer allow. Then the crack of the impact. The scream and the silence afterward. The slow seep of blood, pooling in the cracks between the floorboards.

Call an ambulance. No, no, think about it, just stop and think for a moment. The snaking road and the cold moonlight and the stillness of the silhouetted tree.

Juliet wanted the truth about Guy's death. Lucy wants the truth about it all.

But it was too much truth, and too much knowledge, that led to what happened that night. That ended Guy's life and almost destroyed mine.

CHAPTER TWENTY-FIVE

LUCY . . . I DON'T EVEN KNOW WHERE TO START."

The kitchen seemed to have become the site of confession. Here they were again, in the low light, with things to be said and a lingering smell of dinner. Just the two of them this time, though. Lucy's thoughts strayed to Scott, wondering if the police were questioning him at this moment. If Cora was once again boxing with the air, sweating out her pain. Was it worse to be in a confessional situation with her own husband than with either of her best friends? Of course it was. She'd swap in a heartbeat now, to keep just one thing that was precious to her.

Don't get ahead of yourself. Hear him out. Maybe nothing is as bad as it seems.

She sat opposite Adam. His laptop was between them on the table, like an exhibit in a trial. "Start with the emails," she said, trying to take control. "Who are they from? *Why* have you been getting them?"

He wound his hands around each other in the way he only did when he was extremely anxious and sleep-deprived.

She'd seen him like this before, but not often. It was becoming more and more apparent that "work stress" or "it's just insomnia, I've always had it, there's no particular cause" had only ever been masks for something much more profound.

He shook his head. "I can't, Lucy. I can't."

She banged the table, surprising even herself. "You owe me an explanation, Adam. Can't you imagine what I must be thinking? Emails in your inbox saying, 'I know what you did.'"

"But . . . but they're not the start. You need to know everything. You need to *understand*."

"Okay." Her hands started shaking, so she tucked them under her thighs, unsure why she didn't want to show him her fear. "Tell me, then. Please, I'm listening. Is it about Juliet?"

He fell silent. Lucy leaned forward. She couldn't even tell which emotion was most dominant: her anger, her panic, her frustration. They all rolled into one and made her voice uneven. "Adam! Be honest with me now, finally. Or this . . ." She faltered. "Or this could be the end for us."

His eyes widened. "No, Luce, please don't say that. Please don't do anything rash . . . This isn't what you think."

"Then tell me."

"It . . . it's complicated. Oh, God, it's . . . It goes way back. Scott—"

"Did he do it?" It was a reflex response, the question she was sick of asking but couldn't stop doing so. "Did he kill her?"

Adam held up his palm. "That's not what . . . I don't *know* who killed Juliet." He closed his eyes and they seemed to disappear into the rest of his pale face. "I don't even want to . . ." Then he reopened them and stared at Lucy, startling her with the sudden directness of his gaze. "All I know for sure is . . . Scott killed someone else."

Lucy's shaking spread up her arms, through the whole of her body. She stared at Adam. "Oh, my God."

He was breathing hard, too. "His name was Guy Everley. He—"

"The man from the picture." Lucy jerked her head. *Pictures, plural*, she corrected silently, thinking of the one she'd just seen. "Juliet's flatmate. Cora's . . ." She pointed at the laptop again. "Cora knew him, too?"

Adam looked at her for several beats. "You know a lot about him."

"I've been . . . researching."

He raised his eyebrows, then nodded slowly, as if deciding he wasn't so surprised by this, after all. Getting to his feet, he leaned on the back of his chair and shifted his weight from one foot to the other. "He and Cora were sleeping together."

Lucy's mouth fell open. Even though she'd just seen a photo of Cora cozying up to Guy, she was still shocked. Cora's insistence that there'd never been anyone but Scott was ingrained in her, too.

"She's never even mentioned . . ." Lucy began, then trailed off. Of course she hadn't. Her current husband had killed her former lover. It wasn't gossip over cocktails. It was the kind of thing you'd never, ever want to speak of.

"She was *infatuated* with Guy." Adam shook his head as if this pained or exasperated him even now. "But he treated her like dirt, absolute dirt. Always asking her for money, saying it was for textbooks, then going out and getting shitfaced instead . . ."

Lucy thought of the comments she had seen on Guy's

photo of the "spontaneously purchased" champagne. Friends had bantered, *classic Guy*, and, *whose money have you bought that with?* But Scott had come steaming in: *Is that supposed to be fucking funny?*

Defending Cora? Lashing out at a rival? Lucy had seen him get furious on Cora's behalf on a few occasions in the past. If a waiter had been rude to her or a drunk person had stumbled into her in a bar. But for that instinct to lead to *murder*?

"Was Scott jealous?" Lucy asked. "Were he and Cora a couple at the time? Did he know she was sleeping with Guy?"

"He and Cora weren't together then. Later, we told people they were. It was important nobody knew she was ever involved with . . ." He paused and waved a hand as if he was getting ahead of himself again. "But at that point, he and Cora were just close mates. The three of us were. And Scott hated how Guy treated Cora. So did I, of course, but it really got to him, really wound him up. The way he'd pick her up and put her down at will. Ignore her in public, saying he wasn't a 'couple kind of a person,' but then expect her to go round there in the middle of the night when he wanted company. And the frustrating part was, she did it. She was so obsessed with him that she'd go running when he snapped his fingers. Then she'd come back to me and Scott the next day, in tears *again*, because Guy refused to acknowledge she meant anything to him at all."

"Poor Cora," Lucy said, lowering her eyes. "That's . . . damaging." She always thought of her daughters whenever she heard anecdotes about women being treated badly in relationships. Always muttered a silent prayer that they'd never have to suffer in that way. But her best friend had.

However she felt about Cora at the moment, she still hated to think of it. And she couldn't help wondering, fleetingly, what she herself might do to defend a loved one who'd been treated that way if she saw it happening, saw its effects.

"Yeah." Adam slumped over the chair back, and Lucy saw his thinning patch again, the light bouncing off it. It reminded her that this had all happened so long ago. *How* had Adam kept it to himself? Through their whole relationship, their marriage, their closeness with the Waughs. The deception was overwhelming. And surely it had been eating away at him, too.

"Adam?" she prompted, trying to swallow her emotions in favor of getting to the truth. "Tell me. What happened?"

He straightened slowly, seemed to psych himself up like someone plunging into the next round of a fight. Lucy braced herself, too. Once they'd started again, it felt as if there'd be no chance to draw a breath.

"One night, Cora was really upset because Guy had been up to his usual tricks—asking for money, then ignoring her calls—and she begged me and Scott to take her out to cheer her up. We both knew what she really wanted to do. Traipse from bar to bar looking for Guy, seeing what he was up to, who he was with. I didn't think it was a good idea, but Scott thought we should do what she wanted. He was always softer on her . . ." He stalled, his eyes narrowing as if there was some conflict in this. "And admittedly, if we hadn't gone with her, she'd probably have headed out on her own. She was like that then. Impulsive. Tunnel vision when she got an idea in her head . . ." Another pause, and a fond, almost sorrowful look passed over him. Lucy looked away, once again bottling up the feelings that it stirred.

"Cora was drinking a *lot* that night." Adam glanced at the cupboard where they kept their own spirits. "Speaking of which, I think I need . . ." He strode over and flung open the doors, pulling out a whisky that had been in there for God knew how long. They were wine drinkers, normally. But he poured them both a generous measure and Lucy found herself gulping hers, letting it blunt some of the shock in her senses. Whether it gave her any more courage, she couldn't tell. She had a feeling she would need it.

Adam slammed down his drink, making her jump so violently it was like confirmation that her courage was in shreds.

"Scott and I were just trailing after her," he continued, swallowing audibly. "Bar to bar, for hours and hours, trying to keep an eye on her. That was the night the photo was taken—"

"Of Cora and Guy?" Lucy asked, gesturing at his laptop. "The one you were sent?"

Adam blinked. "No." He shook his head. "Not that one."

So many photos, Lucy thought. Would things have been different if none of them had ever been taken?

"The one you found in Cora's uni collection. With Guy and Juliet in the background," he said. "The one you asked me about the other night—about whether there'd been anything between Cora and me."

"And . . . had there?" She couldn't resist raising it one more time.

Again, he shook his head. "I cared about her. I still do, Luce, just like you do. But Scott was the one who always fancied her. Who *really* couldn't stand the way Guy messed her around. Who was maybe just waiting in the wings all along . . . And shit, if we'd known how he'd end up getting his chance . . ." He picked up his whisky and threw the rest of it into his mouth.

"Sorry," he said, discarding the glass and taking hold of the chair again. "I don't know if you're following this. If I'm making any sense . . ."

"Keep going," Lucy said in barely more than a whisper. Following wasn't the problem. She could see it all unfolding, crystal clear, in her mind's eye.

Adam nodded almost resignedly, his features dragging with exhaustion. "That photo in the bar was taken just after we'd tried to talk to Cora about Guy again. Tried to make her see sense *again.* We came across him in Yates, drinking with Juliet and a few others. And he blanked Cora, of course"—Adam ground his teeth—"then got up to leave not long after we'd arrived. Someone was randomly taking photos; I can't even remember who, or how we ended up with a copy. As soon as she realized Guy was about to leave, Cora started flirting with me, trying to make him jealous. The picture got taken just as she was looking over at me, and Guy was looking over at all of us, and Juliet was just observing the whole charade . . ."

He paused again, staring ahead as if recalling the scene. Lucy closed her eyes and brought the photo into her mind's eye, like her own window into the memory. Her brain added more details: the smell of stale booze in the bar; the clamor of voices; the dance of exchanged looks and unspoken feelings between Scott, Cora, Guy, and Adam.

"Anyway." Adam blinked himself alert. "*That* photo isn't really the point. This was all buildup to what happened"—he flinched and looked at the floor—"to what happened later."

"Which was what?" Lucy asked, fear returning in a giant swoop.

Adam inhaled as if drawing imaginary smoke into his lungs. "We took Cora home. She was crying so much, it was horrible to watch. It was killing us . . ." He stuttered over his word choice, then frowned and stumbled on. "We put her to bed in her clothes, put some water beside her, a sick bowl just in case. Like we'd done many times before. I remember Scott stroking her head, telling her she was safe with us. But the next morning . . . she was gone."

"Gone? Where?"

"We had no idea. We waited around the house all day, getting more and more anxious. And that same afternoon, Scott and I saw something online. A photo . . ."

"*Another* photo?" Lucy couldn't cope. There was a whole album in her head now, which could surely tell her a story if she could just get it into the right order.

"It was in an email newsletter for the English and Modern Langs Society. Cora wouldn't have received it, but Scott did because he'd done an elective in Spanish, or maybe it was French . . . *Anyway* . . ." He shook his head again, seeming exasperated by his own chaotic thoughts. "It was taken at a social a few days before. And it showed Guy in the background. Kissing Juliet."

"*Kissing?*" Lucy lifted her chin. She recalled what the police had said about them being nothing more than friends. "I thought they were just flatmates."

"They were. But Guy was like that. Everything was just a laugh to him." Anger flared in Adam's eyes again. It was clear he still wasn't over it, whatever feelings Guy had riled up, and perhaps neither were Cora or Scott. Perhaps it was a burden they'd shared all these years. *A burden but also a bond*, Lucy thought with a stab of irrational jealousy. Then she looked back at Adam and it half melted into sympathy. Maybe he'd been trapped by that bond, more so than she'd ever realized. Maybe that was why he used to talk sometimes about moving away, starting afresh, before dismissing the idea as a fantasy.

"We didn't know what to do," Adam went on, speaking more quickly now. "We knew it would kill Cora if she found out . . ." That phrase again. He winced this time and glanced at the alcohol cupboard as if considering a top-up. Lucy nursed her drink, though it was no longer warming her up; she was shivering in her chair. "We discussed getting it deleted from the newsletter, or just making sure she never saw it. And then she turned up. In the same clothes we'd put her to bed in, with her makeup all smudged . . ."

"Had she been with Guy?"

Adam nodded. The spark of anger was still in his eyes. "He'd called her when he'd got home in the small hours. Maybe her fake flirting with me had worked." His mouth downturned as if he hated the idea of himself as Guy's bait. Then his face darkened a little more and he added, "Jealousy's a powerful thing."

Lucy swallowed and didn't respond, despite several things colliding in her head. Cora's jealousy. Guy's. Scott's. Adam's. Even hers.

"Anyway." Adam shrugged but it seemed to distort into a shudder. "She'd got a taxi straight round there."

"And?" Lucy leaned forward. "Had something happened? Had he hurt her?"

"No." Another long, anguished sigh. "No, it was . . . almost worse. She was all loved up again. Saying they'd had a really intense day of talking and . . . well, you can guess what else." He shifted position and took his hands off the back of the chair to pull at his collar. "Suddenly it was all about how *misunderstood* Guy was. How he was lovely, deep down, and cared about her more than he was able to show. It was . . . well, I guess it was the final straw"—he caught Lucy's eye and clarified—"for Scott."

Lucy pressed her hands against her cheeks. "He killed Guy because of *that*?"

"Not . . ." Adam twitched again. "No, not exactly. But . . . he told Cora about Guy and Juliet. He couldn't stand it anymore, and he just blurted it out."

"Shit." Lucy sat back. There was a floating dizziness in her brain now, as if the whisky had reached it. "How did she take it?"

"Worse than even I'd expected." He bowed his head as more memories seemed to assault him, and Lucy went with him again, picturing the scene, not knowing whether to sympathize or scream. "She refused to believe it at first, refused to even contemplate it. Until Scott showed her the photo from the newsletter and she saw the evidence for herself. And then . . . then she *completely* lost it. Shouting and crying. Saying it was the one thing Guy had always sworn, that there were no other women. He had problems with commitment, and he wasn't always reliable, but he'd *promised*, she said, that she was the only one he wanted to be with. It was the deal-breaker for her, you see. She could just about handle all the other stuff, but not that."

Lucy tried to reconcile this image with the Cora she knew and realized it wasn't a stretch. *Scott never looks at other women.* That was still what she seemed to value in a relationship. What she seemed to need. Was this why Cora was so keen to post endless photos of her and Scott online—to showcase their commitment to one another because Guy hadn't ever let her go public about theirs?

"Did she confront Guy?" Lucy asked, dragging herself back. Adam had refilled his glass without her even noticing, but he wasn't drinking it, just holding it against his chest.

"She tried to," he said, seeming to pull himself back from somewhere else, too. "The next day on campus, she tried to talk to him. But he kept brushing her off, telling her not to make a scene. She made him promise he'd come round to ours that evening instead, and she was on tenterhooks all night, jumping at every sound. Drinking vodka as she waited, getting herself more and more worked up . . ."

Lucy inched forward again. Something in Adam's tone was growing more urgent, building in intensity, and it was sweeping her heart rate along, too.

"Then Guy arrived." Adam finally took a gulp of his freshened drink, closing his eyes as it went down. "Cora ran out into the hall to let him in, and they started arguing. Scott and I were listening from the living room. Guy was denying kissing Juliet, saying they were just mates, that she was like a sister—" He stalled. Had he realized he'd just echoed what he himself had said about Cora? Blinking, but not meeting Lucy's eye, he continued. "Cora was screaming about the photo but Guy was still denying it, calling her a crazy bitch, all sorts of horrible names. Then there was a sound"—he lifted his hand as if he was going to re-create it—"like . . . like she was slapping him, not his face but maybe his chest or shoulder . . ." The hand hovered, demonstrating noiselessly. "And Scott and I were looking at each other, thinking, should we go out there? The scuffle seemed to get worse and Cora started shrieking, so Scott and I jumped up and ran into the hall . . ."

Adam broke off, turning half away from Lucy and clamping his palm over his mouth. His shoulders heaved. She stood up and moved toward him. He kept his hand in place as if he didn't trust himself to move it, and his face was stark white. Eventually he lowered his hand all the way to his side, breathing unsteadily.

Lucy was equal parts moved and disturbed by how traumatized he looked. "Was that when it happened?" she asked quietly.

Another slow nod. "Cora pushed Guy and he staggered against the wall. He looked furious but also kind of triumphant, like he was pleased to be provoking her. Then he straightened up and looked as if he was going to lunge for her. And then . . . then . . . Scott seemed to see red. He kind of dived between them, shoving Guy *really* hard. It was honestly like slow motion, the way he fell, the way his head cracked on the shelf . . ." Adam's whole body seemed drawn downward by the memory. He hung on to the back of the chair again. "The angle of his neck when he hit the floor. The blood pouring from his head. Fuck, Lucy. I've never stopped seeing it."

She stared at him. Her head was shaking involuntarily, her teeth chattering. "I can't believe it." She wasn't sure exactly what she meant. That she couldn't believe it had happened, that Scott had done *that*, or that Adam had been carrying it the whole time she'd known him. Or *not* known him. Not known what he'd been going through, and not known that he could lie to her in such a big way. It was an awful tug-of-war between compassion for him, the man she still loved, and a howling sense of betrayal.

For a few seconds her thoughts were suspended, and there was just a ringing in her empty head. Then they seemed to speed up, fast-forward. This was not the end of the story.

"The car crash," she said with a flash of High Pass in her mind's eye. "I still don't understand."

Adam kept leaning on the chair, folding his body right over it as if he was going to vomit. "That's the thing," he said, speaking to the floor. "That's where I . . . became involved."

"Oh, no," Lucy murmured. "No, Ad. You . . . you helped them cover it up, didn't you? Helped make it look like a car crash."

She took his lack of reply as confirmation. And it hurt as much as if he'd done it yesterday, not years before he'd met her.

"How is that even *possible*?"

"It's possible." His voice was soft, still directed downward.

Again, without wanting to, Lucy found herself trying to picture it. She saw them wrestling Guy's body into the driver's seat. Rolling the car off the road, letting it hurtle toward a tree. Adam watched her as if realizing what she was doing. He kept opening his mouth to speak but nothing emerged, and Lucy had run out of words, too.

The shrill ringtone of a phone startled them both out of the moment.

"That's . . . mine," Adam said, sounding as if he'd never received a phone call before.

He looked around, disoriented, then fished it out of the pocket of his crumpled jeans.

"Who is it?" Lucy asked, her voice a croak.

He hesitated. "It's Cora."

Lucy swallowed and checked the clock: It was just past one A.M. "Answer it. Put her on speaker." Catching his look, she insisted: "No more secrets, Adam."

He seemed as if he might protest, but nodded somberly and did as she'd asked. Cora's frantic voice came through without any greeting, and without any of her usual control—though perhaps that had never been real, either. "They've taken Scott in! They've taken the car. It's all falling apart, Adam, it's all fucked—"

"Okay, Cor, okay," Adam cut her off, gesturing as if she could see him. "Stay calm." He sounded anything but. "I'm with Lucy. You're on speaker."

There was a short silence. Lucy imagined Cora pausing, blinking, adjusting what she was planning to say. Maybe trying to wrestle her constructed persona back into place.

"Cor, I've told her . . ." Adam said. "About Guy."

Cora's rapid breathing filled the pause. For a moment it was as if she was standing right next to Lucy, panting into her ear.

"What *about* Guy?"

"That"—Lucy could see Adam steeling himself—"that Scott killed him."

"Adam!" Cora sounded aghast, and Adam paled even further. "You *can't*—"

"She was working it out for herself, Cor. It's time she knew."

"It was an *accident*." Cora's voice rose, and Lucy felt a twist of surprise at her defensiveness of Scott, given that she'd just found out he'd been having an affair. Maybe she was under his spell as much as she'd been under Guy's. Lucy had always thought, somehow, that it had been the other way around—that Scott had been the one entranced by Cora.

"I know," Adam placated her, and Lucy got a feeling he'd done it many times before. That they'd had numerous exchanges like this, shifting guilt around, trying to dissolve it altogether. "It's okay, Lucy understands." He flung a glance at her but she shook her head, recoiling from the suggestion. *No, I don't. How can you put those words in my mouth?*

His shoulders sagged. What had he expected? She felt a blast of anger at his presumptuousness, tearing through her earlier compassion.

When he turned his attention back to Cora, his voice was weaker: "Why have the police taken Scott in?"

"That woman. The one who saw him and Juliet in the Maldives. The one who had the photo of them . . ."

"Ruth," Lucy whispered, her head spinning again.

"She's . . . injured," Cora said. "They think she might've been attacked."

Adam glanced at Lucy. Neither of them spoke up to tell Cora they already knew this.

"And they . . . suspect Scott?" Adam asked, still with his eyes on Lucy's face.

"Oh, God, I don't know." Cora began to sob. "I think so. Something to do with a car that was seen near her house."

"Your car?"

"Fitting the description, apparently. Ad, I don't know what to do anymore. Don't know what to think."

Adam put his hand over the phone as if to mute her distress. He seemed jittery now, pushing his glasses up his nose even though they were already as high as they could go. Red marks scored his skin where he'd pressed the frames into it.

Lucy's thoughts were a whirlwind yet again. The Waughs' car near Ruth's house. It had an inevitability to it, almost a simplicity, that was both easier and harder to accept than anything she'd heard so far.

"Sit tight, Cor," Adam said, removing his hand from the phone. "Just sit tight for now. I'll call you back, okay?"

There was a pause on the line. The rustling of a tissue and a sharper sound, like fingers drumming on a surface.

"It's not just that," Cora eventually said.

"What?" Adam sounded at the end of his tether. "What else?"

Cora's breathing could be heard again, like inside a scuba mask. "Check your inbox, Adam. We've had another one."

I shouldn't have gone there in my own car. I realize that.

I left it round the corner and walked to the house, but it was still stupid.

The truth is, I don't think I knew what I was going to do. Just try to talk to her for a second time, properly, firmly, because she wouldn't listen before.

I've got nothing against Ruth Beaumont. I feel terrible, actually, that she got drawn into this. She was just a woman on her honeymoon who wanted to make friends, wanted a memento of a happy, drunken night. Juliet was the one who lied to her first. Inventing Anna and Jason, another sickeningly happy couple in paradise.

Ruth was drinking a cup of tea when I knocked on the door. Her mug said TOP TEACHER, *was even personalized with a photo of Ruth. That's a lot of effort for a student to go to. I squirm when I think about that now. About how much she must've meant to the young person who gave it to her.*

I've learned that it's better not to think about it at all.

She dropped the mug when I barged my way in, and it smashed on the kitchen floor. Something in the back of my mind must've registered then just how hard that stone floor was. The mug shattered into hundreds of pieces and the sound was so loud I worried a neighbor might come checking on her. It seemed like the kind of cul-de-sac in which that might happen. The kind where people actually look out for each other, and like each other, rather than fake-smiling and avoiding too much conversation.

That was when I decided to put music on, turn it up loud. I remember the surprise in Ruth's eyes when I switched on her Alexa. And I did still try to reason with her at that point. I persuaded her, at last, to send the photoshopped picture to Lucy. To try to convince her she'd remembered it wrong, that it was just two strangers called Jason and Anna, after all.

But I could tell that the second I left, Ruth was going to call the police. She kept her phone held so tightly in her fist that I knew what was on her mind. Knew this wasn't going to be the neat solution I'd hoped it might.

And I couldn't risk it. Couldn't leave another loose end. Not when I've come this far, survived all this time, dealt with so much just to keep my secrets zipped up tight.

CHAPTER TWENTY-SIX

LUCY WATCHED CAREFULLY AS ADAM PULLED HIS laptop toward him and logged on. The light of the screen cast a white-blue glow over his skin. She saw him put in a passcode to get into the laptop, then hold his face in front of the screen to presumably get into the folder Lucy had found. He seemed to know that was where he would find whatever Cora wanted him to see.

"That's . . . *no*," he murmured, frowning at the screen. "That's not possible."

"What isn't?" Lucy asked.

His eyes moved to her. In and out of focus.

"Another email?" she asked. "More threats?"

"But . . ." He shook his head again emphatically. "This shouldn't have happened. Not now."

"Why?" she asked. Then froze in her seat as she put two and two together. The other person who'd known Guy . . . who'd said, in the Workshop Your Words Facebook group, that she needed answers about something from her past. "Was *Juliet* blackmailing you?"

"That's . . . what we thought." Adam sounded panicked, too. "That's what we assumed. She was the only one who knew Cora and Guy had ever been a thing. She used to see Cora sometimes at their flat. She was the only person who could connect Guy to Cora, and to us, in any way."

He stood up and began pacing, touching his face with agitated movements. Lucy took the opportunity to grab his laptop and spin it toward her. An email had arrived half an hour ago.

> Prepare for your lives to come crashing down. None of you are even being honest with one another. Are you?

It sent a cold current down her spine. "You were all getting these?"

He nodded, still pacing, seeming to have a discussion with himself at the same time as with her. "All three of us. They started not long after Scott crossed paths with Juliet again."

"You hadn't heard from her in between? Did you see her at all after Scott . . ." Another whirl of sickness. "After Guy died?"

"No." He stopped abruptly and faced Lucy with his hands on his head, elbows jutting out. His T-shirt rode up and she glimpsed the familiar softness of his stomach, the triangle of hair that pointed to the waistline of his jeans.

His body was like an extension of her own. But how little access she'd had to his mind, his memory, maybe even his heart.

"We were waiting, of course, in the aftermath," he said. "Constantly listening for that knock on the door. We hoped we'd made the crash look realistic enough that there wouldn't even be an investigation—"

"How could you *bring* yourself to do that?"

"We had to—"

"To put a body in a car and . . ." She was too choked to finish and stood up to fetch a glass of water, pouring the remainder of her whisky down the sink.

"Lucy, we had to do something!" Adam hovered around her, hands flapping. "We were all there. All involved, in our own ways. Guy shouldn't have died but . . . Please, Luce, I can't stand the way you're looking at me."

"How do you expect me to look, Adam?" She went back to her seat, drawing her knees up as she sat down.

"Don't you think I've regretted it a million times since?" He sounded close to tears, too. At a breaking point. "Wished I'd walked away? Realized no friendship was worth *that*? But it was too late. It was too fucking late."

Lucy shot up her hand. "Just keep going. Get it over with. I'm wrung out."

She could feel him looking at her with a kind of desperate concern, but she refused to look back now, just hooped her arms around her knees and made herself tiny.

"Juliet," she whispered. "Tell me about Juliet."

Adam let out a moan and strode to the window. When he finally continued talking, it was with his back to her, and Lucy was glad. She focused on the grain in the wood of the table, tracing it to the end of each line and then back again.

"We were never questioned," he said, speaking almost dispassionately now. "There was no real investigation. Guy had enough of a reputation—so did High Pass—that it was accepted as a tragic accident. But still . . . we thought Juliet might be our undoing. That she might've known Guy came to our house that night. But weeks passed and . . . nothing."

"How could you *live* like that?" Lucy said. "Didn't you consider going to the police?"

"Of course we did." Adam's tone turned gruff. "So many times. When it first happened, we *were* going to call the ambulance, the police. But it was obvious Guy was already dead. And Cora was hysterical, convinced it would be the end of all of us. Distraught at the idea that she'd provoked Scott to do it and he might go to jail."

Lucy thought about the fact that Cora had abandoned her architecture training. The therapy she'd had after university. The change in her personality. She thought about how grateful Adam had always seemed to have found Lucy, to be involved in something stable and straightforward. Maybe he'd seen her as his second chance. But what about Scott? He was the one who'd killed Guy and he'd apparently swanned through life with a successful career and a beautiful family.

"Scott was in shock at first," Adam said. "Staring at what he'd done. But then he snapped out of it and said, no ambulance, no police. That we'd deal with it together." Adam's eyes turned glassy, his teeth grinding again. "And we did, because . . . it already *felt* like we were in it together. Whatever we decided, at that point, it had to be all three of us."

"More of a clique than I even knew," Lucy said, almost to herself.

Adam turned and looked at her with sharp interest, as if he'd never realized she felt that way. She'd never talked to him about it, she supposed. She'd been ashamed to feel like any kind of outsider.

He stepped back toward her. "We *were* close then. But in the aftermath of what happened, the dynamics changed. Cora turned to Scott for comfort . . ." Adam shrugged tightly. "And that was that. They became this golden couple and we pretended to the world that Cora and Guy had never even known each other. Like I said, Scott always had feelings for Cor. Would've done anything for her . . ."

Even kill the person she was sleeping with, Lucy thought, drawing her cardigan close around her.

". . . and their relationship had a pretty fucked-up beginning, of course, but it seemed to work for them as the years went on. And *I* met you." He smiled sadly at her. "I didn't deserve your love, but somehow I got it and I was determined to hang on to it, be a good guy . . ."

Lucy closed her eyes as she felt them moisten again. "Juliet," she said. "The emails. Stick to that. Please. I can't . . . handle much else."

She heard him inhale. "Okay. I'm sorry. I just wanted you to know—"

"Adam."

"Sorry." He paused, seeming to collect himself again. "Okay . . . A few months ago, Scott saw Juliet's name in one of his trade mags, and it was . . . a blast from the past. Not a welcome one. Suddenly her name started cropping up everywhere in his field, and he got really freaked out. He didn't say anything to me or Cora at first; he just arranged for Juliet to interview him at Istanbul, so he could try and suss out what was going on, whether her reappearance in his life was pure coincidence or something more. But—and I didn't know any of this at the time, neither did Cor—it seems they hit it off. Just like he told you last night. I think

Scott knew it was a *very* bad idea—how could he *not*?" Adam paused and shook his head. "But something drew them toward each other, maybe even something subconscious about the past, this huge thing that connected them but that they couldn't talk about . . . God, I don't know. Whatever it was, the affair started from there. And then, a month later . . . so did the emails." He looked at his laptop, still angled toward Lucy. She swept her eyes over the messages again, noting the dates, wondering what had been going through the sender's mind.

"They came to all of you right from the start? Cora, too?"

He nodded. "Of course, we *all* freaked out then. For me and Cora, especially, it was a total bolt from the blue. We called each other, got together to figure out what the fuck was happening. And that was when Scott confessed he'd met Juliet again. That he'd been seeing her."

Lucy jolted. "To Cora as well?"

"Yes."

"She *knew*?" The pain of it was unexpected, disproportional.

Adam lowered his eyes. "From that point, yes." Lucy swore under her breath. She couldn't even catalog all the things that had been happening without her knowledge.

"We . . . made a plan," he said softly.

Lucy raised her head and so did he. Their eyes met across the table. The air seemed to spiral in Lucy's throat rather than go in and out of her lungs.

"A plan." It made everything seem more calculated. "To . . . to make Juliet go away?"

Adam jerked backward. "Not to hurt her! Fuck, no, not that, Luce. Never that!"

"Then *what*?"

He rubbed at his arms as if he wanted to scour off a layer of skin. "Scott was going to continue seeing her. We hoped we could turn his idiocy to our advantage, and to be honest, that was the least he could do. He said he'd try to get even closer to her. Try to find out if she knew anything, if she was behind the emails."

"And Cora *let* him?" Lucy couldn't comprehend it. Not after everything Cora had always said about Scott's loyalty. Not after how she'd apparently reacted to Guy kissing another woman. The *same* woman her husband had later cheated on her with.

An image came into her head of Cora twisting and bending in her yoga poses, eyes closed, limbs shaking with the effort. Driving her emotions deep down into her body. A contrast to the exuberant, carefree Cora who'd apparently existed before what had happened with Guy.

"She was furious when she first found out about the affair," Adam conceded. "And devastated. Especially given who it was. But after a while, it became all about making sure nobody ever found out about Guy. Not after all these years. Cora had to put aside her hurt—and it was so hard for her, I could see it was, could see how much she suffered . . ." He closed his fists, a cloud taking over his face. "But we all had to focus on the bigger picture. On protecting our families . . ."

"On protecting *yourselves.*"

He hung his head. "Okay. But our families, too. The lives we'd managed to build."

Lucy looked around their kitchen at the fabric of their life. The girls' abstract paintings and eclectic mix of magnets pinned to the fridge. The shopping list scrawled on the blackboard with added doodles. She couldn't contemplate ever not having it. She glared at Adam and he seemed to get the message this time, without her having to urge him to stay focused on his explanations.

"When Juliet invited Scott to the Maldives, it seemed like the ideal chance for him to do some digging. Maybe even try to get into her laptop, find out once and for all if the emails were from her. But . . . I don't really know what happened out there in the end. Cora was in torment the whole time, back here. Scott couldn't communicate with us much, but he said he hadn't managed to get any answers out of Juliet. I think maybe he *had* fallen in love with her. That he'd ended up torn between that and needing to find out what she knew . . ." He shook his head again, half despairing, half admonishing. He seemed to think Scott was weak, not evil, but all Lucy had really heard was, *I don't know what happened out there.*

"And then . . ." He lifted his palms, his eyes glazed as he stared into space. "After he got back, we heard she was dead. It was the biggest shock of my life when I saw it on the news, and I know Cora and Scott felt the same. And we were all terrified, absolutely terrified, that something would lead back to us."

Now Lucy was the one who stood up and began to pace. Back and forth, back and forth, her fingers pressed so hard into her temples it felt like they might meet. "Adam. You should've gone to the police. If Scott's as innocent as he says he is—as *you* say he is—why would he not have just told the truth? Why wouldn't *all* of you—"

He strode around the table and cut into her path, grabbing her arm. "Think what it looked like, though, Luce! Scott was sleeping with her! We'd all been getting emails—"

"But not from her." Her head whipped back toward the laptop on the table, remembering what had restarted Adam's confession in the first place. "They can't have been from her if you've had another."

He loosened his grip on her arm. "No." His face was ashen. "We must've got it wrong. Someone . . ." She saw, almost felt, a shudder pass over his body. "Someone else knows."

"And someone killed Juliet." Lucy wanted to cry again. "Someone hurt Ruth. Neither of them did anything wrong but they ended up the victims."

Scott, Scott, Scott, every nerve in her body was now yelling. Despite Adam's protestations—delusions?—she felt more convinced of Scott's involvement than ever. Who else had so much to lose? Who else had backed themselves into a corner they couldn't get out of? Nobody knew what had happened in the Maldives except Scott and Juliet. What if Scott had doubled back to kill her? To *beat her brains out*? What if he hadn't actually left when his flight records *allegedly* showed he had?

"I have a strong feeling," Lucy said, staring out of the window into the starless, moonless night, "that Scott isn't going to be released this time."

And I hope he isn't, added a voice at the back of her head. *I hope I never have to see him again.*

CHAPTER TWENTY-SEVEN

LUCY WOKE IN A FOG OF DISORIENTATION. HER head was thick and she was achy and cold. Looking around, she realized she'd fallen asleep on the sofa. The throw was draped over her, smelling comfortingly familiar, but there was no sign of Adam. As she swam up toward full consciousness, everything she'd learned last night came tumbling back. The pipes were humming in the walls, revving up for the day, with something newly ominous about the sound.

Lucy got up and tiptoed out of the room. "Adam?" she called, but silence rang back at her. She padded upstairs and peered into their bedroom. The bed was empty, the duvet still thrown back from when Adam had leaped out of it when Scott had turned up two nights ago. It was hard to believe they hadn't made it to bed since then. No wonder Lucy had fallen into a troubled sleep.

Peeking into Tilly and Fran's room, she jolted to see that it had been rearranged. Their beds had been pushed together, like they did when they had sleepovers, and as she peered into the warm darkness she saw that Ivy and Joe were in there with them. Lucy's heart swelled to see them all snuggled up, contentedly close, little feet and hands poking out of the panda duvet. She wanted to draw a magic, protective circle around the four of them, like in that story she used to read to Fran.

But why were they here? Where was Adam? She searched every room in the house, becoming increasingly concerned, and was just fetching her phone to call him when she saw him through the kitchen window. He and Cora were sitting in the garden, rocking back and forth on the girls' swings, talking as intently as when she'd caught them at Cora's work.

Lucy took a moment, watching them. Then she opened the back door and stepped out. It was the second sunrise she'd seen in two days. The grass was a shimmer of dewy gold. She hadn't bothered to put her shoes on, and her feet were blocks of ice by the time she got halfway down the garden. The smell in the air was pure, smoky autumn, and something about it broke her heart a little more. It had always been her favorite season.

"Just hold it together," Adam was saying as she drew nearer.

Cora was shaking her head, looking as if she was about to cry.

"I'm panicking!" she said. "Aren't *you*?"

"We need to stay calm. Wait to see what happens with Scott," he said. "And . . . we need to delete any emails we haven't already. I'll sort that out. Make sure all traces are gone. If the police were to find out we're being threatened . . ."

"Who's sending them?" Cora said desperately.

Adam kicked at the leaves on the ground. "I have absolutely no idea."

Cora rocked more vigorously and Adam reached out to steady her. Their swings were joined for a moment, their feet knocking together.

"Nobody else could've known what happened back then," Cora said, "Or even that we knew Guy. That photo of me and him . . . Ad, I've been going over and over it in my mind, and I don't even remember it being taken . . ."

"It was a long time ago, Cor."

"But I would've remembered him actually agreeing to be pictured with me! It looks like it was at Guy's flat, so surely Juliet took it . . . but . . . but I don't remember . . . and now that we've had another email . . . It can't have been her, can it? Ad? We must've been barking up the wrong tree . . ."

"I know, Cor." That placating voice again. It was a calm contrast to the Adam who'd told Lucy the story in the kitchen just hours earlier. "I know, but seriously, we *have* to stay strong and trust that—" He broke off and they both looked up, finally noticing Lucy. Their swinging lost synchronicity as they fell silent and watched her advance toward them.

Lucy stood in front of them, unable to speak.

"Scott's still at the police station," Cora said to her after a few moments, her panic seemingly reined back in. "I'm sorry if you don't want me here, Luce, but . . . I couldn't stand just waiting at home by myself."

Lucy looked at her almost with fascination. Moving her gaze to Adam, she included him in her disbelief, which hadn't faded for having slept on it. *Somebody died in front of you. And you all joined forces to cover it up, to change the story of his death. And you never told me. None of you.*

And was Lucy complicit, too, now that she *did* know, because she wasn't on the phone to the police?

"Have you heard anything?" she asked, clearing her throat. "About . . . Scott?"

Please don't bring him here, she added in her head. *You're right that I don't even want you here, Cora, in case that draws him to our house.* But she didn't say it. She still loved Cora, still had some sympathy for her in this mess.

Cora shook her head. "They called to say they'd need the car for a little longer. I don't know if that's a bad sign . . ." She turned to Adam. "Do you think it's a bad sign?"

Adam shrugged stiffly. Lucy's mind raced again. What were they doing with the car? Looking for DNA? If they were keeping it for longer, did that mean they'd found something?

"But they said nothing about Scott," Cora said. "And no word from him, either." She brought her swing to a halt and tapped the toes of her boots against the wet grass. "Oh, God, I can't believe any of this is happening. *Has* happened."

Lucy couldn't tell whether her switch to the past tense was a reference to Guy or to more recent events. Cora caught her eye and flushed, perhaps with shame, perhaps just because of the cold wind that had whipped up.

Adam reached across to Cora and touched her back. Lucy averted her eyes, then snapped them back when she realized she shouldn't have to. She couldn't help feeling like a spare part, even in the circumstances; couldn't help hating the feeling.

Her eyes met Adam's. There was the sense of too much

to say, too much lost. Part of Lucy was desperate to know if *her* Adam was still in there. If their marriage was salvageable. She shook her head to dislodge the thoughts. Things had happened—were *still* happening, just as Cora had said—that couldn't be forgotten.

So why did part of her want to, even now?

If somebody told her she could have back her life, exactly as it had been, if she just kept quiet about their crimes, would she be tempted to accept? She thought of the four kids snuggled up. The sight had triggered something in her, but she had to push it down.

"We'll take Ivy and Joe to school," Adam said, looking back at Cora, "and pick them up if you don't have the car back by then."

"Thanks, Ad," she said, her eyes filling.

Lucy averted her gaze from that, too, and this time kept it averted, blinking hard.

LUCY WAS TAKEN aback when Cora announced she was going to work. Cora must've seen the amazement in her face because she flushed again, then shrugged defensively. "I can't just sit around. I'll go mad."

Lucy nodded, softening a little. Perhaps she would go to work herself, though it seemed unimaginable. She was floating in a state of disconnected exhaustion. And maybe that was the only thing stopping her from screaming. The illusion that nothing was quite real.

When Adam said he would give Cora a lift, Lucy watched them go with a sweep of relief. While the kids still slept in their snuggly four, she fixed herself a coffee, though she already had the jitters, then called the police station and asked to speak to one of the detectives.

She expected to be told nobody was available, so was surprised when DC Marr came on the phone. It seemed a small stroke of luck that it was him, not Aggarwal. He'd been more amenable in the past. "Yes, Mrs. Taylor?"

Lucy's stomach clenched into a rock. Here was her chance to blurt it all out. She imagined Adam and Cora being stopped on their way to Cora's work and both arrested. Could she bear to set that in motion? To explain to the kids upstairs why three out of four of their parents were in a cell? Was she prepared to let go of her marriage, her friendships?

"I just wanted to ask . . ." Nerves made her voice faint. No, she realized, she wasn't prepared for that, not yet, maybe not ever. "About Scott Waugh. Why are you holding him?"

She thought she heard DC Marr sigh. "I can't tell you that, Mrs. Taylor."

"You think it was him, don't you? Who assaulted Ruth?"

"We're reviewing the evidence."

"His car? I know you have his car." And she knew she sounded pushy and almost hysterical, too, but she couldn't stop her mouth from running ahead of her brain.

Marr was silent. Then: "Yes, we *were* informed you were with Mrs. Waugh when the car was taken in."

Lucy blinked into the phone. How did they know that? Had the two officers who'd come to Cora's recognized her? Lucy had never even seen them before. She glanced at her living room windows, suddenly feeling watched.

"Does he have an alibi?" she blurted. "Scott?"

"We're . . . awaiting confirmation on that."

"He . . ." She was so close to letting the words spill from her mouth. *He killed Guy Everley. And Juliet Noor was on the verge of exposing that.* But whatever she said would land Adam in trouble, too. And he was still her husband. "Silly Daddy" to her girls. Pain seared through her as she acknowledged how much those things still meant.

"Yes?" DC Marr prompted. "Is there something else, Mrs. Taylor?"

"I . . . no," Lucy said. "There's nothing else." And she hung up before she could change her mind.

As soon as she had, she picked up a cushion from the sofa and flung it hard against the opposite wall. It bounced back and landed in the middle of the living room. Lucy marched over and stamped on it, letting the angry tears flow.

When she'd recovered—or enough, at least—she grabbed her phone again and called the hospital. She got through to the ICU and asked after Ruth Beaumont, dropping Martin's name and pretending to be a cousin.

"She's conscious," the nurse said with the warmth of someone sharing good news.

"Really?" Lucy's heart leaped. Something positive at last. "She's awake? Is she okay?"

"She's heavily sedated," the nurse said. "So 'awake' is putting it strongly. But she's stable. We hope it won't be long before she's back with us."

"That's wonderful," Lucy said, emotion surging into her words. "Has she said anything? Does she . . . remember anything about what happened to her?"

"We're not at that stage yet. We'll reduce sedation gradually. Then the neurologist and physio will visit her."

And the police, no doubt, Lucy thought, biting her lip.

This time, when she hung up, she retrieved the cushion

from the floor, straightened it out, and hugged it against her chest. And she wondered, as she cradled it: What would Ruth recall, once she was completely awake? Would she hear the music that had apparently been playing when she'd been attacked? Would it be Scott's looming face that she saw?

LUCY DROPPED TILLY and Fran off at their school, then Ivy and Joe at theirs, watching them all hug each other good-bye in a way that seemed both sweetly childish and inexplicably grown-up. They always complained about going to separate schools, and the adults would explain to them about school districts while also exchanging looks of slight regret. They'd often wished the kids all went to the same school, too. And that was when Lucy realized what the children had reminded her of as they'd embraced each other. Of Cora and Scott and Adam and herself. The way they would crisscross over each other to make sure each person hugged every other person hello and good-bye each time.

Lucy sat in the car and let her shoulders fall from the tense position they'd been in all morning. Not knowing what else to do, she gave in and drove to work.

SHE MADE IT through to lunchtime without falling apart. But all morning she swung between hyper and sluggish, her poor students either bombarded with barely sensical monologues or ignored and given hastily printed scripts to study. This wasn't good teaching. It would have been better if she hadn't come in at all.

On her lunch break, she bought a sandwich without even looking at the label, knowing she probably wasn't going to eat it. It sat beside her on a bench as she twirled her phone in her hands and her thoughts once again hurtled into overdrive. The BBC News app pinged with an alert, and she glimpsed the name Juliet Noor, her heart vaulting in automatic response. A press conference was underway. Lucy clicked on the video link and immediately recognized DC Aggarwal, sitting behind a wide desk looking even smarter and more serious than usual.

"Leicestershire Police are now taking a lead role in the Juliet Noor investigation," she was saying, glancing at some notes over the top of her fashionable glasses. "It is still an international matter, but new leads in the area mean the UK part of the investigation will be focused here." She sounded almost proud for a moment, but there was a pinch of tension around her mouth as the camera zoomed in.

Lucy's heart thumped more violently. New leads. Maybe they'd found something else on Scott? Maybe that was part of the reason he was in custody again right now.

"We are now able to disclose the cause of Juliet's death," Aggarwal went on. "It's with regret that I can confirm she suffered multiple blunt-force traumas to the head. Therefore, the investigation is being treated as murder, and we will be working with Interpol and the Maldives Police Service to do *everything* in our power to find the perpetrator." She leaned forward, seeming to peer at Lucy through the screen. Lucy put her hands against her stomach. She'd been right, and Aggarwal had been genuine: The cause of death had been kept under wraps until now. Yet Scott had known; he had known in graphic detail, it seemed.

Next up on the screen was Juliet's mother. It was the first

time any of her family had appeared in public. Lucy's eyes were drawn to her stricken face, her posture half collapsed with grief. She had the same thick, dark hair as Juliet, with a shimmer of silver at the roots, and she kept pushing it back from her face in a repetitive, nervous gesture.

"Juliet was the light in our hearts," she said, her voice breaking. "She made us proud every day. Please, if anyone knows who ended her life—"

Lucy clicked out of the app, unable to stand it. She leaned forward with her head in her hands, not even caring which of her colleagues might pass by to see her melting down.

Her phone beeped with an email alert and she slowly raised her head. It was just a monthly newsletter from a romance author she followed, but once she was inside her inbox, she was reminded that it was full of the emails she'd forwarded from Adam's private folder to herself. She began combing through them again. Opening them, staring at them, closing them back down. Lingering, especially, on the photo of Cora and Guy on the brown sofa. The only photo that existed of the two of them, apparently, thanks to Guy's aversion to being "couply." A picture that had been used to threaten Lucy's husband and friends, to prove exclusive knowledge that might unravel their big secret.

But the emails *couldn't* have been from Juliet, the one person who'd known Cora and Guy were seeing each other. Not that her inside knowledge had stopped her from kissing Guy herself. It seemed a messy love triangle—or perhaps a more complex shape, if Scott and Adam were also thrown into the mix. But the question remained: If Juliet hadn't been behind the threatening emails, who had got hold of this image? Cora had seemed to think it was taken at Guy and

Juliet's flat, though the background didn't reveal much. She'd said she couldn't even remember it being taken. Perhaps because she'd only had eyes for Guy, not the camera.

It had new resonance, now that Lucy knew the whole story. The way Guy was sitting with his arm across the back of the sofa but not really *around* Cora, while she was touching his leg and gazing at him. He looked noncommittal; she looked adoring. And there was a *separateness* to them, even though this photo was being dangled as evidence that they'd been together. You could cut it down the middle and almost, almost have two distinct photos. Only Cora's small hand on his thigh stopped it from being so.

It had such a different feel from all the photos of Cora and Scott that had been presented to the world over the years. Their heads-together pose and their winning smiles. Lucy's sympathy stirred again. Maybe she should've been kinder to Cora this morning. But then she pictured the three of them carrying Guy's body out to his car, driving him up to High Pass to construct the scene of a crash, and she shuddered. A kind of guilt came over her as she looked at Guy's face on her screen, knowing what had become of him while he smiled obliviously back.

Suddenly he seemed like a cautionary tale.

He'd died at the hands of Scott Waugh and he hadn't seen it coming.

FOR THE REST of the afternoon, her mind wouldn't drop it. Wouldn't slow. *Scott's a killer, but of how many people? Scott's a liar, but who else is still not telling the truth?* It was draining, head-spinning, and it was getting her nowhere. There was something she was missing, she was sure.

She tried to take steadying breaths as she drove to Ivy and Joe's school for pickup. Adam had texted to say Cora still hadn't got the car back, and he was tied up with his last client, so could she collect all the children? She'd agreed for the kids' sake, not his or Cora's, sending a short, unemotional text in reply. As she parked outside the school, she saw that Adam had sent another message.

> I never wanted to involve you in any of this, Luce. Wanted it to always stay outside of us. You've been the goodness in my life. That's why I lied, why I never told you. xxx

Lucy closed her eyes and drew in a breath. For a few seconds she battled waves of tears, riding them out like sickness. Then she smoothed back her hair, put her phone into her pocket, and got out of the car.

The playground was alive with end-of-day chatter. Lucy found herself staring enviously at the fresh-looking mums and dads sauntering out of the gates, seemingly untroubled by difficulties in their lives. But then, they probably thought the same about her. There was nothing to give away the things she was carrying inside.

A strange, slow feeling came over her as she turned her head, looking for Ivy and Joe. Usually, if she picked them up, they were waiting with the teacher under the sycamore trees to the left. Lucy's tired eyes drifted from one child to the next. Not Ivy, not Joe. She scanned the rest of the playground in case they were on the climbing frame or the slide.

A flash of blonde hair, but no, it wasn't Ivy. A boy ran past with a ball, but no, it wasn't Joe.

Lucy approached the teacher. She and Cora had often joked about how young she looked, how old she made them feel. She spoke to everybody in the same tone, adults or kids alike.

"Hellooo! Lucy, isn't it! Nice to see you!"

"Hi." Lucy couldn't summon the same chirpiness. "I'm here to pick up Ivy and Joe Waugh."

Miss Perry's smile slipped a little. "Oh, Dad's already beaten you to it!"

The habit of using *Mum* and *Dad* instead of actual names threw Lucy for a second. Her brain scrambled to catch up. "You mean . . ." Coolness shimmered across her skin. "Scott?"

"Of course!" The smile was back, full beam. Miss Perry was clearly oblivious to the fact that she'd just made Lucy's stomach plummet.

"Are you sure?" she asked. "He's . . . elsewhere, I thought. I was supposed to collect them."

"Well, he must've been able to, after all. No problem, is there? They looked thrilled to see him, and not just because he'd brought them both an enormous chocolate bar, I'm sure!"

"Uh . . . no," Lucy said, her mind whirring as she turned back toward her car. "No problem, I suppose."

She was already pulling out her mobile to call Cora, the cold feeling seeping through to her bones. When had Scott been released? Surely somebody would've told her if he'd been planning to pick up Ivy and Joe, after all?

"Cor," Lucy said as she answered. "Cor, Ivy and Joe aren't here."

"What do you mean?" The alarm in Cora's tone set off an even louder ringing in Lucy's head.

"The teacher, the permanently happy one . . ." She was flustered, babbling. "She said Scott picked them up."

"What?" Cora's pitch got higher. "How is that possible? He's still at the police station, as far as I know. Why would he just . . . why wouldn't he call me if he'd been released? And I thought they still had our car . . ."

"I don't know." Lucy was panting as she reached hers, and threw herself into the driving seat. "I don't know. Something doesn't feel right."

"I'll call you back," Cora said, and the line went dead.

Lucy slammed the car into gear and screeched away.

CHAPTER TWENTY-EIGHT

LUCY GOT BACK TO THE HOUSE TO FIND BOTH Cora and Adam standing in the kitchen. Cora had her phone to her ear but wasn't speaking. There was a stale smell in the room, despite Adam's cleaning session yesterday, and dust motes floated in shards of evening sun.

"Girls, you can watch TV," Lucy said, aware that they'd had far too much screen time lately.

Fran took off her coat and deposited it dramatically on the floor. "Where are Ivy and Joe?"

Lucy glanced at Cora. "I told you, they've gone to play at a friend's house."

"*Which* friend?" Tilly said with a deep frown. "*We're* their friends!"

"I know, darling, but people can have as many friends as they like, can't they? You play with other people, too, sometimes."

But not very often, she realized, feeling another corkscrew of guilt that she'd inadvertently made her children as reliant on the Waughs as herself. Tilly looked dissatisfied with her answer, but the draw of Disney Plus was too strong and she slunk away, taking Fran with her.

Lucy watched to make sure they settled and saw them cuddle up close on the sofa—the best of friends today, united by missing Ivy and Joe. Pushing away a longing to join them, she went back into the kitchen and closed the door.

"Have you tracked Scott down?" she asked, glancing between Adam and Cora. Adam had a tired, clammy look about him. Cora was wild-eyed, her movements frantic, which told Lucy what she needed to know.

Cora stabbed at her phone again, walking in a tight circle as she listened to it ring.

"Scott's not answering," Adam filled Lucy in. "And he's not at home, not at his parents'. We don't know where he is. We called the police station and they said he was released an hour ago, along with their car, but told to stay nearby."

Lucy felt her chest squeeze tighter. "Why did they release him?"

"They just said they couldn't legally hold him any longer. He's still a person of interest, though."

"Who's now gone AWOL," Lucy said. "You *did* tell them that?"

Adam looked down. "Not yet."

"Well, don't you think we should?" Lucy asked incredulously.

"We thought we'd see if we could get hold of him ourselves first."

She blinked at him, while he continued to avoid her eyes. Clearly, he and Cora were still nervous about too much involvement with the police. She looked back at Cora as she cursed and hung up the phone.

"Still no answer," Cora said, pulling at her bun. "Not from his mobile or our landline. Where's he taken them? What the fuck is he playing at?"

"I'll try him," Lucy said. "Maybe he'll answer to someone else."

Cora nodded. "Yes. Yes. Worth a try." For just a second, a grateful smile tugged at her lips and her eyes filmed with tears. "Thank you," she said, and Lucy swallowed and nodded back, scrolling to Scott's number in her contacts.

It rang and rang with no answer. Lucy tried to keep her tone light as she left a voicemail, though her jaw felt as if it was made of metal. "Scott, it's Lucy . . ." She realized she had no idea what to say that might encourage him to contact her. She ended up with a slightly lame, "Please call me when you get a chance?"

The silence that filled the room after she'd hung up was leaden.

"He'll turn up," Adam said. "It'll be okay, Cor."

"I don't care about *him*," Cora said with unexpected venom. A turnaround from her defensiveness of Scott when she'd been on speakerphone last night. "If he's going to pull a stunt like this after everything he's already put me through, then our whole marriage is more fucked than I even knew." Her voice was taut with anger. "I just want to know Ivy and Joe are safe."

"He wouldn't put them in danger," Adam said.

Cora closed her eyes and seemed to hold her breath. "Don't be so sure," she said. "I don't think any of us have realized what he's capable of."

"Then we should call the police," Lucy said. "If you're really worried, we should call them right now." Another punch of dread hit her low in the stomach. Ivy and Joe. They were almost as precious to her as her own children. She felt a sense of them being untethered from where they belonged, drifting somewhere unanchored. She hoped they weren't scared. Hoped they were just happy to be with their dad, wherever he'd taken them, whatever he was planning.

Cora was on the phone again, but not to the police. She was dialing Scott repeatedly, leaving voicemails so full of fury that Lucy wondered how she'd ever idolized her friends' marriage, ever been so desperate to be at the heart of their life. Everything was unraveling so fast it made her wonder how flimsily it had been held together in the first place.

Everything's unraveling. Like Guy's car when we stopped pushing and it kept rolling toward the tree, freewheeling beyond the momentum we'd started. That's what this feels like now. A downward roll, faster and faster. I keep thinking about the sound his car made when it hit the tree, the shatter of glass and crunch of metal, and wondering whether I'm heading for a collision, too. We were outside of the car then, setting it in motion before watching it roll, but now I feel like I'm inside it, out of control, with forces pushing me toward an ending.

All I can do is focus on Ivy and Joe. On their innocence, their obliviousness. I love them so much it hurts, makes me hate myself.

I thought I was doing all this for them. Now I don't know what any of it was really for. But they're all I have left and I won't let anyone tear them away.

CHAPTER TWENTY-NINE

UNABLE TO STAND THE TENSION IN THE KITCHEN any longer, Lucy went to check on Tilly and Fran. They ignored her, glued to the screen—but still holding hands, she noticed with a pang of love. She gave them each a glass of milk and a packet of raisins, and watched them palming the raisins into their mouths as if they were eating popcorn at the cinema.

"Love you," she murmured, welling up as she kissed the tops of their heads. They complained she was blocking their view but they still smiled at her kiss, and Fran leaned her head into Lucy's stomach.

"Why does Auntie Cora sound angry?" she asked. "Has Joe broken a window again?"

Joe had kicked his ball through the Waughs' back window last year, and Fran brought it up frequently. It was the first time she'd heard of anybody being grounded in real life and it had thrilled her.

"No, sweetie," Lucy said, thinking fast. "She's not angry, she's just trying to sort out something to do with her job."

"Are Ivy and Joe coming back yet?"

"They're staying at their friend's for now."

"I want to show Ivy the drawing of a big snail I did at school."

"Well, why don't you show me ins—" Lucy was diverted by her phone buzzing in her pocket. She drew it out, then almost dropped it again. A message from Scott had appeared on the screen.

Are you with Cora?

Lucy inhaled and held on to the breath. She turned her head to yell out to Adam and Cora, then paused as she saw that Scott was typing again. Are you with Cora? he repeated.

Then another one, quick on its heels:

Lucy. I can see you're online. Don't fuck about.
Answer me.

The phone felt suddenly hot in her palm. She glanced toward the kitchen: The door was half closed and she could hear Adam and Cora talking in hushed tones. Would it be better to try to handle this herself? Perhaps if she trod a careful line with Scott, he would admit where he was. Her instincts urged her to attempt it before involving the others. Though they were all worried about Ivy and Joe, Adam and Cora had their own agendas, and Cora seemed increasingly unstable.

Could she do this? Was it just foolish heroics, or could she pull it off?

She gripped the phone and began to type.

Tell me where you are.

He replied instantly:

Tell me whether you're with Cora.

Lucy paused, wrestling her thoughts into place. Were they negotiating here? She had a sudden awareness of being out of her depth. But something was driving her onward, telling her she had to try.

You can't just take off with I & J like that. We're all worried sick. I'm on the verge of calling the police. But I'll hold off if you tell me where you are.

Adrenaline bolted through her when her phone began to ring. She didn't feel ready to actually talk to him. She moved to the corner of the room, turning down the volume on the ringer. Then, anxious she might lose her chance altogether, she answered in a whisper: "Scott?"

"Lucy." He was talking quietly, too, but sounded wired. "Can Cora hear you?"

"What are you *doing*?"

"Listen carefully. Don't say too much. Don't tell Cora I'm on the phone."

"Scott, you can't—"

"Just trust me, Lucy. Please."

She balked at the idea. How did he expect her to trust him? She strained to hear any background noises at his end. Was he outside or inside? Was he driving? The slightly muffled quality of the call suggested he might be on his handsfree. She wished she'd called the police already. They could be tracking this call.

"*Where* are you?" she asked again. "I'm going to hang up in three seconds and call the—"

"No, don't do that! I—I've got Ivy and Joe. They're right here, eating chocolate. They're fine, I swear. I'm taking them to Norfolk. I'll send you a pin to prove it if you please, *please*, just stall Cora." He sounded utterly desperate now, with a rough, ragged edge to his voice. "Distract her. Give me some time."

Electric fear shimmied over Lucy's skin. She glanced at the girls again, the TV still blaring, too loud as usual. Tilly shot her a curious look and Lucy tried to smile reassuringly back. Turning away, she darted out of the room and up the stairs.

"Scott," she hissed into the phone, standing on the dark landing. "You can't do this. Bring them back. You're out of control. I know what you've—"

"You *don't* know. I had to get the kids away. Now I need some time to decide what to do. To . . . check whether I'm right."

The fear moved inside her like a dance. "What do you mean?"

"It's Cora. She—"

"*Lucy.*" Cora's voice made her whirl around, made her pulse rocket again. Cora was halfway up the stairs, her eyes huge. "Who are you talking to? Is that Scott?"

Confusion scattered Lucy's thoughts as Cora ran the rest of the way up. "Is it Scott? It is, isn't it? Let me talk to him!" When Lucy remained frozen, Cora dived for the phone. Taken by surprise, Lucy jerked away without really registering what she was doing.

Cora stared at her. "Luce, let me talk to my husband,

please!" She grabbed for the phone again and Lucy shook herself, relinquishing it.

Cora held it to her ear. "Scott?" Then she let out a frustrated sigh, lowering the phone. "Shit, he's gone." She turned to Lucy, nostrils flaring. "What did he say? Where is he?"

Lucy sidestepped nervously toward the stairs. Her head was roaring and she couldn't make sense of anything. "He . . ."

"Lucy!" Cora waved the phone. "Please tell me where my children are!"

She came toward her, peering into her face. Lucy searched hers in return, looking for answers that didn't seem to be there.

"Tell *me* what's going on, Cora," she said. "Why is Scott saying . . . that he needs to get the kids away? From . . . from *you*?"

"Is that what he said?"

Lucy nodded, breathing hard.

"And you believe him? He's a liar. A criminal—"

"I just need to understand—"

"—and he's got my babies and you won't even tell me where they are!"

They blinked at each other like stunned creatures. Cartoons continued to play riotously from the TV downstairs. Lucy imagined Tilly and Fran still obliviously glued, Adam in the kitchen wondering where everybody had gone.

Cora seized her arm. "Are they in Norfolk? They are, aren't they?"

Her nails dug in. Lucy pulled away. Cora's eyes shone and she seemed to grow taller, casting a shadow over the last remnants of Lucy's ability to think straight. She turned and ran blindly toward the stairs. Two steps down, her legs went out from under her. It was a strange, disjointed moment: One second her feet were on the floor, her hand was on the banister, and the next she was falling hard, white ceiling and caramel carpet spiraling around her. She heard Cora let out a cry above, heard commotion and footsteps below, before she landed with a thud in a position she couldn't comprehend, and pain exploded in her head.

CHAPTER THIRTY

LUCE? ARE YOU OKAY?"

"Mummy? Mummy!"

"Open your eyes, Luce, if you can hear me. Say something. Where does it hurt?"

"She slipped. She was running and she slipped. Lucy, we're here, don't worry, we're here."

Lucy came round slowly, groggily, with what felt like a tiny hammer bashing at the inside of her skull. There was a band of hot pain all down one side of her body. The fuzzy shapes around her gradually clarified into Adam, Cora, and the girls, all looking down at her with concern. She was lying at the bottom of the stairs, her arms and legs flung out.

"Mummy!" Tilly and Fran were both crying. Lucy tried to reach for them, to reassure them that she was okay, but there seemed to be a gap between what she wanted to do and being able to do it. Was she lifting her arm? Was she speaking? Smiling? There were two of each person for a moment, then one again, but blurry, wavering, like reflections in water. The humming sound in her brain was like the purr of an engine.

"Are you okay?" Adam said. "Luce, do you need an ambulance?"

She didn't answer. She didn't know. The girls looked petrified. She tried to sit up to show them she was all right. And she could do it, she found. She could sit. Bright rods of pain splintered through her, but she saw the relief on everybody's faces as she made the effort to seem okay.

"How many fingers am I holding up?" Fran said, clearly having seen it on TV.

"Eleven," Lucy said. Then: "Only joking, Frannie. I know it's three." The joke took all the energy she had, but it was worth it to see Fran and Tilly grin. Lucy looked at Adam and Cora, her vision swimming as she moved her head. There was a vague feeling of unease hanging over her. Maybe even fear. But the woolliness in her brain was currently smothering everything else.

"What the hell happened?" Adam said.

"Poor thing slipped," Cora said, looking pale.

Lucy nodded. More pain as she did so. Was that what happened, though? Had she slipped? All she remembered was running and then falling. God, her head hurt. She couldn't think through the thump-thump-thump of it.

"We should get you to hospital," Adam said.

"But we need to go to Norfolk!" Cora said, her voice jittery yet forceful. "Scott's there with Ivy and Joe. Isn't he, Lucy?" Those wide eyes again, fixed on Lucy's face, glimmering with tears or worry or something else, Lucy wasn't sure.

Adam's head turned sharply. "Why is he there?"

"I don't know," Cora said. "That's why we need to go *now*. You need to take me, Ad, *please*. I need support, I'm going out of my fucking mind."

"Shit." Adam pinched his nose and looked down at Lucy again, seeming torn. "But she . . ." He touched Lucy's forehead, peered into her eyes.

"The *kids*," Cora said. "Lucy's worried about them, too. She's the one who managed to find out where they are. Please, Ad, they might be in danger. We can go to a hospital once we've got them back. Please, I'm begging you."

"*Shit*," Adam said again, sounding as if he wished he was somewhere else entirely. "Okay, Cor. Stay calm. We'll all go, okay? And then to the hospital as soon as we can."

Lucy was drifting again, seeing double, becoming untethered from the conversation as it continued to bounce back and forth over the top of her. There were things she wanted to say, she knew there were, but she couldn't seem to get her words in the right order. Couldn't seem to make herself heard.

"Luce," Adam said, "can you stand?"

Now she was being helped upright, Adam's arm underneath her. Being *lifted*, in fact, so her feet almost left the floor. She felt as if she was skating on tiptoes as she was guided to the door.

"Come on, girls," Adam was saying.

"We're going to see Ivy and Joe!" Cora chimed in, and something about it made Lucy queasy. Something about the whole situation. But she was so floppy, still so groggy. She couldn't seem to muster any fight as she was put into the back of the car like a child.

"Luce?" Adam said, his voice distant. "You okay? You're not going to pass out, are you?"

She realized she was in the backseat with her head hanging forward.

"Mummy?" Tilly and Fran were either on side of her. She moved her eyes to look at one, then the other, her vision like a seesaw. Fran pawed at her hair. "Mummy, are you sick?"

"I'm okay," she whispered. It took a ridiculous amount of effort to raise her head. She saw, through unfocused eyes, that Cora was in the driving seat. How had that happened? Why? Adam was on his phone trying to get through to Scott. *Phone*, Lucy thought. Where was hers? She didn't have it and it brought a panicky feeling, only slightly dulled this time by the thicket in her head. *No*, her sluggish brain started to protest as they pulled off. *No, this doesn't feel right, none of it does.*

It was twilight now. People were on the streets for evening dog walks, or putting out their bins. Lucy stared through the window, willing them to notice her and somehow realize she needed their help. The world seemed oblivious. Perhaps nobody would believe her even if she could tell them.

"Adam," she tried to say, but her voice was weak and he had his phone rammed against his ear. "Cora," she tried. As the name croaked in her throat, a frisson of dread ran through her. An image of Cora, looming, demanding to know where Scott was before Lucy had turned and run and tumbled down the stairs. Had Cora *pushed* her? The idea made Lucy's insides contract, reacting to the impossible.

She took hold of the girls' hands on either side of her and squeezed them hard. Fran's was damp, as if she was anxious, too. *Think, Lucy, think.* She willed the fog and the crushing pain to clear from her skull. And she began to sing softly, the first Disney song she could think of, hoping it would soothe them.

In contrast, Cora was driving too fast, swinging round corners, speeding through lights just as they changed to red. Adam kept telling her to slow down.

"I know you're desperate to get there, Cor, but my kids are in the car," he said.

"Well, my kids have been abducted," Cora snapped back. "By a man who, for all we know, might *well* have murdered the woman he was—"

"Shhh," Adam said, darting a glance behind him. "Not in front of . . ." He jerked his head. "We need to stay calm, Cor."

"Stop fucking saying that, Ad. It's *easy* for you to say."

"I know." Lucy saw him briefly touch her thigh. "I know, but the last thing we need is another accident."

Cora's head turned. "What's that supposed to mean?"

"Nothing," Adam said. "Eyes on the road, Cor, *please*."

She turned back to face forward but her arms looked rigid on the wheel. Lucy could see the smooth contours of her muscles below her rolled-up shirtsleeves.

"Scott's caused all this," Cora said. "He's put us all through so much and we've always stuck by him, and now he's using Ivy and Joe in his games. And you're telling me to stay calm, not cause another accident, as if everything's been my doing. Whose side are you on, Adam?"

Lucy wanted to ask the same question. She stopped singing and squeezed her daughters' hands again. Sick, she felt so sick.

"Yours, Cora," Adam murmured. "Always. You know that."

Lucy closed her eyes, hearing the affection of half a lifetime in his voice. They were acting as if she wasn't even here now. She wished she wasn't. Wished she could eject herself and the girls from the backseat with the press of a button. Cora's driving didn't get any less erratic. Lucy saw that Fran had to keep bracing herself against the car door. Lucy's head was clearing slowly, though, like cloud cover breaking up, slivers of light poking through that were painful but at least they were light.

She thought of what Scott had started to say about Cora. About needing to get the kids away. Needing to check that he was right. Lucy stared at the back of Cora's head, at the messy strands that had come loose from her normally tight bun, like a visual for her emotional state. Threads began to knit together in Lucy's brain. Something like revulsion building in her throat, thick as mucous.

I need to get us out of this car. She looked frantically around. *Think, think, think.* Her eyes landed on Tilly. She was still wearing her school fleece with the big zip-up pockets. Lucy had made sure she took her phone to school today, and maybe, just maybe . . . With clumsy fingers, she reached to her right and unzipped the nearest pocket.

"Mummy, what are you—?" Tilly said, but Lucy held a finger to her own lips, raising her eyebrows as if it was all a game. Tilly fell quiet, still watching her with curious suspicion as she slowly drew out the phone.

She felt immediately better, just having it in her hands. She glanced at Cora and wondered if she could phone the emergency services without alerting her. She didn't think she could. Silence had fallen in the car and even the whispered words *police, please* would surely be heard. But who else could she contact? Who could she trust to call the emergency services on her behalf? It would be hard for her mum or dad to help from New Zealand. The realization hit again:

Everybody she was close to these days was in this car. She had nobody else.

Her eyes blurred with tears as she looked down at the family photo screen saver on Tilly's phone. Even if she did manage to contact the police, the fact remained that she'd be turning in her husband, her girls' Silly Daddy. Would they ever forgive her?

They might not have the chance to if you don't do something.

She pulled herself together and tapped in the passcode she'd set up on Tilly's phone. The screen bounced with an Incorrect passcode message. Lucy frowned. Tried again. Got the same message.

Have you changed it? she mouthed to Tilly, gesturing at the screen.

Tilly shook her head. The phone didn't have facial or fingerprint recognition set up. The idea had been to use an easy passcode, Lucy's birthday, so that she and Adam could get into it, too. So why wasn't it working?

Her eyes flicked to Adam. The back of his head as familiar to her as his face, but slick with sweat right now. *Daddy borrows my phone sometimes.* More threads knitting together, crisscrossing, trying to show her a pattern.

Tapping the screen again, she tried the passcode Adam used for his laptop. Incorrect. She tried Tilly's birthday, and Fran's, and Adam's; then paused, not wanting to lock herself out of the phone entirely. She stroked the screen so that the shortcuts appeared, knowing she wouldn't be able to get into any of them but curious to check what they were. Tilly only ever used it for text messages and calls, and not very often for those. So why was email showing as the top shortcut, with a red notification dot next to it? Tilly didn't even have an email address.

A shriek of tires and another swerve made her chin fly up. Lucy was thrown sideways into Fran, just managing to stop her daughter's head from hitting the window. She held her close for a moment, her other hand reaching for Tilly to check that she was okay. Both girls were sheet white with terror.

"*Cora*," Adam said. "Do you want to kill us all?"

"I'm just trying to get there faster," Cora insisted. But she straightened the wheel, seemed to regain some control. Lucy clutched at her seat belt. Norfolk suddenly seemed too far away, though they were making frighteningly good time, towns giving way to flat green fields outside the steamed-up windows.

"What are you doing, Lucy?"

Lucy's torso jumped and she looked up, meeting Cora's blue eyes in the rearview mirror.

"I'm not doing anything."

"You're not warning Scott we're on the way, are you?"

"No, of course not." Lucy cupped Tilly's phone in her palms. "There . . . there isn't even any signal out here."

"What did he say to you, Luce, to turn you against me like this? When he's the one—"

"I'm not against you, Cor! I'm not texting him, I swear!" Lucy held up the phone to show she wasn't. Cora reached to try to grab it and the car wavered into the opposite lane.

"Cora!" Adam yelled. "Pay attention!"

"Get that phone off her, then. I don't trust her anymore."

Even after all that had happened, Cora's words were a blow. Lucy tried to harden herself against them. Adam turned around and his eyes locked with hers. Lucy's flashed a challenge: *Who are you going to choose?*

There was sadness in his face as he begged, "Luce . . ."

Then Cora slammed her foot down and rocketed along the road even faster. She flew over a roundabout while Adam hollered at her to slow down, calm down, and both girls burst into tears.

"This isn't going to help, Cora!" Adam tried to reason with her.

"I'm going to phone the police," Lucy said. "If you don't stop driving like this, I'm going to dial 999."

Cora braked violently. The car skidded with a high-pitched squeal but slowed, bringing a moment of reprieve. Lucy realized she was wheezing, her stomach in knots, her cheeks wet. She heard the familiar but surprising sound of Cora doing her deep, meditative breathing up front.

"We're almost there," she said, on an out-breath. "I just want to get to my babies. So, please, can we just do that? Please can everyone just let me drive?"

A sob of temporary relief escaped Lucy's mouth. Adam turned again at the sound. He'd taken off his glasses, as if to deliberately blur the road that had been disappearing far too quickly beneath their tires, and his eyes looked like slits. Cora made a noise like a swallowed sob of her own, but her posture didn't falter, her gaze stayed fixed ahead as she drove on at a relatively normal speed. Lucy saw Tilly's head turn as they passed the WELCOME TO NORFOLK sign that traditionally made them cheer. They were all silent now, clocking each familiar landmark as they got closer to their destination.

CHAPTER THIRTY-ONE

THEY RARELY SAW THE COTTAGE IN DARKNESS. IT looked different as they pulled up: The roof was like a pair of sweeping black curtains parted over the house, and a lit window in an upstairs room was a single eye peering into the gloom. The bushes on either side seemed to encroach further than usual, looking thicker and bramblier than they appeared in daytime.

Scott and Cora's silver Nissan was parked in the driveway, glinting faintly in the dusk.

"He's here," Cora said, bumping the curb as she pulled to a stop.

"I feel sick," Fran moaned.

"I know, darling," Lucy said, stroking her cheek. "So do I. But it's okay. We're here now. Everything's going to be all right. Just do exactly what I tell you to once we're inside, okay? Promise? For Mummy? Tilly, you too?"

They nodded solemnly. As they all got out of the car,

spots of green-tinted brightness skittered across Lucy's vision and her body felt stiff and sore. Adam tried to smile at the girls, put his arms round them, but they seemed wary of him now, associating him with the terrifying drive because he'd been in the front with the new, unpredictable version of Auntie Cora. Adam looked at Lucy imploringly, as if begging her to assure the girls that he was still Silly Daddy. But she couldn't bring herself to do it, or even look at him. She was clicking into survival mode, braced for whatever was about to happen.

Cora ran into the house, shouting for Ivy and Joe. Lucy hung on to Tilly's and Fran's hands while Adam stayed apart from them. The cottage still smelled of fresh paint. A pile of color charts lay on the stairs—their recent obsession, Lucy recalled with a twinge of disbelief at the normality of it—and Adam's spare overalls were slung over the banister like a limp body.

Scott came rushing down in bare feet, with unkempt hair and an untucked shirt. His eyes were bloodshot. A nervous energy seemed to permeate his movements, like when he'd turned up at Lucy's house in the middle of the night.

"What are you doing here?" His eyes flashed to Lucy, who shook her head, then back to Cora.

"What do you think, Scott?" Cora said. "You can't just take my kids."

"*Our* kids."

Cora said nothing, moving to barge past him. "Are they upstairs?"

Scott caught her arm. "Leave them. I just put them to bed."

"I want to see them." She tried to cast him off but he held firm.

"Scott! You're hurting me!"

"Seriously, Cora, leave them be. They've had an unsettling day."

"Because of *you*!"

He exhaled, closing his eyes but still gripping her arm. "I did what I thought was best."

Lucy bent down and whispered to her girls: "Run upstairs to Ivy and Joe, okay? Close the door and put something on Joe's iPad, if he's got it, and stay up there for now. I'll come up soon, I promise."

They looked at her with big questioning eyes. She gave them a gentle nudge toward the stairs, though it was a wrench to part with them. "Go on, it's okay." She blew fretful kisses and they went, slipping past Scott and Cora to scurry upstairs. Scott's face collapsed for just a moment as he saw them. He glanced again at Lucy, as if he wanted to say something, then returned his attention to Cora.

"In here," he said, manhandling her through the living room door.

Lucy and Adam followed. It felt strange to be back in this room again. The last time, for Lucy, had been when Scott had cut his hand. There were still a couple of dots of his blood in the corner, underneath the stepladder. The air held the tickle of sawdust, and the headscarf Lucy always wore for working on the house was strewn on the unvarnished floorboards. She remembered taking it off because she'd got too warm. Now she felt an urge to pick it up and run it through her fingers.

"I haven't called the police yet," Scott said.

Cora stared at him. "Why would *you* call the police? You're lucky we didn't."

"Because . . ." His face went slack for a second, then all the muscles seemed to tighten at once. "Because it must've been you, Cora."

"What are you talking about, Scott?"

"I never thought"—Scott pushed his fingers into his hair, stretching the skin at the roots—"not in a million years . . . that you'd go to *those* kinds of lengths to make sure the photo of Juliet and me never got seen. Was it really to make sure nothing could link back to what happened with Guy? Or was it actually because you couldn't stand people knowing your husband had an affair? And with her, of all people. That was always the part you couldn't get past, wasn't it?"

"I don't know what the fuck you're talking about." Cora turned and made for the door. "I want to see my kids."

Lucy moved fast and instinctively, blocking her path. She and Cora ended up face-to-face. Cora looked at her steadily, as if to say, *You as well.* She turned to Adam, her last hope. *Your side. Always*, he'd said to Cora in the car. Lucy's insides curled as she remembered. But Adam looked confused now, sweat shining on his brow.

"Are you talking about Ruth?" Lucy asked, turning to Scott.

He nodded. Fault lines seemed to appear around his eyes. He raked his hand through his hair again, this time as if he was trying to claw something out of his brain. Memories? Suspicions? Feelings, perhaps.

"I'm lost now." Adam spoke for the first time since they'd arrived. "This is . . . This has all got out of hand."

Lucy gazed at him. He really did seem baffled. She was trying to work out how much he was party to, and how much he'd just blindly trusted and protected Cora. Loved her, probably. And hadn't Lucy done the same?

She looked back at Scott, keeping Cora in her peripheral vision. "Your car," she said, turning hot and cold as she started to put the pieces together.

He nodded. "It was caught by a speed camera, a street away from Ruth's house. But . . . it *wasn't* me driving it. Yes, I'd been to see her before, but not the night she got hurt. I was still at work. The police managed to get confirmation from the one colleague that came to my office that evening. So . . ." He stared at Cora as if seeing her for the first time. "I realized while I was in custody: It must've been you, Cora."

She stepped backward in disbelief. "*I* was at work, too."

"No, you weren't," Scott said.

Cora thrust out her chin. "Yes, I *was.*"

Scott shook his head, his eyes glassy. "I called them as soon as I was released. Pretended to be annoyed that they'd made you work slightly late that night. Said we'd missed a parents' evening."

"You called my *work*?"

"They got all defensive, and then someone else came on the phone, and she said you'd left at four thirty that day."

Lucy's pulse was in her ears now, almost drowning Scott out. But she'd heard enough. Adrenaline began to race around her system. "What did you do, Cora?" she asked, rounding on her.

"Nothing!" Cora said with eyes like an animal in a trap. "I did nothing! This is insane! It's him . . ." She pointed at

Scott. Husband and wife glared at each other, irreversibly opposed now, it seemed. "He's the liar. The one the police have been after all along."

Lucy battled to stay in survival mode, though her legs were barely supporting her. "Well, Ruth's awake now," she said as steadily as she could manage.

Cora's head snapped round. "What?"

"She's woken up. I spoke to the hospital earlier. And . . ." She risked a small exaggeration. "They said she's talking. That she's surprisingly lucid. Remembering things. So it will only be a matter of time."

"What things?" Cora clung to an innocent tone, but the color was draining from her face.

"I don't know yet. The police are with her right now."

"You're lying."

"*You're* white as a ghost."

Cora stepped back a few more inches, toward the corner of the room, her palms reaching for the wall behind her.

Lucy clenched her fists at her sides. "Shall we call the hospital right now and check?" She edged toward Cora. "Or maybe the police?"

"There's no need for that!" Cora said, looking frantically left and right.

"It seems like there is."

"No, you've got it wrong . . ."

"Then you don't need to worry about me checking."

Cora shook her head, screwing her eyes shut. "No. But. I didn't go there to hurt her. Just to . . . *talk* to her . . ." She opened her eyes to fling another accusing glance at her husband. "Because Scott hadn't managed to persuade her the first time."

"I obviously didn't try as hard as you," he said in a strangled voice. "I felt bad enough talking to her the way I did. It seemed to scare the living daylights out of her. But I didn't lay a finger on her."

"You didn't *succeed*, either," Cora said.

"We should've just let her show the damn photo to the police," Scott said, banging a fist between his eyes. "For fuck's sake, we should've let Lucy go to them." He swung his gaze to her, and Lucy had nothing in return but hollow, unhappy agreement. "We were stupid to try to cover it up when we had nothing to do with Juliet's death."

"But we had to, Scott." Adam sprang back to life just behind Lucy, as if he'd been hiding in the semi-plastered walls. He walked forward, back into her eyeline, his hands moving as he spoke. "What if they'd found out about all the other stuff? What if they'd started tracing things back, realized you were at uni with Juliet? Discovered the emails, the photo of Cor and Guy? Found out you were only in the Maldives to try to figure out—"

"That wasn't the only reason I was there!" Scott exploded. He turned and struck the wall with a flat palm, sending clouds of dust billowing out.

There was a silence. Lucy slid her eyes to Cora and saw the hard fury on her face. Scott leaned against the adjacent wall, head down, bereft.

"None of you get it," he murmured. "What I felt for her was real. But it became all about Guy. Yet again."

"You were invested in the plan, too," Adam said. "You had just as much to lose."

Scott blew out through his nostrils, then straightened and turned to Cora. "I've spent half my life protecting you,

Cora Waugh. Lying for you. *Loving* you, but never finding any fucking peace. And I'm at a loss as to why."

"You never found peace for the same reasons as me," Cora spat.

Scott shook his head. "No. That's not what I meant. I'm not at a loss as to why I never found peace. I'm at a loss as to why I've loved you and lied for you, for *so* long. When I've always known, deep down, what you're capable of."

Cora's inhale seemed to fill the room. "It was an accident," she said, her eyes so full of hovering tears that Lucy couldn't understand how they weren't falling down her cheeks. "Ruth. I didn't mean—"

"How many times have I heard that, Cora?" Scott said, sounding broken.

Lucy had a flashback to the car. To Adam saying, *The last thing we need is another accident*, and Cora snapping back: *What's that supposed to mean?* And she remembered Cora on speakerphone last night, when Adam had said he'd told Lucy that Scott had killed Guy. Cora's response had sounded defensive of Scott—*It was an* accident—but now, in the context of everything else, it seemed more like a knee-jerk response. Guy was an accident. Ruth was an accident. Lucy's slip down the stairs.

Of course, something seemed to whisper cruelly in her ear.

She stepped toward Cora and made herself say it. "You killed Guy. Not Scott. You."

Cora went rigid against the wall. Lucy looked at Adam and he closed his eyes; seemed to close his whole face, in fact, and sink his chin into his chest. There was no mistaking that he'd been party to this detail, at least. That he'd changed vital parts of the story he'd told Lucy last night. Protecting Cora again? Or just punishing Scott, having finally had enough of always feeling like he got everything he wanted?

"Adam said it was Scott . . ." Lucy caught the shock in Scott's face, morphing into anger, and it was further confirmation. "But it wasn't, it was you . . ." She turned back to Cora, who was a shade whiter even than before. "You reached the end of your tether when you found out he'd kissed Juliet. You pushed him and killed him."

"It was an *accident*," Cora said, almost comically repetitive now.

"But you killed him, Cora." Lucy glanced at Scott again to be sure. His nod was full of what seemed like years-old pain.

Cora kicked a paint tin and it glided across the floor. "I didn't mean to!" she half screamed. "I was in love with him. How do you think I felt when I realized what I'd done?"

"Maybe it *was* an accident," Lucy said. "A horrible, split-second thing. And yes, I'm sure you felt absolutely wretched. I can't really imagine, to be honest. But everything you've done to keep your secret since then . . . that's been no accident, has it? Even this last twenty-four hours, you've been trying to shift the blame onto Scott. Both of you have, you and Adam. You've felt things unraveling and you've thrown out your loyalties and looked around for a scapegoat."

Scott groaned softly. That weariness again, like he'd been carrying extra weight around for too long. "I'd like to say that surprises me." His eyes were on Cora, and strangely empty now. Then Lucy saw them slide to Adam. "But you never could stand it, could you, Adam? That Cora and I ended up together. You thought she might be your reward for helping to cover up what happened to Guy, for putting yourself at risk like that . . ."

"No," Adam cut in, his voice thick. "No, I saw it the opposite way." He gazed at Cora and his chin trembled. There was a sense that he was giving in, Lucy thought. Shedding the last of his pretenses. She held her breath as she watched it happen. "Losing Cora was . . . my punishment. For Guy. For my part in all that. For the car crash being my idea . . ." He looked at Lucy with a flush of shame at this admission, and she felt as if she was falling. "For driving the car . . ." He pressed his eyes shut. "I did it for Cor, but somehow you got rewarded, Scott . . . and I got punished."

His words swung hard into Lucy's body. She'd thought there could be no more levels of hurt, but she'd been wrong. If losing Cora was his punishment, what the hell was Lucy? A consolation prize?

Yes, she realized at last. *That's what you were.*

A consolation prize that Adam had been determined to make the best of.

As Lucy tried to come to terms with it, the others became locked in a battle of their own.

"See it that way if you want to," Scott snorted at Adam.

"Since when am I anybody's reward or punishment?" Cora said furiously.

Lucy looked among the three of them and saw just how dysfunctional their triangle was. The dynamic that had started at university, become warped by their secret, and continued as the years had gone on.

If this was friendship, she wanted to run from it. If this was *love* . . . She swallowed and looked away.

"You can't report me," Cora said, as if remembering what was at stake. "If you tell the police about Ruth"—she faced Scott, her hands on her hips—"you have to tell them everything else. That *you* intimidated her first, Scott. That *you* kept information from the police—"

"Ruth's going to identify you anyway," Scott said.

"Not necessarily," Cora said. "I wore a hat and sunglasses when I went there . . ." She gestured wildly at her face. "Tucked my hair away."

"One nudge from us and they'll work out it was you," Lucy swooped back in, trying to sound surer than she was. She felt for Tilly's phone in her pocket. Cora's eyes went to the movement, so Lucy veered her hand away.

Cora's gaze roamed the room, as if she was contemplating her next move. She was back in the corner, Scott and Adam facing her on either side, Lucy directly in front of her but a small distance away. Lucy could see her quaking with the effort of keeping her body in line, her back straight, her emotions contained. Like an extreme version of what she'd been doing ever since Lucy had met her.

She had killed someone. Hurt someone else. Maybe pushed Lucy down the stairs. *Cora*. Lover of yoga and health food and motherhood and sunrises. Cora with the Faithless tattoo and the once-blue hair and the flashes of cheeky, unexpected humor.

So what else might she have done? There seemed no limit now, and Lucy's thoughts began to escalate, her skin fizzing with goosebumps layered over goosebumps.

"Call the police," Lucy said. "Adam, or Scott, call the police."

"No!" Cora said, and lunged sideways to grab the stepladder that was leaning against the nearest wall, dragging it in front of her like a shield.

"Adam," Lucy said. "Call someone. I can't . . . the passcode on Tilly's phone's been changed . . ."

Something flickered in his eyes, and then the shutters came down. But she had seen it, she was sure.

"Cora's right, though, Lucy," Adam said. "It . . . it will all lead back to us. To Guy."

"But you didn't kill Guy, Adam. Cora did. And Cora hurt Ruth. And . . ."

"And what?" This came from Scott, in a flat yet fearful tone that suggested he'd guessed what Lucy was going to say.

Lucy couldn't take her eyes off Cora. The woman she'd shared countless drinks and dinners with, saunas and yurts, laughter and tears. Her best friend, Cor. Her children's Auntie Cora. Always the first person Lucy wanted to text, after Adam, if she'd got some happy news or spotted a new muffin flavor in their favorite café.

"Scott," she whispered out of the corner of her mouth, still looking at Cora. "How did you know Juliet was beaten to death?"

"What?" he said to her left, sounding confused. "Wasn't . . . wasn't it on the news?"

"No, not until today," Lucy said, trying to breathe evenly, but failing. "You mentioned it before that."

"No, it must've been . . . I knew she'd . . . I think Cora mentioned something abou—" He stopped speaking midword, and Lucy heard his breathing get choppier, too. She glanced at him, saw his face straining as if in physical effort, then turned back to Cora.

"And, Cora," she said. "That course you went on at the end of Scott's trip to Tokyo. Tell us . . ." She swallowed a bubble of fear, trying not to falter. "Where was it again? What was it called? Maybe we can look it up and—"

She didn't get to finish. The stepladder flew toward her, crashing against her head.

In any other circumstances, that island might've been a balm for my soul.

I could imagine doing flow yoga on the shore while the waves lapped my toes. Meditating on the white sand, soothed by the golden curve of the horizon. Letting go, perhaps, of some of the tension, the anger, that has solidified inside me like a metal plate. Lucy says I float while others walk, but she doesn't see the struggle that goes on inside me every day. The darkness while I pretend to flood my soul with light.

I could imagine my younger self on the island, too. Twirling on the beach with my head thrown back, splashing naked into the sea with all the abandon I used to have. Before Guy, before Scott. Before my life became about cover-ups and control.

When Juliet Noor came back into our lives, suddenly into Scott's world, my rituals intensified even further. I would do the toughest yoga poses, push and contort my body, meditate for hours with my legs crossed and my back so straight it would start to burn. I'd scrub my body clean, scrub the house clean, focus on Ivy and Joe with an intensity that would make them feel smothered sometimes, I could tell.

But every time Scott came back from a work event and I knew he'd been with her, I stopped myself from asking what they'd done, where he'd touched her, if she'd made him feel good. It took superhuman strength, but my only questions were about how much he thought Juliet knew. The emails? The photo of me and Guy? The crash? He knows how painful it is for me to talk about, to relive, even to think about Guy at all. But I had those conversations because we needed to. And the problem was,

Scott never had the right answers. He'd never found out enough, done enough. He'd just been with her, got lost in her, and forgotten what was important.

That was why I had to go to the island. To a place that might've seemed like paradise to a different version of myself. Why I had to finish what Scott was too weak to do, what neither he nor Adam wanted to admit was our only option left.

CHAPTER THIRTY-TWO

SAWDUST SWIRLED AROUND LUCY, MAKING HER eyes stream. She lay panting on the floor, cloaked by Cora's shadow, her ears ringing yet again.

"You think you're so smart, Lucy," Cora said. She looked taller than ever, but her usual elegance was somehow missing, her fluidity gone. She was a stretched-out, misshapen coil, one foot kicking against the stepladder that lay on its side to her left.

Lucy turned her head to splutter into her hand, shooting stars of pain crossing from ear to ear as she did. Tilly's phone had shot out of her pocket, she saw, and landed next to her face. A notification flashed on the screen. Something about a scheduled action. Adam rushed toward Lucy, but as he got closer he seemed to notice Tilly's phone instead. In one motion, he scooped it up and leaned over Lucy: "Are you okay? Luce? Are you hurt? Dizzy?"

She batted him away and creaked into a sitting position. The room whirled, then settled, like a brief spiral of wind. Cora was now standing with her hands over her face, murmuring to herself. Scott was looking at the door, and Lucy thought of the kids upstairs. Someone needed to check on them. How much could they hear from up there?

Cora dropped her hands. "You need to watch what you're saying, Lucy. You shouldn't be making assumptions if you don't have anything to back them up. Talking recklessly about things you don't understand."

Lucy felt a strange sense of courage now that Cora had attacked her but stopped short of really hurting her. She hauled herself onto her knees. "There are a lot of things *you* shouldn't have done, too, Cora."

Scott's attention snapped back. "Lucy, obviously that's true . . ." He couldn't look at Cora now. "But . . . you can't be saying she . . . killed *Juliet*?" His voice broke slightly over her name. "Whatever else she's done, she can't have done that in cold blood . . ." He stalled as if he wasn't so certain now that he'd said it out loud, then shook his head. "Even practically, logistically . . ."

Lucy clambered to her feet. It was agony, but she didn't want them all towering over her. "But I think she did."

"It's impossible." This was Adam now. "She was here, with Ivy and Joe. Scott was in Tokyo. Someone killed Juliet, and that looks bad for us, given everything else . . . and of course it's crossed my mind, at times, that it was a pretty huge, pretty awful coincidence that she was killed"—he glanced at Scott, who stared back at him—"but the fact is we were all thousands of miles away when she died. That's what I came back to whenever I had doubts. What I—"

"Cora *wasn't* here with the kids." Lucy's heart threatened to burst through her chest. "They were at her mum's, and she was away. Supposedly on a training course."

She remembered how Cora had reacted yesterday when Lucy pointedly asked how her course had gone after seeing her with Adam. Cora had asked what she meant and Lucy had been surprised she'd already forgotten a lie she'd told only a few hours before. But she was convinced now that Cora had thought—feared—that Lucy was alluding to a previous lie. A different course she'd claimed to have been on, covering up a much bigger secret. And Lucy was pretty sure that if she'd known enough to take a closer look through Cora's office window at her wall of certificates, she wouldn't have seen one for the dates when Juliet had died.

"That doesn't prove anything!" Cora said. "Nothing at all." But she had that cornered look again, the animal-in-a-trap eyes that turned Lucy's stomach to liquid.

"Cora?" Scott's voice was low as he advanced toward his wife. "Cora, is this true? You left Ivy and Joe with your mum and didn't tell me? You went away? Where did you go?"

Cora began to back up again, her hands at her own throat. Lucy couldn't help looking at her muscular arms, strengthened by yoga. Strong enough to bludgeon someone to death? It still seemed unthinkable, still made Lucy want to return to the dusty floor and curl up into a ball.

"*No*," Adam said in anguish. "Cora? No. This can't be true. It isn't true, is it?"

Cora opened her mouth but made no sound. For a moment she looked as if she was silently screaming, her hands still pressed against her jugular.

"That wasn't the plan, Cora," Scott said. "What the fuck? That was *never* the plan."

"*Wasn't* it?" Cora said, her hands falling away in a sudden blaze of defiance. "I think it was, but nobody would admit it. Nobody had the guts except me!" She slammed her palm into her own chest. "Least of all you, Scott, all lovesick over Juliet, while we were terrified she was threatening us, threatening our family."

"But . . . but we *agreed*," Adam said while Lucy raged at him in her mind, seeing now how weak he really was. "Scott was just going to talk to her. We just needed to be sure of what she knew, what she planned to do . . ."

"And then what?" Cora demanded. "How did you think we were going to deal with whatever she knew? Which we assumed was quite a lot, based on the emails. 'I know what you did,' they said, or have you forgotten already? 'I could ruin you,' they said. 'Do your kids know what you are?' I couldn't bear it! Waiting for the ax to fall, every hideous day since they started. How else did you think we might stop that, *Adam*?"

"I don't know." Adam clamped a hand over his mouth, looking as if he'd been slapped. "But not this. Not you, Cor. Not after Guy."

It was these words that brought tears back to Cora's eyes. She blinked them furiously away, but Adam continued to stare at her, as if waiting for her to burst out laughing, for the *gotcha* moment so he didn't have to accept what she'd done. Getting nothing, he looked wildly at Scott, as if it might come from him instead. As if Cora and Scott might've concocted this elaborate practical joke between them, because they were the fun couple, after all, they were the ones who liked to surprise and entertain people.

Finally, Adam looked at Lucy. Not with hope that she might let him off the hook of having to accept this, but with a new, dark anger. Anger that she'd been the one to suggest, in the first place, that Cora might've brutally murdered Juliet Noor.

"How did you even . . . ?" Scott's question for Cora trailed off, and he looked as if he'd made himself feel sick just thinking it. They were all surely thinking it, though. Questions were forming in Lucy's mind as quick as she could fight off the unwanted images that came with them. How had Cora actually done it? How had Juliet Noor actually died?

The rain began as I was making my way around the edge of the pitch-black island. Warm and tropical but sudden and heavy; a different kind of rain from any I'd experienced before. My app had warned me that the weather was turning, the monsoon season set to begin. But all I thought was that the darkness and rain might play to my advantage.

The island reshaped as my eyes adjusted. I saw the black outlines of palm trees and the pointy roofs of the bamboo huts facing out to sea. Beyond them, the waves were getting choppy and the rain disturbed the surface that was earlier so serene. I lingered behind a tree, checking if anybody was around. The guests were sleeping, it seemed, the staff gone home. It was the dead of night in paradise, which most people dream their way through.

As I crept forward, I went back to feeling grateful for the rain. Though my hair was plastered to my skull and my vision was clouded with droplets, the noise of the downpour masked my arrival. And it meant no guests were out on their verandas, not even for a late nightcap, as I slipped around the back of the huts.

For a moment, as I approached, I was struck by the fact that I was there, I was doing this, and I wondered if I'd completely lost my senses. Scott was in Tokyo; Ivy and Joe were with my mum; not even Adam knew what I was doing. He'd been needier in the preceding weeks, constantly in touch, but I'd managed not to let on what I was planning to do. I'd never trodden such a fine line between feeling in and out of control. My plan wasn't flawless, far from it, but Scott had left me with no choice, left too many dangling threads. He's always acted like he's the strong one, the protector, the capable partner in the craziness that is our marriage. The one who looked after me at uni, in some kind of weird competition with Adam, and helped me keep "my" secret all these years. But as things got critical, I realized I was the strong one. When it came to it, I was the one with the follow-through, the real commitment to our survival.

I found the right hut, the one I'd been watching for most of the afternoon. The terrace was dark and slick with rain but there was a light on somewhere inside. I imagined Juliet's and Scott's silhouettes in there a few days earlier. Drawing together, moving together. Skin on skin. Her hair falling into his face. The images repelled me, paralyzed me, but then a hot surge of jealousy and anger had the opposite effect, pushing me forward like a hand at my back.

I glanced to the left and right, checking for faces in the rear windows of the spaced-out huts, then climbed over the railing to Juliet's veranda. Something caught my eye on the far side of the terrace. As I blinked and leaned closer, I realized it was an oar. My heart seemed to turn over. It felt like a sign. I slid it carefully toward me, held it at my side, and walked slowly toward Juliet's back door.

There, I took a moment to catch my breath. Digging deep into my resolve, gripping the oar so hard my arm spasmed. The light in Juliet's hut had gone out. Maybe she'd gone to bed. As I tried the back door, I realized the strange whistling in my ears was not the wind but the sound of my own labored breathing. I should've felt relieved to discover the door open, but the ease with which I was able to step inside unnerved me. At that moment I was looking for reasons to stall. Urging myself onward at the same time as hoping for obstacles and delays.

Spurning my hesitation, I crept across the living area. Part of my brain was scanning for any evidence that Scott had been there, anything carelessly left behind, but there was nothing I could see. I was planning to clean the place afterward, of course. Change the sheets, scrub away our prints, get rid of Juliet's laptop and phone. He wouldn't have thought it necessary to do that before he left to fly back to Japan. He was never going to tie things up in the way I was. Probably because he couldn't bring himself to say a permanent good-bye to her.

A pair of gold sandals lay on the rug, spilling granules of sand. A cherry-red bikini was draped over the back of a chair and I imagined her in it, sunbathing with Scott, her olive skin and her seductive curves. Then I could hardly breathe. I froze in the middle of the room. Can I do this? Am I actually going to? *I looked again at Juliet's things and they seemed to scream,* She's a person, *despite my vow to think of her only as the source of all my problems. I closed my eyes, shook my head, tried to quieten the voices, remember what she'd done. The emails. The threats. Guy. Scott. Thinking she could play games with people's feelings and lives. Slowly, I pushed open the bedroom door. I saw a bed with pale, rumpled sheets; a white robe hanging on a hook, which looked fleetingly like a person. But the room was empty. I peered through the half-open door to the en suite and found that empty, too.*

Juliet wasn't there. Her smell was there, her essence, but not her.

My arm sank, lowering the oar so its end touched the floor. But that was when I saw it. Her laptop yawning open, the screen lit as if I'd only just missed her. And on it, the so-called novel she went out there to work on. I inched a little closer, my breath evaporating as I caught the word crash. *I knelt down with my face too close to the screen, as if I'd be able to read quicker that way, absorb the words through sheer proximity. Though she never actually used his name, it was clearly all about him. How much she cared about him even though he infuriated her. The good times they'd had as "flatmates and friends." And his death. The way it left her reeling . . . and once the shock had worn off, left her wondering. What was he doing on that road? What made him lose control if there was no other car involved? Why were people so quick to assume it was an accident of his own making?*

My heart thumped hard and fast. This was confirmation, at last, that this had been on her mind the whole time she'd been messing around with my husband. Confirmation that it was only a matter of time before she was going to act on the threats she'd been sending. So I knew I couldn't give up. Couldn't leave. I had to find her on the island, had to finish what I came for.

The bedroom walls felt as if they were closing in. I stepped out of the room but it was just as airless in the living space. I flailed to the front door, oar still in hand, and stuck my head out into the warm, wet darkness. Though it was sticky and humid, the rain revived me. I let it stream down my face. Then I opened my eyes and slipped all the way out of the hut. Across the boardwalk, through the palm grove, along the shore like a nocturnal animal, skulking low and silent.

Where are you, Juliet? How can you have vanished on a tiny island? *For a moment I thought maybe someone had beaten me to it. Maybe she'd disappeared of her own accord, or maybe the ocean had swept her away. I thought of her novel and its thinly veiled cry for justice. I imagined it published, causing a stir, Guy's case reopened after all this time. Was that what she was planning? What the vague threats in the emails were actually about? I pictured Scott and myself in handcuffs while our babies watched on. And it fired me up again, pushed me to do another faster circuit of the island.*

Finally, I spotted her. A figure at the far end of the beach, walking away from me, dressed in white but with a curtain of contrasting dark hair. Out for a walk in the pouring rain, it seemed. Tilting her head up to it, so that the moonlight rippled in the wet silkiness of her curls.

I wasn't prepared for how it felt seeing her again. I'd thought about it before, of course, in unguarded moments, on darker days. I'd imagined what might happen if she ever reappeared from wherever she's been all these years. But I've also tried so hard to forget about her, about everything connected to her. I've built a career, a family, a safety net for us all. Until the day I heard her name again, on Scott's lips, confessing how foolish he'd been, and the cracks seemed to suddenly show.

It remained just a name for a while. A name with a mess of feelings attached, but just a name, at least, something I could keep at arm's length, decide what to do with. But then, seeing her. The easy way she moved, like she didn't know or remember a thing—except I knew she did, knew all too well. I watched her from a distance, mesmerized, paralyzed, and then I moved toward her, small step after small step. Following her as she swished through the rain to the edge of the shore, where the ocean was a black, depthless swell.

"Juliet?" I said, gripping the oar.

Her dark hair flew out as she spun around.

That was the no-going-back moment. A moment that seemed to have ripples gliding off it, forward and backward in time.

CHAPTER THIRTY-THREE

THE AIR IN THE LIVING ROOM WAS THICK WITH shock. The four of them blinked at each other through it, as if in the hazy wake of an explosion.

"I can't believe it," Scott said. "I can't believe . . ." He held his hand up like a barrier between himself and his wife, and they all saw that he was shaking uncontrollably.

Lucy swayed on the spot as her brain repeated what Scott still couldn't say out loud. *Cora murdered Juliet Noor.*

She had to push through the shock and do something. Phone the police. What might Cora do now that she felt she'd got nothing left to lose? Lucy looked at Adam and mimed a phone call with her hand. His eyes darted. She looked pointedly at his pocket where he'd stashed Tilly's phone, and signaled again. Adam flinched, shrugged, looked back at Cora and Scott.

"I've been going through *hell* wondering what happened to Juliet after I left the island," Scott was saying. "Griev-ing, and fucking terrified, but trying to hold everything together for *your* sake, Cora. Trying to balance all the lies, keep up the pretense . . ." He glanced wretchedly at Lucy. She thought of the confrontations they'd had. Him denying the affair, then admitting to it. Never letting on that Cora knew about it. But, it seemed, never thinking she might've gone to the Maldives and killed Juliet herself.

Lucy swore under her breath, trying to get Adam's attention again. Why was he guarding the phone? Why did she feel like there was more he was hiding? He stared helplessly at Cora and Scott as they screamed at each other. Lucy edged to the door and slipped out of the room.

She took the stairs two at a time and burst into the largest bedroom. The kids were in a huddle on the floor, watching Joe's iPad like Lucy had told them to, but pale and worried-looking, the older ones especially. Lucy's heart bled for them. Just following her instructions, sitting tight while all hell broke loose below.

"Are you okay?" she said, gathering all four of them into her arms. "I'm so sorry."

"Mummy," Tilly said, grabbing Lucy's sleeve, "what's going on? Why is everybody shouting?"

They gazed at her, wide-eyed and expectant. *Say something to make it all better.*

"Bad things are happening right now," she said, swallowing, "but it . . . it's going to be all right."

The younger ones nodded trustingly, solemn faces trying not to cry, but Tilly frowned and pulled herself up to kneeling. "What bad things?"

"I—I'll explain later, darling." Impatience flurried in Lucy's chest but she tried not to let it show, smoothing Tilly's hair behind her ear. "Til, about your phone . . ." She had to get into it. Not just to phone the police, but to see what was on there, what Adam didn't want her to see. "You're sure you don't know the passcode?"

Tilly wrinkled her nose. "I *do* know the passcode."

Lucy gaped at her. "But in the car you said you didn't!"

"No, I never."

"Tilly, you *did*!" Lucy couldn't keep a note of outrage out of her voice, then felt guilt-stricken, especially as Tilly's chin started to wobble.

"No," Tilly said, "you asked if I'd changed it. And I didn't . . ." She hesitated, seeming pensive. "Daddy did."

Lucy's mouth formed an O. "Shit," she said softly, earning her four surprised looks. She'd forgotten how literal Tilly could be. She leaned forward, putting her hands on her daughter's shoulders. "Then what is it, Til?"

Tilly blinked anxiously. "He told me not to tell anyone. In case my phone got hacked."

"But you can tell *me*!"

Tilly hesitated again. Lucy resisted a terrible urge to shake her. Adam had got their daughter keeping secrets from her, too. It was the peak of a mountain of betrayals.

"Tilly, please, it's important. And it's me. I'm not going to hack your phone!"

"Okay." Tilly fluttered her eyes. "Sorry, Mummy. It's 2006."

Lucy felt another low twist of nausea. The year Guy had died. What kind of sick idea was that?

"Thank you." She kissed Tilly's forehead. "Good girl." She stood up and looked down at their confused expressions. "Darlings, I have to go back downstairs now, but stay up here, keep doing what you're doing, and it will all be over soon. I'm so proud of you . . ." She was already backing toward the door. "I love you. Stay here until I come back."

She closed the door on their soft protests, though it felt like the most unnatural, awful thing to do, and hurried downstairs.

Back in the living room, the volatility in the air had climbed even further, or perhaps it just felt that way in contrast to the kids' quiet, unified distress. The warring adults didn't even seem to notice Lucy slipping back into the room.

"You're both looking at me like I'm a monster," Cora was saying, "but I'm not the one who started it all." Her eyes seemed to have little fires in them, her gaze veering between Adam and Scott. "I wish you'd never even told me about Guy kissing Juliet. Just look at everything it's caused."

Lucy watched Scott for his reaction. Was Cora seriously still trying to blame him? But Cora's gaze rested on Adam, in fact, and he seemed to shrivel beneath it.

And it was he who answered after a long pause. "I was trying to be a friend."

"Oh, *were* you, Adam?" Cora shot back. "Really? You weren't just jealous?"

Adam's face colored, like a teenager being taunted by his crush. It made Lucy's skin crawl to witness it. And something had flagged red at the back of her mind, something wrong about the dynamics of the discussion.

"I didn't make you push him," Adam said, twitching with agitation. "You did that. You lost control."

"That's not what you said at the time. 'It was an accident, Cora. This doesn't have to mean the end for you.' I wanted to go to the police but *you* convinced me not to!"

"Wait—" Lucy tried to butt in, unsure if she was hearing

things right. Neither of them acknowledged her. It was just like in the car, as if they'd forgotten she existed.

"You didn't take much convincing," Adam said.

"I couldn't even think straight! From the moment you told me about him and Juliet, I was out of my mind! You sprang it on me when I thought things were good with Guy. I was happy and you pissed on all of it."

Lucy's head began spinning again. Cora was aiming it all at Adam. You *sprang it on me.* You *convinced me not to go to the police.* In his version of events, that had been Scott. Lucy recalled some of the phrases he'd used and realized, with another rush of wounding clarity, that they'd all, actually, been referring to himself. *It was the final straw for Scott. He couldn't take it anymore. He just blurted it out. We both cared about her, but he'd always been the one who had feelings for her.* Now Lucy was watching Adam, and those deflected feelings for Cora, unraveling in front of her. She felt suddenly hollow, like an empty space waiting to be filled up with the next dose of hurt.

"You weren't happy," Adam was saying to Cora. "You were just deluded because he'd been nice to you for a day. I had to do something. Had to tell you, *show* you, what he was really like. And you had to see it for yourself. I had to make sure of that . . ." He looked to Scott for some kind of support, but Scott blanked him. Adam's face was bright red, the shade of rising panic. Lucy had never seen him look quite like it before.

Another dark wave of understanding came over her. There was something, again, about Adam's turns of phrase. *I had to show you what he was really like. Had to make sure you saw it for yourself.* Several things seemed to thud into place at once, and Lucy found herself speaking up, louder this time, before she'd even followed her line of thought all the way through.

"But it wasn't a coincidence," she said, "that you saw that photo of them kissing. Was it, Adam?"

"What?" He flinched and then frowned at her. Lucy felt a tilting sensation, like seasickness.

She moved her feet further apart, as if to form a solid base. "You . . ." She was going to say *you took it* or even *you staged it*. But then it occurred to her. Adam's specialty. His MO. Maybe it went further back than she'd even realized. "You faked it," she said instead, with a feeling like she'd just smashed a glass pane to set off an alarm.

She watched the jolt of his reaction. The flash of his now-familiar guilty look. It seemed she hadn't reached the peak of his betrayals when she'd thought she had.

"*What?*" Cora said, whipping to face Lucy and almost overbalancing.

Lucy was caught up in her own momentum. "You accuse *me* of being obsessed with photos," she said to Adam. "But you've got an obsession with *changing* them. Changing the story they tell. You did it with Scott and Juliet, in the Maldives . . ." She glanced at Scott, who was blinking rapidly. "And long before that, you did it with Juliet and Guy, the picture of them kissing, which I . . . I don't think they ever did. Nobody except you has ever claimed they were more than just friends. *And* . . ." She faltered, doubting herself about this last part; then faith flooded back, painful as it was.

"And with *Cora* and Guy," she finished. "The photo that supposedly came from Juliet, which Cora couldn't even remember being taken. And therefore, I assume . . . the *emails* that supposedly came from her."

"Wait . . ." Scott took a big stride forward, while Cora had been rendered speechless, frozen in place, her hands raised with the fingers half-closed, as if they'd got stuck.

Lucy pointed to Adam's pocket. "Give me Tilly's phone."

His hand shot to it. "Why?"

"Give it to me!"

"No . . . I don't . . ." He stepped backward, as if he thought she was going to tackle him. Actually, it was Scott who looked more likely to, but confusion seemed to have stalled him. He hovered restlessly, his eyes shifting from Adam to Lucy and back.

"What's on there, Adam?" Lucy asked. "What have you got to hide?"

"I just don't understand what you want with it."

"It's my daughter's phone, too."

"But you can't even . . ." It was his turn to look like an animal in a trap, as if taking over from Cora. He drew the phone out and stared at it. Lucy held her breath. She was relying on the fact that he didn't know she had the new code. She watched him shrug with exaggerated nonchalance, one shoulder higher than the other, and finally hand it over.

His whole body jerked as she tapped *2006.*

"Lucy—" he said, lunging for the phone.

She leaped away from him, spinning so he collided with her back, and went straight to the phone's mailbox. It asked her for the passcode again. That wasn't normal, was it? Lucy guarded the phone as she keyed it in, feeling the intense scrutiny of her audience, their different levels of confusion and concern.

Then a sense of anticlimax crashed over her. The inbox was empty. The Sent folder, then? She slumped as she discovered it empty, too, wondering if she'd got it all wrong. Glancing up, she caught a flare of relief in Adam's eyes, bordering on triumph, and her fury surged back. She scrolled quickly until she spotted a folder called Scheduled Items. With a hammering heart she clicked into it, pushing Adam away as he reverted to trying to grab the phone.

And there they were. The messages Lucy had thought she'd find, but it still made her sick to see them. On Tilly's phone, of all places. When Adam tried to seize it again, over her shoulder, she whirled round to face him.

"Why don't you show them, Adam?" she said. "Show your friends that the blackmails were actually from you? Scheduled emails, sent from your daughter's untraceable phone?"

The guilty panic in Adam's eyes didn't fade. He finally snatched the phone, but with a defeated fall of his shoulders.

"Is this a fucking *joke*?" Scott said, closing in on Adam, who put up his hands like a shield and backed away.

"Ad?" Cora had started hyperventilating. Lucy flicked her eyes between her and Adam, the mirroring high color in their cheeks.

"Cor . . ." Adam begged, sidestepping Scott in favor of appealing to her.

"Am I hearing this right?" Cora hissed. "You made it up about Guy and Juliet? And you . . . you sent the emails? Faked . . . *how* many photos?"

"I . . . I had to make you see sense," Adam stuttered, practically crawling at her feet. "The Guy and Juliet thing . . . I did that for *you*. I had to get you away from him and it was the only way to convince you."

"Oh, my God." Cora's eyes rolled back into her head. It was as if she was rolling back in time, too, reassessing everything. "Adam, do you know what you've—"

"And the emails . . ." Adam's gaze flailed again between Scott and Cora, before fixing on Scott with bald hatred, like a mask had been removed. "I was just *so* fucking angry. So gobsmacked that this idiot could be *that* stupid."

Scott looked him up and down with a mixture of bafflement and contempt. "What are you talking about?"

"Juliet."

"But—"

"I knew about the affair long before you admitted it to Cora and me. Long before you were *forced* to."

This seemed to throw Scott onto the back foot. He pulled himself up tall, as if to compensate. "What the *fuck*?"

Adam was flinging out words with the abandon of somebody who'd reached the end of the line. "Don't you realize that every time you ask me for help with your computer, every time you treat me like IT support for your *much more important* work, I have a look at your emails, your files?"

Scott's confusion flipped back to outrage. "Why would you do that?"

Adam snorted with hostile laughter, the grating tone of it making Lucy wince. "Because I don't trust you! Just like you don't trust me. But we're stuck with each other, tied by what we did for Cor."

Lucy glanced over at Cora, but she didn't respond, not even to protest against Adam's white knight interpretation. She remained frozen, her lips parted, her eyes unblinking. The only chink in her disturbing stillness was a tiny, barely perceptible shake in her arms.

Scott stepped even closer to Adam and raised his fist. "You always were a snake. And so pathetic, so jealous . . ."

"Rather that than have your arrogance!" Adam ducked a punch that didn't even come, making himself look as pathetic as Scott was claiming. "To believe you could start messing around with Juliet, of all people, and there'd be no consequences . . . To not realize how fucking lucky you are . . ." Adam gestured furiously at Cora. A flinch in her color-drained face was the only indication that she was listening.

Scott shook his head, holding the bridge of his nose. "That was what it was all about. Time and time again, Adam. Cora. Always Cora."

"You were playing with fire, Scott!" Adam erupted. "Even being in touch with Juliet again was insane! But to be sleeping with her? It was messed up on so many levels!"

"*I'm* the messed-up one?"

"I had to snap you out of it, scare you away from her—"

"Then why send threats to Cora as well?" Scott challenged.

That made Adam stall. His eyes darting again, his neck reddening. "To . . . to make it seem believable. It had to be all three of us—"

"No, Adam." Scott resumed shaking his head, half smirking, half grimacing, "No, you're kidding yourself. You wanted Cora to find out about Juliet. You wanted to blow our marriage apart."

"Well, that would've been nothing more than you deserved!" Adam grabbed the front of Scott's shirt. He held on to it for a moment, thrusting his face into Scott's. But Scott was full-on smirking at him now, in a grim told-you-so kind of way, and Adam seemed to deflate, as if realizing he'd exposed himself again. Lucy's sympathy for him was gone. What remained in its place was impossible to process as her supplies of adrenaline wore thin.

"But just look what you caused instead," Scott said, graveness returning.

Adam released his shirt. Closed his eyes. He hadn't glanced at Lucy in several minutes, and she was glad; she didn't know how she would handle it. Perhaps the only way to cope, in this moment, was to pretend there was nothing between them.

When Adam next spoke, it was in a whisper that seemed to come from low in his throat. "Once you confessed about the affair, and we were all talking about the emails, about what to do . . . I couldn't come clean. I felt like I had to cover my tracks, make sure you really did think they were from her. Except . . ." He stopped dead, staring straight in front of him. "Except that I failed to unschedule them. I thought I had, but then another one got through somehow after we found out Juliet was . . ." He covered his face, dragged his hand slowly down it. "I never dreamed she'd end up dead. I just got carried away, and the plan took over, and I was too far in to stop it . . ."

"No, no, no." Cora came to life at last and began chanting under her breath like a meditation, shaking her head as if denying what she was hearing. "No, no . . ." The chanting got louder, making everyone in the room turn toward her. "None of this even needed to happen!" she eventually screamed, lunging at Adam.

Adam's hands flew up in front of him, shoving her away. Cora was flung backward, her arms wide and wheeling. Lucy saw Scott dive forward to break her fall. Heard him shout something incoherent as he failed to catch her and stumbled to his knees. Cora's heel clipped the edge of the stepladder that was still lying, glinting, on the floor. Her body twisted and for a moment she was suspended, as elegant and beautiful as ever, until time seemed to catch up and she was still falling, her head smacking against a low corner beam. The one Scott had always wanted to remove but Cora said would be sacrilege, such a beautiful old beam. She hit it with a solid, reverberating thud. And then she dropped like a rag doll, crashing down into a pile of paint tins. They exploded in a shower of terra-cotta, and more dust erupted from the floor, like smoke attempting to veil what had happened, how still she was, how silent.

CHAPTER THIRTY-FOUR

TILLY AND FRAN. TILLY AND FRAN. THE WAY FRAN used to call her big sister "Tiggy" because she struggled to pronounce her name when she was very young. The way Tilly would push Fran away if she tried to join in with the puzzle she was doing or the picture she was drawing, but then would cuddle her a second later if she thought nobody was watching.

The way they used to hang on to Adam's arms like little monkeys and he would lift them high, their feet cycling in the air. Their living room picnics on rainy days, as a family, when Fran would insist on paper plates and plastic forks.

Those elaborate dens the girls would make with Ivy and Joe, and persuade the adults to climb into as well. The sight of Cora's bare feet as she crawled beneath the propped-up swathes of duvet and Lucy followed her, laughing, the kids delighted to show their mums the interior of their creation. And Scott poking the den from the outside to make it shake, make everybody squeal, never quite allowing it to collapse.

Lucy saw and thought all of these things but they were

muddled, fragmented, as she struggled to understand where she was. She could smell sawdust and paint, and something more human. Could hear muffled footsteps and the bang of doors. She tried to open her eyes but they'd never felt heavier, and there was a crushing pressure behind the bones of her face.

"Lucy?" said a voice.

"Fran?" she murmured. "Til?" It made no sense: They'd never called her Lucy and she knew it was neither of their voices.

"I'm a paramedic. Try to stay awake for me, okay? You're doing really well, but you fainted, and you seem to have some injuries. Can you tell me how you got those?"

The spiral of the stairs. The crash of the stepladder. The floor rushing up as she'd finally blacked out. How could she know which injuries belonged to which? She tried to explain but her words kept folding back up.

"Don't worry for now," said the soothing voice of the paramedic. "Keep calm, keep breathing. I'm going to put a support around your neck, just in case."

Lucy felt a jolt of pain to all corners of her body as she was gently maneuvered and her neck was enclosed by something thick and warm. The paramedic kept asking her questions, encouraging Lucy to fight against the heaviness of her lids. Lucy tried to focus on colors and shapes. She was still in the living room of the cottage. She was at a strange angle and everything else looked wrong, too.

Memories came back in tiny, whirling pieces. Cora. She couldn't reach for her, couldn't ask about her. But she could see now her blonde hair splayed across the floorboards on the other side of the room, with new streaks of red, like a bold choice of highlights. *She used to dye her hair vivid colors,*

Lucy thought distantly. *She used to do a lot of things until she stopped.*

Lucy felt a hand grip hers. She thought it must be one of the paramedics but it held on for too long and it was too familiar. Tearing her gaze from Cora, she turned her head back the other way and realized it was Adam, crouching beside her. His glasses missing; his facial muscles apparently in collapse. There was a second, just a second, in which Lucy was flooded with love and gladness that he was there. Until more memories came back and she gasped as they piled on top of her like bricks.

Adam looked as if he was trying to speak but couldn't find the words. Lucy had nothing, either, just a hole inside her, as if the core of her had been removed. Then his hand disappeared and so did he. Lucy realized there was a police officer behind him, that he was being led away from her rather than walking away of his own accord. He glanced toward Cora's motionless form, then bowed his head as if in acceptance of his fate. Or maybe with guilt, maybe grief. Lucy didn't know what he must be feeling after everything. He already seemed to not belong to her anymore.

LUCY WAS ALLOWED to close her eyes, at last, when she reached the hospital. Nurses bustled around her; machines beeped; faces loomed close and voices reassured. Once they'd removed her neck brace, she sank into the cool pillows and dreamed again of Tilly and Fran. But the dreams gave way to nightmares and her girls were replaced by Juliet, by Scott, by Cora and a parade of accidents.

Lucy woke with a gasp and searched around her for an

indication of reality. There was nothing to tell her what her new reality was going to be.

"My daughters," she said, unsure if she was speaking at the right volume, if anyone was listening. She said it a few more times until she felt fingers touch her arm.

"Are you okay, love?" said a female voice with a gentle Norfolk accent.

"My family," Lucy croaked. "Are they okay?"

"Your husband's in custody, I believe," the voice said, almost apologetically.

Lucy brought the speaker's face into focus. The main thing she saw was warm, sympathetic eyes, and they made her feel better even though the words didn't.

"And your friend . . ." The nurse pulled the curtain around the bed, then sat down. Lucy knew that was a bad sign. Her blood started fizzing, her reaction already a mess of different emotions.

"Cora?" the nurse said. "Is she your friend?"

Lucy nodded reflexively, the full answer too complex to attempt. Her ears blocked and unblocked as if she was underwater.

"I'm so sorry. She . . . didn't make it. The head trauma was too severe."

All Lucy seemed able to do was nod. *Yes, yes, I hear you, I hear you, I just can't process, not yet, but I've heard you.* She pulled in shaky breaths and couldn't identify all the feelings she was battling with, only that it *was* a battle.

The nurse squeezed her hand. "I'm sorry. You've been through a lot."

Lucy lay back, staring at the ceiling, and two quiet tears fell out of the corners of her eyes.

Time seemed to slow and distort, then her pillow was

damp and she was sitting up again, remembering. "My daughters, though. Where are they?"

"Ah, yes. Sorry. I do have an update on that for you." The nurse fished a piece of paper out of the pocket of her tunic. "They're with social services at the moment."

"Oh, God." Lucy pictured them sitting with strangers, not knowing what was going on, wondering why their mum and dad had abandoned them.

"They're fine, according to the reports we've had. Coloring, eating crisps." The nurse gave her another encouraging smile. "Is there anyone who could collect them on your behalf? Grandparents?"

"My parents live abroad," Lucy said. "There's my husband's mum, though. She's in Northamptonshire . . ."

But what will I even say to her? Adam's mum idolized him. This was going to destroy her.

This was going to destroy Tilly and Fran.

"Have the police been here?" Lucy asked.

The nurse nodded, a little more somber now. "They want to interview you down at the station when you're strong enough."

The ordeal wasn't over yet. Lucy wondered what the police had already pieced together and what she would need to tell them. Truth and blame had been flung into the open by the events of the last twenty-four hours, and there was no escaping it anymore.

Cora. Her face came into Lucy's mind, smiling, glowing, the way she used to be. Stretching those long arms above her head.

"Are you all right?" asked the nurse in concern. "Do you have pain?"

Lucy realized she was clutching her side as the memory

of Cora, the *before* Cora, hit hard. Other images tumbled after it, ending with Adam being led away, head down, by the police. Her husband had killed her best friend. The fact that those labels no longer felt true didn't make it any less hard to accept. And it had happened in a terrible kind of reenactment of their night with Guy, the night that had started everything.

Yes, Lucy thought, her head falling into her pillows. *Yes, I have pain.*

CHAPTER THIRTY-FIVE

A PROPER FORMAL INTERVIEW THIS TIME. A ROLLing tape making a permanent record. A lawyer next to her who was not particularly reassuring. Arrested or not—and DCs Aggarwal and Marr insisted she wasn't—the formalities made Lucy tenser than ever. The sense that this time was for real, and there was no room for skirting the facts.

"Firstly, can you tell us, in your own words, your relationship to the suspects Adam Taylor and Scott Waugh?"

The first word that landed on Lucy was *suspects*, sending a fresh zip of nervousness down her spine. As it passed, all that remained was the question and the acknowledgment that the answer could be simple or complicated. Husband. Friend. *And what am I left with now?*

She swallowed another pang of loss and stuck to the simple answer. Even that was greeted with raised eyebrows and note-taking. Her *relationship* with the *suspects.* Lucy shifted in her chair. She knew the detectives had to treat her with suspicion and scrutiny, too, perhaps even more so than they'd seemed to before. Had to ask her about things she'd already told them, because this was evidence that could be used in court. And besides, she remembered with a tightening of her stomach, she had not always been entirely honest with them.

"How much did you know about the deaths of Guy Everley and Juliet Noor?"

Lucy paused. The question seemed too nebulous, spanning two weeks of her life but years of her husband's and friends'. All she felt able to answer was: "Nothing." It was both true and not true.

"Your husband never confided in you?"

"No. And he didn't know about Juliet, about how she died. Not until I did."

"You mean that Cora Waugh killed her?" Aggarwal didn't even say *allegedly*. Lucy knew that they had managed to trace Cora's journey to and from the Maldives. Knew that the evidence had fallen quickly into place since Scott had relayed Cora's confession to them in the aftermath of their showdown.

Lucy nodded, lowering her eyes. The evidence could confirm that Cora was the murderer, but it still couldn't help her to fully comprehend it.

"Did you suspect anything about either incident?" Marr asked.

Lucy's palms were damp. The temperature in the room was ridiculously high again. It was a different room from last time, though. An interview *suite*, they had called it, as if she'd gone up in the world. "Well, I came to *you* about the photo of Juliet and Scott . . ."

"But you claim you didn't suspect any foul play at that point?"

Foul play. Claim. The words fell accusingly. Lucy wiped her hands on her skirt. She felt grubby. She'd come straight from the hospital to here and she longed for a shower, the softness of her own bed, even if her house would feel lacking, changed. She longed to collect Tilly and Fran from her mother-in-law's and wrap her arms around them until they squealed that she was holding them too tight. She'd spoken to them on the phone from the hospital, and the brave bewilderment in their voices had broken her heart. The sooner this interview was over with, the sooner she could see them.

"I was never quite sure," she said, looking at the detectives one at a time. "I *was* worried that something even more sinister than an affair might be going on. But I had no real idea, no proof . . ." She glanced at her lawyer, wondering whether she was shooting herself in the foot. She hadn't committed a crime, the businesslike woman had assured Lucy before the interview. So why did Lucy still feel as if the police wanted to pin something on her?

"And what about Guy Everley?" DC Aggarwal asked.

Lucy followed a thread back through the nightmare of the last two weeks. So much, so much, so much.

"I discovered that Juliet went to the same university as Scott and Adam and Cora. And then you mentioned Guy's name to me. But I didn't get as far as making any concrete connections, really, until it was too late. I suspected something amiss, but I didn't *know*." She leaned forward, trying to drive it home. "And would *you* want to believe your husband and best friends might be capable of these things?"

The detectives exchanged a glance. DC Marr seemed to mellow, as he had before, inclining his head. "No," he conceded, "I don't suppose any of us would."

"How about Ruth Beaumont?" DC Aggarwal moved things on. "Did you suspect Cora Waugh of attacking her?"

"No." Lucy shook her head vigorously. "No, not at all, not until Scott said it hadn't been him driving the car." Even so, guilt washed over her. She wasn't sure why she felt so responsible for what had happened to Ruth, in particular, but she did. She thought of Martin at her bedside, berating himself for not asking Ruth what had been troubling her. Thank God it looked like she was going to be okay.

The detectives questioned her for a while longer, pressing her on the specifics of the last fortnight but also asking broader questions about Adam and Cora and Scott. At times it felt like an interrogation; at times a test of how well she knew her husband and the Waughs. A test she both passed and failed. She knew them intimately, yet hardly at all. And she was mourning a version of them that was both true and false.

A version of her marriage, too. Her whole life. It was still unfathomable, really, that it could have collapsed so thoroughly in such a short space of time when it had taken years to build, with memories and familiarity and what she'd thought was a solid love.

"What do you know about the threatening emails that they'd been receiving in the run-up to Juliet's murder?" DC Aggarwal asked, making Lucy tense up again.

The emails. Yes, the emails. She still had more questions than answers about those.

"I only found out about them very recently," she said.

"They all thought they were coming from Juliet. But they received one even after she had died. And then . . . when we were . . ." She pictured the sawdusty room, the claustrophobia of the four of them in there. "When we were at the Norfolk house, I realized . . ."

"Realized what?" It was hard to tell how much the detectives already knew about this. Their poker faces were back.

"That Adam had been sending them. That he'd got them on some kind of schedule . . . and failed to cancel them after Juliet had died."

"Did he say why he did that?"

Lucy closed her eyes. She didn't want to have to relay what he'd said, stcp into his frame of mind. It felt like the worst part of everything he'd done. Cora had murdered Juliet but Adam had set it in motion, just as he had with Guy.

"To scare Scott away from Juliet." Fragments of the scene in the cottage skittered through her mind. *You were playing with fire, Scott! Even being in touch with Juliet again was insane! But to be sleeping with her?* "To punish him, spook him, maybe . . ."

No, Adam. No, you're kidding yourself. You wanted Cora to find out about Juliet. You wanted to blow our marriage apart . . .

Well, that would've been nothing more than you deserved . . .

None of this even needed to happen . . .

Then Cora's fall and the paint tins and the mushroom cloud of dust.

"Mrs. Taylor, do you need a break?"

Lucy realized she was doing it again: clutching her stomach, doubling over. She straightened up and shook her head. She needed to get this done.

"Has he said anything?" she asked the police. "Has Adam explained about sending the emails?"

They looked at each other and seemed to weigh up, as in previous times, how much they should reveal.

"I'm as surprised by it as you are," Lucy insisted. "I want answers myself."

DC Aggarwal leaned forward, elbows on the desk.

"We conducted the first part of a long interview with your husband an hour ago," she said.

Lucy held herself back from asking how he was, even though part of her still cared. She didn't want to jeopardize whatever information they might be about to share.

"His version of recent events mostly tallies with yours," the officer said, and Lucy allowed herself a flutter of relief—surely that was a good thing? She glanced at her lawyer but the woman was as silent as she had been for most of the interview. "We've analyzed the emails, and the system he set up for sending them was quite sophisticated. From your daughter's phone, as I believe you worked out. To himself, as well, to make it look less suspicious. An odd combination of acting on high emotion and planning meticulously."

Maybe that's Adam, Lucy thought. He had been careful, all these years, to show her only the calm and meticulous parts of himself. And perhaps she had been carefully ignoring any clues to the contrary.

"Except his own setup outsmarted him, in a way," Aggarwal continued. "Because, as you know, he failed to stop it from sending one after Juliet was already dead."

Dead because of emails he sent. Paranoia he created. Lucy gripped the smooth plasticky edges of the table, trying to keep her feet flat on the carpet.

DC Marr picked up a beige folder and flipped it open in front of Lucy. "You've seen this photo before?"

Lucy glanced at it briefly and nodded as DC Marr explained for the tape what he was showing her. It was the picture of Guy and Cora on the brown sofa, Guy with his arm across the back and Cora in her pink tie-dye top. Both so young-looking. Both dead before they'd ever been captured looking old.

"We analyzed this, too," he said. "It definitely looks as if it's been photoshopped. Pieced together from other photos to create a moment that never actually existed."

The phrase bounced around Lucy's head. *A moment that never actually existed.* That was what Adam had constructed, time and time again, as if he'd become addicted to it. The man who'd harped on about the importance of honesty and the damage lies could do. Now she suspected he'd been thinking of his own experiences, the destruction *he'd* caused. In effect, he'd photoshopped himself into a good person, a reliable husband. An image of someone who didn't really exist.

"And . . . this one, too, in fact," DC Marr said while Lucy was still lost in thought. This time, his verbal description for the tape snapped her back. "DC Marr is showing the witness an image of Guy Everley and Juliet Noor kissing in the background of a photograph taken at a university social event."

Lucy's eyes fixed on it. She hadn't actually seen this picture before, only heard about it, and extrapolated that it might've been a fake, too. Now she peered closely and she could see that their mouths didn't fit together quite right. You wouldn't notice it at a glance. You might even think they were just awkward kissers, these two people who were supposed to be good friends, nothing more. But Lucy could see Adam's handiwork now that she knew to look for it. His manipulation, yet again, of the story.

DC Marr moved the photo away. DC Aggarwal cleared her throat.

"Adam was insistent that you knew nothing of any of the crimes," she said. "He very much wanted us to know that." She lifted her chin. "And for the record, you are making that claim, too?"

Tears pricked Lucy's eyes again as she confirmed. She didn't know how to feel about the fact that Adam had made a last-ditch attempt to protect her. Nothing could undo the things he'd already put her and so many others through. But she saw him in her mind's eye, his glasses steamed up as he came into their house from the cold. Tilly and Fran running to greet him, giggling as he exaggerated being unable to see them through his fogged lenses. He might've cultivated a persona for himself, put it through a flattering filter and cropped out the bad bits, but it had been a nice persona, all the same.

"I think we can leave it there," DC Aggarwal said, reciting the time for the tape and then reaching to turn it off.

Lucy sat back, relief sweeping over her, hugging herself at the thought of seeing her girls.

Everything has to be about them now, she thought, but there was something haunting about the words, something reminiscent of Cora and the others, and the justifications they had clung to as they'd tried so hard to keep their secrets.

EPILOGUE

Eighteen Months Later

IT WAS A STRANGE THING TO GROW ACCUSTOMED to, visiting a prison. The first time Lucy had done it, even driving into the car park had felt daunting, and the girls had stared up at the barbed-wire boundaries with saucer-like eyes. Now the three of them passed through security with almost no fuss, and Tilly and Fran practically skipped down the corridor toward the visitation room, excited about seeing their dad.

Fran had been quicker to adjust than Tilly, which had surprised Lucy. Fran was usually the more anxious of the two, but Tilly being older worked against her somehow. She understood much more. The first few visits, Lucy had seen her looking around at the security guards and the other prisoners, her sharp mind taking it all in.

Lucy still felt a storm of nerves when Adam actually appeared. It could almost be mistaken for the feeling she used to get when they were dating, seeing him walk toward her across a busy bar. Yet this stomach flip had a much, much darker core.

He was allowed to hug the girls. "Hello, my favorites!" he said. "You've grown again!"

He and Lucy didn't touch. For the sake of Tilly and Fran, they said *hello, how are you, it's good to see you.* Lucy had visited him by herself just once, near the start, so that they could talk things through. She had come away knowing their marriage was over, but not knowing how to deal with it, this thing she'd never thought would happen to *her.* Her body had responded over the next few weeks, with crying fits and vomiting and insomnia, but her mind still hadn't fully caught up. Therapy was helping. *You'll get there*, her mum kept telling her during their video chats, which had gone from weekly to daily since everything had happened.

"What have you got to tell me?" Adam asked Tilly and Fran.

"Ivy and Joe are coming to play tonight!" Fran said.

Adam glanced at Lucy. "That's . . . great. How are they doing?"

"They're moving house," Fran said, her excitement punctured as she remembered. "With their nana and grandad."

"You'll still see them," Lucy reassured her. "We'll visit them all the time."

"Where are they moving to?" Adam asked.

"A fresh start," Lucy said, unsure why she felt reluctant to tell Adam exactly where. "And Scott will join them once he's out."

"Ah." Adam nodded. "Of course. Well, that's . . . good, I guess." He looked pensive for a moment, then recovered his overly cheery smile for the girls and started asking them about school.

They came alive, talking over one another about their

lessons and their teachers, giving Lucy a chance to sit back and reflect. They were doing okay, weren't they? The school counselor was helping them, too.

We're all doing okay, she thought, but couldn't help questioning why she felt the need to keep articulating that, reciting it like a mantra.

Whatever gets you through. Another thing her mum often said. It turned out she was a pretty good listener, when Lucy let her in.

In the immediate wake of last year's events, Lucy had tried, stubbornly, to get by without opening herself back up to her family, or the friends she'd had before the Waughs had become all-consuming. She'd kept herself at arm's length from everyone except Tilly and Fran, as if she had something to prove, or to protect herself from. But she'd gradually realized it was a lonely way to be. There was no shame in admitting she still craved friendship, and confidantes, adult company after her kids had gone to bed. Gradually, she'd reconnected with old friends, even tentatively made some new ones.

And Scott. She had written to him in prison. He had written back. They'd talked about Cora, about the things that had happened, not just recently but across the whole of their friendship. The real parts and the not real parts and the gray areas in between.

You were our safe place, Luce, he had written. *The one without any exhausting secrets. We'd have torn each other apart if you hadn't been there to keep things normal, make things nice, even fun, more often than we deserved. We all loved you. That was never a lie.*

Lucy had cried when she read that and not known how

to respond. But when he came out, maybe she would see him. Maybe they needed to talk some more.

Checking her watch, she remembered she needed to text one of the school mums, Sofia, to confirm their plans for tonight. Ivy and Joe's grandparents had said they would watch all the kids while Lucy went out. A rarity these days. It still made her feel guilty to have fun, to forget. But when it happened, when the fog lifted and she realized she was laughing and chatting with the heaviness temporarily gone from her heart, she would appreciate it all the more. Would never take lightheartedness for granted again.

"Are you okay?" Adam asked her, perhaps seeing that she'd drifted into thought. It was normally him who did that, suddenly straying far away. Lucy would always wonder if he was thinking of Cora.

She blinked. "Yes," she said. "I'm okay." After a pause, she forced herself to add, "And you?"

He shrugged. The girls were distracted and he could let the act drop. Lucy tried not to focus too hard on the sallowness of his skin, on the fact that he'd lost so much weight his glasses looked big on his face. *My ex-husband is in prison.* Sometimes it did still feel beyond surreal. He'd pleaded guilty to Cora's manslaughter as well as perverting the course of justice along with Scott. But he'd been cleared of conspiracy to murder. That meant Lucy could just about look him in the eye when the girls were around. Meant she didn't have to associate him with the word *murder*, not directly anyway. Yet the word floated in the air, gnashed its teeth at the edges of her thoughts whenever she was with him—and too often, still, when she wasn't.

Some nights, lying awake in the small hours, she had three contrasting pictures in her head. One of Adam trailing behind Cora and Scott, caught up in their messes, helping to sweep them under the carpet. And another, which she knew, deep down, was more accurate, in which Adam was at the center of it all, his lies and motivations the crux of everything.

And then she'd think of the other version, the Adam she'd fallen for and married and had children with, and she'd pack him away in a box, like a photo album from a past life. Separating their story from the others—because otherwise, how could she bear it?

THERE WAS ALWAYS a sense of release when they got home after a visit. Even the girls seemed to feel it, despite how much they liked seeing their dad. They would have a manic half hour of running around the garden or bouncing on their new trampoline, and Lucy would feel the need for fresh air, too, stretching her legs by walking laps around their lawn. It made her feel guilty sometimes: their freedom compared to Adam's lack of. Guilt was just another confusing thing she had to contend with in the tangle of it all. Guilt about what had happened to Juliet, and to Guy, but guilt about Adam and Scott being locked up, too. About Cora being gone.

She heard the doorbell go from inside the house, dragging her out of her thoughts before they got too dark.

"Girls, Ivy and Joe are here!" she called, and they jumped down from the trampoline, scattering grass through the house from their bare feet as they charged to answer the door.

Lucy composed herself. Seeing Ivy and Joe was always

tough. Their brave little faces. And she still half expected Cora and Scott to follow them into the house with a bottle of wine. As she made her way into the hall, her eyes automatically went to the framed photo on the wall at the foot of the stairs. It was of the two families, the Waughs and the Taylors, taken at a barbecue at the Norfolk cottage. All eight of them were somehow managing to sit on only three unstable-looking camping chairs. The kids were sitting on knees, not necessarily their own parents'; Lucy was on Adam's lap, too, with Ivy on hers. They were all grinning. Lucy had put her phone camera on a timer and balanced it on the barbecue, which was already lit—*nothing like a high-risk photography setup*, Scott had joked. The sun gave the whole scene a honeyed glow, like a dream, a memory—which was what it had become, Lucy supposed. Even the cottage belonged to somebody else now.

She kept the photo on the wall for the sake of the kids. To remind them of happier times, and to show Ivy and Joe, when they came to visit, that their mum hadn't been forgotten, despite everything. That was what Lucy told herself anyway. But sometimes, late at night, she would stand here and gaze at the picture. And she would admit that it was there for herself as much as for anybody else.

ACKNOWLEDGMENTS

Once again, I am extremely lucky to have a long list of wonderful people to thank. This book was written during an eventful year—you could say with almost as many twists and turns as a novel plot—so the support of my editors, agency, friends, and family has been vital, and hugely appreciated.

As ever, an enormous thank-you to my awesome agent, Hellie Ogden, for her guidance, wisdom, enthusiasm, reassurance, and care. Thanks to the whole Janklow & Nesbit team, in fact, especially Ma'suma Amiri, for so much moral and practical support. And to Emily Randle for looking after me superbly during your time at Janklow (especially as I ended up stranded abroad for most of it!). You've all been amazing.

It's been an absolute privilege, yet again, working on this book with my incredible editors, Kimberley Atkins at Hodder and Danielle Dieterich at Putnam. Thank you for loving the premise and the main character of this novel from the start, and, more importantly, for helping me do them justice. Your feedback is always transformative, and you've also been supportive and patient when I found myself writing under tough circumstances. I'm so happy we got there in the end, and so proud of the result!

Thank you to the ever-brilliant teams at Hodder and at Putnam, including Amy Batley and Olivia Robertshaw for all your editorial support and professionalism; Helen Parham, Janice Barral, and Madeline Hopkins for your eagle-eyed copyediting and proofreading (I don't know how you do it!); Ollie Martin and Kristen Bianco for all your great work on publicity, and Callie Robertson and Brennin Cummings for inspired marketing. You all continue to be a dream to work with.

Thanks also to the people who have helped me with research, queries, and ideas while working on this story. A particular shout-out goes to Erin Smith, whose career and travels inspired Scott's and Juliet's. Apologies for all the artistic license I've taken! And a giant thank-you to the members of Leicester Writers' Club, who were my first readers and helped to vastly improve and shape this novel from its early drafts. The amount of talent in the Club always keeps me on my toes, and your feedback led to some significant changes that have made this an infinitely better novel. I'm so grateful to know you all!

Despite some of its challenges, this has been a rich and rewarding year, not least because of some of the new people I've met and new creative spaces I've found myself in. Thank you to the Leicester Speculators for welcoming me at your Wednesday-night writing sessions, where I got more words down than I ever normally would in an evening, and got to know another group of talented and inspiring people. Thanks to Jim Worrad for all the chats about this strange and wonderful business we're in! And to all my bookish friends on social media, including bloggers, readers, reviewers, and fellow authors, who fill my Twitter feed with much-needed positivity.

As well as new friends and networks, there are so many people who have always been there for me, and continue to be. Mum, Dad, Gramms, Christine, Yassin, Idris, and Aryn: You're the best family anyone could wish for, and it makes me happy to see my books on your shelves. You inspire the family elements that are so important to my stories (the good bits!), as do all my friends who have little ones, and that's been particularly true of this novel. Thank you also to my extended family, and to the new families I've been welcomed into this year (Carol and the Watsons and Stanilands; John and Clara and the Irvings). Your support means the world, and your messages, kind words, and photos of my books in far-flung places keep me going.

Thank you to all my long-term friends who I'd include in that bracket of "extended family." To the people who are always first to preorder my books and wait excitedly for their delivery on publication day (you know who you are!). To Lisa Bentley for all the chats while you've been on your own journey to publication this year. To former colleagues and old friends for inviting me to give talks or do book signings (Mike, Amy, Dave, Sheena, Margaret). And to everyone who puts up with the fact that I'm a bit obsessed with taking photos, just like Lucy is in this novel. Again, all the nice bits about friendship in this story are inspired by you!

Last but definitely not least, Phil. My best friend and one of the best people I know. Not only do you support, inspire, encourage, and counsel me, you've also helped me improve this book in so many practical and invaluable ways. From talking through plot points to reading and editing chapters, you've made me realize that living with another writer is extremely useful, especially one as gifted as you! Thank you for being there through the stressful times, celebrating with me in the happy times, and caring about this book as much as I do. I couldn't have done it without you.

ABOUT THE AUTHOR

Helen Cooper is the author of *The Other Guest* and *The Downstairs Neighbor.* She is from Derby and has an MA in creative writing and a background in teaching English and academic writing. Her creative writing has been published in *Mslexia* and *Writers' Forum;* she was shortlisted for the Bath Short Story Prize in 2014 and came third in the Leicester Writes Short Story Prize in 2018.

HelenCooper85
HelenCooperWriter